All
the
Little
Ways

All the Little Ways

Laura Lekkos

GALLERY BOOKS

New York   Amsterdam/Antwerp   London
Toronto   Sydney/Melbourne   New Delhi

Gallery Books
An Imprint of Simon & Schuster, LLC
1230 Avenue of the Americas
New York, NY 10020

For more than 100 years, Simon & Schuster has championed authors and the stories they create. By respecting the copyright of an author's intellectual property, you enable Simon & Schuster and the author to continue publishing exceptional books for years to come. We thank you for supporting the author's copyright by purchasing an authorized edition of this book.

This book is a work of fiction. Any references to historical events, real people, or real places are used fictitiously. Other names, characters, places, and events are products of the author's imagination, and any resemblance to actual events or places or persons, living or dead, is entirely coincidental.

First Gallery Books hardcover edition June 2026

GALLERY BOOKS and colophon are registered trademarks of Simon & Schuster, LLC

Simon & Schuster strongly believes in freedom of expression and stands against censorship in all its forms. For more information, visit BooksBelong.com.

For information about special discounts for bulk purchases, please contact Simon & Schuster Special Sales at 1-866-506-1949 or business@simonandschuster.com.

The Simon & Schuster Speakers Bureau can bring authors to your live event. For more information or to book an event, contact the Simon & Schuster Speakers Bureau at 1-866-248-3049 or visit our website at www.simonspeakers.com.

Interior design by Silverglass

Manufactured in the United States of America

10 9 8 7 6 5 4 3 2 1

Library of Congress Control Number has been applied for.

ISBN 978-1-6682-0699-7
ISBN 978-1-6682-0701-7 (ebook)

Scan here to get book recommendations, exclusive offers, and more delivered to your inbox.

For my husband

All
the
Little
Ways

1

Victoria

Every courtship was a dance, and even though this seduction was professional, it was no exception. Victoria had been pursuing Nash Winton—*the* Nash Winton, as in the elusive, eccentric billionaire Nash Winton—for the better part of a year. Now, Victoria was closing in, her body rife with the delicious anticipation of consummation . . . well, metaphorically, anyway. Victoria was so thrilled, she could do another dance—the sort of dorky, fist-pumping jig that one only did alone, or in sitcoms.

Victoria arrived at the restaurant early. The host greeted her warmly and led Victoria over to the table, which was situated smack in the center of the place, where Nash could see and be seen, just as he liked. Victoria thanked the host and discreetly slipped him a hundred for securing her the last-minute reservation of a prime table.

Then, Victoria assessed the lighting, choosing the chair that would bathe her in the most flattering glow. She sat and crossed her legs, which were intentionally unsheathed from their usual trousers and instead clad in a formfitting pencil skirt with a generous slit. Most of the time, the boys' club prevailed. But sometimes, the hint of an extra little *something* worked to pique the interest and capture the attention of a man who didn't need any club, a man whose fortune rendered rules irrelevant, a man who had already blazed a trail of indisputable conquests and relished a challenge, a man who was seemingly one of the few tycoons without any interest in playing with rockets.

Five minutes later, as Victoria was faux-casually scanning an index report on her phone, Nash sauntered in, making his presence known as he waded through the restaurant, stopping at various tables, first to level a boisterous greeting at a movie-studio head in gym shorts and then a "Howdy, ya handsome devil" to a hedge funder who recently closed a deal to control the majority of high-end retail in the United States. When Nash reached their table, Victoria put down her phone and gave him a friendly smile. Victoria's bottom line was abundantly clear to both of them: She wanted Nash's money—not for yachts or Birkins, but to make an indisputable case to everyone at her wealth-management firm that she should at last be named managing director, having landed this ferociously sought-after whale.

Victoria stood to greet him and Nash's hand grazed the small of her back as they embraced.

"Vic—can I call you Vic?"

Victoria loathed nicknames and would likely pretend not to hear someone if they dared to abbreviate her name. She looked directly into Nash Winton's intelligent eyes. "Let me handle your portfolio and you can call me anything you want."

The dance had begun. Nash's mouth twisted upwards with amusement. "All you care about are my assets?" Nash asked.

"I could say the same thing to you," Victoria teased.

Nash took an unsubtle, appreciative glance towards her figure. It was then that Victoria knew, without a doubt, that she had him. Her whale was on the line.

Just a few days later, Victoria would marvel at how everything could come spectacularly undone in an instant, how a carefully constructed life was no more impervious to complete disaster than a sandcastle was immune to the threat of a wave. But at 1:15 p.m., Victoria was still forty-seven minutes away from losing Nash and forfeiting the role of managing director to her coworker Mark Berg, a position they both had been contending for since day one. It was a designation that, if meritocracy were as fashionable as nepotism, Victoria should have been a lock for, even though she lacked the prep school connections, the Ivy League pedigree, and the sprawling ancestral manse on Nantucket that came with them.

Victoria glanced around her corner office, taking a rare moment to appreciate her surroundings. She let her gaze pass over the midcentury modern couch, the artfully arranged objects on the coffee table, and the pearly white cymbidium orchid that was thriving despite her flagrant neglect. It all came together to create a sense of tasteful, if studied, luxury—the interior design equivalent of a sweater from the Row, of which Victoria owned several. Something understated and expensive but without a giant label on it that screamed, *Hello! I'm loaded, can't you tell by this logo?*

Victoria lightly tapped her heels on the area rug beneath her desk. She didn't struggle with nerves before pitches, didn't crumble under pressure or quake at the idea of public speaking. The opposite, in fact. Victoria lived for the thrill of bringing in a new asset and multiplying a fortune on their behalf. Victoria could deliver a TED Talk to rousing applause without so much as considering a beta-blocker, glancing at a confidence monitor, or breaking a sweat, and had in fact accomplished this very feat five years prior, just shy of her thirty-ninth birthday, allowing her to check yet another item off her list of life goals. Becoming her firm's youngest and first female managing director instead of Mark Berg, a Wharton grad born and raised in Brentwood who managed to insert this information into most of his conversations, would satisfy another. A movement in her peripheral vision caught Victoria's eye and snapped her back into focus. She shot a glance out the floor-to-ceiling glass expanse that separated her corner office from the cubicles housing the assistant pool. Her assistant, Harper, met Victoria's gaze with an exuberant wave, then launched into a series of hand movements that Victoria couldn't interpret.

"What?" she mouthed. Harper leapt up from her chair in platforms and a collared crop top—ostensibly an oblique nod to business casual—her three-inch heels not impeding her speed as she galloped over to the glass wall demarcating Victoria's office from gen pop.

Harper mimed being stabbed and Victoria screwed up her face in confusion, then pointed to her door, indicating that since Harper was already convulsing at her threshold, she might as well come in. Harper pushed the door open a few inches and stuck her head through like a puppy sniffing out the location of a treat.

"You're going to kill!" Harper whisper-shouted. "Your slides are lit."

"Thanks, Harper."

"Mark Berg thinks he has rizz but he's one ass-grab away from getting hashtag canceled! Do you want to, like, close the shades and dance around to 'About Damn Time'?"

"Oh. That sounds . . . fun. Maybe another time." *With a karaoke machine, in hell.*

Harper flashed Victoria a thumbs-up and clomped away.

Several minutes later, a muted chime alerted her to a Slack message and Victoria shifted her attention to one of the three screens on her desk. A chat box started with *Hey, B!*

It had taken a few months for Victoria to get used to her assistant's syntax, an adjustment period before she realized that Harper was teeming with youth in a way that required an onslaught of slang, emo-jis, and exclamation marks to communicate.

Messages from Harper popped up, rapid-fire.

B like boss, not bitch!
OMG I would never call u that!
LOL!
Literally!

Victoria wondered if Harper was literally laughing out loud at the thought. She, like the rest of her generation, seemed to have a flawed relationship with the word *literal.*

The messages kept coming:

I know u don't want to dance but do u want anything else before
the BIG mtg!?! Like a latte? Or a matcha? Or a green juice?
Endorphins! Yay!

There was a case to be made that what Victoria needed was another assistant. One, for example, who showed a fleeting interest in the world of finance, or who practiced a more judicious approach to her use of exclamation marks, or who had a résumé devoid of the glaring nepotism that had landed Harper the position in the first place. Because yes, Harper's parents were longtime clients. If pressed, Victoria would have suggested that they take a little time to get to know their offspring and then, correspondingly, find another field—*any* other field—better suited to Harper's interests and talents. Victoria was glad she hadn't been consulted, though. Despite Harper knowing the lyrics to every Taylor Swift song but being unable to create an Airtable to save her life, Victoria was charmed by her.

Victoria tapped out a quick reply: *Thanks, Harper. Appreciate it, but I'm good.*

Harper wrote back, *U know u r! SLAY ALL DAY!*

A smile tugged at Victoria's mouth and she shot another glance out of her office, hoping to lock eyes with her assistant, but instead Victoria intersected gazes with Mark, who was walking by in a flash of Zegna and hair pomade. Mark's head snapped away from Victoria, but not before she caught his death stare.

Victoria's stomach suddenly coiled—a familiar pang of hunger mixed with something else altogether, a bitter, foreign sensation. She tensed. Her digestive tract twisted again and Victoria chastised herself for skipping breakfast in favor of an acidic orange juice; she didn't have time for GI rebellion. She considered asking Harper to bring her something to eat but rejected this idea in the time it took her to stand up from her desk. The litany of questions and opinions that would follow was simply not worth it. *What kind of snack? DF and GF? I swear my skin is literally glowing since I cut out dairy. You deserve some carbs, girl! I mean woman. I mean BOSS.*

Victoria set off towards the office kitchen, walking down the hallway, which was decorated with muted but still significant modern art. When Victoria first traversed this hallway as a summer associate, she'd been wowed by the whole mise-en-scène. The army of Purple Label suits, the number of zeros on the figures funneled into funds and trusts, the sometimes intricate, sometimes flashy vanity deals brokered to satisfy clients' whims. Victoria had listened to the easy banter of the other summer interns over take-out salads from La Scala, wondering how they had all learned so much, so quickly, about tennis clubs and Cap d'Antibes and the significance of Teterboro. A few weeks into the summer, Victoria had realized they hadn't *needed* to learn these things; their fluency was innate, whereas Victoria, who'd grown up in landlocked, blue-collar Fresno, where mozzarella sticks and fountain Coke signified the height of fine dining, had to figure out which parts of Florida were acceptable (Palm Beach, Wellington, and Miami—but only during Art Basel) and if "The Brando" was a nickname. It wasn't.

Now, Victoria smoothed her pencil skirt and silk blouse, about to enter the kitchen, when she heard the chatter. She paused, peering in through the inch-wide crack between the wall and the doorframe.

"I almost bought her whole I-don't-need-a-man act," said Ellen, a middle-aged mid-level HR manager.

Deborah, an assistant to one of the partners, predictably agreed. Deborah loved nothing more than feeling included. Except, perhaps, for combing through eBay for rare trolls to add to the sprawling collection that lined her cubicle.

"I heard the wedding cost a million dollars!" Deborah chirped with satisfaction. "A *million*."

Annalise, the most junior member of the trio, gasped. "No way."

Victoria felt a frown forming on her face and tried to tamp it down. Surely, she wasn't . . . hurt? This woman collected trolls.

"Do you think it will last?" Annalise tested.

"I give it a year," Ellen said.

"Six months," challenged Deborah.

Victoria's stomach lurched again. She chastised herself—why did she care? She usually deflected spiky, petty remarks without a second thought. Maybe that was the way she was built. Maybe it was a habit born of necessity. Maybe this was just how women were with one another.

Victoria marched into the kitchen. "What's the over/under on a year?" she asked.

The women's heads turned in unison. Ellen's mouth dropped open. Deborah and Annalise froze in place and flushed, not with shame, Victoria suspected, but at the bad fortune of being caught.

Deborah recovered first. "Victoria, hi," she said.

Annalise joined in. "We were just talking about this girl I know—who recently got married!" she added lamely.

As she stood there looking at the three women—Ellen focusing on the air two feet to the right of Victoria's head, Deborah staring at the floor, Annalise suddenly consumed by an emergency with a fingernail that required her full attention—Victoria stifled a sigh.

"Ladies, ladies. Are we really going to pretend you weren't talking about me or are we better than that?" Victoria asked, keeping an upbeat, playful lilt to her voice. Like she was in on the joke. Like it was a joke.

There was a sharp intake of air from Ellen as Victoria went over to a cabinet, opened it, and selected a box of Simple Mills almond-flour crackers. Deborah's left eye began twitching in a way that a casual observer might think required medical attention, but it was just her tell—the signature, irksome physical response that acted up when Deborah behaved poorly, like a punitive Tourette's.

Victoria felt a quick pang of guilt when she noticed Deborah's eyeball dancing in its socket, but she also knew her point had been made. She tucked the box of almond-flour crackers under the crook of her arm and thought that Simple Mills had just complicated their day.

"It wasn't anywhere near a million," Victoria informed them. She was a wealth-management advisor, for God's sake. Did they really think she'd blow that kind of money on one day?

Victoria flashed the women a thousand-watt smile, then walked out, holding her head high. She knew details of this encounter would be disseminated, deconstructed, and debated until the story no longer bore facsimile to what had occurred, but she had bigger priorities.

Moments later, Victoria was scarfing crackers and completing a post-presentation mental victory lap at her desk when her phone buzzed on her desk with a text notification. She assumed, without having to look, that it was her husband, checking in on her before her meeting.

Victoria picked up her phone. His text read, *Checking in . . .*

Victoria called him and Ace picked up immediately.

"A phone call? From the office? Did someone die?" Ace asked.

"No. No deaths. Just crackers," Victoria answered.

"Crackers? Are we speaking in code?"

"Sure, as long as it's code for 'I'm sitting here taking down an entire box of crackers.'"

"Careful, you know what they say about crackers. It's a slippery slope to sourdough."

Victoria's mouth curved upwards. Her orchid gleamed in the early-afternoon sunlight spilling in through the window. "I love sourdough."

"I know you do."

"Now I want a big stick of sourdough."

"Is *that* code?" Ace joked.

Victoria chuckled. "You wish. And you know what? It's your fault I'm in this carb hole."

"Moi?" Ace asked.

Victoria could picture the sly half grin, half smirk that Ace was undoubtedly wearing at that exact moment.

"Yes. I'm wondering if I can go back in time, un-meet you, and not be shoving crackers down my throat," Victoria said.

"String theory! Let's do it."

"Actually, I could still meet you," Victoria mused, looking out her window down onto the tony streets of Beverly Hills. "I'd just have to stick to my guns in the parallel life where I'm not in this situation and never give you the time of day."

"To be fair, you didn't. Not at first."

"Not for a long time."

"Good thing I was irresistible," Ace said.

"More like relentless," Victoria replied. "And now here we are. Here. We. Are."

"Indeed," Ace said. "Pumped for your meeting?"

"I am," Victoria answered. She didn't believe in beating around the bush, and with her husband, she never felt like she should.

"Go land your white whale," Ace said.

"And here I was expecting a joke about how I already had."

Ace laughed his way off the phone while wishing her good luck and simultaneously making it clear that Victoria didn't need it. She didn't rise to meet an occasion; she was already there, ready and waiting, prepared to harpoon it.

Victoria walked out of her office and tossed a friendly smile to Harper without breaking her stride so her assistant would know to carry on. There was no need for Harper to join Victoria on her battle march; she didn't need to pause her important work adding items to her Shopbop cart, decoding illiterate texts from last week's one-night stand, and trading memes of the day with friends who were also serving in the ranks of corporate incarceration with only the internet to lighten their sentences.

Victoria passed the smaller conference room—the one reserved for internal meetings and clients who preferred the sensation of intimacy over grandeur—and veered to the right, towards the large conference room. The big dicks, the major leagues. Most of the principals were already assembled in leather rolling chairs around the long mahogany table. A large flatscreen displayed the firm's name, cued up for Victoria to present her deck.

As she entered, Victoria passed an approving eye over the Russ & Daughters spread she'd had flown in from New York. A few months prior, Nash had mentioned that it was his favorite deli; Victoria had collected this kernel of information and squirreled it away until she could transform knowledge into action. The billionaire's preferred refreshments now sat waiting: a precipitously tall tower of bagels, plump and doughy; a platter of gleaming smoked salmon; mounds of cream cheese flecked with forest-green chives; a bowl of satiny sablefish; and a vat of caviar so deep it would please an oligarch, the small onyx beads of roe glittering like treasure.

Victoria looked at the suits convened around the table. As usual, Mark avoided her gaze and inspected the infantry of LaCroix cans lining the middle of the table before finally selecting Pamplemousse, then checking his watch like he couldn't wait for this to be over.

At precisely two o'clock, Victoria's white whale crested the shores of the conference room wearing custom cowboy boots, faded Levi's, and a crisp Charvet shirt tucked in to show off a belt with an over-sized buckle. His silver mane was slicked back and glinted like mica under the recessed lighting.

"Excuse the boots. I just came from my ranch," Nash announced, referring to his expansive property in Montana recently featured on the cover of *AD*. An assistant ferried over a bagel and lox. As Nash sat down, the sharp, pungent smell of the smoked fish wafted over to Victoria.

A wave of queasiness descended like a thick fog rolling in without warning. Victoria felt a gag rising in her throat and managed to swallow it down, but her stomach roiled uncontrollably. She tried to prevent evidence of her nauseated state from showing on her face. She tried to proceed as if her body hadn't been overtaken by forces beyond her. She really tried. But goose bumps sprang up amid the sheen of sweat suddenly covering her body, and there was no stopping this. The morning's ill-conceived orange juice and half-digested almond-flour crackers forcibly ejected themselves . . . onto Nash.

Revulsion covered Nash's face as he recoiled, the viscous, milky-yellow soup of Victoria's stomach acid seeping down his white shirt. A cracker fractal slid off his chest onto the table.

The room was deathly silent. The sour, acrid stench of sickness permeated the air. One of the assistants dry-heaved, then turned to retch into a nearby wastebasket.

Still in shock, Victoria put her hand up to her mouth. Little driblets of vomit clung to the bottom of her lips.

"Oh my God. I am *so* sorry," she said, then vomited again onto the table.

Nash remained motionless—a statue of stunned disgust. Everyone else stared at her, aghast, except for Mark, who didn't bother to try to conceal the titillated grin splitting his face like a Muppet. For maybe the first time in her adult, professional life, Victoria didn't know what to do next.

"I'm pregnant," she blurted. Then, she fled the room.

2

—

Liz

8 WEEKS: IPHONE APP ICON

Liz pulled the chicken out of the oven and inspected it for the "life-changing" qualities that a sitcom star turned lifestyle blogger had touted on TikTok. Liz doubted that this twice-basted bird could make her boyfriend of eleven months suddenly declare his undying love or give Liz the courage to quit her soul-crushing job. Still, Liz had to try. Even though she was about as far from a yoga-mat-toting, green-juice-chugging blogger as Preston was from proposing.

Liz sprinkled parsley on top of the chicken and, with full hands, jabbed at her phone with her pinkie finger before it plunged into lock-screen mode. She saw the time: five minutes to seven. *Shit.* Liz whipped into action and spun through her apartment. She hid dirty pans and threw away used paper towels, hopefully removing any signs of effort so that this dinner, which she had labored over, would seem effortless. *Oh, what? This four-course gourmet meal? It was nothing!*

Liz tried to arrange the place mats to cover the various water rings and other blemishes on her table. She fluffed the throw pillows on her worn-in Jennifer Convertibles couch, tore off her rarely used apron—a gag gift from a bachelorette party that boasted penises dressed as vegetables—and cued up a Romantic Dinner Vibes playlist on Spotify.

As soon as Al Green started flowing through the Bose speakers, Liz paused. "Let's Stay Together" seemed . . . a little on the nose? Maybe even desperate, or like she was trying to convey some kind of super-textual message like the sync music in the background of *The Catch*, the reality dating show she edited, if combing through hours of B-roll for something scandalous that had inadvertently slipped through the net counted as "editing." Liz knew she should feel grateful to have a job on a top-rated show, but instead Liz felt her faith in mankind plummet with every day she spent witnessing gaggles of women fight to lock down "a catch," fully aware of the other catch that the double entendre of the show's name promised: One of the men wasn't straight. Liz had worked for this arguably homophobic cultural blight upon humanity for six of its eight seasons, vowing with each ersatz fight or booze-soaked hookup that she'd finally get on LinkedIn and get out of reality TV. Meanwhile, Preston loved his job in the sports department of a top agency. He met whatever professional tasks he faced with the boundless enthusiasm of a golden retriever. Like the world owed him something, and wasn't it fun?

The buzzer sounded. Either Preston was on time or Postmates was ringing her again because her stoner next-door neighbor had ordered enchiladas, then fallen into an indica stupor and forgotten about his craving. Liz took a deep breath to steady her nerves. Would she *ever* feel secure in a relationship, free of the sense of impending doom that clung to her like bad perfume? Or were relationships just like this—as precarious as a polar ice cap? Liz went over to the buzzer as it sounded again, loud and squeaky, like a goat bleating.

"It's Domino's," Preston joked when she answered it.

"No tip if you forgot my breadsticks again," Liz said, and let him up.

While she waited for Preston to climb the two flights of stairs to her apartment, Liz changed to a Dinner Mood playlist and paced her tiny kitchen. As soon as she heard footsteps approaching, she channeled her best breezy blogger and plastered on a smile that she hoped came across as chill, low-key, and appealing.

"Sweet," Preston said, taking in the Pinterest-worthy tablescape. He offered her a bottle of wine and kissed her on the cheek. Liz hoped he directed his affection there—where he might greet his sister or his mother—instead of kissing her on the mouth because she was wearing visible lip gloss and not for some other reason. Like he'd suddenly lost all romantic interest in her. "You went all out," Preston said.

"This?" Liz said, gesturing casually to the spread she'd agonized over for a week. "Oh, it's nothing. Are you hungry?"

"Starving," Preston said, taking off his suit jacket and slinging it over the arm of the couch. Liz loved how comfortable he was in her place. Even if he didn't have a key. Even if they never discussed their future. Even if their relationship seemed more like a mislabeled situationship they had slid into rather than something with legs they had intentionally sought out. Even—

"Should we pop that open?" Preston asked, pointing to the bottle of wine in Liz's hands.

"I'll do it!" Liz rushed off to find a bottle opener. Preston sat down at the table and started thumbing through emails on his phone.

"Just have to check something." Liz wasn't sure if he was talking to her or himself, so she just nodded while pouring cabernet.

"I'll put it on silent in a sec," Preston added.

"It's fine!" Liz insisted.

Preston tapped out a few more emails, then put his phone on vibrate—his definition of silent—and slipped it back into his pocket.

"This dinner looks bomb," Preston said, glancing at the roasted chicken, Mediterranean farro, kale salad, and sweet potatoes. He helped himself and Liz fussed over him, acting like it was normal for them to have a home-cooked meal together on a weeknight. Preston ate heartily, laying on the compliments, while Liz tried to choke down a few bites of influencer-endorsed chicken. It was perfectly cooked, but Liz was too nervous to enjoy her culinary triumph. She waited for Preston to consume enough wine to take the edge off a workday, then she cleared her throat.

"There's something I need to talk to you about . . ."

Preston looked at Liz curiously and then a flash of something else—fear?—flickered across his face before he said, "Actually, there's something I wanted to talk to you about too."

Liz's heart sank so low in her chest she was sure a rescue party would deem it a lost cause.

"Okay," Liz said, her throat constricting and dry . . . like overcooked chicken. "Do you want to go first?"

"No, no. Ladies first." Chivalry was not dead, though Liz wished, in this moment, that it was taking a breather. She didn't know how to go about this, only that she needed to, somehow.

"Well . . ." Liz took a big gulp of air. "I know we weren't planning this, and we don't ever really talk about us in a where-is-this-going kind of way and—that's fine! Not everything has to be so target oriented just because we're in our thirties and our friends are hitting those milestones and society—you know?" Preston looked blankly at her but nodded. "Anyway, this was—*is*—a big surprise, and obviously, you have a say in it, we'll figure it out together—"

"Liz," Preston interrupted, his brow furrowed. "What's *it*?"

She looked at him. At his classic, even features and his blue-gray eyes that changed color like a mood ring.

"I'm pregnant," Liz said.

Preston stared at her. The shock seemed to spread across his face gradually, like a rash, from top to bottom. First, his eyebrows darted up, then his eyes widened, and finally his mouth opened to form a perfect circle. "Seriously?"

"Seriously," Liz confirmed, as if she would ever play a pregnancy prank on someone whose feelings for her still felt undefined, as if she would ever joke about something so huge. Liz twisted her hands in her lap underneath the table. Preston sat there wordlessly for what felt like an eternity. A torturous eternity. A torturous eternity from which Liz could wave at him from across the expanse of a galaxy and send him a postcard: *Hi, from Hell!*

"Are you sure?" Preston said.

Liz felt a little piece of herself crumble like a brick from an abandoned building. While it was ridiculous for her to imagine that Preston would have reacted by leaping up, shouting like Oprah, and telling Liz that this had made him realize his deep love for her, it was still a fantasy she had unfortunately entertained.

"Yes . . . positive."

In case Preston needed proof, Liz got up, went over to a drawer, and pulled out ten at-home pregnancy tests. She carried them over to the table and placed them in front of Preston in a haphazard heap of EPTs, some of the sticks jutting out at odd angles like a bizarre game of Jenga. Preston eyed the tests from a distance, either unwilling to touch them and validate their contents or reluctant to handle plastic sticks that had been held under a stream of her urine. Liz watched Preston's facial expression anxiously, trying to tease out its shifts like a meteorologist.

"They're all positive?" he said.

Liz nodded. A candle dripped wax on the table and Liz didn't wipe it away, beyond caring that it would congeal on the wood and have to be scraped off later with a butter knife.

"Wow," Preston said. "*Wow.*"

Liz peered into the question marks in his eyes and marveled that someone who had been inside her body on a semiregular basis over the course of almost a year could do something, or *not* do something, and suddenly seem like a complete stranger. Her expression, which she was trying to keep under wraps, must have escaped onto her face, because Preston leapt into preservation mode.

"Sorry, I'm just really shocked."

"I get it. But, yeah, it's not a joke. I'm pregnant. Knocked up. With child. Or at least, pre-child. With sperm that joined up with an egg."

"'Joined up,' like they formed a band?"

Liz lifted a corner of her mouth into a tentative smile. Was Preston cracking jokes? That seemed like a good sign. "A tiny, two-member band," she said.

"Wow. This is *wild*. Preg-nant." Preston paused between syllables to break the word into two parts, enunciating like English was his second language instead of first and only. Before he could utter the word *wow* one more time, Liz rushed to supply some facts.

"I'm eight weeks along. I'm not completely regular so I didn't think anything of it last month, but then I started feeling nauseous and I looked at the calendar . . . so I got the tests."

Preston cracked a few knuckles, a habit he had been trying to break for as long as Liz had known him. Which was to say, since they had both swiped right on an internet stranger eleven months ago and then, unbelievably, made plans to meet up in person. Plans that, even more unbelievably, seemed to go well. Until . . . now.

"You don't have to say anything this second. It's a lot," Liz added, more to reassure herself than him.

Preston met her gaze. "Sorry. I know I keep saying *wow* and sitting here like an idiot."

"Not at all. I mean, you are saying *wow* a lot, but you're not an idiot."

Preston smiled at her a bit sheepishly, but also gratefully. "You're not alone in this. Two people formed that band, and we'll decide how to handle it as a team." Liz assumed he meant whether the band should break up or stay together and she felt her chest tighten at the second option. She wasn't ready to talk about that.

"Should we think about it?" Liz suggested, suddenly feeling like her lungs weren't getting enough air and trying not to suck in asthmatically. "Let it sink in?"

"Good idea," Preston agreed.

Liz got up and retrieved a plate of tahini chocolate chip cookies, another blogger-sanctioned delight. "I made dessert, if you want some." She used her arm to make room by sweeping the pile of EPTs off the table, onto a chair. In the second after, she regretted this move; it was gross, and Preston might not have been done eating.

Preston put his hand on his stomach. "Thanks, but I'm full from the chicken."

Or unforeseen news that he needs to digest, Liz thought. And then she remembered.

"Was this what you wanted to talk to me about too? Were you going to tell me you're pregnant?" *Jokes. Bad jokes.*

Preston laughed, but it sounded strained. "How'd you know?"

Liz chuckled but the problem was, she didn't know. She didn't know what Preston was going to talk to her about before she had dropped a bomb on him, and Liz didn't have the courage to ask him.

"I don't remember what I was going to say. It obviously wasn't important," Preston told her, and Liz wondered whether one or both parts of that statement was a lie.

Soon after, Preston said he had to leave because he had an early branding meeting the next day with an outfielder. He told her the player's name and Liz feigned recognition, but it was impressive in and of itself that she knew he was talking about baseball instead of basketball. Preston lived for men running around in uniforms trying to put balls in nets, over walls, or in holes. Liz knew nothing about these nets, walls, or holes, except that they were very important to these men, and therefore to Preston.

"I'll call you tomorrow," he said.

They hugged goodbye and then Liz stared at the back of Preston's head as he walked out as if maybe, just maybe, his wavy hair held some clues about what he was thinking. After the door closed, Liz sank onto the couch and drew a soft, nubby blanket over her legs, too tired to clean up the dinner plates she had tossed in the sink and too nauseous to deal with the cloying scent of cleaning supplies. She thought that while it could've gone better, it certainly could have gone a lot worse.

When the buzzer sounded again a short while later, Liz groaned. She was scrolling through some true crime shows in her queue and had paused at one that another editor had told her was especially violent and murderous, though she had just come across a meme warning that people who watched true crime shows to unwind might be seriously disturbed themselves. Liz didn't want to unpack why she felt televised trauma relaxing, but she also didn't want to get up to manage her pothead neighbor's Dorito Locos Taco order. Nevertheless, Liz mustered the energy, walked across the room to the buzzer, and called into it "You have the wrong apartment" before allowing the delivery person up.

Two minutes later, there was a knock on her door. Annoyed, Liz flung it open, ready to redirect the Postmate, only to find Preston, holding a container of breadsticks. "I wanted to make sure I'd get a tip this time."

Liz stood there too flabbergasted to react.

"Can I come in?" Preston smiled and handed her the cardboard box. Liz wordlessly accepted it and stepped aside to let him in. Preston waited for her to close the door behind him but remained standing, as if he wanted a clear escape route after he had accomplished whatever pressing task had led him back there.

Liz clutched the warm box of breadsticks and wondered if they were a parting gift, Preston's way of letting her down easy. Nothing said *I don't want you to have my child and I don't want you to be my girlfriend anymore, but I hope we stay cool* like a dozen gooey breadsticks.

"Why do you look scared?" Preston asked, inspecting her.

"I'm not!" Liz insisted, terrified.

"I didn't want you to think I was only bringing this up because of, you know." Preston gestured to Liz's midsection. "But it really is what I wanted to talk to you about earlier." Preston paused and Liz held her breath.

"I think we should move in together," Preston said.

3

—

Victoria

10 WEEKS: KUMQUAT

Victoria's usual routine, after stepping out of her heels and putting her bag down on the console table in the foyer, was to settle into Ace's end-of-the-day embrace. Today, she flung herself into his arms like she had been ejected from a T-shirt cannon at a Lakers game. She buried her face in Ace's chest and inhaled his familiar scent, the woodsy muskiness somehow complementing the freshness of Dial soap, which he insisted on still using even though Victoria had read somewhere that the dye was carcinogenic.

"That bastard. He wouldn't sign?" Ace asked.

"No. It was worse. Much, much worse," Victoria replied, her voice muffled. She pulled her head back and looked up at her husband, whose brown eyes were brimming with affection. "I threw up on him."

"What?" Ace exclaimed, his eyebrows lifting.

"And then I panicked and told everyone I was pregnant."

"I thought you weren't saying anything until—"

"After I landed managing director and I was showing, I know," Victoria said, unable to stifle a flare of irritation. "Hence, the 'I panicked' of it all."

Victoria peeled off her jacket and stalked towards the kitchen. She smelled something simmering on the stovetop. Bossa nova emanated from the sound system. A bouquet of peonies sat on top of the gray-and-white Calacatta marble island, their ballet-slipper-pink blooms newly burst open, and two place settings were arranged on the dining room table. It looked like a fucking movie set.

"I'm sorry," Ace said as he followed her into the kitchen. "What can I do?" Victoria threw her jacket across the counter, knocking a few petals off a peony. She sat on a barstool and kicked off her heels, which skittered across the floor.

"A dirty martini would be great, but I can't even have that, can I?" Victoria shot Ace an aggrieved look, then shook her head. "After everything . . . I can't believe this."

"You're human," Ace said. "We've all—"

"Vomited on a billionaire in front of your entire company? After working for decades to be taken seriously? To be taken seriously *as a woman*, and then that very thing—that *womanhood*—is the thing to betray me?" Ace opened his mouth to respond but Victoria silenced him with an icy look. "Don't try to make me feel better. There's nothing you can say."

Ace put his hands up. "I won't even try. I won't point out that it's not your fault. I might, in fact, try to make you feel worse."

"Impossible. How?"

"You don't smell great," Ace replied, shooting her a smile as he went over to the stove and adjusted the heat setting.

"You do realize I won't get managing director now? Not after that disaster. Not now that they know I'm going to be out on maternity leave."

Ace opened his mouth, but Victoria beat him to it. "Don't try lecturing me about workplace equality. The idea that women aren't discriminated against for having a uterus is complete and utter horseshit! Sure, that would be nice. That would be fair: Don't punish our gender while we propagate the human race. But that's not reality."

Ace waited patiently for Victoria to finish her tirade. She knew she was preaching to the choir. Ace would never try to mansplain about workplace equality. He was the guy who couldn't eat lobster rolls after learning that crustaceans often walked claw in claw. Ace knew how many times Victoria had been mistaken for an assistant. He understood that the condition of walking-into-a-conference-room-while-female was tenuous at best and arduous at worst. He was deeply aware of how, unbelievably, Victoria still had to fight to be compensated for her worth.

"I'm going to wash the vomit out of my hair!" Victoria yelled before storming out of the room. Her dramatic exit was impaired when she tripped over her discarded shoes, stubbing her toe. "Damn it!"

Victoria limped to the closet—her sanctuary. Once there, she parted a row of hanging clothes and dove into it like Moses crossing the Red Sea. This was the only place she cried, not that she would ever admit it. Just like Victoria didn't do nerves, she didn't do tears. Over the years, she had cultivated the tough emotional shell of an armadillo, which she considered not just key to her success, but also vital for her well-being. Only by herself, in the dark confines of her closet, safely tucked away from the world, would Victoria occasionally allow herself a good cry.

An initial, indignant tear made its descent down her cheek, soon followed by its brothers-in-arms. While Victoria hoped the tears would prove cathartic and wash away some of her fury, she also tried not to think about Nash's reaction, what her coworkers were saying, how much Mark Berg was gloating, or how she had taken out her frustrations on Ace.

It was remarkable that her relationship with Ace had even happened. Victoria had been on a tear of mutually agreed-upon, no-strings dalliances when she attended a client's wedding in Montecito. She had been sitting by herself in a quiet corner of the hotel bar, downing a martini before the reception and dreading the gauntlet of social pleasantries she was about to endure, when Ace had interrupted her solitary pregame. Victoria hadn't bothered to look up before blurting, "No thanks. I'm not interested. I prefer being single."

Instead of being rebuffed, Ace asked, "Why's that? Have you been dating a bunch of clowns?" Victoria looked up to register this annoying stranger who had invaded her space. If an oak tree were cast as the star in a romantic comedy, that would be the man standing before her: handsome, tall, sturdy, capped with an impressive shock of salt-and-pepper hair. Oh, and he possessed what would doubtlessly be described as an "irresistible" twinkle in his eyes.

Victoria replied, "I don't date clowns."

That was true enough. Victoria didn't date clowns; she slept with perfectly acceptable guys for three to six months before finding perfectly reasonable excuses to extract herself. But Victoria didn't owe anyone an explanation about her personal life. She returned her eyes to her phone.

"No, you don't date clowns," Ace corrected himself, sizing her up further. "You don't date. Or you do, but you don't *relationship*."

"*Relationship* isn't a verb," Victoria responded. Clearly, this guy would have to go away now, understanding that her bar for entertaining someone's advances started at basic grammar.

"The lady deflects," Ace hit back, then tossed her a grin enclosed by parentheses of dimples.

A charming grin, those twinkling eyes, *and* dimples? Victoria was sure the damn things had never failed him. She drained the last drops of her martini and stood up.

"Nice to meet you." She didn't think she needed to voice the sentiment *Have a nice life, which I will never be a part of again.* It hadn't been the most eloquent exit line, but it was a solid plan. That is, until Victoria found her seat assignment for the wedding reception, located the hodgepodge singles' table her place card directed her to, and saw The Oak Tree sitting there.

"Should we try this again?" he said, giving her a broad grin and extending his hand. "I'm Ace."

What was Victoria to do? She introduced herself, made polite conversation, and allowed Ace to order a drink for her. At the end of the night, if forced, Victoria would have to admit that she had enjoyed his company. Then again, the people at the singles' table of a wedding were like the dregs at the bottom of a bag of potato chips. The unfortunate aunts and weird friends from college did not pose fierce competition.

Ace had asked to see Victoria again while escorting her to the hotel elevator. He handed Victoria his card and watched as she stepped inside. Victoria pressed the button for her floor. Ace pointed to the card in her hand, indicating: her move. Victoria had considered calling him. Emailing? Texting? Did men his age even text? Was there a complimentary communications course at the Genius Bar for men over the age of fifty-five with the purchase of an iPhone? What would she even say? What was the chance that this guy would be different from everyone who had come before him, that he was worth the time, the risk, the energy?

Victoria had reminded herself that her life functioned flawlessly exactly as it was. She dismissed the entire episode with Ace and left his business card in the trash can of her hotel room.

When an enormous bouquet arrived at her office without a note a week later, Harper—instinctual Gen Z digital sleuth that she was—immediately did a reverse Google image search and discovered that they were purple torenias. *Also known as Clown Flowers, LOL*, she had Slacked.

Victoria had felt something inside herself shake loose—an excavation of sorts. In hindsight she could label it. It was hope.

As she sat in their closet, inhabiting a world they now shared as a unit, Victoria thought that it was either unbelievably terrifying or downright extraordinary how one person could bend the trajectory of your life. She could smell the shallots wafting from the kitchen and her stomach—that traitor—growled with hunger. After shedding her work clothes, Victoria threw on a silk robe and rinsed her face, the cold water offering a small internal reset. When she walked back into the kitchen, Ace looked up from the stove, where he was tasting sauce from a wooden spoon. "I know," he told her. It was all he needed to say.

Victoria went over to wrap her arms around him and whispered the words into the soft fabric of his shirt anyway. "I'm sorry."

"Are you also hungry?" Ace asked.

"Yes, but I might throw up on you."

"You're my wife. You can vomit on me anytime."

"You should have put that in the vows," Victoria said.

Ace spooned puttanesca into their dishes and they sat down at the table, side by side.

"Do you want to talk about it?" he asked.

"It, the dumpster fire of my career? Or it like *Rosemary's Baby?*" Victoria pointed to her stomach. "I think you impregnated me with the devil. I've felt perfectly fine this entire time and then, at the most inopportune moment, this little fucker decided to act up."

Ace switched his focus from Victoria's face to her abdomen. "You keep putting your mom through the wringer and we're going to have words on the other side of this thing, you hear?"

Victoria froze, a rictus grin on her face.

"What?" Ace asked, putting down his fork.

"I'm going to be someone's *mom.*" Victoria paused, the words heavy on her tongue before she uttered them. "What if this was a huge mistake?"

"My love," Ace said, turning to her and placing his hand on her knee.

"I know I shouldn't say this out loud . . . but I'm having second thoughts." She looked at Ace. "Some people shouldn't be mothers."

"That's true. But you're not one of them."

"I don't like children."

"Who does? From what I can tell, it seems like they're always sticky and loud and demanding. But there must be a reason people keep having them."

"What if the maternal instinct doesn't kick in?"

"It will. I know we're old and we don't know the first thing about parenting, but we're in it together."

"What if I'm not any good?" Victoria looked at him searchingly, raw and exposed. "You know how my mom was. How she is."

"You're not her," Ace said firmly. "You're nothing like her."

Victoria thought about her mother, who had birthed her with an enthusiasm that faded in steep increments once she failed to detect any commonality. Family lore had it that as soon as Victoria began talking, she was brimming with questions, having found a voice for her insatiable curiosity. *Why are tongues wet? Why did they build the pyramids? Where do we go when we die? But how? But why? Why, why, why?*

Victoria's mother met this onslaught with confusion and then fatigue and irritation. By age five, Victoria had taught herself to read so she could find better resources to quench her thirst for information. Victoria's mother then operated with the polite remove of someone hosting a foreign exchange student in her home. She would be gracious until the semester was over, but she wouldn't try to bridge the language barrier or forge any sort of lasting bond.

Victoria met Ace's gaze and swallowed hard. "What if this is the one thing we have in common?" Victoria asked him, speaking so softly her words were barely audible. "What kind of mother feels ambivalent about being pregnant?"

Ace took Victoria's hands in his. "I've been on this planet for six decades. Not to toot my own horn, but there have been a lot of women who have wanted to procreate with me. But until I met you, I never thought about settling down and having a family. So, what does that tell you?"

"You have Alzheimer's?"

Ace tipped his head back and laughed. "I fucking love you."

Ace got up and scooped Victoria's favorite gelato into martini glasses for dessert. Then she picked up the rogue peony petals from the counter while Ace rinsed the dishes and loaded them into the dishwasher with the precision of a brain surgeon. By the time they were turning off the music and shutting down the kitchen for the night, Victoria's low-grade queasiness had subsided, and she was feeling almost like herself again. *Almost.* This course correction made her hopeful that the horrendous incident earlier in the conference room was a one-off and she'd be able to go on acting like nothing was changing for at least another month, when she entered her second trimester. After all, Victoria wasn't even showing. Until this afternoon, she hadn't experienced any evidence that she was pregnant.

As they were getting ready for bed, Victoria ducked back into their closet and, in an attempt to feel like herself again, put on the white La Perla set that was Ace's favorite. She opened the bottom drawer that housed Ace's skiwear. It was where they hid their sex toys so their housekeeper didn't have to face the discomfort of knowing too much about her employers. Victoria rifled through GORE-TEX turtlenecks and heated ski socks until she reached a layer of equipment that wasn't sold at base lodge mountain stores. She was startled to see a tuft of fluffy fabric sticking out from under a two-pronged vibrator. Victoria pulled out the unidentified object and puzzled over it for a moment: Was Ace exploring a furry fetish?

And then Victoria realized.

She marched into their bedroom. Ace was settled in their California king, reading glasses perched on his nose, Barbra Streisand's thousand-page autobiography in his hands.

Victoria held it up. "I thought we said we weren't doing this?"

Ace looked up and his face immediately became blanketed by a bashful grin.

"I know, I know. I'm sorry!" Ace said. "I couldn't help myself."

"But you put it with our sex toys?"

"It's the only designated hiding spot in the house. Aside from the safe."

Victoria nodded. She had to give him that.

"Besides," Ace added. "It *is* a rabbit."

Victoria looked down at the object in her hand, which she had only given a cursory look. Genus: stuffed animal. Species: bunny.

"We said weren't going to buy anything," Victoria said. Ace was Jewish and superstitious. Victoria was agnostic and in denial that they were having a baby. Agreeing not to fill the house with pacifiers and onesies had become an easy show of solidarity.

"Zei gezunt," Ace said. "Now can we talk about your outfit?"

Victoria remembered that she was wearing nothing except Ace's favorite bits of strategically placed French lace, but her mood had swung from lust into less prurient territory upon discovery of The Rabbit, not to be confused with her sex toy, the Rabbit. Victoria looked down at the offending object. It wasn't that Ace had gone against his own insistence that they not buy anything ahead of the baby's arrival. It was the expression on Ace's face that betrayed deep reserves of excitement that Victoria didn't share.

"I'll be right back," Victoria said, eking out a smile to her husband.

She strode into the bathroom and looked at her reflection in the suspended mirror above the his-and-hers sinks. Then she peered up at the ink-black expanse of night visible through the skylight. *Get it together*, she told herself.

Victoria entered the toilet room where the Japanese commode heralded her arrival by opening its lid with a cheerful jingle. She sank onto the heated seat and pulled down her lace thong, where she was stunned to see a vibrant Rorschach stain on the small triangle of available real estate. She stared at the color, trying to make sense of it; usually period blood had a rusty-brown hue. This was crimson like Snow White's apple, cartoonishly bold. It was a red carnation. It was a funeral flower. Victoria called out her husband's name, having the good sense to know that something was very wrong.

4

———

Liz

10 WEEKS: MINI COCKTAIL SAUSAGE

Liz gave her thirty-day notice to her landlord and started packing her things as she waited for Preston to bring up the pregnancy again. It was agonizing, a true test of her willpower, but Liz was determined not to ask Preston for his thoughts before he was ready. Two weeks after their initial conversation, and a week before Liz was set to climb that next rung of adulthood—cohabitation—she still hadn't found out what those terms were. She was about to learn that the conditions for discovery involved six vodka tonics.

But before Liz began debating how many hair-depilation devices and sweatshirts were too many to cram into a U-Haul, Preston invited her to go with him to his coworker Sameer's birthday party. It was at a dive bar in Koreatown, the kind of place that was so uncool it was cool. Preston had texted Liz to remind her about the party, as if it weren't implanted in her memory with the force of a thousand Sharpies. Liz comforted herself that even though Preston had yet to bring up the elephant in the womb, at least their plans weren't being canceled. They were still a couple, and they were still on steady ground. Right? Maybe?

As she tripped over herself trying to figure out what to wear to the party, Liz questioned whether steady ground really existed for anyone. Her therapist, an impossibly rational Gen X PsyD named Jayne, always reminded Liz that by validating a feeling, she perpetuated it. *Feelings are not facts,* she said. *They often are the mind's most creative fiction.* The day before, Jayne had urged Liz to envision an alternative default setting. *What if, instead of ending,* Jayne had said, *a relationship lasted?* Well, yeah. That would be great. Only Liz had never known that to happen. Liz was well versed in all varieties of rejection. The swipe right that wasn't reciprocated. The unsubtle *Do you want me to call an Uber for you?* while she was still half naked in a guy's bed like food simmering in the pan even though the stove had been turned off. The glaring inactivity of her phone. (Who knew you could feel the calls and texts you weren't receiving?) The pat lines delivered unceremoniously: *I'm not looking for anything serious. I feel like something's missing. I met someone else. I'm getting back together with my ex, but do you wanna fuck?*

Liz frowned, recalling how Jayne had laughed, as if Liz were paying $120 an hour, after insurance, for the express pleasure of entertaining someone with her misadventures in dating. But still, Liz tried to remember how, in the next breath, Jayne had encouraged optimism. Liz had tried to explain how she thought the best approach was to keep her expectations low. If Liz could pre-manage disappointment, it would be bearable. But Jayne had not been impressed by this.

Liz threw on a black sweater, gave it a cursory mirror check, then tore it off and looked at the other options splayed over her bed. If Preston ghosted her forever or rekindled things with his ex-girlfriend, an impossibly toned, bi-curious Pilates instructor named Jessica with fake, perfect hair and real, perfect tits, would Liz really be surprised? She pulled on another sweater—this one navy blue—and hoped for the best.

When she walked into the bar that didn't have a sign outside and was filled with kitsch inside, Liz was relieved to see that she wasn't too off the mark. Some of Sameer's friends were dressed casually, although it was the kind of casual that involved $400 Dunks, while others had come straight from work and were still wearing suits. Liz thought that her jeans and sweater split the difference satisfactorily. But then she watched Sameer's wife Pia lope away from the bar to greet someone in a miniskirt, a tattered rock-band T-shirt, and four-inch stilettos. The vibe was *I just threw this on and I look like I stepped out of the pages of* Vogue. Liz had to work a messy bun for at least an hour to achieve the right kind of undone effect and couldn't believe how naturally things— namely looks, men, and luck—came to some people.

"You made it." Preston smiled.

"Hey, of course!" Liz hugged him and worried that she had come across as desperately overeager instead of merely (and appropriately) enthusiastic. The night passed in a blur of inside jokes and industry banter. Liz tried to nod and laugh at the right times and smiled extra hard when Preston threw his arm around her shoulders and told Sameer and Pia that they were moving in together. Finally, guests started to filter out, which was a relief, because Liz's feet were killing her. She followed Preston to the valet stand, noticing that he was slurring his words a little, which made sense since he'd been slamming back vodka tonics all night. Liz didn't want to point out that Preston was plastered in case she seemed judgmental, so she just offered, "Do you want me to drive? I Ubered here because I wasn't sure about the parking situation."

Preston turned. "Great!" He was unbothered, jolly, and drunk as he paid for the valet and got into the passenger seat of his BMW. Liz slid behind the wheel and adjusted the seat settings.

"I guess you're my designated driver now," Preston said. "That's a perk!"

Liz flicked on the turn signal and pulled into traffic, wondering if this was when and how they were going to talk about The Pregnancy. Liz rooted her hands at five and nine and tried to tone down her chest palpitations; it was like a flock of birds had made a nest there and were flapping their wings to the beat of a Tiësto song. "Yeah, no need to Uber for a while." Then she snuck a glance at Preston to make sure he wasn't passed out against the passenger-side window. He wasn't necessarily alert, but he was awake, so Liz asked, "Should we talk about it? Not now, if you don't want to . . . but sometime? It's a big thing and it wasn't something we were expecting."

"But you're expecting," Preston said. "Wait! That was my first dad joke." He smiled at her, and Liz felt completely and totally . . . in love? Or maybe it was the hormones coursing through her body. She asked herself if she should push for a real conversation, then shoved this thought from her mind. Obviously, they were on the same page! So what if Preston was drunk? Didn't alcohol lower inhibitions, basically making it a truth serum? Preston was making dad jokes! He was smiling! He was going to be a dad. Their little band was going to stay together.

Liz and Preston were going to be parents.

A few days later, Liz replayed this moment as she soaked in the bathtub, cramming her limbs uncomfortably so she could fit inside. As the water turned tepid, Liz found herself obsessing over the idea that on the same night she had prepared the elaborate dinner and sprung the pregnancy news on him, Preston had likely been planning to end things. Liz had no evidence of this, but a good detective didn't need any to posit a theory.

Liz arched her back and let the bathwater cascade over her torso, careful not to spill water onto the mint-green floor tiles of the apartment she'd soon be vacating. If the results from her ten-week appointment that afternoon showed that the pregnancy wasn't viable, no one would be the wiser. They'd just think Liz had let herself go and slacked off on the strict exercise regimen that allowed her to eat most major food groups and still hold steady at an acceptable size six (four in J.Crew, but everyone knew that didn't count).

Liz forced herself to get out of the tub. She stretched her legs, which ached from being constricted too long, then stepped through the maze of boxes and inspected herself in the full-length mirror. She was suffering hormonal breakouts that had focused their attention on her chin, so she was sporting a goatee of pimples. She had immediately developed a dark line of fur, a stripe stretching across her navel, which made her feel like a skunk. And while her belly area was protruding, especially at night after a full day of eating, other areas of her body were too. Unless the baby was also growing in Liz's ass, it was safe to say that pregnancy was hurling its insults upon her, not its kindnesses.

Half an hour later, Preston met her at the doctor's office, rushing into the waiting room ten minutes late. "Did I miss anything?" Preston asked, a bit breathless. Liz had the unkind thought that her very fit boyfriend wasn't out of breath but rather putting it on for effect to make up for not being on time.

"Just my weigh-in," Liz answered. "So, no. Nothing at all. Not a pound."

Preston sensed her discomfort and rubbed Liz's back. "Babe, don't worry. You look great." Liz smiled. "You aren't fat, you're pregnant," he added.

But after Liz gave what felt like an arm's worth of blood and she and Preston were led into a generic exam room, Dr. Rosenblatt, an experienced but stone-faced man in his sixties who had a good rating online and accepted Liz's health insurance, also took note of her "accelerated weight gain." Dr. Rosenblatt warned Liz that rapid weight gain could put her into the high-risk category for pregnancy. Liz wanted to protest that they hadn't even ruled out chromosomal abnormalities and they were already talking about how much she was eating, but she nodded and kept quiet. While gesturing for Liz to insert her feet into the cold metal stirrups, Dr. Rosenblatt cautioned her against giving in to every craving. "Right now, your baby is the size of a kumquat," he said, inspecting her cervix.

"Or a mini cocktail sausage!" Preston announced.

Dr. Rosenblatt looked at him quizzically.

"There's an alternative week-by-week comparison guide," Liz explained.

"It's more fun than fruits and vegetables," Preston said.

Dr. Rosenblatt just nodded, his fingers several inches deep in Liz's vaginal canal. Though it was uncomfortable, it wasn't painful. Still, Liz resisted the urge to clench at the physical intrusion. Dr. Rosenblatt continued, "A kumquat—or a cocktail sausage—doesn't need a couple thousand extra calories. It only needs a couple hundred."

Before Liz could ask for clarification on when she would have free rein to eat as much as her appetite demanded, Dr. Rosenblatt moved on. "Let's take a look and see if there's a heartbeat," he said, referring to this possibility as casually as if he were discussing the availability of a reservation on OpenTable.

Preston shot Liz an excited look. Dr. Rosenblatt explained that he would be using a transvaginal ultrasound not only to check for a heartbeat, but also for early detection of abnormalities. Without further ado, he slapped a condom on the ultrasound wand, applied a dollop of lube, and inserted it several inches into her body. Liz tried to focus on the matter at hand rather than processing why she was mortified by having a condom-covered piece of medical equipment inserted into her in front of the person who had impregnated her. She looked at Preston, but he didn't even seem to notice the value-sized container of lube.

As Dr. Rosenblatt continued his examination wordlessly, Liz held back the tears that threatened as she sank into the amazing horribleness of the moment. Was there anything more capable of creating such an insane mix of emotions? Liz either stood on the precipice of parenthood with all its hope and love and expectations . . . or not. Preston's hand instinctively moved to hold Liz's and she grasped on to it. Dr. Rosenblatt, Liz, and Preston all looked at the ultrasound machine's screen as if it held the answers for the rest of their lives, which, for two out of the three of them, it did.

Liz couldn't breathe. The silence accompanying the appearance of a black-and-white blur on the screen felt oppressive, interminable. But then, finally, Liz heard a steady whoosh-whoosh-whoosh sound.

"There's the heartbeat," said Dr. Rosenblatt.

"Yes!" shouted Preston, fist-pumping like he did when any of his clients won any sort of sporting event.

Liz tried to swallow the enormous lump that had formed in her throat. She had promised herself that she wouldn't be dramatic, but she burst into tears that flew from her eyes like a sprinkler, staining her flimsy paper gown.

"Sorry," Liz said. "I'm just so relieved." She stared at the image on the screen: It looked like nothing, a black-and-white smear, but now this incomprehensibly small cluster of cells was a life they had created. Liz couldn't believe that such magic could exist within four such nondescript walls, that such a fantastical but common-place feat—procreation!—was happening all the time, all over the world, and that she was being allowed to participate in it.

"Is that what I think it is?" Preston asked, pointing proudly to the screen.

"No," Dr. Rosenblatt said. "We can determine gender from the blood test, though."

"Oh," Preston said, disappointed. "I thought it was a boy."

"I don't think we should find out the gender." Liz had only just come to that decision, having not allowed herself to mentally go there before they knew if there was a heartbeat or not. "What do you think?" she asked Preston. "Let's be surprised?" Before Preston could answer, Liz added, "If the blood tests show it's viable, of course," addressing Dr. Rosenblatt, but really reminding herself.

"I don't know if I can wait!" Preston said.

"It's fun to wait. There aren't too many real surprises left in life anymore, you know?" Liz said this to the room, but she willed Dr. Rosenblatt to weigh in, supporting her position.

"What do you mean?" Preston asked. "This baby was a surprise!"

Liz cleared her throat uncomfortably. She hadn't specifically told Preston that she didn't want their doctor to know the baby hadn't been planned, but she'd hoped they had an unspoken agreement, the kind born of instinct, from being reasonable people.

Liz willed Preston to let it go, but mental telepathy failed. Preston pointed to her abdomen and informed Dr. Rosenblatt, "That was an accident. What's a bigger surprise than that?"

"I wouldn't call it an accident," Liz said. Dr. Rosenblatt didn't comment. "It's . . . unplanned," Liz offered.

"How's that different?" Preston asked. "Accident, unplanned—same thing. Right, Doc?"

Dr. Rosenblatt continued jotting notes in Liz's folder. Liz took the opportunity to shoot Preston a look that she hoped came across as kind but also crystal clear: *Shut the fuck up. (Please.)*

Preston did, but they continued the conversation in the elevator after the appointment.

"There's a stigma when you say it was an accident. Dropping a glass on the floor, getting into a fender bender. Those are accidents," Liz said.

"So is getting pregnant when you thought you were using birth control," Preston challenged.

"I was," Liz said, failing to meet his eye. "The pill is only ninety-nine percent effective. No one talks about the other one percent!"

Never mind the fact that the efficacy rate dropped when combined with antibiotics, which Liz had been prescribed for a bout of strep throat. Never mind the fact that the rate went down even more if the pills weren't taken diligently each day. And especially never mind the fact that on one Friday evening, Liz had glanced into her toiletry bag and noticed three little pink egg-shaped pills for Wednesday, Thursday, and Friday that she had neglected to take. And then Liz hadn't dry-swallowed the forgotten pills on the spot. She hadn't told Preston that he should pull out. She hadn't mentioned it at all. Liz had tempted fate. She had, if not flat-out invited the pregnancy, at least opened the door and put out a welcome mat.

Liz rationalized that this didn't make her a bad person. No one told the person they were with everything. The world would cease to function! Preston didn't need to know that Liz waxed her naturally furry mustache once a month, or about Liz's hand in the pregnancy. She hoped that the guilt gripping her internal organs would eventually dissipate.

The elevator arrived and Liz darted forward, as if to outrun her own thoughts. Preston followed her into the lobby of the medical building. Momentarily stunned by the burst of sunlight streaming through the glass doors, they both put up their hands to shield their eyes from the glare.

People of all ages filled the lobby, but Liz zeroed in on a new dad toting a car seat, his newborn swaddled and tucked inside it like a pearl in an oyster shell. His wife, beside him, was still swollen from the battle her body had waged, and fatigue was evident on her face, but she beamed with love and joy and pride. They were so happy—the whole tableau was so tender—that it almost hurt for Liz to take it in.

Liz looked away and Preston must have caught her pained expression. "Sorry!" he said quickly. "I get it. We won't say the pregnancy was an accident."

Liz thanked him. They exited the building and Preston walked Liz to her car, gesturing that his was across the parking lot.

"I really don't want the baby to know that he or she was unplanned," Liz said, getting worked up again. "A child who thinks they weren't wanted can struggle with those feelings their entire life." Liz gave him what she hoped was a calm, unbothered smile but it probably looked how she felt, which was deranged.

Preston took Liz by the arm. "Are you all right?" he asked. "I have to get back to work, but . . ."

I'll stay here if you're going to have a mental breakdown in the parking lot of the medical complex.

"I'm fine!" Liz assured him brightly. Chill, easygoing Liz was back, the break in character a blip, an acute but brief outbreak of irrationality that had been contained—no need to phone the CDC!

"I'll come by your place later to help you finish up the boxes," Preston said, giving Liz a peck on the lips.

As Preston jogged away, Liz slumped against the passenger door of her old Audi. She frowned, then thought about her own mother as she unlocked her car and slid behind the wheel. She hadn't informed Angela she was pregnant yet. She had told Preston she didn't want to tell anyone until they got the results of the genetic testing back and knew that the pregnancy was viable—a totally reasonable and typical approach. Then again, reasonable and typical never fared well around Angela.

Which was probably why, a few days later, when Liz and Preston received a stellar DNA report, Liz still balked at the idea of picking up the phone. She rationalized her hesitance: It was big news, better conveyed face-to-face. Plus, Angela was probably joining a cult in some backwoods corner of the globe with bad cell service. Liz couldn't imagine trying to deliver her pregnancy news over the static of a poor connection, the conversation devolving into a frustrating game of Mad Libs while they struggled to make out each other's words. The real issue, however, was that announcing her pregnancy wouldn't be like poking the bear. It would be like ramming it with a stick, midwinter, and shouting, *Get the fuck up, bitch! Feeding time!*

That night, while Preston was scooping takeout onto plates, and after he'd announced that he wanted to try going vegan, Liz made her case. She had solid reasons to delay telling Angela about the mini cocktail sausage—the baby.

"Of course you'd want to do it in person," Preston said. "So it's great timing."

"What's great timing?"

"Your mom's coming here next week. Didn't she tell you?"

Liz's face burned. "No. I mean yeah, I just didn't know it was definite. You know what she's like."

"She sounded sure," Preston said happily. "Which is awesome. I can't wait to tell her."

Liz nodded numbly. Preston had only met Angela once, when she made a pit stop in LA with a boyfriend who had some ridiculous name Liz couldn't remember. Angela and Kale or Lyon or Tide had been on their way to a holistic health retreat in Joshua Tree, which Liz translated to mean a weekend of magic-mushroom-fueled past-life regressions with sound baths and vortex vibrations. Whatever those were.

Liz had steeled herself to introduce her mother and boyfriend and prepped Preston with the basics: Angela was a free spirit, Liz's childhood had been chaotic, they were on fine terms if not exceptionally close. But to Liz's dismay, Angela and Preston had hit it off. The Angela who had shown up that day was fun and warm, like she had upgraded to the breezy bohemian model of herself. Angela had offered freshly rolled joints, trilling that it was legal now, and a bottle of skin-contact orange wine, insisting that it was *the* color to be drinking. She told rambling, amusing stories, pausing to let her stupidly named boyfriend add something here and there. Liz had remained pretty much monosyllabic. After the visit,

Angela had traded in Kale or Lyon or Tide for an energy healer she'd met at the orgy in Joshua Tree, and Preston said he didn't understand why Liz told him that her mom could be difficult. He thought Angela was terrific!

Preston smiled at Liz across his vegetable chopped salad. "How should we tell her?" he asked, spearing lettuce with his fork. "I want to plan something special."

Liz took a sip of water to avoid answering. Though she was loath to endorse any of Angela's claims about her intuitive gifts, Liz did have to admit that her mother had an uncanny ability to tease things out. For more reasons than one, Liz was dreading the reunion with every fiber of her being.

5

—

Victoria

10 WEEKS: KUMQUAT

Everything's okay," Dr. Waldman announced, covering the distance between the door of Victoria's hospital room and her bedside in four efficient strides. Sitting up in her hospital bed, Victoria watched Ace leap to his feet, his face rearranging itself from a tight mask of concern to a slightly more relaxed state. Victoria realized she was having a similar physiological response: muscles slackening when she hadn't noticed they were tensed.

"I'm not having a miscarriage?" Victoria asked. "Because when I Googled—"

"Never Google," Dr. Waldman advised. "You'll self-diagnose with five different conditions, and if you're pregnant, the first is—"

"Preeclampsia? Toxoplasmosis? Molar pregnancy? Obstetric cholestasis?" Victoria filled in. Ace's head whipped over to her, his eyebrows shooting up with surprise.

"Your baby is fine," Dr. Waldman reassured Victoria, smoothing her white doctor's coat, which was still crisp despite the late hour.

"And my wife? What happened?" Ace said.

"Most likely a subchorionic hematoma," Dr. Waldman said.

"At least that doesn't sound terrifying," Ace replied facetiously. Behind him, there was a pain-assessment-tool poster to help patients communicate their level of discomfort via a series of exaggerated cartoon faces. Ace frowned, resembling the orange grumpy face in the middle. Moderately severe pain.

"In layman's terms," Dr. Waldman continued, "it means bleeding from one of the membranes that surround the embryo."

"What?" Ace cried.

"I know it sounds scary, but this should resolve on its own," Dr. Waldman said. Victoria tried to relax and gave Ace a look to suggest he attempt the same.

"Thank God." Ace sat back down next to Victoria in the visitor's chair that was pulled as close as possible next to her bed.

"I guess we overreacted," Victoria said, feeling a little silly for bolting to the hospital and for having Dr. Waldman's after-hours service page the doctor with a request (it admittedly came across as more of a panicked demand) for her to meet them there as soon as possible.

"Not at all," Dr. Waldman said. "I'm sure the internet told you that there are unfortunately much more worrisome reasons for bleeding, especially with a geriatric pregnancy. It's important that we ruled them out."

"And you did, definitively?" Ace asked, a twinge of hysteria creeping back into his voice. "All of them?"

"Baby and mother are both fine," Dr. Waldman confirmed. She pulled out her iPad, scrolled through Victoria's chart, then looked up at them. "Since you're here, would you like to know the gender?"

Victoria and Ace locked eyes. At the same time, they said, "Yes." Ace clutched Victoria's hand between his palms.

"It's a boy," Dr. Waldman told them.

Ace exclaimed, then started sobbing. Victoria's head swam, and suddenly, all the reasons she had decided to try for a baby crystallized before her: the recurring dreams about a towheaded toddler with a stubborn cowlick or wayward pigtails; visions of Ace teaching a tiny person how to ride a bike, running behind the wheels until wobbles segued into triumph—the nebulous but still vivid sense of a person Victoria had begun to conjure up before that should have been possible, as if the act of imagining a child was itself a critical part of bringing him or her into existence.

"I'm just glad the baby's okay," Ace blubbered. "And you're okay. We're all okay . . ."

"It makes it more real, doesn't it?" Dr. Waldman said, smiling. Down the hall, beyond a closed door, an alarm went off, faint but persistent.

Victoria nodded. "I didn't expect that." But it was undeniable: The assignment of gender, no matter which one, transformed an embryo from an amorphous idea into a distinct entity. A baby.

"I'm going to give you two a moment while I fill out your release forms," Dr. Waldman said, and excused herself.

Victoria had never fully appreciated her concierge doctor's expertise and attentiveness until she and Ace were speeding to the nearest hospital with their hearts in their throats. If the scare was some sort of test—*you want this baby, bitch?*—it had worked.

When they had started trying, Victoria had urged Ace to temper his expectations, even going so far as to supply him with gloomy statistics and unsettling medical jargon, but his hope was like the Olympic flame. And then, it was rewarded. Despite Victoria's warnings and all the data working against them, it was absurdly easy for a forty-three-year-old woman and sixty-year-old man to get pregnant. Naturally, no less! It was like a cosmic joke. Since their fertility limbo had only lasted two months, it didn't allow ample time for Victoria's ambivalence to resolve itself.

She turned to her husband, the puddle. "Are you glad it's a boy? A little you."

"I'm just so happy he's okay," Ace said between tears. "Obviously, all I wanted was a healthy child . . ."

Victoria traced the lines of her husband's handsome face with her gaze, trying to imagine it duplicated in an infant.

"It's not about whether we're having a boy or girl," Ace added. "It's that I'm doing it with you. You're it, Victoria. Ever since I first laid eyes on you."

"You mean when I rejected you without looking up?"

Ace laughed, the tears finally subsiding. "Okay, maybe I fell for you right after that. You're my person. And now you're the person who's going to make me a father."

They kissed, then leaned their foreheads against each other's. "We're doing this," Victoria said.

"It's happening," Ace answered. "My heir is being brought into the world, at long last."

"Ace Junior?" she joked.

"Yes! A.J.!"

Victoria pretended to gag. "Over my dead body."

Ace's mouth turned down. "Too soon," he said.

"Ace, I'm okay. Are you?" she said, gesturing around.

Ace allowed himself a long, steady exhale. When he was a teenager, his mother had died slowly and painfully of ovarian cancer. Hospitals brought up a lot for him.

"I am," Ace said, taking her hands in his again. Victoria gazed into the face she knew so well she could draw it from memory. "We're doing this," she repeated, letting him know that it was finally beginning to sink in. "You and me . . . and the baby."

You and me and the baby.

The words ran like a refrain through Victoria's head as a nurse brought in the discharge paperwork and they thanked Dr. Waldman for rushing over to take care of them, pocketing pamphlets about maternal health. Ace treated Victoria like a Ming vase even after she had been cleared from the mandatory wheelchair ride to the hospital's perimeter, insisting that she take his arm for the three steps to the car, gingerly depositing her in the passenger seat, and then driving at the literal speed limit the entire way home, even though everyone was honking at them. Victoria was touched, so she didn't remark on how Ace had adopted the pace of an elderly snail. Sometimes marriage meant going thirty-five miles per hour.

They arrived home after midnight, bone-tired from the ordeal, and headed straight for their bedroom. Everything looked the same since they left the room a few hours and a different world ago, like the space had been hermetically sealed in their absence. Victoria and Ace peeled off their clothes, which didn't quite remove the lingering antiseptic scent of the hospital. Ace sniffed his armpit, nostrils curling, but confessed, "I'm too tired. Let's shower in the morning?"

Victoria agreed. She was weary but also strangely wired. In the chaos of the evening, she had all but pushed the day's earlier events out of her mind, but now she remembered—and commented—that she had to confront them at work the next day.

"You're not actually thinking of going to the office tomorrow?" Ace asked as they both walked into the bathroom to give their teeth a quick brush.

"You heard Dr. Waldman. The baby and I are both fine," Victoria said.

"You need to rest!"

"If I call in sick, which I have never done, it's only going to make everything worse," Victoria said between brushes.

Ace tucked Victoria under the covers as if ensuring her comfort would also translate into her—and the baby's—health and safety. Then he lay down beside her and was fast asleep less than thirty seconds after his head hit the pillow. Victoria peered over at him. She knew that her husband had been deeply affected by the scare, but he was also peacefully comatose. Unlike Victoria. She slipped out of bed carefully so she wouldn't disturb Ace, but he didn't stir.

Victoria threw on slippers and padded out of their bedroom, gazing around their house like she was seeing it for the first time, but really it was that she was looking at it through a new lens. Children hadn't been on the radar when they'd bought the house, a modern Spanish-style home perched on a leafy promontory off Coldwater Canyon. This house, the first house where she had cared about things like crown moldings, would get messy and marked with the stamp of a child, its chevron-patterned hardwood floors scuffed by toys, the White Heron baseboards striped with crayons when no one was looking. It would experience a different iteration of Victoria and Ace as they made the leap from a twosome able to abuse their freedom and luxuriate in selfishness if they so chose to *parents*. They would soon share one primary goal—raising a human—with all the attendant changes, responsibilities, and sacrifices this monolithic shift entailed.

Bet you didn't see that coming, Victoria wanted to tell her wainscoted walls as she stepped into the soon-to-be baby's room. They had never outfitted it to serve as a guest room, instead using it as a spillover storage space for extraneous odds and ends—spare suitcases, old memorabilia, and the like. Victoria tried to imagine the bookshelves filled with fairy tales and children's stories, the Farrow & Ball Au Lait walls covered with whimsical wallpaper or a jungle-animal mural, the corner occupied by a rocking chair rather than an extra-jumbo pack of paper towels. She sat down on the floor, trying to anticipate what it would feel like to inhabit this space with a child. The house's exterior lights, which illuminated the olive trees in the backyard, filtered in through the windows and cast stippled shadows on the floor of the darkened room. Her mind was still racing, but it had begun to slow. Should she . . . talk to him?

Victoria put a hand on her still-flat abdomen. "So . . ." she began, her voice a self-conscious whisper before stopping altogether. She felt ridiculous.

"Hi," she began again. Should she introduce herself? *I'm your vessel, your mom, your home for the next thirty or so weeks. I hope you'll find the stay to your liking and give me a five-star review.* Victoria shook her head at herself. The lack of sleep was hitting; she was losing it. But she did have things to say.

"I didn't think I wanted to be a mother," Victoria told her unborn child. "The whole idea that a woman has to reproduce in order to be fulfilled, in order to *fulfill* her purpose on this earth, that really stuck in my craw, you know?" She imagined her little boy nodding while he floated, suspended in amniotic fluid like an astronaut in space. "But you know what? If more women were honest about being conflicted about motherhood, maybe the world would have less crappy parents and fewer messed-up kids. Obviously, I changed my mind," Victoria continued telling her unborn child. "And that's the thing about life. One person can come into yours and change everything about it. That's what your dad did and now it's your turn. Because I want you. I want you very, very much."

A shadow passed across the floor and Victoria looked up to see Ace standing in the doorway. She wondered how much he had heard.

"I couldn't sleep, so I thought I'd talk to our unborn child like a lunatic," she told him.

"My dear, if you're a lunatic, I don't know what to call half the women I dated in the great big bad before," Ace said, sitting down next to her. He put one of his hands on top of hers and Victoria admired it. She had always been a sucker for large, strong hands that were more like paws. "What have you two been talking about?" Ace asked.

"The basics," Victoria said. "Integrity, equality, individualism . . ."

"Great." Ace smiled. "All that's left for me to do is teach him how to throw a football."

"Meaning, you're going to learn how to do that?" Victoria teased.

"YouTube," Ace said. "I'm sure there's a video for how to explain to everyone at the playground that you're the dad, not the grandpa."

"We're really talking about how you're old when it's fundamentally impossible for a medical professional to reference my pregnancy without putting the word *geriatric* in front of it?"

Ace offered Victoria an unbothered shrug. "We're young at heart."

They walked hand in hand back to their bedroom as Ace enumerated the reasons they'd make better parents at their advanced ages than if they had embarked upon the journey when they were less experienced, an argument Victoria had heard before and couldn't say she disagreed with. Still, Victoria thought as she tried to fall asleep next to Ace for the second time, she really would have liked to have made managing director before she took on the mantle of motherhood. Her last thought, before she finally drifted off to sleep, was that she was scared motherhood would make her less ambitious—and equally scared it wouldn't.

Victoria chose her favorite power suit that stopped just short of *fuck you* shoulder pads. The lack of sleep showed on her face, most particularly the sallow under-eye circles that Ace pretended not to be able to see. Victoria said if that was the case, he needed to get his vision checked, then smeared on a thick concealer. She wasn't one to make the same mistake twice, so she took the time to shove a piece of sourdough toast in her mouth and offered Ace her cheek to kiss on her way out the door. She made it to the office in fifteen minutes and girded herself to confront her coworkers' reactions.

"Victoria!" Richard Delancey, one of the partners, exclaimed as soon as she stepped off the elevator into the lobby. "We didn't have a chance to congratulate you yesterday."

Victoria paused. Why would he want to congratulate her on what had been an unmitigated disaster? Her confusion must have been apparent because Richard clarified, "The baby!" Richard looked like he was threatening to hug her. He also seemed . . . genuine?

"Oh, yes. Well, I did run out of here like I shit the bed on signing a star client," Victoria said. "That didn't exactly leave ample time for a postmortem."

Richard flashed her a sympathetic look. "You win some, you lose some." He shrugged. "Cliché as it sounds, my kids are the best thing I've ever done. Including the unemployed dipshit who's the reason there's smoke coming from my Amex."

"Note to self: Watch my credit score," Victoria said.

"There you go," Richard chuckled. "That's all you need to know about parenting."

Victoria laughed. Did she and Richard just bond?

"I'm happy for you," Richard reiterated before heading to his office.

As she walked to hers, Victoria was met with similar sentiments by everyone she encountered. Only Mark came across as anything less than authentic when he asked Victoria how she was feeling (probably hoping for hyperemesis to sideline her for the rest of the pregnancy) and offered his condolences for the conference-room debacle.

"Do you mind if I take a shot at Nash?" he asked, his shellacked hair immobile as he cocked his head. "It looks like I'm our only hope to get him at the firm, after all," Mark added.

It took reserves of well-honed resolve for Victoria to maintain a poker face. She couldn't believe—well, she could—that Mark would have the audacity to swoop in so quickly. With the events of the previous night—the hospital visit, the mere four hours of sleep she had managed before reporting to the office—Victoria hadn't had a moment to craft a contrite apology to Nash. However futile the endeavor might be, she was at least planning to try to salvage the relationship and see if there was any hope he might still sign with her. But Mark was giving the impression that it was a fait accompli. Victoria didn't think Nash would take a liking to Mark. He was proficient at his job but his personality carried the finesse of a Brillo pad. Nevertheless, the idea of it still burned. Victoria offered a thin-lipped smile to Mark and said, "Go for it."

She walked away, fury building. Was this how it was going to be now? Victoria could play at being one of the men, but not when she was marked in a way that shouted her femininity.

She was so preoccupied she forgot to consider Harper. As Victoria rounded the corner towards her office, her assistant's shriek made her jump.

"We're having a baby!" Harper exclaimed. "I am SO! SO! SO! Excited!"

"Thanks, Harper." Victoria smiled at her assistant, who held the distinction of being the first person to jump up and down in that hallway, and this included a client of Victoria's who learned that he had quadrupled his net worth to a cool $400 million.

Harper lunged forward to hug Victoria. When Harper pulled back, her eyes beelined for Victoria's stomach. Victoria prayed Harper wouldn't toss out any horrible phrases like *bumpwatch* or *baby-loading zone.*

"Mark's such a dick. Coming in like that and trying to poach your client? *Rude!*" Harper rolled her eyes. "Screw him. You kill at work and you have a guy who worships you and you're having a baby. You win." When Victoria heard it spelled out like that, it almost sounded like she could have it all, even though she knew the mere concept was a colossal fallacy propagated by the patriarchy. "I'm still trying to figure out one thing I'm good at," Harper continued. "Besides being a genius with a Beautyblender."

Victoria put her hand on Harper's shoulder to usher her into the office with her. "I'm a little terrified to have this baby, to tell you the truth."

"Why?" Harper asked. "You're going to be such a good mom."

Victoria nearly halted in her tracks. It had rolled off Harper's tongue so easily. To try to corral her emotions, Victoria continued over to her desk, sat down, and powered on her monitors.

"Thanks, Harper. That means a lot. I hope so."

"I know so!"

"I have managed to keep that orchid alive," Victoria said, gesturing to the elegant bloom. "So maybe that bodes well."

Harper looked at the orchid, then flushed a deep pink.

"What?" Victoria asked. "Harper . . . ?"

"I tried plant CPR. I put an ice cube in it every week but . . ." Harper shook her head. Victoria looked at the thriving orchid with confusion.

"I got you a new one before you noticed it was dying . . . slash dead."

"Oh," Victoria said, the implication registering. "I can't keep a plant alive." A moment of uncertainty transpired between them, but then Victoria started laughing, which gave permission to Harper to join in, and soon the two of them were giggling like seventh graders on the school bus.

"I can't believe you swapped out my dead flower," Victoria said.

"My parents did it with my goldfish when I was six," Harper explained, her face gleaming with amusement.

Victoria chuckled. She had been patting herself on the back when she could not, in fact, keep anything alive. It was only later, when Victoria thought about how much weight she had placed on the orchid's ability to thrive despite her inability to provide it the proper care, that she decided she would buy a horticulture manual, if that's what it took, because she *was* going to keep Orchid II alive and flourishing from here on out.

6

———

Liz

12 WEEKS: JELLY MUNCHKIN

Liz had hoped that something—a turtle migration, a peyote harvest, a NXIVM meeting—would call Angela away and require her to reschedule her visit, but no such luck. While Preston uncorked bottles of orange wine, Liz shoved boxes of random belongings into the second bedroom, out of the way, and tried to mentally prepare herself. She heard the first notes of mystical flute music stream through the speakers in Preston's (now their?) house and stopped short. A line had to be drawn. Northern Plains Flute Key G was that line.

Liz rushed into the kitchen, where Preston was wiping down counters.

"Please tell me this is a joke and you're going to change the music before my ears start to bleed," she said.

"Your mom loves this flutist! Flautist?"

"She also loves occult magic and fringe theories."

Preston listened to the music for a second. "But it's kinda nice, no? Relaxing?" Liz just looked at him. "Okay, I'll switch it."

"Thanks. And honestly, we don't have to make a fuss," Liz said, gesturing to the fruit platter, wineglasses, and gift box on the counter that actually contained a sonogram photo.

"It's your mom!" Preston replied. "We never get to see her."

"We don't roll out the red carpet for your family."

"They live two hours away." Preston switched the music to a Pandora yacht rock station.

Liz bit her tongue to keep from saying that yes, Preston's family lived in Orange County, less than two hours away, but she had only met them twice. She told herself that this said more about Preston's relationship with his family than it did about how serious their relationship was. It seemed like Preston's interactions with his parents, his older sister Piper, and his sister's husband Brooks were fine . . . but also like they were actors in a play instead of real people? The whole dynamic reminded Liz of the way she spoke to a cashier at the grocery store. *Did you get your holiday shopping done? You see the game last night?* Preston's family had been perfectly pleasant on the two occasions they had dinner, but Liz also couldn't escape the idea that they wouldn't have noticed if she had gotten up to go to the bathroom and never come back.

"She's going to be here soon!" Preston announced, and Liz snapped out of it to see that he was looking down at his phone. Liz wondered whether Preston had received a text from her mother or if Angela had enabled location-tracking services for him. "Do you want to set up the cheese board while I straighten up the living room?"

Liz mustered a smile and crossed to the fridge to get some Camembert.

"Don't put out the Camembert!" Preston reminded her. "Stinky cheeses remind Angela of bathroom mold."

"Does Her Highness have any other likes and dislikes we common folk should know about?"

Preston shot her a look. *Ha ha.*

Liz opened the fridge and pulled out some inoffensive cheeses. As far as she knew, Preston hadn't told anyone else about his bizarre, secret guilty pleasure: the royal family. He could name every one of Queen Elizabeth's beloved corgis. He had watched each episode of *The Crown* at least twice. And Preston had told Liz that when England's longest-reigning monarch passed away, he had taken it hard, been downcast for weeks. Now that Preston was making a fuss over Angela's visit like she was Camilla's long-lost cousin, Liz had another reason to be worried: She needed their conversation to stay within domestic borders. She didn't want to freak Preston out with a laundry list of topics to avoid, but the royals—and really, Great Britain overall—fell under that umbrella.

Liz knew from experience that her mother would be only too happy to launch into a tirade about colonialism, the monarchy's pedagogical hierarchies, or its longstanding systems of oppression. Liz remembered standing in the Painted Desert in Arizona, age ten, on the way to her new home in an intentional lesbian community in Santa Fe led by a woman named Ocean whom Angela (going through a sapphic phase) was enamored with. Liz had been trying to take in the pastel brushstrokes of nature, but Angela was ranting about caste systems and sociopolitical overlords. It was tough to relax and enjoy the view when your adult needed a benzo large enough to topple an elephant whenever anyone used the word *princess*.

Liz sighed as she lined up seed crackers like obedient soldiers on the marble cheese board. She promised her unborn child—for what wouldn't be the first time—that she would do things differently. Liz wouldn't allow the same mistakes to tumble down the generational line; she would use personal history as a primer instead of a playbook. Even though she was becoming a mother, she could not, would not, turn into *her* mother. Given that Liz didn't consult tarot cards for major life decisions, there wasn't much danger of that, but Liz still had to make the point to herself.

The doorbell rang. "She's here!" Preston exclaimed as he bounded over to the entrance. Liz tried to mentally prepare herself to walk on eggshells for the next hour; she'd never developed an emotional callus thick enough to contend with Angela.

"We're set with the plan?" Preston yelled over his shoulder.

"We'll give her the gift box when we sit down," Liz confirmed, and braced herself for carnage.

The door swung open. "Angela, hi!"

Liz watched from the kitchen as her mother stepped inside and opened her arms, the familiar jingle of bangle bracelets announcing her arrival like a wind chime at Spahn Ranch. Angela swept Preston into a fond embrace and Liz couldn't help but watch with fascination. Angela was big on physical touch with everyone except the person she had once shared a body with. It was like Liz had hit her quota in the womb.

"You look great. Are you getting younger?" Preston said. Thrilled, Angela waved this off in a faux show of humility. "Seriously, you gotta tell me your secret," Preston said, laying it on thick.

"Only if you tell me yours," Angela teased. *Code word: tiara,* Liz thought.

"Deal." Preston grinned.

Angela giggled. Was she flirting? Liz wouldn't have put it past her, but given Liz's expectant state, the idea left a particularly sour taste in her mouth. Liz stepped out into the foyer at the same time Angela whispered to Preston, "I'll tell you my secret: tantric sex."

Liz stifled an eye roll. That was hardly a secret. Neither Preston nor Angela could qualify for a discussion on secrets, however. Liz was haunted by the image of those three pink pills. But Preston and Angela had stopped fawning over each other and were walking towards her.

Liz stood awkwardly, unsure whether to go over and open her arms. "Hmm . . ." her mother assessed. "I'm picking up on a new vibe. Did you do something to your hair?"

"No," Liz said. "It's the same." Angela narrowed her eyes and kept them trained on Liz.

"Something's different." Liz squirmed under her mother's penetrating gaze until she couldn't take it anymore.

"I'm pregnant."

Angela's eyes widened.

"Liz!" Preston turned to her, disappointed.

Liz mouthed, "Sorry!" It had taken all of thirty seconds for Liz's resolve to evaporate; the news had slipped out as if it were a burden she needed to unload rather than a source of joy to be heralded. Liz glanced over to the gift box on the kitchen counter. She had blown it.

"Pregnant!" Angela repeated, stunned. Liz had never managed to throw her mother for a loop . . . until now. Liz allowed herself a tiny moment of satisfaction.

"At least that explains it. I was going to say you look a bit . . ." Angela made a meal of searching for the right word. "Sturdy."

Liz absorbed this with the stoicism of a Secret Service agent and refused to take the bait. "Do you want some wine?" Liz asked brightly.

They sat down in the living room and Liz hoped her mother was impressed by the accomplishment she had added to her résumé: live-in girlfriend.

"Knocked up," Angela commented, sipping greedily from a glass of orange wine and nodding at her surroundings, like now the change in address made sense.

"She's twelve weeks," Preston said. "We're waiting to find out if it's a boy or a girl."

"Thank God you're not doing one of those horrendous gender reveals," Angela opined. "Those people in Virginia who got their legs blown off by the blue smoke from that cannon deserved everything that was coming to them."

Liz pursed her lips. She was tempted to suggest that suffering the loss of a limb might be a tad punitive for a questionable party choice, but they were far too early into the visit for her to risk provoking Angela.

"We'd never do a gender reveal," Preston assured Angela. "So tacky. Finding out is going to be the best surprise."

"Plus, this way, you're allowing the child to make decisions about what gender he, she, or they identify as rather than letting society decide 'You're a boy, you're a girl,'" Angela sniffed.

Liz's brow furrowed. "I'm all for someone deciding their own identity, but this is less of a political statement and more like, we're not finding out if it's a boy or girl until the baby is born."

Angela's face hardened. "You're going to pander to an antiquated social construct that doesn't honor individual choice? I always hoped you'd think outside the box, Liz . . ." Angela shook her head.

Liz should have known that if a gendered baby came out of her uterus instead of a *they*, she would be a de facto disappointment to her mother.

"You should try the leaf rattle," Angela advised.

"The what?" Liz asked, baffled by this non sequitur.

"The chakapa? From Peru?" Angela replied as if she were explaining the basics of life to a complete moron.

"Unfamiliar with the chakapa," Liz said tightly.

"It's a tool to heal blockages." Angela addressed Preston, like it was clear that Liz was a lost cause. "It can also cleanse your energy and bring in balance and harmony."

Liz didn't trust herself to respond. An awkward silence stretched out between them.

"You know what? We *are* going to have a nonbinary baby shower," Preston said, looking hopefully at Angela to see if he had successfully fluffed her spirits. Liz's head whipped over again. Preston flashed her a look like *Just go with it.*

"A baby shower?" Angela said, her face souring.

"I know," Preston said. "But I'm sure Liz's friends will want to do something for her."

Liz sat silently as Preston reframed Liz's hypothetical gender-neutral baby shower as a nonbinary celebration of life and the infinite diversity of the human experience. She wondered if Preston was placating Angela or if he knew the difference.

The conversation went downhill from there.

Angela warned Preston that Liz had been a colicky baby and hoped their child would inherit Preston's disposition. This led into an announcement about how brutal the first six months were. "No one talks about it," Angela declared, "but babies are miserable. All that crying, screaming, and spitting up, while they suck the life force out of you? Plus, they're ugly. Anyone who calls one of those bald, shriveled-up things cute is lying!" She glanced over at Liz. "Seriously. You looked like Bernie Sanders fucked a hamster with alopecia."

Liz suggested that since some parents seemed to love their infants, maybe Angela wasn't a baby person. (Or a toddler person, or a kid person, or a tween person, or . . .) Angela's eyes narrowed but she didn't deny this. "We'll see," she said smugly, taking another sip of wine. "At least you didn't destroy my body," she told Liz. "I've always had an exceptional metabolism," Angela gloated to Preston. "Part of my divine goddess energy."

Liz shifted uncomfortably and forbade herself from looking down at the spread of her thighs on the couch cushion. She would not let her mother get under her skin. "You were also really young when you had me," Liz reminded the room. "That must've helped."

"No. Some things are sacred gifts from the divine." Angela gave her buoyant breasts an appreciative pat. Liz curled her fingers and dug her nails into her palms. All she'd wanted, her whole life, was a mother who did Zumba instead of ketamine; instead she got an identity-hopping narcissist who protested the middle school's anti-drug program. *Yes, I dare to go up against DARE!* Angela had shouted up and down the front steps during homeroom.

"What time do you need to get going?" Liz asked Angela, checking her watch and trying to steer the visit to an end. "Didn't you say you had a moon gathering later?"

"A moon circle, Liz. A moon *circle*." Angela tossed a look in Preston's direction. "Considering how many I brought her to when she was little, you'd think she would remember."

"I'm guessing I was asleep since they were probably past my bedtime."

Angela scoffed. "You know you didn't have a bedtime!" Liz stayed quiet and Angela interpreted it as a damning silence. "Here we go again," she said. "You didn't have a chore chart—someone call Child Protective Services!"

Someone had, when Liz was in fourth grade, but Angela packed their things into their ancient station wagon and crossed state lines before anything came of it. Liz didn't point this out.

"I wish my mom was as cool as you," Preston told Angela.

Liz almost snorted, thinking about how different Angela was from Preston's mother. Angela considered a pile of towels a perfectly acceptable substitute for a crib and usually neglected to mention Liz's existence, especially when it conflicted with Angela's persona as an artistic muse, grassroots political activist, dedicated Burner, or middle-aged modern urban witch. Then there was Preston's mother Cricket Lancaster, an Episcopalian blonde from Connecticut who had sought refuge in the country clubs of Orange County after she bravely made the trail west to California as a condition of her married life. Cricket never encountered a toile pattern she didn't like and loved being a mother as long as she could outsource childcare to a team of nannies, housekeepers, and tutors.

"I guess we'll be meeting soon," Angela said. The thought of these two women in the same room sent a chill down Liz's spine.

"Definitely before the baby shower," Preston agreed.

"You'll have to let me know when that is," Angela said, twisting her lips with disapproval. "Rain and I are going to Esalen next week to decompress and then I'll be working on new pieces for the art fair in Taos."

"Who's Rain?" Preston asked. Liz didn't know the answer either, but she also didn't care. Liz was used to an endless parade of her mother's flings, each one more inappropriate and fleeting than the last.

"My soulmate," Angela said. The bottle of orange wine was sweating in the ice bucket.

"Another one?" Liz blurted. Oops. She hadn't meant to say that out loud.

Angela glared. "Some people are love magnets, Liz. They have an irresistible energy and otherworldly capacity to attract and connect with others."

Liz took an almond from the cheese board and placed a protective hand on her bloated stomach. The dairy she had eaten was causing fireworks of gas and she was still at the stage in her relationship where she didn't want to admit any bodily functions to Preston, which was an issue she was going to have to figure out fast now that they were sharing a living space and, also, if the delivery-room horror stories she had heard weren't urban legends.

"Anyway," Liz said, desperately hoping her mother would leave soon, "you're in love and I'm pregnant. Big day for everyone."

"We'll look into that leaf rattle!" Preston chimed in.

"I'll loan you mine," Angela offered. "Excellent for unblocking chakras. Speaking of well-being, what about that pharmaceutical poison you're so fond of?" Angela asked, turning to Liz. "Did you go off your meds?"

"Wait. What meds?" Preston asked, his eyes darting back and forth between Angela and Liz.

"The Effexor," Angela said. Preston's eyes narrowed.

"You're on Effexor? You didn't tell me that."

"Can we talk about this later?" Liz said, staring at the cheese.

"Haven't there been studies about kids born with three hands, or ADHD, or dumb-dumb IQs because their moms kept popping that garbage when they were pregnant?" Angela said.

"I don't think there's been one documented case of Prozac causing a three-handed baby," Liz said, seething.

"Wait, so you're on Prozac?" Preston asked.

"No. I was making a point."

"So, you're not on something?"

Liz had sampled every mood stabilizer on the market, but this was something she'd planned on discussing, along with her choice to stay on Effexor, at another time. A time when she was prepared, when the tape on her moving boxes wasn't still sticky, and when, most importantly, her mother was nowhere around.

"Can we please talk about this later?" Liz asked again. "There's nothing to worry about. I wouldn't do anything to endanger the baby's health."

"How did I not know this?" Preston asked. Liz pushed down the gnawing truth that her antidepressant was the least of it, while Angela seized the opportunity to refresh her wine. She poured herself a full glass, which glowed like a late-harvest sun.

"A lot of people are on antidepressants," Liz said. "I bet half the people we know are on something, or else they're microdosing on their lunch breaks."

"I have an incredible shaman who leads guided ketamine trips," Angela said. "You should try it, Liz. You might have some real breakthroughs."

"I'm not going to do ketamine," Liz said through her teeth. "I'm pregnant."

"But you're still taking the Effexor," Angela said.

Preston leaned back so he could better scrutinize Liz.

"It's a really low dose, prescribed by a doctor," Liz said just as the doorbell rang.

"That must be Rain!" Angela said. "Do you mind doing the honors?" she asked Preston like a teenager at prom who wanted to make a grand entrance for her escort. Preston stood up obediently. While mother and daughter waited for the men to return, they marinated in the palpable friction.

Preston walked back into the living room with a diminutive man boasting central casting facial hair—*show me a yogi boyfriend* without *a white feathery plume extending from his chin like a billy goat*, Liz thought— and stacks of Tibetan prayer bead bracelets. Angela sprang up. "My darling. I've missed your light." They embraced with eyes closed, then Angela turned to Liz and Preston. "This is my lover, Rain."

"Honored to meet you all," Rain said, bowing at them over his prayer hands.

"You're probably picking up on an odd energetic frequency," Angela told Rain. "You've come at a bit of a strange time."

"I didn't know Liz is on a mood stabilizer," Preston muttered under his breath.

"I meant the pregnancy," Angela said. "I'm going to be a grandma... But we obviously won't use that word."

7

Victoria

Shortly after Victoria's disaster-riven pitch, Mark was named managing director of the firm. Across the conference room table, Victoria watched as Mark accepted the role with forced humility, pledging to maintain the firm's track record while continuing to elevate it to great heights. That Victoria was able to maintain eye contact with her nemesis turned superior without vomiting again in the exact same place where she had done so during the biggest pitch of her career seemed like an accomplishment worthy of applause, if not a Finovate Award, a.k.a. the Oscar of the financial and tech worlds.

"No hard feelings?" Mark asked Victoria, popping a mini blueberry muffin into his mouth. The company-wide meeting had concluded and everyone had begun filing out of the room.

"Of course not," Victoria responded, even going so far as to extend her hand. Mark hesitated a moment, as if a Trojan horse could be tucked into the curve of her palm, then shook it.

As Victoria walked away, she reminded herself that even though Mark had gotten the position over her, and even though Nash Winton had replied to Victoria's message with a terse, perfunctory response that didn't invite further communication, Nash also hadn't jumped at the opportunity to get into business with Mark. Though it was a blow to the firm that neither Victoria nor Mark had signed him, it did provide Victoria some comfort.

Victoria didn't have much time to dwell on Mark's new title or worry about how his oversight would affect the corporate environment, however, because when she got back to her office, she found Deborah, Annalise, and Ellen planted in front of her desk. A janitor showing up in scuba gear and a bird mask would have been less odd, so Victoria took a quick look around to make sure she was in the correct place. Her computer monitors blinked hello, her Birkin rested on the coffee table, and Orchid II sat cheerfully in the corner, its pearly blooms still at full mast.

"Victoria, hi," Deborah began, her tone hard to place.

Victoria offered a tentative smile rather than responding, *What fresh hell is this?*

"We have great news!" Ellen said, throwing her arms up in the air like a cheerleader about to execute a lift.

"We're *so* happy for you!" Annalise said, gesturing in the general direction of Victoria's midsection, which was beginning to protrude ever so slightly, as if it were emulating a waxing moon. "And we want to help you celebrate this happy time."

"We got you an appointment at Mother's Haven—today!" Deborah said, her voice straining to be heard over her cohorts.

"So you can do your registry for the baby shower!" Annalise explained.

"Which we're throwing you," Victoria thought she heard Ellen say, but no, it couldn't be.

Victoria looked between their pleased faces. "You're throwing *me* . . . ?"

"A baby shower!" they all said within seconds of one another. The words reverberated like an echo. This was on-brand, given that Victoria felt like she had fallen down an elevator shaft and entered a different dimension.

"We called over to see if you had registered but they didn't have a record of you," Annalise said.

"Mother's Haven is *the* place," Ellen said. "Your appointment is at eleven."

"Today?" Victoria said, trying to process all of this and also buy time to figure out how she was going to wiggle out of having a baby shower thrown for her by three women whose only real connection to her was that they enjoyed talking about her behind her back. "That's—I appreciate it," Victoria said, treading carefully, "but my day is—*packed.*"

"Not anymore!" Harper announced, popping into Victoria's office as if she had been hovering outside, waiting for her cue. "I switched some things around in your calendar."

"Great," Victoria said weakly. She didn't think Harper knew how to access her calendar. The words were forming on Victoria's lips when she noticed the expansive look on her assistant's face. Victoria's gaze panned over to Ellen, Deborah, and Annalise, who wore similar expressions. Could it be? They were simply trying to do something nice for her?

"The day my daughter was born was the best day of my life," Ellen said.

Deborah nodded solemnly. "Having children is the greatest gift."

"There is no harder or better job than being a mother," Annalise offered.

Victoria looked at them, at their indelible sincerity. Deborah, Ellen, and Annalise didn't understand her and had even delighted in picking her apart, but maybe gossip was just their sport, and it was harmless? More to the point, here they were, crossing her threshold with an olive branch because they were thrilled for her, plain and simple. When Victoria thought of it like that, how could she rebuff such a gesture?

"Well . . . I guess if my calendar is clear, I'm out of excuses," Victoria said.

"Yay!" Harper cheered.

"This is going to be great!" Deborah said. "You're going to love Mother's Haven!"

"Have so much fun!" Ellen commanded before the women abandoned their anchorage in front of Victoria's desk.

"I will," Victoria promised, knowing she would do nothing of the sort.

———

When she arrived at Mother's Haven, located in a freestanding two-story bungalow on a quiet but prime street off Melrose, Victoria sized up the storefront and immediately took umbrage with not only the smiling stork—a stork, really?—that accompanied the bubbly script lettering across the window, but also the childlike font itself. She forced herself to tear her eyes away from the stork's grin and pushed open the door. Victoria told herself that the sooner she started, the faster it would be over and she could be back at her desk researching the new treasury bond she wanted to check out.

Inside the boutique, an explosion of paraphernalia was organized to suggest a sort of merry chaos, the fun chaos of parenthood, where painting might become cooking might become scooting might become—who knows?! The possibilities were endless, as were the offerings of the store. Overwhelmed by the sheer volume of *stuff*, Victoria paused to let her eyes pass over the many aisles filled to the brim. Despite feeling intimidated, Victoria was also wary. Cave women hadn't had access to this cornucopia of gear. How had they managed to keep their offspring alive?

As Victoria walked over to the register, she vowed not to be sucked into an industry predicated on flooding expectant mothers with fear by telling them that they needed an army of gadgets to be up to the task. Otherwise—cheerful grin!—your child will feel unloved in his or her formative years and possibly fail at everything in life—smiley face! Victoria waited patiently behind four women, three of whom had paired diamonds with athleisure. The fourth possessed a height her bad posture couldn't disguise and looked like she was in the early stages of pregnancy. Her sweatshirt was stained on the shoulder, something she perhaps had just realized; Victoria watched her try to arrange her light brown hair to cover the spot. Meanwhile, the non-pregnant friends were all squealing over a tiny stuffed mouse in a tutu, which rested inside a delicately painted cardboard matchbox.

"This is the cutest thing ever! You have to get this. Mike is threatening to divorce me if we throw the dice again. He said four kids is crazy, but I really want a girl," one of the friends said emphatically, her auburn ponytail swishing with each statement.

"You have to get it, Liz," the next friend, a blonde with a chic bob, agreed.

"I don't even know if I'm having a girl," the pregnant one reminded her friends.

"And four kids *is* crazy," the blonde told the boy-mom. "The mess alone!"

"I know, I know, but I need some ballet in my life," the boy-mom said. "If I have to go to one more eight-hour soccer tournament in Chatsworth?" She shuddered.

Victoria watched the Liz woman covertly check the price tag on the mouse.

"It's Maileg," the raven-haired third friend explained. "It's a European brand. Lark has all their mice and accessories."

"I'm buying it for you!" the blonde announced.

"Well, thanks," Liz said as her friend planted the dancing European rodent on the counter and pulled out her wallet, for which at least five reptiles had to perish. "I've always wanted a dancing mouse, but only if it was overpriced and European. Budget American mice? No way."

The blonde tensed. "Liz, this is your child you're talking about. You can't buy anything budget or American, ever! Especially not car seats. Promise me."

As Victoria was trying not to mutter "What the fuck?" to herself, Liz turned. She and Victoria looked at each other and their wide-eyed, scleral show said it all: *What the actual fuck?*

The blonde was staring at Liz expectantly, so she eventually swiveled her head back. "Repeat after me. American car seat: no. European mouse: yes."

Victoria's voice cut through the air. "Actually, American manufacturing is superior in many industries."

Everyone shifted to look at Victoria. Liz's friends regarded her with a whiff of annoyance, but Liz held Victoria's gaze once again. It was one of those looks between strangers that conveyed entire conversations, a silent dialogue unfurling like a CVS receipt.

They were interrupted when the boy-mom gave Victoria an uninterested "Good to know," then slung a ropy, toned arm around Liz's shoulder. Victoria thought she had the distinct look of someone who prayed at the altar of Tracy Anderson four times a week. "I'm going to hate you so much if you get a girl," she told Liz. Victoria flashed her pregnant compatriot an exaggerated worried look and Liz shot her back a faux-frightened expression.

"Should we grab a coffee? Not for you, though," the blonde said to Liz, picking up the gift bag and depositing it in Liz's hands.

Liz murmured thanks and started following her friends out of the store. As she passed Victoria, she shot her a shy smile, which Victoria returned. Victoria felt the impulse to run after this complete stranger. *Wait! Come back. Let's know each other. We can be each other's port in the storm.*

But that would be crazy, and before Victoria could telegraph anything more substantive via facial expression, the door closed behind the women with a tinkle of bells. The moment was over. Victoria stepped forward to the woman manning the register, who wore a name tag labeled Maureen. She inspected Victoria without comment, a stern librarian life-swapped into a world of frilly onesies and animal rattles.

"Hi, I have an eleven o'clock appointment. Victoria Miller."

Maureen turned and beckoned to a perky sales assistant, who skipped over and planted herself by Victoria's side. Caitlin with a C said she was thrilled to guide Victoria through the registry process. Caitlin held up her iPad and explained that they'd go through the store together, and when Victoria saw something she liked, it was as easy as a click and add. Since Victoria was more sure of what she *didn't* like than what she did, she asked Caitlin if they could start with the necessities. Victoria's head swam as Caitlin spouted words and terms at an alacritous clip and they began blending together into an indistinguishable soup, until it started to sound like a peppy sort of prayer.

Liki—Doona—sensory—swaddle—Willow—bassinet—Brezza— Everlywell—booster—Babyzen—teether—Pipa—Tripp Trapp—carrier— Bestaroo—Inglesina—Björn—microplastics—Skip Hop—WAYB— Bugaboo . . .

Victoria thought the phrase *It's Greek to me* was overused, but in this case, it was fitting. Victoria was more proficient with actual Greek, or at least able to order moussaka and kolokithokeftedes and dolmadakia and frappés at a seaside mom-and-pop joint in Crete, like she and Ace had done last summer. She let herself drift off in memories of sapphire and cobalt water that turned teal at the shoreline, of lazy afternoons sipping rosé and snacking on tzatziki and pita triangles at beach clubs, of balmy summer nights spent naked underneath the sheets, salt from the ocean water still on their skin, and then their tongues.

The sound of a gentle throat clear snapped Victoria back to the present.

"Sorry," Victoria said. "What did you say?"

Caitlin repeated the question, which was about self-soothing and it was apparently a loaded one—what were Victoria's thoughts on the polarizing pacifier: forbidden or beloved?

I don't know! Victoria wanted to shout, but she also didn't want to let down her baby-store docent. If only Caitlin were to ask her about empirical asset pricing. Because then, *then!* Victoria told Caitlin she was undecided and skated by this question. She thought she might escape Mother's Haven with no one the wiser as to her glaring insufficiencies, but then Caitlin asked her, "Nanit or Vava?"

What the ever-living fuck? Are those car seats? Parenting methods? Robots?

"I think it will depend on the car?" Victoria guessed.

Caitlin's face fell like a guillotine. Victoria was tempted to grab a plush lamb from the nearest shelf and tell Caitlin that it was going to be okay. Instead, she explained that her husband was superstitious and didn't want to buy anything until their child is born. Still, Victoria confessed to Caitlin, she recognized how behind she was on preparations.

"Don't worry," Caitlin said. "A lot of parents don't want to jinx it." She held up her iPad and assured Victoria that they had tackled the essentials. Then she added, in a conspiratorial tone, that asking friends to purchase things for you was an authorized loophole, even if you were Jewish and worried about endangering your children's survival. Caitlin told Victoria that, in fact, some of her clients bought everything and sent it to a different address, while others stored it all in their garages and didn't bridge the divide over the threshold until they were released from the hospital. Victoria smiled gratefully, but her relief didn't last long because Caitlin's eyes abruptly darted around the store like she had just shoved a rubber giraffe teether down her pants and was about to suggest they walk out without paying. Caitlin lowered her voice and asked, "You did sign up for Dawn, though?"

"What?" Victoria asked.

"Who," Caitlin corrected.

"Who?" Victoria parroted.

"Dawn Hampton," Caitlin said, pausing to allow for a reaction. "Dawn's class?" she added, scanning Victoria's face for recognition. Coming up short, she rushed to inform, "Dawn Hampton is the leading parenting expert in the city."

Caitlin took Victoria by the arm and led her to the counter to see if they could plead her case with Maureen, who apparently oversaw class registration. Surrounded by trucks, tiaras, and toy espresso sets, Victoria wondered if there was a place in the mom-wife world for women like her who thought mixers were what you paired with alcohol, who didn't possess an encyclopedic memory of lullabies or have any interest in making pancakes shaped like bears.

While she waited for Caitlin and Maureen to decide her fate, Victoria noticed that someone had joined the line behind her. She turned slightly to see that it was the woman from before—Liz—but this time she had returned without the gaggle of ballerina-mouse-pushing friends.

"Hi," Victoria said, wondering if Liz had come back in the hopes that Victoria would still be there. Then she felt as foolish as a wallflower with a crush. Was Victoria losing it? Had her first foray into mom world sent her over the edge, imagining, and even worse, yearning for a connection with a total stranger?

"Hi!" Liz said. "Me again. I escaped."

"Are your friends going to issue an Amber Alert?"

"They're having twenty-dollar lattes at Erewhon," Liz said. "They'll be fine. The dancing rodent is getting returned, and hopefully, they'll never know." She held up the gift bag and a pastel rainbow of ribbons fluttered in the air.

"When are you due?" Victoria asked.

"October eighth," Liz said.

"I'm due October third!"

Liz's eyes slid down Victoria's frame. She looked as if she were trying to detect the pregnancy that Victoria alleged. "No way," Liz said. "We're due the same week! I'm Liz."

"Victoria."

Liz held her hand out to shake Victoria's, then seemed to think better of the gesture—like it was weird to offer your hand to an adult, pregnant stranger in a baby store—but it was too late. Her retracting hand hung limply in the air like the claw in one of those arcade games that were rigged to never catch a prize. Little did she know, Victoria had fought the urge to run after her. Victoria shook Liz's hand enthusiastically to put her at ease.

"Nice to meet you," Liz said.

"You too. Did you also know to sign up for some essential class the second you got pregnant?" Victoria asked.

"Dawn's class?" Liz said.

"That's a yes."

"As soon as I told my friends I was pregnant, they said I had to register for Dawn." Liz smiled apologetically at Victoria, as if she felt guilty for securing a precious spot.

"Good for you. And I'll be fine," Victoria said. "I can always buy the book, right?"

"She did write a book. *Hey, Bae Bae.*"

Victoria grimaced at the horrendous title. "Let me guess: She has a podcast too?"

"*Dawn of a New Mom,*" Liz said.

Victoria looked at her, aghast.

"I wish I was joking."

Caitlin left Maureen's side and headed Victoria's way, her shoulders hunched in defeat. "I tried my best," Caitlin said, her face awash with concern, as though the ship were going down and Victoria hadn't procured a seat in a life raft. "It's too late to squeeze you into the October babies' class. We're going to have to wait-list you and hope for the best." Victoria prayed that Caitlin meant a mother might change her mind rather than tragedy creating a vacancy.

"No problem," Victoria said, not wanting to dwell on it. "Thanks, Caitlin."

"I'm in that class," Liz said. "If a spot doesn't open up, I could fill you in on anything important we talk about? If you want . . ."

Witnessing Liz's uncertainty as she extended the offer was like watching a baby deer try to find its footing for the first time. Not that Victoria was any more adept at talking to strangers, forging connections with other women, or making friends as an adult. She simply chose not to attempt those things.

"Yes! What a great idea!" Caitlin said, nodding. "Motherhood: It takes a village—and a WhatsApp group!"

Victoria had neither a village nor a text chain; she didn't even have a guest list of friends to invite to the baby shower that Ellen, Deborah, and Annalise were foisting upon her.

"Why don't you two exchange numbers?!" Caitlin directed. She seemed to doubt that Victoria and Liz had ever been asked out on a date the old-fashioned way. That said, she appeared thrilled with how well they followed instructions ("Now you put her number into your phone and then you call her phone so she has your number and can store it"). Once the exchange was completed, Caitlin bowed her head and radiated beneficence upon them like she was the pope presiding over an official baptism.

"This is the kind of magic that only happens at Mother's Haven," Caitlin pronounced without a trace of irony. Victoria and Liz locked eyes. And as Victoria watched Liz clench her jaw to tamp down her amusement, she thought there was a chance they might actually become friends.

8

———

Liz

14 WEEKS: BICYCLE BELL

Did you return the mouse?"

Liz froze, clutching a piece of pretzel bread in her hand.

"No?" Liz said, lifting her voice upwards. Madison, Cara, and Freya studied their menus. Now that Liz was almost a mom, they had invited her to join their weekly Friday moms' night out—a sacred occasion where they laid claim to their favorite booth in a sceney restaurant in West Hollywood, let the espresso martinis flow, and complain-bragged about their kids and husbands. Liz had been looking forward to joining—and to trying the restaurant's legendary eggplant Parmesan—but things were already off to a rocky start. Liz took a bite of pretzel bread. She'd hoped they would all be gossiping over martinis (and her mocktail) like an idyllic '90s *Sex and the City* vision of female friendship, but instead she got . . . this: Singapore math and flatulent husbands.

When she was younger, all Liz had wanted was a best friend—someone to pass notes to in class, to giggle over crushes with, and to have sleepovers with on the weekends, filled with makeup Caboodles and Ouija boards. She'd yearned for the classic American dream: childhood edition. Unfortunately, Liz had moved around too much, pulled by the unpredictable tides of Angela's moods or the predictable threat of her debts. Every time it seemed like Liz might be making some headway socially, she was uprooted like a garden weed. Eventually, Liz gave up. She loved to read and watch old movies on AMC; she understood the anatomy of solitude.

Liz had made a brief stab at reinventing herself and adjusting the social calculus when she went to college, but she discovered that a new haircut and optimism didn't translate into becoming close with her roommate or being able to belt out the words to "Pour Some Sugar on Me" while dancing on top of a bar. Personalities couldn't be remade overnight at will. Patterns were entrenched, and Liz wasn't a social butterfly or even a popular moth.

It was after college, when Liz stumbled into an entry-level job as an assistant to a TV editor through Wesleyan's alumni network and moved to LA, that things changed. Cara, an assistant across the hall, had launched a spirited campaign to befriend her. It hadn't taken Liz long to realize she was the only other person in the office under the age of fifty aside from Ilia, a second-generation Russian who flooded his conversations with anecdotes about Siberia.

Liz would sit, wide-eyed, as Cara spilled about the affair she was having with their married boss, Peter, and detailed their trysts, decoded his intentions, and showed off the dick pic of the day. Before Liz knew it, she was a warden of dalliances, gatekeeper of dick pics. Over time, in deference to Liz's critical post, Cara felt obliged to include Liz when she made plans with her real friends, Madison and Freya. In this way, Liz was slowly absorbed into their group, an osmosis that might have otherwise been unlikely.

When Cara, Freya, and Madison approached thirty and locked down husbands in rapid succession, Liz knew her time by their side was limited. *Our dick-shopping days are over!* Freya had announced. It was true. Their stint in the clubs was finished. Single life and nightlife were behind them. The bell for last call had rung, and thanks to Liz, everyone had gotten home safely.

Once the tasks of bridal shower organizing, bachelorette planning, and wedding wrangling were dispensed with, Madison, Cara, and Freya started procreating. They were busy, preoccupied, and increasingly unavailable. When Liz did see them, she tried to coo over their babies or discuss preschools, but she was terrified of holding their newborns and didn't know anything about Montessori versus Reggio Emilia. Still, she had been surprised when her pregnancy news—casually dropped over a group text—elicited a flurry of excitement.

Cara, Madison, and Freya had started texting her at all hours with advice (*get in as much sex and sleep while you can*) as well as links to Japanese bottle sterilizers and reminders to play Mozart to her embryo. Liz's friends seemed thrilled and relieved that Liz had made it to the other side, but also maybe a bit mystified that she wasn't at the club handing out mints alongside the bathroom attendant.

"You should get the kale salad," Cara said, jarring Liz back to the present. "Iron is good for the baby."

"I'll have the kale salad, with chicken, please," Liz told the waiter. Eggplant Parmesan would have to wait.

"Our kale salad is bomb," the waiter promised with the enthusiasm of someone praying his impossibly symmetrical features would be noticed by a casting agent and vault him out of the service industry. He walked away and Freya checked out his ass, drawing a conspiratorial look from Madison.

Liz observed the new dynamic between her friends, mentally taking notes about how marriage and motherhood had changed or solidified aspects of their personalities. Cara had replaced her taste for married men with a competitive bloodlust when it came to her children's achievements. She was big on the performative aspects of parenting. *Mother* as a verb. Freya seemed to have changed the least, although since Liz saw her last, she had acquired a new face. She'd married a socialist who had a trust fund equivalent to the GDP of a small European nation. Even though Freya got exactly what she said she wanted, Liz questioned whether she was as content as she said she was or advertised on social media.

As Liz watched Freya polish off her first cocktail before the appetizers arrived, Cara asked, "Liz? Are you listening?"

Her thoughts had drifted off again, a paper sailboat in a current. Liz looked over at Cara and made an *oops* face. "Sorry!" she added. Freya gestured to the hot waiter for another cocktail.

"Don't worry," Cara said. "The hormones can make you so loopy. I was just saying that it's never too early to figure out your values and the kind of boundaries you're going to set."

"Gentle parenting is my religion," Madison said, looking at Liz intently.

"I didn't know you converted," Liz joked.

"I did," Madison said, as serious as a priest in church. "It's my bible."

"Gentle parenting is a bunch of hype," Freya said.

"No, it's not," Madison shot back. "Because of gentle parenting, now I know that my early-childhood trauma was the cause of all the issues I had when I was a teenager. If only my parents hadn't used such brutal tactics. But it was a different time. They didn't know better." Madison's mother and father were nationally recognized physicians, a cardiologist and an oncologist, respectively.

"What kind of tactics?" Liz couldn't help but ask.

"Raising their voices, withholding affection, *punishing* me," Madison answered gravely.

"Doesn't every kid get punished? Isn't discipline an important part of parenting?" Liz asked. She tried to banish the hopeful tone from her voice. Oh, how she had wished to be grounded. Obviously, Angela didn't believe in curfews. Or rules. Or parenting.

"No!" Madison and Cara yelped in unison. Freya downed another drink. Was that her second or third?

"Punishing kids only encourages the behavior you want to prevent," Madison said. "Plus, it creates a divide between the parent and child."

"I'll give you my copy of the book," Cara told Liz.

"Gentle parenting." Freya snickered. "Doesn't work for some kids, let me tell you."

"If it's not working, that's on the parents," Cara said. "It works if you do it right." Freya shrugged. Liz wondered if this was what happened when your blood alcohol level and bank account balance tipped the scales—did you simply stop caring what anyone else thought?

"I'll tell you what works," Freya said. "Time-out! No dessert! No TV time!"

Madison flinched. "It really all goes back to healthy limits. That reminds me! Did I tell you about this mom from dance class . . ."

As Madison prattled on, Liz caught a glimpse of a gelatinous eggplant Parmesan on the tray of a passing waiter. Her hormones shouted, *Me want that!* Her better judgment said, *Remember what the doctor told you: You're not eating for two. Don't give in to every craving. Stick with kale. Yuck.*

Liz doubted that Cara, Madison, and Freya had ever pounded Twix bars or double-fisted french fries, two fantasies that had been playing out in Liz's mind on repeat. She was sure the woman from Mother's Haven hadn't ingested one extra calorie. Liz thought Victoria looked like the kind of person who had a private chef serving up gourmet meals and a professionally organized pantry stocked with superfoods. Liz knew Victoria operated in a league far, far beyond her. Sure, it was the immaculate designer clothing, the perfectly manicured appearance, and the tasteful jewelry that gave off "quiet luxury" vibes, but it was so much more. This woman had a presence, like she had everything figured out. Victoria exuded a confidence and grace that astounded Liz, who never corrected someone if they got her name wrong. Liz found it exhausting to inhabit a vessel that could constantly betray her. Dandruff, ingrown nipple hairs, buccinal farts—the possibilities were endless. A sliding scale of terror.

Cara slapped the table. "Omigod, did you hear what Madison said? Dying."

"Dead! I am a corpse," Madison agreed.

"The deranged dance mom sent an Uber for Sparrow!" Cara said. "Can you believe it?"

"Is Sparrow . . . a person?" Liz asked. Madison and Cara looked at her strangely.

"Obviously!" Cara said. "Why would she send an Uber for a bird?"

"Right, sorry." Liz cringed internally.

"Anyway," Freya said. "Could we please talk about something a little more spicy?" She turned to Liz. "How's the pregnancy sex? I wanted it *all* the time."

"Good!" Liz lied, then stuffed another piece of pretzel bread in her mouth so they couldn't expect her to go into any more detail.

"Uh-oh," Madison said, tilting her head suspiciously at Liz. Good lord. When had Madison started moonlighting for the FBI? Did she have a lie detector test nestled in her Celine Triomphe?

"You gotta take care of your man too," Cara told Liz.

All three women nodded their heads like they were bobbing for apples—or mimicking blow jobs.

"Totally! We've just been busy," Liz said. "But it's all good."

Cara, Madison, and Freya regarded her like they doubted it was all good, or even half good, which it wasn't. The truth was Liz and Preston hadn't had sex since they saw the baby on the ultrasound at the doctor's office for the first time. Preston told her that he didn't want their child seeing his penis. Liz tried to explain it didn't work like that—their embryo wouldn't look up one day and see a dick hurtling towards him or her like a phallic asteroid. But Preston couldn't be swayed. If he was determined to wait out her pregnancy, that would be nearly a year without sex. Which was worrisome for all the obvious reasons. There was also Liz's bigger fear: that potential penis exposure to the baby wasn't the real reason Preston didn't want to be intimate with her.

"Get the wedge," Cara advised. "It's a sex pillow."

"Life-changing," Madison said. "All bow down to the wedge!" She lifted her arms, then prostrated like she was praying to Allah.

"I'll give you mine," Freya offered.

"Thanks," Liz said, though the idea of accepting her friend's used sex pillow made her as uncomfortable as a pair of handmade clogs from Etsy. The hot waiter brought their entrées, Freya threw back another martini, and Liz forced down a brittle kale salad while fielding unsolicited advice on birthing methods.

When Liz returned to Preston's house, he was still out. She walked around listlessly, observing the decor like it was a showroom. Since the house had been fully furnished when she moved in (Preston's mother Cricket had dispatched her decorator from the OC the second Preston closed on the house), Liz gave away most of her furniture, even her beloved Jennifer Convertibles couch, which obviously had no place here. She had been trying to unpack in an unobtrusive way so it felt like a seamless transition into a shared space rather than a hostile takeover. Preston had encouraged her to feel at home and told Liz to let him know if she needed more organizers in her closet (she was living in a house with his-and-hers closets!) or storage space in the garage, but Liz still felt like a visitor who had booked an extended stay at a luxe Airbnb. She walked into the kitchen and opened the pantry, wondering if this feeling would go away. Liz's name wasn't on the deed. She hadn't picked out the travertine dining room table. She hadn't weighed in on what kind of towels she liked, or if the neighborhood was kid-friendly, or—wait, should she have offered to pay half the utility bills?

Flummoxed, Liz frowned as she looked at the array of healthy snacks, all sanctioned by Preston's trainer and devoid of any nut oils, cane sugar, corn syrup, xanthan gum, or taste. She had decided that part of blending into her new environment like a squid capable of adaptive coloration meant adopting Preston's healthy-eating program, but Liz would kill for a bag of neon-orange Cheetos. She considered texting Preston to see when he'd be home and stealth-ordering some artificially flavored, artery-clogging junk food in the interim, but instead tethered her phone to the charging cord and walked away so she wouldn't be tempted.

Liz headed for the second bedroom, where she had stashed her boxes in the closet, and tried to get organized. She unpacked some books and added them to the bookshelf in the living room, but then she opened a box containing assorted knickknacks, half-melted Voluspa candles, a dozen Hopi kachina dolls (Angela had been enraptured by Native American culture for a while), and never-used wrap gifts from Liz's horrible job like a Hydro Flask branded with the show's name. Liz tried to imagine how Preston would react to finding a feathered figurine decorating his mantel, or even better, what his mother Cricket—or Cricket's decorator—would say about a tomahawk adorning one of her beloved Assouline coffee-table books. Liz shoved the kachina doll back into the brown cardboard moving box and put it in the closet to deal with another time. Then she gathered an armful of generic flowery-scented candles and flimsy phone-charging docks (the work holiday gift two years in a row, because a production assistant had dropped the ball on ordering *The*

Catch earthquake kits, never mind the irony that the show itself was the natural disaster). Liz carried everything outside to the trash cans and unceremoniously dumped the load into the black bins. She should have done a more scrupulous clean-out when she was packing up her life and choosing what items would accompany her to the new, adult, cohabitating phase of it.

Liz walked back into the house, entered the bedroom, and was about to turn on the TV, but stopped when she realized she hadn't asked Preston if she could record some of her favorite true crime shows, mainly because she wasn't sure if it was weirder to seek permission or not to. Anxiety was forming in the pit of Liz's stomach and she wanted to treat herself, but there wasn't a Sour Patch Kid or televised triple homicide in sight.

Liz starfished listlessly onto the bed and looked up at the ceiling. Lights from the neighbor's house crept in through the slatted blinds. She heard a burst of Taylor Swift from a car passing by. Maybe it was too quiet; maybe that's why Liz was . . . what, exactly? Lonely? Liz wasn't even alone! Liz had a boyfriend who would be coming home soon, to a house they lived in together. She needed to get a grip before she ended up on a holotropic breathwork retreat with her mother.

Liz was rising from her perch on the bed when she heard a noise that sounded like the front door shutting. Liz froze in terror and listened. Preston would use the garage entrance. But if it wasn't him . . . Oh God. Liz stayed perfectly still, but she didn't hear anything else. Maybe she had hallucinated. She held her breath. And then she heard it: footsteps. Liz panicked, mentally scrolling through the recent alerts on Citizen about the rise in crime.

Liz darted over to the bedroom door and locked it, then grabbed a ceramic vase and clutched it desperately. She had seen action heroes slam objects against villains' heads in movies—hopefully that worked. But then, just as quickly, the footsteps receded, and Liz exhaled a shaky breath of relief. Still trembling, she questioned whether she should call 911, but she didn't want the trespasser to overhear her and get violent. The last thing Liz wanted to do was inflame the situation. *Take the signed Jordan jersey*, she wanted to say. *Take the Assouline coffee-table books, take the coffee table, take the coffee maker—take whatever you want and leave!* But the trespasser was in no rush. Liz heard things being picked up and moved around, as if the thief were picky about what to steal. It seemed like an hour had gone by even though it was probably only a few minutes. Growing desperate, Liz searched "how to text 911" on her phone. She was about to SMS her distress, but the footsteps suddenly got closer again, and then someone was trying to open the bedroom door, jiggling the handle repeatedly.

Liz fled into the bathroom, shut the door behind her, and called 911. Her entire body had gone to ice and she was shaking so hard that her teeth were clacking against each other.

"911, what's your emergency?"

"There's an intruder in my boyfriend's house!" Liz whisper-screamed. "I mean MY house! There's someone in the house!"

"Is the person in the house now?" the operator asked.

"YES! Please come. I'm—alone. I'm all alone." Liz dropped her head and convulsed with silent, panicked sobs.

"What's your address, ma'am?"

Liz gave it, then stayed on the line with the operator until she heard the distinct wail of sirens crescendoing up the hill.

"POLICE!" someone called out, then thumped on the front door. Still shaking uncontrollably, Liz thanked the operator for not abandoning her and hung up the phone. She unlocked the bathroom door, crept out into the bedroom again, and listened to the cops bang down the door to enter the house. A loud squeak spoke to the hinges being tested and then there was a flurry of movement, sounds of a tussle, and then . . .

"What do you think you're doing?" No, it wasn't . . . It couldn't be . . . Was that . . . Her *mother's* voice?

Liz closed her eyes. Of all the horrors Angela had perpetuated, this was a new low. Liz opened the door to see Angela, wearing a sheer caftan and turquoise beads, surrounded by four of LA's finest. The flashing lights of the squad cars strobed through the windows.

"Angela! What are you doing?" Liz saw the cops side-eye each other.

"You know this person?" one of them asked.

"I'm filming this," Angela said, whipping out her phone and directing it at the cops.

"Yes. I'm—she's my mother. What are you—I'm sorry to bother you with a false alarm," Liz said, rubbing her temples.

"Your mom?" another cop asked incredulously.

"I'm so sorry," Liz repeated, at a loss.

"You should be apologizing to me," Angela told Liz. "Calling the cops on your own mother? Who does that?"

"I thought you were a burglar! I was terrified!"

"I can tell. You look horrible. And you," Angela said, glaring at the policemen. "This is going on Facebook Live."

"If you're both okay, this seems like a family matter. We don't need to write up a report," one cop said.

"I guess you're the good cop," Angela quipped.

"Next time, make sure it's an intruder. And not *your mom*," another cop said.

Liz apologized again to the policemen and showed them out. As soon as the door closed, she sprang on her mother. "What were you thinking?"

"I came by to drop off the chakapa," Angela said, pointing to some sort of leaf fan resting on the counter of the open kitchen, like this was the most normal and obvious thing in the world. "Preston gave me the lock code to the front door."

"And you didn't think to tell me?" Liz asked. "What were you doing in the living room anyway? What were all those noises?"

"The feng shui in this place needed some zhuzhing." Liz noticed that her mother had rearranged the armchair and the side table; she had to admit, the room did look better.

"You can't do that!" Liz said. And then, a little more quietly, she implored, "You can't keep doing this to me."

"What? Helping?"

"Showing up whenever you feel like it," Liz said.

"Fine. I'll go now," Angela said, posturing like she was severely wounded, but Liz knew better. Her mother had the thick skin of a calloused, bronzed Floridian snowbird who had spent ninety years worshipping the sun and now looked like a purse. "Enjoy the chakapa."

Liz blinked her eyes closed for a moment as the martyr made her way to the front door. Liz's body was still humming with adrenaline, but she felt strangely disconnected. The whole episode was too surreal.

The door clicked closed behind Angela, and Liz trudged over to make sure it was locked. Then she leaned against it, considering. The thing that really tore at her was the realization that besides her therapist, whom she paid to listen to her, Liz didn't have anyone she could confide in about this ordeal. Her friends would be titillated, then digress into stories about their demanding in-laws, and an anecdote about Freya's mother-in-law scheduling a family gathering during her baby's nap time couldn't compare. Preston was Angela's number one fan and would no doubt find it amusing.

Fuck it, Liz thought. Maybe it was the kale salad, maybe it was the sex pillow, maybe it was the chakapa, but something had sent her over the edge. She picked up her phone. She could hear her shrink's voice in her mind. *What's the worst that could happen?* Jayne would ask, a plaque of woven wall art behind her.

Victoria doesn't write me back? Liz thought. And then she realized: So what? Liz was the daughter of a narcissistic, chakapa-wielding maniac. She had survived far worse.

She was about to text Victoria when Liz saw an unread message waiting for her like a shimmering jewel. During the chaos of the evening, she must have not heard the notification. Liz read Victoria's text: *Nice meeting you at Mother's Haven. Do you want to have lunch sometime?*

Liz clutched the phone to her chest and thought that maybe there was some semblance of order and equity in the universe. This was better than a family-sized bag of Flamin' Hot Cheetos.

Later, Liz would revisit this moment and wonder, had she known what was to come, if she would have made different decisions. But then again, hindsight was as useful as half a pair of shoes.

9

Victoria

16 WEEKS: AVOCADO

Ace stood in the doorway of the closet, watching Victoria select an outfit to wear to brunch.

"You're putting so much thought into this, if I didn't know any better, I might suspect you're going on a date," he said.

"I am," Victoria said. "A friend date. My very first friend date."

"May wonders never cease," Ace said, and whistled. Victoria held up a dress. "That's nice," Ace said. "But more importantly, where's she from? What does she do? What's she looking for? Something serious, or just a friend fling?"

Good question, Victoria thought. Did people actively seek out specific kinds of friends? What *was* Liz looking for?

"I'm kidding," Ace assured her.

"I know—but we're due at the same time, and she seemed equally out of her depth and possibly also suspicious of the parenting industrial complex pushing EWG-verified diapers."

"What's an EWG-verified diaper?"

"Exactly."

Victoria pulled on a simple A-line dress. "Zip me?" she asked Ace.

Ace did, then circled around to plant a kiss on Victoria's forehead.

"Good luck. And let me know if you want me to text you halfway through and say the roof caved in so you have an out if it's going badly."

"The roof caved in? That's like the dog-ate-my-homework of dating. Did you ever use that excuse?"

"No," Ace said. "Should have. Would've saved me a lot of time and trouble. You can test-drive it!"

"Your faith in my ability to make a new friend is overwhelming."

Victoria went over to her vanity to put on some makeup and Ace left to play golf. She thought Ace had exercised remarkable restraint from poking more fun at her—a friend date? At her age? Not to mention, Ace accumulated friends without even trying. Then he nurtured these relationships, valuing new acquaintances and long-standing connections alike, so Ace's circle only moved in one direction: expansion. When they had first started dating, Victoria stopped short of declaring this a character flaw, but she certainly flagged Ace's extensive social network as a glaring incompatibility between them. Ace assured her that he wasn't planning on dragging Victoria to any event she didn't want to attend. As long as Victoria didn't mind if he grabbed lunch or played pickleball with his buddies from time to time, they'd be fine.

Their guest lists for the wedding had been comedically imbalanced, but so what? Allison, their wedding planner, had suggested they avoid designating typical bride and groom sections for the ceremony, and Victoria agreed—no need to take a fluorescent highlighter to an already obvious fact. Victoria had only a paltry handful of guests to invite to the wedding compared with Ace's biblical scroll (he had been forced to edit down his list several times), but his friends were inclusive and laudatory in their toasts. They had poked fun at Ace, the legendary bachelor no one ever thought would settle down. But after the laughs, Ace's closest friends also held up a glass to Victoria and Ace, declaring that they had never seen him look so happy; the couple's love lit up a room. Tears were shed. Not hers, but still. Victoria was so touched that after the wedding, she decided to take a stab at befriending Ace's friends' wives after all. Victoria even agreed to a couples' trip to Palm Springs. Once they were in the desert, though, the men absconded to the golf course, leaving Victoria to report to the spa with the other ladies. She soon realized that without the wedding to discuss, they had no common ground. These women weren't interested in dissecting the latest from Davos and hadn't heard of Jessica Ann Levy's podcast. Victoria was equally lost when it came to their topics of choice. Victoria told herself—and Ace—*I tried.* Victoria didn't need a coterie of friends to parse the details of her day with—she had Ace. Between her career and her husband, she was more than fine . . . until it had struck her at Mother's Haven like a bolt of lightning in a graphic novel: *I could really use a friend right now.*

Twenty minutes later, Victoria pulled into the elegant apostrophe of a driveway in front of the Bel-Air and an army of uniform-clad valet attendants greeted her. They took her car without giving her a ticket and Victoria strolled over the carpeted bridge, past the iconic swans, into the hotel. She had suggested the Bel-Air because even though the prices were exorbitant, Victoria shamelessly loved the Old Hollywood vibe and how it felt like a luxurious oasis within the tree-lined bowels of Bel Air. As the hostess led her over to one of her favorite tables on the patio, Victoria hoped this would be the perfect place to kick off what would evolve into a meaningful friendship.

But when Victoria clocked Liz walking in and getting her bearings, she realized she might have made a serious error in judgment. Victoria saw Liz glancing down at her tunic and leggings like she was regretting not only her outfit but every decision she had ever made that had led her to this point. As Liz reluctantly followed the hostess, who charted the course towards Victoria at their table, Liz cowered like she wanted to shrink into herself and disappear before she reached her destination. As Liz reached the table, Victoria hopped up and outstretched her arms, trying to put her self-conscious friend date at ease.

"Liz, hi!"

Liz tentatively hugged her back. "Sorry I'm late."

"You're not at all. I'm glad we could find a day to do this."

Liz sat down. What now? Victoria questioned whether she should address the awkward nature of this, or if that would only make things more uncomfortable. Feeling a prickle of moisture on her brow, Victoria picked up the menu in a desperate attempt to land upon an easy topic to discuss. "Are you hungry?" she asked Liz.

"Starving," Liz admitted. "Always."

"Me too," Victoria said.

"Really?"

"I want everything," Victoria said. "Should we order a bunch of things and share?"

Victoria watched Liz's eyes turn into saucers as she glimpsed the prices on the menu. Victoria had thought it was mutually understood that she had invited Liz and would be paying, but now, looking at Liz, who appeared to be mentally cataloging what she could pawn to cover her share of the bill, Victoria stepped in to clarify.

"This is my treat, by the way."

Liz's head whipped up. She hesitated—her eyes darting around as if they were unsure where to land but certain that Victoria's face was not a viable destination.

"I invited you as my guest. But there's also a good chance I'm going to be texting you with a million questions because I'm not in *Dawn's baby group*, so it's the least I can do," Victoria said.

"Okay . . . thanks."

Victoria motioned the waiter over and ordered a pastry basket, pancakes, eggs Benedict, avocado toast, a fruit plate, and a side of truffle fries.

"I think I love you," Liz told Victoria when the waiter walked away.

Victoria laughed. "My husband pretends he understands, but I don't think anyone other than a pregnant woman can know how it feels when you need all the food in the world, but also something so specific, that very second, or you might snap."

"Totally," Liz agreed. Victoria waited for her to keep talking, riff on that—wasn't that how conversation worked? But Liz was busy sneaking glances at her surroundings again, which seemed to subdue her and reintroduce a reluctance to engage. A trio of Chanel-clad octogenarians was sitting nearby, their perfectly shellacked helmets of hair offset by a collective thirty carats of diamonds. Across the way, the star of a hit limited series on Apple settled into a booth with a squadron of agent and manager types.

"So . . ." Victoria started. It really was like a first date. "Where are you from?" Make that a blind date.

"All over, really," Liz said. "We moved around a lot."

"Your family?"

"Me and my mom. My dad's been out of the picture since I was young."

"I'm sorry," Victoria said, for lack of a better response.

Liz shrugged. "Where are you from?" she asked, as if eager to punt the focus to Victoria.

"Fresno. The raisin capital of the world," Victoria said, and saw Liz's eyebrows rise a smidge in surprise. "I moved here right after college, though, so I've been here an eternity now."

Liz smiled, but she didn't say anything else. Victoria racked her brain for the next question. This was hard work.

"How did you meet your husband?"

Liz shifted uncomfortably. "No husband."

"Sorry!" Victoria said. She felt her face growing hot. "Wife, partner—"

"Oh no," Liz said, laughing a little. "I meant we aren't married. Boyfriend—Preston."

"Please excuse me, I'm ancient."

"No, you're not," Liz said.

There was another awkward pause. Victoria scrambled to fill the dead air.

"How did you and your boyfriend-not-husband meet?" Victoria meant it to be irreverent, not flippant, and hoped it came off that way.

But Liz's face reddened.

"Um . . . online," she said.

"How everyone finds someone these days!" Victoria said. "How did we even do it before the apps?" Victoria couldn't think of anything worse than building a profile of factoids and manipulated photos in order to swipe at other people's digital avatars, but this opinion didn't seem germane at the moment.

"Did you meet your husband online?" Liz asked. It wasn't an off-base assumption given Victoria's glowing endorsement of the internet-hosted meat market a few seconds prior. Victoria had to stop herself from blurting *Hell no.*

"We met the old-fashioned way," Victoria told Liz. "Woman rejects man at bar."

"Rejecting a guy? In person? Impressive." Liz smiled at Victoria, who was buoyed by the better tempo the conversation was taking.

"What do you do?" Victoria asked Liz. She was running out of small talk and would soon need to dash to the bathroom and Google "great first date questions."

"I'm an editor for a TV show," Liz told her.

"Nice! I don't have a creative bone in my body, but I imagine it's great to work in the arts."

"I imagine it's great too," Liz said. "I wouldn't know. I'm in reality TV. It's not exactly high art. Or art at all."

"Unscripted is so popular, though," Victoria said, trying to think of something positive to say about a category of television she disliked on principle and had never personally sampled.

"Yeah, our culture's going to hell," Liz said. "I'm pretty sure my show was dreamed up by the devil himself."

"Which show?"

"*The Catch*," Liz replied.

"I don't know it. But I don't watch a lot of TV in general," Victoria said apologetically. "I'm sure it's great."

"It's not. I promise. It's a dating contest, so basically, thirty women are isolated in a house, plied with endless amounts of alcohol, and encouraged to stab one another in the back to compete for three dream guys. They're total 'catches,'" Liz said, putting the last word in air quotes. "Whoever gets proposed to at the end gets a hundred grand—for the wedding, wink wink, but really it's about potential endorsement deals, followers, and obviously, true love." Liz rolled her eyes. Victoria smirked. "There's a catch, though. Only two of the guys are straight. One's just pretending."

"No," Victoria gasped. "That's an actual show on the air?"

"It's insanely popular."

"In this day and age, how has everyone involved not been canceled?"

"Ratings?" Liz offered.

Victoria shook her head, baffled. "I'll have to check it out."

"Don't. Trust me. In the last episode I was editing, Kylie and Kelly started a fight with Kelsie because she lied about hooking up with Finn, but Kelsie was too drunk to defend herself, so she got out of the Sprinter van and laid down on a speed bump in the middle of the street and shouted, 'Now I'm really in your way, bitches!'"

Victoria looked at Liz, wide-eyed. "Are those their real names? Or do the producers change them for narrative purposes?"

"It was probably part of the casting process, but you never know," Liz said. "Working on it really is death by a thousand cuts."

Now Liz looked glum rather than amused, as if the titillating nature of the show had worn off and soured. Victoria tried to steer the conversation into safer territory. "When you say editing, what exactly do you do? Decide what gets included in an episode?"

Liz shook her head. "That's above my pay grade. I go through B-roll and make sure we didn't miss anything exciting. The cameras are on twenty-four seven, so there's a lot of footage to go through."

"I'm guessing that's a little depressing."

"Seeing humanity at its worst? Beyond," Liz said.

"What attracted you to editing in the first place?" The waiter delivered the pastry basket and both women dug in, but Victoria was thrilled that she didn't need to fall back on discussing the array of carbs; conversation was now rolling.

"I think the idea that there are so many ways to tell a story. When we read a book or watch a show or a movie, it's the final cut, but that's only one way the story could've turned out. Sometimes a filmmaker releases deleted scenes, sure, but you still don't really see the alternate version of the story. Including or deleting one scene can change the whole effect."

Victoria smiled. "I never thought about that."

"Just not my show. It's impossible to change something that can only be different degrees of horrible."

"Then why don't *you* make a change? Why don't you do something else?"

Liz offered another slumped-shoulder shrug. "Once you're in unscripted, it's pretty hard to break into something more highbrow. Editing multiple seasons of *The Catch*, believe it or not, doesn't exactly make you attractive to people doing quality work."

"That might be the case, but you equated your job to death by a thousand cuts, and the longer you stay, the harder it will be to segue into something else."

Liz bristled. "It's not that simple," she said, her tone growing stony. "I can't just quit." The waiter arrived with the rest of their food and had to arrange the plates like puzzle pieces on the tabletop to fit everything. Liz and Victoria sat in silence while he accomplished that.

"When you think about quitting, what's the hardest part?" Victoria continued, unable to stop herself.

"I need a job. A paycheck. Benefits and health insurance. Especially now. Do you know how much it costs to have a baby?"

"Twenty-five thousand."

Liz blanched. "Uh . . . what?"

Liz's reaction indicated that she had meant the question rhetorically, or Victoria had supplied a number much higher than what Liz had in mind. Either way, Victoria had made a gaffe, allowing her concierge OB's fee to roll off her tongue so easily.

"Or less. Or more," Victoria said. Liz's face fell further. It was like Victoria was *trying* to make it worse. "Whatever the number, obviously, it's a lot. The health care system in this country is fundamentally broken." Why didn't Victoria get an actual soapbox to stand on?

Liz gave little more than a grunt in response. Victoria didn't blame her.

"Look, I understand. It's always been nonnegotiable to me to be financially independent," Victoria said, trying and failing to do damage control.

Liz picked up a fry. "Must be nice," she said. The subtext was clear: *Easy for you to say "Do what you want" when you reek of privilege.*

They finished their food quickly, making inconsequential chitchat, both racing towards the conclusion of the brunch like it was the finish line of a marathon. Victoria paid the check, Liz thanked her, and Victoria told her, "It's my pleasure," though she was sure neither of them had enjoyed themselves very much. How had it all gone off the rails so quickly?

Victoria and Liz walked outside to the valet, and like an ill-fated date that both parties knew would not be followed up on, they exchanged half-hearted pleasantries.

"Have a good rest of your day."

"You too. Have a great weekend."

The valet attendants brought the cars around and Victoria and Liz awkwardly said goodbye. As Victoria watched Liz walk away, she thought, *I'll never see her again.*

10

Liz

16 WEEKS: ÉCLAIR

Liz got into her car, thinking it must have been the first time an Audi as old as hers had been parked at the valet. Buff Range Rovers and curvy Aston Martins glistened in the sunlight as Liz drove away, replaying how badly the brunch had gone. Even though she and Victoria looked like "before" and "after" photos in a make-over story, Liz had nurtured a morsel of hope that maybe they weren't so different after all. Maybe they could become friends. But . . . no. Hard no. Did Victoria not realize how condescending she had been, or did she not care? Was she so used to dishing out guidance over sixty-dollar pancakes that she had lost touch with how she came across?

When Liz got home, Preston greeted her from an armchair in the living room. Liz saw that he was marking up endorsement contracts, making neat little notes in the margins with a black ballpoint pen. His demands looked like an army of ants colonizing the white pages.

"How was the brunch? With your new mom friend?"

"Fine," Liz said.

"Where'd you go?"

"The Hotel Bel-Air."

"Swanky! Should I be jealous?" Preston joked.

Please. Please be jealous.

Liz chuckled and switched topics. "Do you want to try that vegan Mexican spot tonight?" Liz was trying to support Preston's meatless enthusiasm even though she despised tofu anything and thought seitan tasted like a microwaved eraser.

"We have the Clippers game!" Preston said, thrilled. "Remember? We're in the box, with Travis and Lulu."

"Right," Liz said, trying to cover her dismay. Preston's friend Travis and his girlfriend Lulu were perfectly nice, but they couldn't keep their hands off each other. Liz always felt uncomfortable around their constant PDA and nonstop declarations of love and infatuation, unsure where to look and deeply insecure about her own relationship in comparison. "I must've spaced on it."

"But we're good?"

"Yeah! It will be fun!"

It wasn't fun. Afterwards, Liz's cheeks burned from forcing a smile for so long. Between the brunch with Victoria and the basketball game with Travis and Lulu, who might have made a baby of their own during halftime if such a thing could be achieved through a layer of clothing, Liz just wanted to get into bed and put the whole day behind her. She decided that a self-care Sunday was in order so she could clear her head before she had to report to work on Monday and delve into the grand shit show that was *The Catch,* season 8, episode 8.

On Monday, it took less than an hour for Liz to determine that the prenatal yoga class, cheap foot massage, and manicure she had indulged in were not enough. Not even close.

"Liz-o," her boss, Cam, said as the expensive, heavy scent of his Byredo cologne collided with the stagnant air in her editing bay. Cam slid across the desk and perched on the corner of it. Like they were best friends. Like workplace etiquette wasn't a thing. Like Liz wanted his ass four inches from the Trader Joe's cactus she had bought to brighten up her little corner of hell. "What's shakin'?"

Liz looked at Cam's empirically attractive face; now that she had gotten to know him, it was as appealing as an iguana's. It sat atop a wiry frame that, try as he might (and he had, with creatine, HGH—you name it), Cam could never get to bulk up and align with what he considered the peak male form. Liz thought that if Cam hadn't achieved success in reality TV, he might've become a con artist. But Cam had thought up *The Catch* and it had taken off. He had EP cash, a Porsche, a model/influencer girlfriend, and a standing boys' trip to Cabo with Ryan Seacrest. Many people found her boss clever and charming. Liz just tried to keep her head down and get her work done without having a mental breakdown.

"I'm almost done with B-roll for episode eight," Liz told him, her words clipped.

"Love it. Liz-o, you're so solid. Buuuuut . . ." Cam said, drawing it out like he was about to announce a raffle prize she had won. "A birdie told me you missed some primo bathroom action in episode siete."

Liz looked at her monitor like it might open up a porthole for her to dive into. "I did?"

Cam cocked one of his manscaped eyebrows at Liz, any pretense fading fast. "You tell me."

"There was some stuff, with Allegra and Jazz, in the bathroom, but it didn't seem . . ."

"Juicy enough?"

Decent, Liz wanted to say. *Humane. Moral.*

"They were both really drunk," Liz told him. "Jazz was dry-heaving, and Allegra was crying, and it didn't seem . . . juicy. It just seemed sad."

"Drama, Liz-o! That's what slaps! That's what people want to see."

"They didn't remember any of it the next day," Liz said. "It felt kind of wrong to put that out there."

"That's what they signed up for, Liz," Cam said more sternly, dropping the nickname to show he meant business. "Your job is to bring anything like this to me. I decide what's gold. And if you hadn't noticed, I'm pretty damn good at it."

"I'm sorry. It won't happen again."

"I'll let it slide this time. Maybe you're not yourself because you're pregnant."

Liz was hit with a wave of vertigo. When she recovered, she pulled at her oversized button-down, which was obviously not fooling anyone.

"Would you rather we think you're going HAM on the Häagen-Dazs?" Cam said, winking.

Liz forced a half-hearted laugh. It was nuts. Everyone she worked with acted like there was no HR department at all, like the lack of ethical boundaries in their show had seeped over into real life and *The Catch* production offices were the gun-slinging, ass-slapping, epithet-dropping Wild, Wild West.

"I was going to tell everyone soon," Liz said.

"Guess we beat you to it. Congrats!"

"Thank you," Liz replied, praying he would leave now.

But Cam still wasn't budging. Not for the first time, Liz wished she had the ability in life, like in TV and movies, to cut away from a moment, to smash to a new scene, to dissolve out of the undesirable and fade into a new set of circumstances.

Cam shot her finger guns and finally got up. "Good chat."

Mercifully, Cam left the editing bay. Liz tilted her head back in her desk chair and looked at the track lighting bifurcating the cottage cheese ceiling. She didn't like how it had been conveyed, but Victoria was right: This job was soul crushing. She needed out. Unfortunately, Liz was also right. She needed gainful employment. Her ancestors hadn't invented fire, planted a stake in oil fields, or presciently gobbled up valuable real estate; she didn't have the freedom that being independently wealthy yielded you to make attractive life decisions based solely on their merit or personal happiness. Liz couldn't afford to quit and surf the uncertainty of unemployment without knowing when her next paycheck would appear.

Liz tried to wrest control of her thoughts and focus her attention back on episode 8. When she had paused it to talk to Cam, the fiery Allegra, who was one of the more popular contestants, was making out with Dylan, who was doing an admirable job of pretending to be straight, though sometimes he laid it on a little too thick with mentions of "bro code" and had a habit of sticking his hand up the female contestants' shirts like it was a fishing expedition and he wasn't entirely sure what he'd encounter. Allegra hadn't caught on to the fact that Dylan was the gay catch, or that he had made out with no fewer than four other contestants during their "seven minutes in the closet." Which was exactly like the adolescent game that sixth graders cooked up in basements all over America, only with a supposedly sexy, romantic, and grown-up closet, designed by a buzzy HGTV personality. It was supposed to be clever. But the "seven minutes in the closet" portion of the show was another sad detail of many that, together, manufactured a delusion that two people wholeheartedly embraced. It was a farce—an utter mockery of love, romance, and relationships. Then again, the reductive and abhorrent train wreck that was *The Catch* provided entertainment that hinged upon an illusion that was mutually agreed upon by viewer and participant. Real love wasn't found through competition and contests under the blaze of set lights; its reward wasn't a partnership with Zales, and everyone knew that. And yet . . .

Liz wished she could wake these people up. She wished she could flee the editing bay. She wished she could go back and take a different path in the choose-your-own-adventure version of her life. But she couldn't do any of that.

Liz clicked play. On the screen, one of the women threw a green smoothie into Allegra's face. Cam was going to love it.

―――――――――

Liz hustled to get across town to Mother's Haven, where she was attending her first new mom's class with Dawn. Determined not only to fly in the face of the example Angela had set, but also to enter into motherhood in the most knowledgeable, prepared manner possible, Liz was looking forward to learning about feeding schedules and CPR. She made a mental note to ask Preston if he knew how to do the Heimlich.

When she arrived, Liz climbed the stairs to the second floor and entered a hybrid classroom-playroom. There was a large, colorful rug that covered the floor, with various toys sprinkled about the periphery. *You'll be playing here soon enough with your little ones*, they promised. One of the walls was mirrored and the other three were covered with murals and photos of previous classes of mothers and babies. The infants were arrayed for their photo ops with their backs on the carpet, arranged so they looked like flower petals around a Frisbee bearing the logo for Dawn's class.

None other than Dawn Hampton herself greeted Liz and the other new moms as they entered, checking their names off a list and pointing out the cubbies where they should store their shoes. Only socks and bare feet were allowed on the carpet. Liz was wearing loafers but fortunately had remembered to bring a pair of spare socks. She didn't want to lead with her bunions when meeting a new group of women. She tugged on her socks and found a seat with her back to the mirrored wall. As women kept filtering in, Liz snuck glances at her classmates. They had already coalesced into little clusters and were talking animatedly. *How?* Either they knew each other beforehand or they had forged alliances in the four minutes it took to get from the parking lot to the second floor.

"Did you choose a pediatrician yet?" Liz heard one woman ask another.

"We're going with Dr. Daniels. You?"

"Same! He's the best. And the offices are—" She did a chef's kiss.

Liz watched them exchange a heartfelt look.

"I'm so glad we're doing this together."

"Our babies are going to be best friends."

"They don't have a choice!"

The two women hugged. Their swollen midriffs grazed like bumper cars and they laughed before they broke apart—a peak momcore moment. Flooded with envy, Liz fixed her attention on a poster on the wall. The new-mom class was yet another sorority. Just as Liz was telling herself that it didn't matter, she was here to learn how to take care of her baby, not compliment someone's Hatch jumpsuit, she saw her walking into the room.

Liz was puzzled, but it was Victoria striding into the room in skintight leather pants, a white button-down shirt, and three-inch heels. Liz watched her give her name to Dawn and take off her shoes.

"Who wears leather pants to baby group?" said the woman next to Liz.

"Seriously," said the woman on the other side of Liz, who now found herself in the middle of a shit-talking sandwich. "And heels!"

"It doesn't exactly scream *maternity wear,*" Liz opined, and the women looked at her approvingly. A line had been drawn and Liz was on the correct side of it.

Across the room, Victoria placed her heels in a cubby, then looked over, directly at Liz.

Liz held her breath. She had once run into a one-night stand at Whole Foods two years after their forgettable, sweaty tryst. Liz had been piling her cart with chickpea puffs and plantain chips—snacks masquerading as health foods—when he had rounded the corner with a pretty girl on his arm. Liz had immediately clocked the ring on her finger—and the fact that he still had all his hair. She hadn't known whether to say hi and introduce herself—*I'm Liz and I've already met your fiancé's penis*—or pretend it wasn't happening, she didn't recognize him, she wasn't actually in aisle 9 at all, these weren't her chickpea puffs or Nayonaise. This situation, with Victoria, felt similar. What was the protocol for greeting someone you never thought you'd see again after a test brunch that had gone terribly?

Like the one-night stand who had pretended Liz was wearing an invisibility cloak and walked right by her, Victoria also took the reins and solved the dilemma for her. She gave Liz a wave, then came over and sat down next to her.

Liz saw the other women give her side-eye—she knew this creature?

Liz attempted a casual tone as she addressed Victoria. "Hi. I didn't expect to see you here!" *Or ever again.*

"Me neither. They called me yesterday and said there was an opening," Victoria explained.

"That's great," Liz said, processing the news that they were going to be in the class together after all.

"Actually, what they said was that they had lost one of the moms," Victoria added.

"Wait, what?" Liz asked, alarmed.

"They clarified that she was moving to Chicago, but still. Not the best wording to lead with."

Liz braced herself for Victoria to ask if she had updated her résumé yet, but Dawn closed the door to the classroom and called all the moms to order. She sat down in the circle with them and introduced herself, telling them how, many years ago, she had noticed a hole in the market. There were postpartum baby groups, but there wasn't a course for expecting moms, led by an expert, that would give them the resources they needed and allow them to foster a community that would continue after their babies arrived. Dawn's idea gestated and then . . .

the class was born. Dawn told them that yes, in the years since, she had written books and appeared on *Good Morning America*, but Dawn's heart and soul remained here: with the new moms, in this classroom. Even if the lighting on set at *GMA* was more flattering! The women laughed, and as Liz glanced around, she saw that they were soaking up Dawn's words like manna from heaven.

Dawn then asked the women to say their name, their baby's due date, if they knew whether they were having a girl or a boy, and one thing they wanted to learn. Liz lost track of all the women and their corresponding October due dates. Their answers were so similar about what they hoped to learn—holistic teething remedies, the latest data on cord blood banking, anti-Ferber methods for sleep training—that no one stood out. Until it was Victoria's turn. "Is it true that bubble baths can give your baby a UTI?" she asked. Hiccups of dismay and pejorative giggles spread around the circle like a SoCal wildfire. If Victoria noticed, she didn't seem to care. "Maybe it's an urban myth, but I heard that you shouldn't do bubble baths under the age of two, for a boy or girl," she said bluntly.

Liz looked at Victoria to see if she was aware that she was causing an international baby-group incident. But Victoria was casually looking around the room, meeting everyone's gaze without compunction. Dawn cleared her throat. "Remember, everyone, no question is too weird or wacky. This is a safe space." Dawn then assured them that they would spend a class covering bathing methods and hypoallergenic products.

When the class concluded, the groups of moms formed right back up. Liz pulled out her phone and pretended to check an influx of important emails. Victoria stood and stretched her legs. Liz overheard a cluster of three women talking, their voices too many decibels above a polite stage whisper to suggest they'd even considered it.

"She doesn't look pregnant," one woman said with a snicker, fingering her loose braid. They were all rocking wispy, ankle-length peasant dresses, like they had raided a DÔEN sample sale together.

"Maybe she's not," said the doughy-faced but pretty one.

"Surrogate. Good call," the redhead in the trio said. "She does look a little *old* to be pregnant."

"I am old," Victoria said, walking over to the group of women. "But I'm not using a surrogate. I'm pregnant. Naturally, no less. If you have any other questions, feel free to ask."

Liz watched the women redden with embarrassment. Liz had to hand it to this woman: Victoria had done what Liz had fantasized about many times but had never been able to muster the courage to accomplish. She had stood up for herself.

Victoria flashed them a smile, then collected her heels, slipped them on, and strode out of the room. Liz scrambled to gather her purse and information packet, then hastily threw her loafers on over her socks in order to catch up to Victoria, who was already down the stairs, exiting Mother's Haven.

"Victoria," Liz yelled, once she got outside to the sidewalk flanking the tree-lined side street. "Wait up."

Victoria turned and did, a polite expression resting delicately on her face like an outfit on a hanger.

"I'm sorry," Liz said. "That was shitty. I shouldn't have been a part of that, earlier, talking about your outfit."

"I'm pretty tough. I just wish people would say it to my face."

"You're right." Liz drew in a deep breath. A motorcycle zoomed by, interrupting the otherwise quiet setting. "At brunch, I realize you were probably only trying to help—"

"But I came across as privileged and out of touch and bossy," Victoria said.

Nailed it, Liz thought. "A little?" she suggested.

"I'm sorry. I'm good at zeroing in on the bottom line, playing hard-ball, and voicing my opinions. It's served me well at work, but this wasn't work. I could have used a filter."

The admission settled nimbly in the air between them.

"Do you want to go for ice cream?" Liz asked suddenly.

Victoria's mouth curved upwards in surprise. "I'd love to."

They walked to a gelateria nearby and ordered double scoops.

"Outside or inside?" Liz asked, then she and Victoria found a corner table on the patio and dove into their stracciatella and dulce de leche.

"I'm bad at this," Victoria said. "Small talk. Making friends. Relating to other women, in general."

"Really?" Liz said. "I figured you had a tight-knit group of equally flawless women who did spa days together and went on shopping trips in Paris."

Victoria burst out laughing and a bit of stracciatella sprayed from her lips like a puff of confetti. "Hardly." She wiped her mouth with a napkin. "I've really only had one friend and we only started hanging out because we were in the same AP classes in high school. But then our lives took different directions and I insulted her about the path she chose and now we're twice-a-year-happy-birthday-text friends. So, not many friends in my stable."

Liz took this in, trying to recalibrate the version of Victoria she'd had in her mind.

"I don't have anyone to invite to my baby shower," Victoria said, her tone matter of fact. "Except maybe my doctor. I think she would come. Part of the concierge fee?"

"Let me guess—it's twenty-five thousand dollars?" Liz asked pointedly but not unkindly.

Victoria laughed. "Yep."

"I'm not good at the whole friendship thing either," Liz admitted.

"Really?" Victoria asked, her turn to be surprised.

"I've always felt like I'm on the outside, looking at the cool girls, taking notes, trying to fit in."

Victoria nodded thoughtfully.

"I think a lot of people feel that way," she said. "Most people just don't have the courage to admit it." Liz considered this, taking another spoonful of gelato. "Is it like that with the women you were with at Mother's Haven?" Victoria asked.

Liz deliberated about how much to divulge; even though Victoria seemed to put a premium on let's-cut-the-shit honesty, laying bare the innermost contents of her mind wasn't something Liz was used to doing. There was also the danger that once she revealed a little, everything would come tumbling out. Secrets were as slippery as marbles and best kept bundled up in a tight drawstring bag. "They're my friends, but I always feel like I'm wearing or doing or saying the wrong thing."

"Liz, I'm no expert, but that doesn't sound great."

"No?" Liz said, irony filling her tone. She licked the frosty spoon. Maybe she and Victoria *did* have something in common. And that it was a friend deficit—who would have thought?

As their gelato melted into sweet soupy puddles, Liz and Victoria sat at the table trading details of their lives. Liz thought about all the times she had read something extolling the power of female friendship, whether it was a piece of highbrow literature or a coffee-mug quote. All the poignant musings and quippy sound bites on female friendship had seemed valid in theory but hadn't resonated for the simple fact that Liz couldn't relate. *Maybe this is it,* Liz thought as she sat on the patio, enjoying the last slips of afternoon sun with Victoria. *Maybe this is what everyone has been talking about all along.*

11

Victoria

20 WEEKS: ARTICHOKE

Victoria skipped into the kitchen in her workout pants and squeaky new Nikes. Despite having to contend with Mark's unctuous grin as he presided over the week's company-wide meetings, the days had flown by as if they were hurtling towards an end goal. Victoria had cheerfully informed the gossip-turned-planning committee—Deborah, Ellen, and Annalise—that she was diligently making her invite list for the baby shower. So what if Victoria only had one name on it? Two, if she counted her concierge OB! Victoria slid behind the kitchen counter.

"Do we have ingredients to make a smoothie?" she asked Ace, as if she needed a prop in hand to complete the "pregnant workout lady" costume. He eyed her suspiciously from his post in front of the espresso machine.

"Who are you and what have you done with my wife?" Ace asked.

"I told you! I have plans today with my new friend Liz."

She opened three cabinets of pots and pans and place mats before Ace pointed her in the direction of the Nutribullet.

"Seriously. What's happening here?" Ace asked.

"We're going for a walk together."

"You, as in the person who has said, many times, that walking is a geriatric excuse for exercise?"

Victoria threw half a banana, a scoop of almond butter, and a handful of berries into the Nutribullet.

"Friends walk together," Victoria announced, rifling through the pantry for protein powder. "And I have a friend."

"A real-life human woman?"

"Indeed. And I'm going to keep her." They both laughed, Ace's dimples making deep indents in his cheeks.

"No more four-hundred-dollar brunches that are going to make Liz feel uncomfortable," Victoria said.

"Four hundred dollars? How much did you order?"

"Half the menu. But now, we're going to do nonintimidating, inexpensive friend things."

"Wholesome." Ace hid a smirk. "What's she like?"

Victoria thought for a second. "She's funnier and smarter than she realizes. I haven't gotten a read yet on what the situation is with her boyfriend. She has a terrible job she needs to quit—"

"Is she a friend or a project?"

"Who says she can't be both?" Ace looked at Victoria knowingly. "Liz is great. She could just use a dose of confidence. I think she's in a pivotal place. Maybe if she had an executive coach . . ."

"Lucky for her, now she has a very successful, fully realized exemplar of corporate womanhood by her side."

"Make fun of me all you want," Victoria said, turning on the Pulse button of the blender to drown out his words.

"You know I do nothing but live in pursuit of putting a smile on this beautiful face," Ace shouted over the noise.

He caressed her cheek and they kissed deeply. Behind Victoria, the smoothie churned, and then the motor of the blender started to burn, emitting a fatigued, grisly sound. Ace jabbed his hand blindly in the general direction of the appliance and turned it off without breaking their embrace. It was only after a few more minutes that he pulled back.

"When do you have to leave?" Ace asked suggestively.

"If I skip the smoothie, I probably have time," Victoria said.

"Race you to the bedroom!" Ace said, then took off in a sprint down the hallway.

Victoria tilted her head back and laughed. Then she followed her husband to their bedroom and peeled off her workout outfit to reveal her naked, pregnant form.

"Yes, please," Ace said.

Victoria moved to the bed and allowed her husband's caresses to arouse her, grateful that pregnancy, thus far, had not impeded either of their libidos. She lost herself in his touch, succumbing to the skilled movements of Ace's hands, then guided him to enter her. Ace pulled Victoria's head towards his and kissed her as their bodies collided, building friction towards its eventual exquisite climax.

Afterwards, Victoria rested her head on Ace's chest. He stroked her hair gently and Victoria thought about how lucky she was.

"I love you," Victoria said, then craned her neck to look at the clock on Ace's bedside table. "I have to get going, though."

"A few more minutes," Ace said. He reached his hand down to rest on the curve of her belly, which was growing more pronounced. "I'm going to miss you both when I go to London."

"Us both?" Victoria repeated, amused. "Also, you're already thinking about this? You're not even going for two months."

"Of course I'm thinking about it. Are you sure you don't want to come?"

Ace had made his money in commercial real estate, but he was also the silent partner in several restaurants along the California coast, one of which had sown offshoots in New York, Miami, Aspen, and now, London. Ace was flying over for the opening.

"I'm going to be taking time off after the baby as it is," Victoria said. "I have to plant my stake in the office and make sure Mark doesn't get any ideas about poaching my clients."

"Fair enough," Ace said. "But I'll miss you. Hookers just don't do it like this."

"You better believe it."

Ace watched Victoria as she got out of bed to get re-dressed.

"Are we going to do playdates with your new friend after the babies come? Mom and dad things? Birthday parties on the weekends at those indoor playground germ factories?" he asked.

"You sound very eager for all of that. Including the germs."

Ace grinned. "I can't wait to be a dad."

"They said it would never happen . . ."

Ace stood up, came over to Victoria, and lovingly cupped her face in his palm. "Thank you for proving them wrong."

———

Victoria walked on the sun-dappled dirt path next to Liz. Tall stalks of wheat-colored grasses sprang up around them and wildflowers dotted the hills. The area was teeming with native species of vegetation, and though adult Victoria generally appreciated the great outdoors as commodified by a five-star resort, she was spellbound as Liz led her down the trail and a not insubstantially sized lake came into view, its slate-gray ripples shimmering like a mirage.

"I live fifteen minutes up the road," Victoria said, gesturing in what she thought was the vague direction of Coldwater Canyon, "and I had no idea this was here." Victoria studied the alluvial vignette and marveled that they were ten minutes from the bustle of Beverly Hills.

"It's kind of a hidden gem," Liz said, pointing over to her right, where a serpentine trail made its way up the mountain. "You can hike over there without running into crowds of influencers in full faces of makeup or tourists with selfie sticks and little dogs in baby carriers."

"Why get a dog you have to push in a stroller? And at what point do you stop calling that kind of animal a pet and start calling it something else?"

"I never had a pet," Liz said. "I always wanted one, but Angela said it was enough work to take care of me."

"Angela is your mom?"

Liz nodded. "I never called her that, though. She introduced herself to me as Angela and it stuck."

"That's hard to imagine. Isn't there a reason all kids say *mama* or *mommy*?" Victoria observed.

"Yeah, but Angela only sees one version of things: hers. Unless she's microdosing. Then she sees everything. All her lives. Because she has access to the Akashic records."

"*Oh.* I'm starting to get a sense of her."

"She's . . . a lot," Liz said. "She legally changed my name when I was four because I wasn't living up to it."

"Seriously? What was your name?"

"Sage." Liz rolled her eyes. "So obviously, she did me a favor. But yeah. Angela told me that I was turning out to be a more conventional child than she'd hoped for and I couldn't handle the weight of such a unique name."

"Your mother said that to you when you were four years old?" Victoria looked over at her friend, agape.

"It's a miracle I turned out halfway normal. Sage is the name of the daughter Angela wished she had . . . and I guess Mom is the name for the mother I wished I had." Victoria looked at Liz, her chest clenching with sympathy. "I see all these women posting on Instagram, thanking their babies for choosing them to be their mommies, and I'm like, *What? Your baby didn't have a say in the matter!* Because—trust me, if I had been given a choice, I would have picked differently. Angela and I were just stuck together, two people who had nothing in common except DNA."

"I know the feeling," Victoria said, a light breeze sending tendrils of hair against her cheek. She brushed them away. "I always felt like an alien that had been plucked from my real home and deposited into this foreign place, with people who didn't know what to do with me. I used to wish I had been adopted because then there would have been a logical explanation."

Liz flashed Victoria a commiserative look, her hazel eyes warm and, Victoria thought, particularly attractive in this light; flecks of green leapt out from deep pools of amber. "What's your family like?" Liz asked. The seemingly innocuous question threw Victoria into rumination, sending her back in time.

Thanksgiving at the Millers' was not the joyful, raucous affair associated with the commercially wholesome holiday. Instead, it consisted of what was perhaps the more common American tradition: an obligatory exchange of strained family dynamics over a meal that culminated in multiple stomachaches. Sixteen-year-old Victoria dutifully helped her mother prepare for two days beforehand, not because she had any talent in the kitchen or interest in slopping Hamburger Helper into casserole trays, but because it was assumed of her, like her younger brother Jimmy was expected to glue himself to the couch next to their father and scream at the TV screen. The difference was, Jimmy enjoyed his role. Victoria had suggested to her mother that they might include something green this year to offset the sea of starches, and she did not take kindly to this, insulted that Victoria thought her casseroles (main ingredient: box or can), cream of mushroom soup, and stuffing dotted with crushed Lay's potato chips (it looked like potpourri) needed any accompaniments. The dining table would be dressed once again in its array of beige, white, and orange carbohydrates, like the Pilgrims had intended it.

When Victoria's extended family arrived an hour later and they sat down for the meal, Victoria wished that she had come down with an acute case of smallpox. Her cousin Kristine told everyone that she had seen Victoria entering the college counselor's office that week. Victoria and Kristine seldom crossed paths, and when they did, Kristine didn't dare tarnish her patina of popularity by acknowledging her cousin who had no interest in normal teenage rituals like cutting class, giving hand jobs under the bleachers, and sneaking booze into school dances. All heads turned to Victoria, who felt the burn of gazes threaded with judgment.

"You're a junior," Kristine accused.

"I have a lot of AP credits," Victoria said simply, hoping her family would drop it rather than reveal that they didn't know the significance of this. But the plan backfired. She saw annoyance sprout on her mother's face; she probably thought Victoria was trying to make them feel dumb.

"What does that mean?" her mother snapped.

"I might be able to skip senior year and go straight to college."

"You already skipped a year," her dad said, like he didn't understand why Victoria would want to do something unusual not just once, but twice. He had turned down a promotion the previous year, disinclined to take on a greater workload and responsibility.

"Seriously?" Kristine asked, unable to imagine the horror of not attending one's senior prom.

"I get your room!" Jimmy yelped. "Can I, Dad? Can I have her room?"

"You wouldn't live here?" Victoria's aunt asked. "Where would you apply?"

"Stanford, Berkeley, USC, UCLA . . ." Victoria caught their looks and stopped reciting the rest of her college list. Her mother's face assumed the color of an eggplant, a vegetable that had never graced that table.

"I'm not sure," Victoria hedged. She looked at her mother and tried to change the topic. "The stuffing is great." Her mother frowned, the deep grooves that probably had Victoria's name on them carving themselves irrevocably into the topography of her mother's face.

"My family is very simple," Victoria told Liz. "They're content with what they have, satisfied without needing more, which is obviously a good thing." Victoria trailed off, not entirely sure how to phrase the rest of it.

"What's the bad thing?" Liz asked.

"They looked down upon intellectual curiosity, drive, and ambition. All the qualities I had and they didn't. They didn't like that." The truth was, they hadn't liked *her*, or at least that's how it felt.

"What would they have against ambition?" Liz asked.

"They couldn't relate to it. I think they were threatened by anything that disrupted their status quo. When they watched game shows every night, I'd go off to my room to read by myself and they'd roll their eyes. They probably thought I looked down on them, but I couldn't help being who I was, even if it was a rejection of everything they were."

"Do you still talk to them?"

"Quarterly check-ins," Victoria said. "We're as close as you can get to not having a relationship without being formally estranged. I always call them, otherwise I'd never hear from them, and the conversations are always stilted and awkward. What am I supposed to say to people who never told me they were proud of me for getting into Berkeley? Who I didn't invite to my wedding because . . . well, a lot of reasons."

Liz looked at her. "Do they know?"

Victoria shook her head. "I told them I was getting married, but said we'd probably just go to the courthouse, and they didn't ask any questions."

"Do you think they would have come?"

"I don't know," Victoria said after several moments. "I told myself that I didn't want to find out—I didn't want to be disappointed again. But maybe I was equally scared of them showing up. I couldn't bear to watch them see my life through their eyes."

"I get that," Liz said. "I know what it's like to have someone not show up for you. Or to have them show up, but not in the way you need, and that's almost worse."

Victoria nodded, and wished she didn't feel the same stirrings of emotion she always did when she thought about her family. The pain of their rejection had once burned intensely, and while over time it had fermented into something less potent, or so she insisted to herself, it still stung. The wound may have crusted over, but Victoria didn't know if it would be like a bad knee that acted up when it was going to rain.

"I should probably let it go," Victoria said, "but calling them every few months seems like something I should do, like getting a dental cleaning. I don't expect anything anymore, though." It was true—Victoria had no expectations. But if she was being completely honest with herself, Victoria was also still holding on to a sliver of hope, a vestigial token of her younger years, that one day her family would surprise her. That their inability to relate to her wouldn't impede their ability to love her.

"Look at us. It makes you think happy childhoods really are a myth," Liz said.

"You don't need Freud to figure out that my upbringing played a role in my ambivalence towards motherhood."

Liz nodded. "I don't want to do anything like Angela. Sometimes I get scared, though. What if I'm nothing like my child either? What if I can't bond with my baby?"

"That scares me too," Victoria said. "Motherhood scares me."

"You don't look like you're scared of anything," Liz said.

"Plenty of things," Victoria said. "Bad Botox, for one."

Liz laughed.

"Hazard of being in LA, though."

"Yeah, I'm not sure I belong here, but at least I'm more used to it now," Liz said.

"This city is strange. But it also has a strange magic. There's a beautiful alchemy that's possible in Los Angeles that you can't find in other places."

"They should talk about that on those star tours instead of pointing out where O. J. Simpson used to live," Liz said.

"That's a stop?" Victoria asked.

"They tore down the house. But they show you where it used to be, in Brentwood," Liz said. "Probably not during the regular tour. My friend Freya made us do a true crime tour for her birthday one year."

"Was it fun?" Victoria asked.

"No, it was weird and creepy. But she was fresh off a breakup with a guy who had a raging coke problem, so she said murder matched her mood more than champagne."

"Aside from the murder tours, which are obviously enticement enough," Victoria said, "why did you move here?"

"I was into film and I lucked into a job through my college's alumni network. But I think moving to California was always my secret goal, deep down."

"Why was it a secret?"

"I knew my father lived in California," Liz said. "But I couldn't tell Angela that I still thought about this person who had abandoned us when I was a kid. She would've lost her shit."

"You knew where your dad lived?" Victoria asked.

"I used to let myself Google him once a year, on my birthday. It was like some form of internet emotional cutting, but I stopped when I turned thirty. I told myself I was too old for that. No good had come out of it—or would."

"You never considered contacting him?"

"No," Liz said, shaking her head so that her ponytail swung emphatically. "That's not why I came here. I wasn't ever going to hit him up and be like, 'Remember me, the kid you wanted nothing to do with?'"

"Why not? You could get some closure, at least."

"I honestly never even considered it. My shrink says that wanting to move here was probably a subconscious choice—the pull of a place that had intrinsic value. The thing—the life—he chose over me."

Victoria processed this, trying and failing to keep her face a blank slate.

"It could be worse," Liz said. "I didn't wind up on a pole."

Victoria laughed, and then, as if they both needed to focus on less mentally taxing subjects, the conversation turned to their first impressions of Dawn's class and the cliques of disciples that had already formed.

"How about that group chat?" Liz said.

Victoria remembered that after she had joined Dawn's class, she had received an invitation to join the WhatsApp group. She had mentally set it aside and promptly disregarded it.

"I completely forgot," she said, pulling out her phone from her jacket pocket. Victoria navigated to WhatsApp and made a face at the group name: Dawn's October Mommies. It was accompanied by a string of pregnant-woman emojis.

Victoria scrolled through. "Two hundred and sixty-seven messages!" she exclaimed.

"You haven't looked at it at all?"

"No. Why are there two hundred and sixty-seven messages? What can these women possibly be texting so much about?" Victoria looked through the barrage of messages, picking up key words here and there. "'Who's getting the Snoo?'" Victoria read. "'To Nanit or not to Nanit?' 'Anyone have reccos for hypoallergenic onesies? TIA.'"

Liz made a face, expressing a sentiment that Victoria felt on a visceral level. Victoria kept reading: "'What bottles are you ladies getting? TIA' . . . TIA, TIA, TIA. What's *TIA*?"

"Thanks in advance," Liz said.

Victoria's head shot up. "Thanks in advance? Why do they say that? And how do I unsubscribe from the group chat?"

"Please don't leave me alone in there," Liz said. "TIA."

Victoria laughed. "Please don't say that again. TIA."

They spent the walk back finding ways to insert *TIA* into various contexts. *Please don't cum inside me, TIA. Extra mustard and ketchup, TIA. Kindly go fuck yourself, TIA.*

When they reached their cars, Liz's mood seemed to downshift. Victoria noticed that she looked pensive and was chewing her bottom lip.

"What is it?" Victoria asked. "I know we got off on the wrong foot at brunch, but I promise you can tell me anything. I won't overstep."

"I've been thinking . . . about my job . . ."

Victoria nodded and tried to keep her face neutral. While mentally, of course, she was plunging into a PowerPoint presentation to chart the course forward, she forced herself to stay mum and allow Liz to lead the charge.

"I can't quit without having something else lined up. And obviously, this is the worst time to be trying to change jobs." Liz pointed to her pregnant body. "I have to be responsible about this. But I do want to see what else is out there."

"Yes! I mean—good idea."

"I had a feeling you'd say that."

"I've never been good at hiding my opinions," Victoria said. "I also know, even though it didn't come across initially, that passion and a paycheck don't always go hand in hand."

"You're lucky that they do for you," Liz said.

"I am. Is my job always ideal, though? No. I really wanted to be named managing director of my firm but it went to a self-impressed, backstabbing weasel."

"Why do the douchebags always win?" Liz lamented. Victoria was touched by her new friend's automatic loyalty.

Liz frowned, and Victoria was worried she had overstepped again, but then Liz asked, "Would you take a look at my résumé? If the offer still stands?"

"Of course. Anything I can do to help."

"TIA," Liz said with a small smile.

"TIA," Victoria told her back.

12

Liz

Liz studied the Tulum-inspired decor of the restaurant as Preston mumbled assurances that he'd only be a couple more minutes on his phone. Basket lights emitted a soft golden glow, the furniture was all made of rattan and beachy off-white rope, and hammered terra-cotta tiles covered the floor. It came together to invoke a sense of relaxed, if appropriated, exoticism. *Don't you feel like you're on vacation?* Despite it being the tenth restaurant of its kind to pop up in the past year, with the foodie blogs reporting on the Tulumification of Los Angeles. Liz took a sip of her mocktail, a bland imitation of a margarita without any of the ingredients that made one tick. Preston drank half of his Casamigos Blanco margarita in one pull without breaking eye contact with his device.

Liz would have preferred a taco truck, but this temple of fancy plant-based Mexican fare seemed as good a setting as any for the conversation Liz wanted to have with her boyfriend. Now that she had voiced her desire to quit her job, it felt real, so Liz figured she should probably tell Preston she was thinking about it, given that they were a unit and that's how coupledom worked. Talking to each other about the minutiae of their days, discussing big decisions, disclosing (most) aspects of their lives . . . that's what adults in a relationship did, right?

But Liz hadn't wanted to broach this conversation over another home-cooked meal because she had a strong suspicion that if she did, memories would crop up of the last one she had engineered. Liz tried to forget Preston's blank-eyed stare when she had told him that she was pregnant—and the way his vocabulary had dwindled to one word: *wow*. Deep down, Liz knew that the casual, easygoing equilibrium their relationship had always been defined by couldn't last forever. She was halfway through the pregnancy, and she and Preston had important subjects they needed to tackle soon. Who was going to take care of the baby? Private school or public? Would they split costs or prorate them based on income? But one step at a time: her employment.

Ever since Cam had settled his ass next to Liz's plant and reprimanded her for not serving up the dregs of humanity, Liz had been crawling with resentment and disgust towards *The Catch* and anyone who enjoyed working for it. It was like art and cinema and literature didn't exist. Even though art and cinema and literature were often about sex, that wasn't the point. There were other things to do on a Saturday night than try to make out with a steroidal RN whose abs looked like a rack of lamb.

Preston finally put his phone down. Liz didn't wait until the light on the home screen had blinked off. "I hate my job and want to quit," she said. So much for a preamble. Preston screwed up his face and looked like he'd had either too much or not enough of his margarita to process this.

"What? I thought you liked your job. You're on a hit show!"

"I did. At one point. Maybe? But now I hate it," Liz said. "It makes me understand why people have psychotic episodes in the workplace and HR has to flag their files and recommend IOPs."

"What's an IOP?"

Liz should've known Preston wouldn't be familiar with this term. His family believed in gin, not therapy. "Intensive outpatient program," she said. "Anyway, the point is, I hate my job, and seeing how much you're obsessed with yours, and how my new friend Victoria loves what she does—it only makes me feel worse."

"Well, she's right," Preston said. "Your job is so much of your life. Of course you should do something else if you don't like it. What are you thinking?" Preston asked. "*The Bachelor* or a *Housewives* franchise?"

"No. I don't want to go from one vile reality show to . . . another kind of reality show."

Their waiter delivered a basket of chips and a ceramic bowl filled with guacamole the color of Kermit the Frog. The bowl reminded Liz of a pinch pot she had made in second-grade art class but never saw emerge from the kiln because Angela had moved them to Twin Oaks, an intentional community in Virginia, before it was fired.

"That makes sense," Preston said. He looked skeptical, though, like he was trying to process the discrepancy between Liz being staffed on a show that was a cultural phenomenon and Liz suddenly declaring she no longer desired any involvement in said success.

"I know that life isn't a rom-com, and at a certain point, you can't have these unreasonable, crazy dreams about what you want to do, like 'I'd love to be a prima ballerina or own a vineyard in Tuscany.'"

"You want to be a ballerina?" Preston asked.

"No. I'm not eight years old," Liz said. "I just think there's a difference between settling and selling your soul." Liz looked into Preston's eyes. "I hope there is, anyway." Liz also hoped there was a difference between pursuing a dream and chasing the contrails of a self-indulgent artist's fantasy à la Angela. There had to be a sweet spot where passion and paycheck and purpose converged.

"I had no idea you felt this way," Preston said. "Of course you shouldn't sell out." Liz beamed at him, overflowing with gratitude.

"What do you want to do?" Preston asked.

Liz took a deep breath. "It's probably going to sound as ridiculous as wanting to be a ballerina, but I'd really love to edit features—indies. Small arthouse films that say something. That mean something," Liz said, feeling so self-conscious about this admission that she was tempted to pick up the bowl of Kermit-green guacamole and shovel the whole thing into her mouth.

"A24, Searchlight kind of stuff?" Preston asked.

"I mean, that's the dream," Liz said. "But I'd probably have to start out smaller than that. Like, really small. Work for free for a bunch of USC Stark kids doing their student films or something."

"Don't sell yourself short," Preston said. "That's the first thing I tell my clients when we're negotiating a deal. Always ask for more. Always act like you deserve more. Otherwise, you're never going to get it." Liz nodded. "So yeah, you gotta do it," he continued. "Edit an indie! Bring home an Oscar! Or, you know, an Independent Spirit Award."

Liz giggled despite her doubt, pleased with his encouraging response. Preston lifted his margarita.

"To your new career."

Liz clinked her glass against his and enjoyed the sound they created together. It made everything feel real and substantial. It made her feel like she and Preston were united in this. It made her feel a little buzzed despite her anemic, virgin cocktail. "Thanks for having my back," she told him.

"Of course. Obviously, indies are really tough, though. Getting financing, operating on a low budget, dealing with psycho actors who want to talk about a scene for four hours, securing distribution . . ." Preston must have seen Liz's expression falter because he trailed off. "But it's not like I have a ton of experience on the feature side. I just hear talk in the office. A guy I know had a passion project, great fucking movie. Charlize starred in it! Premiered at Toronto. No one saw it."

"That sucks," Liz said, shifting unhappily on the white-and-beige chair cushion.

"The point is: You gotta shut all that stuff out!"

Was that his point?

"This is gonna be great." Preston nodded energetically, like he was at a Tony Robbins seminar.

"It probably won't be great at first," Liz said. "But I'll work my way up, I'll work hard, and hopefully it will work out."

"It will. And in the meantime, I'll support you. You don't have to worry. I'll get you a credit card."

"No," Liz said quickly. It was an automatic response, one she didn't have time to parse before the words flew from her mouth. "That's not necessary. I can't ask you to pay for me." Preston looked at her, uncomprehending, and Liz tried to figure out the reasons for her vehemence. Maybe it was because Victoria had discussed the importance of a woman being financially independent and Liz didn't want to disappoint her friend. Maybe it was how Preston had phrased it. He wanted to do this *for her*, rather than thinking of them as an *us*, with the offer intended to serve them as a unit. Or maybe it was that some fledgling part of Liz wanted to achieve success in her own right so that she could embrace the feeling of satisfaction if and when it came, so that she could claim it without having to attribute any of it to someone else.

Liz reached across the table, not towards a crispy chip and dollop of guacamole, but for her boyfriend's hand, and said, "I appreciate it, Preston, really, but I have to do this on my own."

"I'd get more points," he offered feebly, before dropping it and asking if she wanted to split the jackfruit tacos and jackfruit enchiladas, which sounded like the same concoction of ingredients in nominally different forms.

When they got home from dinner, the jackfruit was sitting in her stomach like a lump of lead, right next to the spot where about the truth of their baby's conception had lodged itself permanently. Still, Liz was inspired to put on a loose (forgiving) nightgown, light a few candles, and try to seduce her boyfriend. If only she knew how to go about such a thing. Even before she was pregnant, Liz usually let Preston initiate. But tonight she was feeling brave, emboldened by Preston's positive reaction to her career goals.

"Hi," Liz said, attempting a breathy, sexy voice while crossing the room from her closet. She probably sounded like an asthmatic who needed an inhaler. Preston was already in bed, wearing boxer shorts and his faded Dartmouth T-shirt, fumbling with the remote.

"Hey," he said automatically. "Want to watch Bill Maher?"

"I was thinking we could do something else first," Liz said, arranging herself on top of the duvet cover in what she hoped was an attractive, come-hither pose.

"What?" Preston asked. He looked genuinely curious, like Liz might be suggesting a game of thumb war or a walk around the neighborhood.

"You know . . ." Liz said.

Preston looked over. He noticed the silk nightgown. And the candles. Synapses fired and then he said, "Aww, babe."

But not in the good way of saying it. Preston said it in the rejection-couched-in-niceties kind of way. Liz frowned. She felt silly and embarrassed and, obviously, repellant.

"It's not because I'm not attracted to you—I swear!"

"Then why don't you want to . . . do it?" Liz internally shook her head at herself. *It?*

"I told you, I'm freaked out about the baby seeing my dick," Preston said.

"But it doesn't go into the uterus. That's not how it works."

"Do we really know that, though?"

Liz looked at him, incredulous. Did the father of her child really just ask her that? Did he think the world was flat too?

"I know I'm being nuts," Preston said, "but I can't get the idea out of my head. You're doing your thing, and then all of a sudden, your dad's dick is coming at you like a torpedo?"

Liz just looked at him, then made a sound to signal that she had heard him, which was about all she could offer.

"Hey," Preston said, grabbing Liz's arm, then traveling down it to knead her hand, like massaging her extremities was a suitable consolation prize. "I promise, it doesn't have anything to do with you. As soon as the baby's born, we'll be back at it."

Liz smiled and went off to the closet, where she silent-screamed into a pile of jeans that no longer fit her. She couldn't take another failed attempt. A secretly sexless pregnancy this would be.

Work that week was excruciating. On Monday, when the whole staff gathered for a morning meeting to watch dailies, Liz watched Cam eye-fuck a new assistant while baby-talking with his girlfriend on the phone. On Tuesday, they received a report that the paramedics were called overnight because Kylie had an acute case of alcohol poisoning. No one was too concerned, however, because while one contestant was getting her stomach pumped, two others had given up on the male prospects and hooked up with each other. Everyone was delirious with excitement.

"Ratings gold!" crowed an entry-level producer who played pickleball with Cam.

"Threesome! Throuple!" Cam shouted, amped up like he was at a MrBeast fan event and pronouncing it incorrectly: *threw-ple.* "That would *crush!*"

Liz needed out. And fast.

She finished going through more B-roll of late-night antics, then emailed the cut to Cam and left the office an hour early, allowing more than enough time to get across town to the third new-mom class. When she arrived and ascended the stairs, Dawn's perky, signature brunette bob coming into view, Liz realized how much had changed since the first class. It was no longer a question of who she would sit next to, but whether she or Victoria would arrive first and stake their spots together on the kaleidoscopic carpet. During the second class, Liz and Victoria had whispered in each other's ears the whole time. Their alliance and attachment, ad hoc at the first class, was now well established. Liz rested her purse beside her to save a spot for Victoria.

Finally, her friend glided in at a brisk, eager clip.

"You look weird. What's going on?"

Liz contemplated various versions of the truth. *I'm fantasizing about murdering my boss. I might have tried to get pregnant on purpose. I'm not a good person and I don't deserve you as a friend.*

"Nothing!" Liz said. "What's going on with you?"

"I'm pregnant. Have you gotten any bites on LinkedIn yet?"

"No. I'm starting to lose hope," Liz admitted. "Maybe indies are as impossible as Preston said." Dawn was closing the door to the room to begin class, but Victoria swiveled her head like an owl to look at Liz.

"You're not giving up, are you?"

"No," Liz said, lowering her voice to a whisper as Dawn announced the topic of class: sleep schedules. The women clapped and cheered. Hurrah! Answers to the questions that were plaguing them most—how would they go about getting their infants to sleep through the night? How soon after birth could they anticipate getting some rest again?

"I'm all in my head, though," Liz continued. "Maybe I should try to pivot to something more realistic, like scripted or another reality show."

"Is that the goal? A less heinous version of what you're doing now?"

In the background, Dawn plunged into her lecture. Liz listened for a second to Dawn, who was advising them about wake windows for newborns. "We can talk about it later. I don't want you to miss the sleep talk."

But Victoria waved this off. "I hired a live-in baby nurse."

"So you're auditing this class for fun?"

"You know what's going to keep me up at night?" Victoria said. "Thinking about you wasting your talents, working for someone who should come with his own warning label. You don't have to wait for the perfect opportunity to materialize to quit. You can temp or wait tables to pay the bills in the meantime—whatever it takes."

Dawn kept advising about nap schedules, but Liz was too preoccupied to listen. The more she thought about the indignity of her job and the outrageousness of Cam's behavior, and the more she played back Victoria's words in her mind—*This is your life. What do you want to do with it?*—the more fired up Liz got. She knew that if Victoria were in this position, questioning what to do, the answer would be obvious. *Quit your job. Take them down—all the men who treat women like things and all the women who sit there and watch them do it.* With a sudden ferocity of decisiveness that she rarely felt, much less exhibited, Liz plucked up her phone.

The words came naturally. The email wrote itself. Liz was sure it would be likened to a feminist *Jerry Maguire* manifesto of sorts. *Fine. Good. Let them,* she thought. If her coworkers needed to wrap their heads around her missive by drawing an association to an iconic Tom Cruise film, so be it. Jump on a couch. It wouldn't detract from the headline—I'M QUITTING—or dilute the essence of Liz's words—THIS WHOLE PLACE IS SEXIST AND RAPEY AND YOU'RE A SAD BUNCH OF MORALLY REPUGNANT HACKS WHO CAN'T EVEN PRONOUNCE THE WORD THROUPLE CORRECTLY. AND PRO TIP: YOU DON'T HAVE TO WEAR

THE ENTIRE BOTTLE OF COLOGNE! YOU SMELL LIKE A DUTY-FREE STORE, YOU LECHEROUS DESK-CREEPER! Liz didn't forget to touch upon the show itself: THERE'S A SPECIAL PLACE IN HELL FOR EVERYONE WHO HAD A HAND IN THIS OFFENSIVE, CRAPTASTIC TRAVESTY. THAT'S THE REAL CATCH! AT SOME POINT, EVERYONE WILL HAVE TO ANSWER FOR WHAT THEY'VE DONE TO FEMINISM AND DECENCY—COMMON DECENCY!!!—SO LOOK FORWARD TO THAT!

Liz felt fire in her veins along with a certainty that she was doing the right thing. Her thumb hovered over the screen, but only for a second. Liz pressed Send and the manifesto hurtled off into cyberspace, heading to Cam, all the producers, and the HR department.

She put the phone back in her purse and didn't look at it for the rest of class, pretending to pay keen attention to Dawn's directives even though her mind was whirring like a car's air-conditioning system set to max. When class was over, Liz gathered her purse on autopilot and prepared to stand, but found herself incapable of completing the task. Had she really written that? Had she really done that? In the middle of a new-mom class? Yes. Yes, she had. She had completely lost her shit. Over email. Along with a sense of disbelief, Liz was also proud. Maybe all the instances when she had failed to stand up for herself had led to this one stunning, transcendent moment of assertion.

"Wanna go for ice cream?" Victoria asked, handing Liz her purse. Liz still hadn't budged from her spot on the floor. Liz looked up. She felt like she was operating in slow motion.

"Ice cream. Yes. Sure. Let's do it." Liz was grateful to be handed a direction. She would give Victoria the update when they weren't surrounded by pregnant women. Liz followed Victoria out amidst a chorus of their classmates thanking Dawn for her wisdom and complimenting her comprehensive explanation of sleep-training methods.

"Ten weeks or ten pounds!" one mom cheered.

"Let the sleep training begin!" another said enthusiastically.

Victoria tossed a look at Liz while slipping on her shoes, another elegant pair of heels. "How much are they going to hate me when they find out I'm getting a night nurse?"

"I'm sure you're not the only one," Liz said.

"A night nurse maybe," Victoria said. "But a twenty-four-hour live-in?"

"How long do you have her for?" Liz asked as they exited down the stairs.

"Six months," Victoria said. "And before you ask—it's a fortune. But I'm going back to work as soon as I can and Ace is old—he's not going to be up at two in the morning with our newborn. Or maybe he is—he's so excited it wouldn't surprise me. If he wants to take a shift instead of Magda—great, we'll have options."

Would Preston wake up with the baby at night? Liz realized this was another thing barreling towards them that they hadn't talked about. Then she realized she no longer had maternity leave. Because she no longer had a job. Because she had sent an accusatory, expletive-filled email of resignation. A beam of late-afternoon sunlight, diffused but still strong, hit Liz's face through the cirrus-smudged sky and she suddenly felt lightheaded. She put a hand up to her forehead to steady herself.

"Are you all right?" Victoria asked.

"Yeah, I'm fine."

"That's weird." Victoria had taken out her phone and now was looking warily at a text message. "Sorry," she said, snapping her focus back to Liz. "You look a little pale. Do you feel okay? We're going to talk more about your job situation and figure out a plan."

"I was a little dizzy, but it passed," Liz assured her. "What's going on?"

Liz watched Victoria fight the urge to check whatever was happening on her phone.

"I didn't read the text yet," Victoria said. "It's just odd. My friend Jen, who I told you about, texted me and it's not either of our birthdays . . ."

"Check it."

Victoria looked at her phone, her face creasing with confusion. "'So sorry about your dad,'" she read.

"Sorry about what?" Liz asked.

"No idea." Victoria typed and then there was a chime as she received an immediate response. She cocked her head. "Oh. That makes sense. He's dead."

"What?!" Liz exclaimed.

Victoria looked up with a bewildered expression.

"My dad died. Apparently."

"Oh my God. Victoria, I'm so sorry."

For the first time since Liz had met her, Victoria looked like she didn't know what to do. It occurred to Liz that she had quit her job, and rather hysterically at that, due to the influence of someone who had been accidentally informed of her dad's death over text. It probably should've alarmed Liz, but she actually found it fitting. Or maybe she was still hysterical.

13

Victoria

28 WEEKS: EGGPLANT

The morning after Victoria had been notified of her father's sudden death via text message, she walked into her office with her usual commanding stride, her bravado tempered when she took in her surroundings: The same early-morning light streamed in through the window, but today its brightness felt harsh and wrong. Orchid II was flourishing and the tidy landscape of Victoria's desk greeted her as it always did. All of which served as a stark reminder that despite cataclysmic personal events, the world churned on. But then, as if to assure Victoria that this day was *not* like every other day, Harper charged into her office with the subtlety of a Category 3 storm.

"Victoria! I got your email last night. I'm SO sorry. Obviously, I was so honored you, like, *shared* that with me." Harper put her hand over her heart. "But it's so terrible."

"Thanks, Harper. I'm going to work remotely for a few days while I go to the funeral."

"Omigod, you're in *mourning*. I'm sure you'll need more than a few days."

Victoria considered. Was she in mourning? She was shocked and saddened, of course, in the way you were supposed to feel certain emotions in response to specific events. Truth be told, Victoria felt like she was grieving the loss of a possibility that would now never materialize, much like her actual father.

When Victoria had called the landline of the house she grew up in—digits emblazoned upon her mind despite their habitual disuse—her mother had answered and Victoria asked, in what she hoped was a measured, reasonable tone, whether anyone was planning on telling her that her father had died. Her mother had chided Victoria for making it all about her. Then she had handed the phone to Jimmy, who told her that their mother was taking it really hard and he probably would've remembered to call Victoria eventually. Victoria then asked if any arrangements had been made. That they had managed to plan a funeral in record time before—or without—bothering to notify her felt like an additional blow.

"Was he old?" Harper asked.

"Seventy-three. So, relatively. To you, that must seem ancient, of course—"

"No! Not at all!" Harper protested too vehemently. Victoria remembered being Harper's age, when fifty felt futuristic and old age would surely be accompanied by flying cars.

"It was a brain embolism." Victoria thought about her father's fate. There was no way to predict or prevent such a thing. It was a trick of faulty wiring, a malignant shooting star.

"Sometimes when I sneeze when I'm driving, I get worried I'm going to crash my car," Harper said solemnly. "There's a lot of scary stuff out there and so much of it is completely out of our control. We have to, like, live in denial about our mortality or we'd just be paralyzed."

As Victoria was taking in the astuteness of this observation, she saw a flash of a familiar salt-and-pepper coif heading down the hallway accompanied by—Victoria felt like she had been slapped in the face. Nash was meeting with Mark? Harper saw her expression and followed Victoria's gaze to the source.

"Ugh. Do you want me to spread rumors about Mark in the assistants' Slack channel?"

"It's okay," Victoria said, trying to maintain her equilibrium. She was surprised that Nash was willing to meet with Mark and disheartened to see that her estimation of the billionaire—and his ability to size up a person—had fallen short.

Before she could spend more time mourning the loss of Nash to her odious coworker, Victoria's cell phone rang, and she had to deal with the loss of her father. Ace had just landed in London and had no doubt received Victoria's text saying that everything was fine, but please call her when he could. Victoria gestured to Harper that she needed to take the call and Harper backed out of the room, making a heart shape with her hands.

"What's wrong?" Ace asked immediately.

"My dad died. I didn't want to tell you over text. Which, incidentally, was how I learned about it."

"What happened?"

"Brain embolism. He dropped dead in front of the TV."

Victoria thought about her parents. Regardless of their lack of affection for her, they had tethered their lives together for nearly fifty years. Victoria wondered how her mother would go about her daily routine when half of its focus had been erased. And if—no, when—this happened to Victoria and she lost the person she had built a life with, how would she cope? How did anyone bear it?

"I'll book the next flight back," Ace said.

"No. I'm fine."

As Victoria said it, she wondered if she truly was. Maybe she was still in shock, but she felt strangely dissociated from the fact of her father's death.

"I know how strong you are, and even if you are quote-unquote fine, you're my wife. I want to be there for you," Ace said.

"I know and I appreciate that, but we can talk on the phone. There's no need for you to physically be here. I would tell you." The silence that followed conveyed Ace's skepticism. "I would," Victoria insisted. She didn't want to explain to Ace, who had never met her family, that introducing him over a casket would only intensify the awkwardness and hostility thrown her way. Victoria looked out the window, down to the manicured streets of Beverly Hills, which were only now beginning to awaken. A shoeless homeless woman, her matted hair sticking up at haphazard angles, scavenged through a trash can in front of the window display for a men's clothing store selling $2,000 sweaters.

"I'm looking up flights."

Victoria drew her gaze away from the window. "Ace—seriously, don't. You won't even make it in time. I'm leaving for Fresno in an hour. The funeral is tomorrow morning."

"Tomorrow? What are they, Jews?"

"Jimmy said my mother didn't like the idea of him lying around in a morgue because my father didn't like being cold."

"Even though . . ."

"Correct."

"Jews also avoid cemeteries and funerals when they're pregnant," Ace said, his voice taking on a different cadence. "The spiritual and emotional state of a mother directly impacts her unborn child. The mother's emotions and surroundings are imprinted on her developing embryo. Attending a funeral or entering a cemetery is an emotionally charged event best avoided to protect the mother and fetus."

"Are you reading from the internet?" Victoria asked.

"Only so I could explain it properly."

"I respect the Jewish traditions and that makes a lot of sense, but I'm not a Jew. I have to go to my father's funeral despite . . . everything."

Victoria couldn't put a finger on why the need was so strong, but she also knew that if she didn't go to Fresno and pay her respects and remind everyone that she was part of this family, the last tenuous string connecting her to her origins would snap. Maybe Victoria should have been ready to let go, but she wasn't.

"I understand," Ace said. "I'll come with you."

"I don't want you turning around and spending another twelve hours on a plane. You could get a blood clot. I love you and I'll call you when I get there and I'll tell you if I need you, I promise."

"I can't allow my pregnant wife to drive almost five hours by herself into the belly of the beast."

"My friend Liz *did* offer to come with me . . ."

———

Victoria's GPS directed her up Thrasher, and then she saw Liz standing in front of an attractive mid-century modern house, an overnight bag resting at her feet. Liz waved. Victoria pulled over and stepped out of the car.

"Are you sure about this?"

"I'm coming."

"What about work? And Preston? He's never even laid eyes on me and he's fine with a random woman absconding with his girlfriend?"

"You're not random, you're my friend. I've told him all about you. And I think he missed the funeral part and thought it was some kind of fun girls' trip because he kept telling me to have a blast and send him pics from the road." Liz made a conspiratorial, hapless gesture—*men, what can you do?* Victoria smiled for the first time that day.

"Your evil boss really okayed the time off?"

"About that . . ." Liz said, picking up her overnight bag. "I kinda quit."

"What do you mean 'kinda'?"

"Not kinda. I quit. I completely quit."

"Liz, that's great. Good for you!"

"Well . . . there's a little more to it. I might go viral." Victoria shot her a quizzical look. Liz pulled out her phone, scrolled, and handed it to Victoria. She read Liz's diatribe, her eyes widening and her face modifying itself every few seconds with a medley of emotions in quick succession.

"Liz! This is incredible."

"So you see, I'm free to go to Fresno for as long as you want." Liz marched over to Victoria's car, opened the trunk, and put her bag in. "I'm probably going to need a few pit stops, though. The baby's tap-dancing on my bladder."

Victoria walked over to the car, her mind still playing catch-up with all that had occurred in the last twenty-four hours. "You're an angel for coming with me and you're a hero for writing that email and you can have as many bathroom breaks and road trip snacks as your heart desires."

"TIA," Liz said, and they shared a smile. Victoria input the destination into her GPS even though she could navigate from the 5 to the long stretch on CA-99 that would deliver them to Fresno without its guidance. Any sort of assistance, however, felt like a salve. Victoria had not made this trip, or seen her family, in five years. As if sensing her thoughts, Liz asked, "When's the last time you were there?"

"Five years ago." Victoria started the car. "My brother Jimmy was being named teacher of the year at the local middle school. I had just done my TED Talk—"

"Wait! What? I didn't know you had a TED Talk! On what? I need to see it!"

Victoria smiled, flattered by Liz's effusiveness. "It was about how women can take control of their financial futures despite it being such a male-dominated world, which could lead to advances in gender equality on a global level. Unfortunately, people in town had gotten wind of it, and when I went back for my brother's big day, they were laying it on thick and asking if I was on a first-name basis with Bill Gates or had my own plane."

"Yikes. So your brother felt like you stole his shine?"

"You guessed it. My parents were furious. They acted like I did it intentionally, as if I drove up there not to celebrate him, but to sabotage my brother. And I haven't been back since then, so this should be fun. Buckle your seat belt," Victoria said with a half smile. She pulled onto the freeway, which was mercifully flowing this morning rather than clogged with thick ropes of traffic. Victoria realized that despite the reason precipitating it, she was already enjoying this road trip. It was the first she had ever taken with a friend. The absurdity of that—and of the idea of two pregnant women belting out classic tunes like "Free Fallin'" on their way to the armpit of the great state of California for such a solemn occasion—suddenly struck Victoria as hysterical. She cracked up, and Liz looked over with alarm.

"What's happening?"

"It's funny," Victoria said, hiccupping with laughter. "And ridiculous. It really is." Victoria's hysteria slowly abated. "Sorry." She signaled and switched into the HOV lane.

"Don't be," Liz said. "I think any reaction after a parent dies is completely normal."

Victoria smiled at her. "I'm glad you're here with me."

"Me too. Thank you for inviting me."

"Fresno? For a funeral? What could be better than that?"

"My boss's face when he got my email calling him a rapey hack?"

Victoria cracked up all over again.

As they discussed everything from politics to Victoria's baby shower to the sublime, almost indescribable experience of feeling their babies move inside them, the extended metropolis of Los Angeles gave way to suburban strip malls, and then stretched into flat, endless plains as they made their way farther in-state. They stopped at several rest stations for bathroom breaks and sustenance, Liz leading the charge to select the requisite road trip items—warm, doughy pretzels dusted with salt crystals, oversized Big Gulp slushies the shade of stoplights, french fries sweating oil from the fryer they had emerged from, and a handful of Snak Club bags filled with sour watermelons, gummy bears, toffee peanuts, and chocolate trail mix. Victoria picked out two trucker hats, T-shirts bearing the rest stop's name, and furry novelty sunglasses made in China.

When Ace called to check on Victoria with one hour to go to Fresno, she answered over the car's Bluetooth and told him she was having a great time. Ace sounded slightly baffled by her jubilant tone, but relieved, and thanked Liz for being such a good friend to his wife. Then a Miley Cyrus song came on the radio, and while Liz sang along and bopped her head to the beat, Victoria shimmied her shoulders since she didn't know the words. Their faces shone with the pleasure of camaraderie as they crossed into Fresno, the "best little city in the U.S.A." according to the sign on the side of the road.

When Victoria arrived at the home she had grown up in, her mother instantly appeared at the threshold, clad in all black with the countenance of the grim reaper himself, perhaps to spectate at Victoria's arrival like she might accidentally drive over the gravel front path or trample her prized begonias. Jimmy emerged in the doorway behind the bereaved widow and inspected Victoria's car like he had never seen a Range Rover in person before.

"I better go face the execution squad," Victoria said, already weary from the effort.

They got out of the car and Victoria's mother and brother both did a double take, their eyes sliding over her body to determine whether Victoria had shape-shifted or if she was pregnant. From their expressions, both were equally possible. Their gazes bounced to Liz next; Victoria's mother stared at the two women with an uneasiness that suggested she was confronting evidence of a contagion infiltrating her home.

"Hi," Victoria said. "This is my friend Liz."

"Nice to meet you both," Liz said politely.

Neither her mother nor brother returned the favor. They stood there, as welcoming and impassive as the security detail outside the White House. "As you can see, I'm expecting," Victoria said. "Liz too. We're due at the same time." The silence that ensued could also be described as pregnant.

"I thought you married a guy," Jimmy said finally.

This was going to be ten times more insufferable than the awards-day TED Talk debacle. Victoria cleared her throat. "Ace—my husband—is in London and couldn't make it back in time. Liz was kind enough to come with me."

"Oh," Jimmy said, literally scratching his head.

"I guess you'll be wanting to come inside," Victoria's mother said.

Not particularly, Victoria thought. But she offered a polite smile of assent and her mother sidestepped to allow for entry. Victoria and Liz trundled inside the modest house and Victoria was struck by the sense of inertia it exuded. In five years, so much had changed in her life, and yet it was as if here, in her childhood home, time had stood still. The same scent had always clung to these walls—musty floral potpourri. The faded wallpaper, the yellow curtains hanging like overgrown bangs on the kitchen window over the sink, the linoleum flooring, the telephone extant in its wall mount, the round wooden table wedged into a corner so it had only ever really fit three chairs comfortably, not four—nothing had changed.

"Everyone's out back," Jimmy said. Victoria and Liz followed him wordlessly; her mother stayed behind, busying herself with some unnamed, important task.

They entered the screened-in porch where mourners were gathered alongside a folding table of refreshments—two-liter bottles of every variety of soda imaginable, clear plastic boxes of cookies cracked open like clamshells to display their contents, and a large plate of crackers next to a can of Cheez Whiz. The small room couldn't contain all the guests, so they spilled out into the backyard, where tufts of dirt still outnumbered patches of grass and a storage shed battled with the elements to prove its fortitude. When Victoria and Liz entered, the pockets of conversation abruptly ceased. Victoria put up a hand in greeting to the general vicinity.

"Victoria's here," Jimmy announced needlessly. "And she's pregnant. And she brought a pregnant friend. But they're not lesbians."

"Thank you, Jimmy," Victoria hissed under her breath.

He turned to her. "What?"

"Never mind." Victoria shot Liz a plaintive look. "Do you want a drink? Or an Uber to the hotel?"

"I'm totally fine," Liz assured her.

"That makes one of us. I have never not wanted to be sober any less than this exact moment."

Liz sympathetically rubbed her shoulder. Victoria saw her cousin Kristine approaching and mentally rectified her previous statement: Make that *this* moment.

"No way!" Kristine said. "This is nuts! Congrats, Cuz." Victoria saw that middle age had not tempered Kristine's fondness for a full face of makeup. Her eyebrows looked like they had been drawn on and her hair was striped with highlights. Kristine cracked her gum and looked at Liz. "You too."

"Thank you," Victoria and Liz murmured at the same time.

"Let me tell you, it's murder on the body. I still piss a little when I laugh—or cough—or sneeze, but I love my little fuckers," Kristine said, gesturing behind her to two gangly teenage boys who were calmly beating the shit out of each other in the driveway. "My Benny's got a mean right hook," Kristine bragged.

"How—nice," Liz said.

"Does he box? Or wrestle?" Victoria asked, trying to seem interested and avoid looking at a small child who appeared to be licking rocks and eating dirt nearby.

Kristine furrowed her brow and frosty-blue eye shadow caked in the corners of her eyes. "In one of those tight-ass spandex onesies? Over my dead body!" she said. Then Kristine seemed to realize the impropriety of this statement given the context and crossed herself. "Sorry, Father." She looked at Victoria. "And sorry about yours."

The afternoon passed in a similar way. Victoria accepted condolences, braved her mother's contemptuous silence, and withstood the shock of a whole town that never thought Victoria would find someone who wanted to love her or procreate with her. When guests eventually filtered out, Victoria and Liz escaped to Jimmy's former room, which her mother had turned into a sewing room. Victoria's childhood bedroom had been claimed by Jimmy the second she left for college, all chess-team trophies and SAT study guides swept away to erase any evidence of her presence.

"I don't know why I came here," Victoria said, her face drawn and her mood dismal.

"Because he was your father?" Liz suggested delicately.

Victoria's phone chimed and she checked a text from Jen, who said she couldn't get away from the kids' soccer practice, but she'd see her at the funeral in the morning. "My friend Jen," Victoria explained to Liz, gesturing to the phone. "I owe her an apology."

"Why?"

"I looked down on her," Victoria said. "I did to her exactly what everyone here did to me my entire life: I judged her for her choices. She was the closest thing to a kindred spirit I had, so when she dropped out of college to get married and told me that all she wanted in life was to be a stay-at-home mom, I was horrified. I could have been disappointed *for* her, but I shouldn't have told her I was disappointed *in* her."

"You could still tell her that."

"You're right," Victoria said. "Jen will probably think it's because I'm pregnant now so I see the value in her choices, but that's not it. If she's happy managing her kids' schedules and volunteering for school plays, who am I to say she should be more than a stay-at-home mom?"

"I think she'll appreciate that," Liz said. "But don't go getting soft on me. I need someone to boss me around and tell me what to do with my life now."

Jimmy walked into the room at that moment, interrupting Victoria and Liz laughing together in the corner. He raised an eyebrow, as if he had confirmed his belief that things were more than platonic. "Ma and I were gonna go through some of Dad's stuff."

"So soon?" Victoria didn't understand what the rush was, but Jimmy shrugged. She turned to Liz. "It's been a long day. Why don't you take the car and check into the hotel? I'll catch a ride and be over in a bit."

"Are you sure?"

Victoria gave Liz the reservation number and her car key, promising she wouldn't be too long—and instructing Liz to send a SWAT team if she was. Then she joined her mother and brother in her parents' bedroom. Victoria felt uneasy in these quarters, as if she were a child walking in on something illicit. Jimmy didn't exhibit any such discomfort in invading their parents' domain; he plopped on the bed and watched their mother carry over an armful of their dead father's clothing from the closet.

"We didn't have a will," their mother announced. "Your father always said, 'What's the point in paying a lawyer when I can write it down myself?'"

"He wrote down his wishes?" Victoria asked.

"He didn't have time, Victoria. He died before he had the chance!"

Victoria pressed her lips together. Her brother flashed her an annoyed look: *Why do you have to upset her like that?*

"Sorry," Victoria said. "And to be clear, I don't want anything. I'm only here . . ." She paused. Why was she there? "To pay my respects."

Her mother scoffed. After a full day testing her self-control, Victoria was running on empty. "Is that funny?" she asked her mother.

"It is, considering you'll show up for a funeral but didn't want us at your wedding."

"Some of the neighbors saw the announcement in *The New York Times,*" Jimmy explained.

Victoria's mother turned to Jimmy as if the topic weren't worth further discussion. "Take whatever you want of his clothes. Anything else we'll give to the church donation bin. I'm going to keep his wedding ring, and I thought you should hang on to his watch."

"Thanks, Ma."

"He loved that watch."

Victoria felt as unwanted as a hemorrhoid and as out of place as a financial analyst at a rave. She tried to determine a non-obstreperous way she could remove herself from the situation. But when Victoria shifted on her feet, her ankles suddenly feeling as heavy as the emotional pall cast over the room, they both looked over at her.

"Are you going somewhere?" her mother asked.

"No."

Her mother then opened the bottom drawer of her father's nightstand and, from underneath a pile of old remotes, chargers to nonfunctioning phones, and other assorted junk, pulled out a manila folder. She glanced at it with confusion, flipped through briefly, then handed it to Victoria without pageantry.

Victoria took the innocuous-looking folder, wondering if this was the moment she had hungered for in her youth, when she would finally learn that she *had* been adopted and all the photos of her pregnant mother had been Photoshopped. But the contents of the folder caught her by even more surprise. Inside, Victoria found every newspaper article she had either written or been featured in, old term papers, report cards smattered with straight A's, written commendations from her teachers, a National Merit Scholarship award, and copies of every single college acceptance letter. It was a comprehensive capsule of the achievements Victoria never thought her father had noticed. Tears sprang to her eyes and Victoria choked them back, her throat suddenly raw with the effort.

"I need to stretch my legs," she croaked, then fled the room before her mother or brother could say anything. Victoria traversed the hallway and living room of the house in six strides, then flung upon the front door and took a large gulp of air, reeling. When Victoria looked up, she saw that Liz was sitting in the Range Rover, waiting for her. Her friend hadn't gone ahead to the hotel without her. And then the tears came. Liz wordlessly got out of the car and held Victoria in her arms.

"It's okay," she soothed, offering up the instinctive incantation of a mother comforting a child after they had fallen and skinned a knee. "It's going to be okay."

Victoria and Liz stood there, two expectant mothers who had never been properly mothered, who had not been shielded from the disappointments and injustices of life but still could find themselves surprised by its largess and, more to the point, loved. Victoria let the tears cascade down her face, weeping for all that could have been and all that still could be, for the exquisite agony and joy of being human.

14

Liz

33 WEEKS: SMALL CHIHUAHUA

Liz dunked a packet of herbal tea into hot water and set up her at-home workstation at the kitchen table. She told herself: Today was the day she'd find a job! In the weeks since she and Victoria had gotten back from Fresno, Liz had been energized to the task, partly to make her friend proud of her. Liz had sent out her résumé upwards of forty times, applied for more than a dozen jobs, and spiraled towards an existential breakdown on multiple occasions. As she scoured job listings, sending out queries at the hyperactive pace of a tennis ball machine, Liz tried not to think of Angela's mantra: *Manifest, manifest, manifest!*

Liz poured a packet of stevia into her mug and shook off her mother's incantation like it was a mosquito. Preston had told her that Angela mentioned she might be coming into town soon, but Liz hadn't heard from her mother personally and "soon" could mean anything to Angela. Regardless, Liz had received this update from her boyfriend with dread. But Liz had bigger concerns than the usual drama her mother brought with her. If Liz didn't land on a lead soon, she'd look into temping, although that wouldn't provide the health insurance she needed, and her COBRA extension was available for only six months. Even though Liz understood Victoria's message—wait tables or do whatever else she needed to do to collect a paycheck until her ideal position materialized—Liz seriously doubted anyone would hire a pregnant woman when scores of aspiring actresses and models were clamoring for service positions, a.k.a. jobs where looks were leveraged for tips.

"Hey, babe," Preston said as he came into the kitchen, dressed in a suit that immediately announced his occupation, in Los Angeles, as either an agent or a lawyer.

"Morning," Liz said. She watched him go about making his grass-fed, ghee-infused coffee. She had tried it once and gagged so violently she thought she might bruise her throat. Butter coffee was repulsive—to hell with its benefits for cognitive function. Also, hadn't that whole trend peaked years ago, along with the Master Cleanse?

"What's on tap today?" Preston asked.

"Same thing. Desperately seeking employment."

Preston looked over at Liz while using an immersion blender to emulsify every disgusting ingredient in his keto coffee. "I'll follow up with my guys in the feature department and see if they can hook you up with something. Sameer's gotta be able to help."

"I hate to ask for favors . . ."

"Babe, this town is built on favors! It's the only way anything gets done."

"I guess as long as you don't feel weird about it . . ." Liz buried her face in her mug and questioned why she felt conflicted about Preston's offer. She *was* grateful, but she also felt pathetic to have to resort to her boyfriend pulling strings . . . even if it seemed like Preston delighted in his proximity to said strings and, even more, to the greater web of a network they formed.

"Obviously I want to help," Preston said, taking a long, ritualistic sip and savoring his revolting morning beverage. "And again, I respect that you want to work. I'm all for it. But I don't want you to stress. I'll support you as long as you need. And if you want to take some time off and focus on the baby, I'm all for that too. My mom didn't work and she was perfectly happy."

Liz decided not to point out that Preston's mother had opted out of the workforce in favor of tennis games and country club lunches, not involved parenting. Also, did Preston think Liz was anything like Cricket? Because if so . . . that would be problematic. There was a greater chance of Liz becoming a literal cricket than of her resembling Preston's mother Cricket. Liz's head suddenly ached. She asked him, "Are we still planning on going down there on Sunday?"

"Yeah! They're excited to see us." Despite Preston's insistence that his parents had been surprised, yes, but *pleasantly* surprised to learn they were going to be grandparents when he had told them over the phone a couple months prior, Liz was nervous about the upcoming visit to her quasi in-laws. She didn't know the Lancasters well but could guess they were the kind of people who leaned hard into conventions. Like marriage before baby. The first time Liz had met Preston's parents, Preston's dad crowed that their country club now boasted three Black families in its membership ranks and Preston's mom announced that "a gay" did her hair before informing the table that love is love.

"We'll have lunch at the club. Piper and Brooks are coming too," Preston said, scooping up his phone and car key, off to another fantastic day rolling calls at the office.

Liz smiled weakly. "Great." Preston's sister Piper was maybe even more intimidating than his parents with her flawless porcelain complexion, haughty and indifferent horse-girl air, and laundry list of accomplishments: Junior Olympian in jumping, high school valedictorian, Princeton undergrad followed by Columbia Law.

Preston gave her an appraising look. "Why do you look weird?"

Liz froze. "What do you mean?"

"When I said my sister was coming, your face got all wonky. Do you not like her?"

"What do you mean? I barely know her." Thanks to social media, Liz knew Piper's favorite brand of cocoon sweaters, where she liked to have date nights, and the names of all her best friends, but that was irrelevant. "She's your sister. Of course I like her."

"I know she can be a little . . ." *Aloof. Unapproachable. Arrogant.* "Tough, but that's only typical protective-big-sister stuff."

"Wait, what do you mean? What has she said about me?"

Preston reddened. "Nothing." Liz looked at him imploringly. "Nothing bad!"

"So your sister disapproves of me. Terrific."

"I never said that!"

"You kinda did, though."

"No—she likes you, and look, I told my parents not to tell her about the baby, so it can be a fun surprise. It's going to be great."

Liz didn't think this sounded so great, but what was she going to do? It was Preston's family. She was still obsessing about it, though, when noon rolled around and she decamped to the local coffee shop, saying hi to her favorite barista, a twentysomething with facial piercings and green streaks in his hair who wore his sense of self effortlessly. Axel recognized her now that she had become a regular. He called her "Blueberry Muffin Mom." The blueberry muffins were covered in frosting and should've been classified as cupcakes, but since the morning had been less than stellar, Liz allowed herself a consolation pastry. She was nibbling and scrolling through LinkedIn when a flash of expensive silk in her peripheral vision caused her to whip her head up.

"I thought I might find you here," Victoria said, sitting down across from her.

"Hey! I'm so sorry last night didn't work out," Liz said. She and Victoria had been trying to arrange a double date since they still hadn't met their significant others, but after finally finding a date that worked for everyone, Preston had a work thing come up and they had to cancel.

"Don't worry," Victoria said. "It happens. But I wanted to see you and make sure that you weren't drowning your sorrows in an extra-large latte."

"I don't know why I'd do that. Except I'm unemployed, pregnant, and got an email from *The Catch*'s legal team threatening to slap me with a restraining order if I say anything else disparaging about Cam or the show. Guess I can't count on him as a reference."

"I'd be severely concerned about anyone who valued the rapey hack's opinion," Victoria said.

Liz gave her a small smile. "How are you doing?"

"Okay," Victoria said, tilting her head as she considered the question. "I'm still processing everything."

"It's really good you went." Liz didn't say that she had wanted to bitch-slap Victoria's sullen, contemptuous mother and her insipid sidekick, Jimmy. How could Victoria's family treat her like that? Liz thought back to her fifth-grade school performance of *The Wizard of Oz*, when she and Angela were living in Oregon. Liz had landed the role of the Tin Man and practiced her lines for months, all the while silently pleading that Angela wouldn't yank her out of school, dragging her to some illusory new life before the weekend of the show. Liz had been so relieved to make it to the stage, her face coated in shiny silver face paint, her limbs encased in aluminum washing machine tubes; she was practically high as the curtain rose. She remembered scanning the audience for her mother's face, the bright stage lights making the task difficult. Before she could lay eyes on Angela, the production began. Liz hadn't missed a line. She nailed every cue. She evinced no shred of the stage fright she'd feared might be her downfall. At the end of the show, parents swarmed Liz's classmates with praise and cellophane-wrapped bouquets. Liz waited for her mother to appear. She stood alone in the auditorium for what felt like an eternity. No one noticed the girl who had remembered every one of her lines about not having a heart. Finally, Liz had retreated backstage and rubbed her face raw trying to remove the silver makeup.

"I'm glad I went too," Victoria was saying. "It also gave me a chance to clear the air with Jen. I don't think we'll ever be close again, but I said my piece and it seemed like she appreciated it."

"Will she be at the baby shower on Saturday?"

"She doesn't know if her husband can handle all three kids for the weekend but she's trying to get her sister to pitch in so she can come."

"That's great," Liz said. "Are you excited?"

"Excited for it to be over."

Liz laughed. Behind the counter, a cappuccino machine hissed and released steam into the air. "Who's coming?"

"Ellen, Deborah, and Annalise, who are throwing it, my assistant Harper, maybe Jen, my OB, and almost all the women from Dawn's class."

"That's nice!"

"Is it?" Victoria raised an eyebrow. Liz knew Victoria had gone back and forth on whether to invite their classmates. "Or is it a sad and pathetic attempt to fill seats, the pitiful move of a woman who doesn't have any friends?"

"You have friends."

"I have you," Victoria said. Liz felt her chest swell with warmth. "But apparently a six-person baby shower would not suffice." Victoria held her hands up. "Did you decide on a date for yours?"

"I still have to get back to Cara," Liz said.

"Liz Reynolds, for someone who was championing the sacred occasion of the baby shower mere minutes ago, are you avoiding your own?"

"No. And by that I mean, yes, obviously. I don't want to think about Angela being around you or any other friend I want to continue having in my life. But I also have to invite Preston's mom and sister this weekend. One thing at a time." Liz tried not to think about how it was one thing of so many things. *Focus on the task at hand so you don't get overwhelmed,* her therapist often encouraged, like emotional triage was on par with the standard operating procedure of an emergency department on a Shonda Rhimes show.

"Fair enough," Victoria said. "And if you want me to run interference with Angela or talk about polo with Preston's mom the whole time, I'm happy to."

"I couldn't ask that of you," Liz said.

"Sure you could. You're my best friend."

Liz's grin stretched to the far corners of her face. She turned the words over in her head. Victoria was her best friend.

Liz walked into the lobby of the Four Seasons. A three-foot floral arrangement, architectural in scope, rose above a shiny lacquered round table. Liz paused to admire it, then found a discreet sign in a gold frame listing the private events being held that day. She headed towards the Wetherly Gardens and Terrace and saw that Victoria's coworkers had spared no expense. It was luxurious but tasteful, a bucolic garden dreamscape come to life. And—crucially—there wasn't a diaper tower or baby bottle station that would offend Victoria to her core. A single long table, twenty chairs on each side, had a pale blue tablecloth and was set with bone-white china. Calligraphed place cards sat at the top of each plate, and the table was decorated with simple, elegant clusters of ranunculus in silver vases. The temperature was perfect, like the weather had been prearranged. Birds were chirping, lending their natural soundtrack as an accompaniment to the coffeehouse acoustic set filtering in from the speakers, butterflies fluttered through the air, and the sheer magnificence and abundance of the garden almost made it seem fake.

"Liz, you're here!" Victoria said, stepping away from a trio of women gathered in front of a gracefully gurgling fountain. Victoria found Liz's side and hugged her, not letting go of Liz's arm.

"You look beautiful." Liz thought Victoria had never looked more stunning in the feminine cream sheath dress she was wearing, its precise tailoring the only evidence of what Liz assumed was its considerable designer expense.

"Hiiiii!" a leggy twenty-something squealed as she loped over to them in a miniskirt the size of a postage stamp.

"Harper," Victoria said, greeting her warmly. *Ah*, Liz thought, *the assistant.* Victoria introduced them and then Harper looked around and exclaimed, "This is a-maze-ing! It's my first baby shower. Obsessed! And I'm finally meeting Victoria's best friend!" Without any forewarning, and with the ease of someone whose advances had always been welcomed, Harper wrapped Liz in a hug.

Thirty minutes later, after the guests had helped themselves to the passed hors d'oeuvres and started sitting down at the table, Jen hurried in and Liz saw Victoria's face light up with pleasure that her old friend had made the effort to attend. Liz greeted Jen, who said it was nice to see her at a happy occasion instead of a funeral, and then both of them were touched to see that they had been assigned the seats on either side of the guest of honor.

The lunch passed like a dream, the event humming with harmony. Conversation and laughter flowed around the table, and the setting was so perfect that if a rainbow had appeared, arching over them, Liz wouldn't have been surprised. She thought: *This is what all baby showers should be like.* Two of Cara's had been dampened by her obvious displeasure that she was having another boy, the shower for

Madison's twins had included a double amount of everything cringey (a blind diaper-changing challenge, a pacifier scavenger hunt, a craft corner for decorating bibs), and Freya's baby showers had been so over-the-top (one had called for black tie) that they must've been planned by Liberace himself. This, on the other hand, was understated and flawless. And yes, an insane amount of estrogen was rocketing through Liz's body, magnifying her emotions, but the whole thing was just so . . . lovely. The ambiance, the joyful chatter around the table . . . Liz felt like she was wrapped in a cocoon of divine feminine energy; she felt like she was connected to life and the world of women in a way she had never experienced before. Liz looked over at Victoria and saw that she also seemed like she was enjoying herself.

"I told you," Liz whispered to Victoria. "Isn't this nice?"

"I'll deny it if you ever repeat it," Victoria said. "But it actually is."

Liz smiled. There was something about being part of the undeniable womanhood in the room that was like getting caught up in a great song at a music festival, the syncopating beat and enthusiasm of the crowd carrying you like the current of a wave.

One of Victoria's coworkers stood up and tapped her spoon against a glass—was it Ellen or Deborah? The room quieted. Liz snuck a glance at Victoria, but she appeared at ease, even if all eyes were turning to her for the toast.

"I'll keep this short and sweet," Victoria's coworker said. "Mainly because we were warned not to do anything Victoria would hate, which rules out . . . a lot?" She paused for polite laughter. "I'm kidding! But I am pretty sure a gushy speech is a no-no. So, Victoria, I'll just say that we're so happy for you. We're excited to see how becoming a mom challenges you and frustrates you and drives you nuts— am I right, ladies? Because that's part of it—it's beautiful and brutal, but being a mom is like nothing else you'll ever do. From the bottom of our hearts, congratulations, and welcome to the club."

Everyone cried out "Cheers" and clinked their glasses against one another's. Jen asked Victoria if she could say a few words, and Victoria mockingly rolled her eyes. "I suppose it's a free-for-all now."

Liz had prepared some thoughts for her toast but nervously ran through them again, listening with one ear as Jen began.

"Most people assume Victoria never got anything less than an A, and they'd be right—almost. The one bad grade on her transcript, which she probably still loses sleep over, knowing her—"

"Don't remind me," Victoria interrupted, with a smile.

"Was home ec. It was a requirement, and even though Victoria could solve the toughest equations in precalc, our beloved Victoria couldn't unfold an ironing board." Jen paused for a smattering of laughter. "One time, she sewed over the teacher's finger. Another time, Victoria almost blew up the classroom because she put tin foil in the microwave."

Liz saw that Harper was slapping the table. This would be a hard act to follow.

"But it was the childcare portion of the class where Victoria really shone," Jen said. "We had to carry around an egg for a week, learning how to protect something so fragile. The goal was: Don't let it crack. It was a tough task and most of us didn't make it the whole week. But Victoria went through a whole carton of eggs . . . on the very first day!"

Victoria shook her head, her face glowing with amusement.

"Everywhere she went—splat! There was a trail of eggs. Victoria's yolk kiddos were all over the place. Which is why Victoria Miller got her one and only failing grade."

"And now you know why I don't care for omelets," Victoria said.

"But Victoria has come a long way since then," Jen said. She turned to face her old friend. "I'm glad we reconnected. We've known each other a long time and I've watched you accomplish so much, but I think the best is yet to come."

Victoria and Jen embraced, and then Liz unsteadily stood up. She was never at ease with public speaking, but she wanted to express to Victoria how much her friendship meant to her.

"I'm excited for you too, Victoria," Liz began. "I'm excited to be moms together. But I'm most excited for your baby. He doesn't know this yet, but he's the luckiest little boy in the world because he has a mom who's fearless. You stand up for yourself and for other people, and you're so brave and smart and fierce that I think sometimes it's easy for people to miss how loving you are too. You want the best for the people around you. You admit when you're wrong and you apologize, which is rare. You can seat-dance while going eighty miles an hour on the freeway like nobody's business. I have no doubt that you're going to be an incredible mom, Victoria, because even if you couldn't keep those eggs from breaking, you haven't let me crack."

The force of Victoria's embrace almost knocked Liz over. Around her, she heard sniffles.

"I LOVE BABY SHOWERS!" Harper cried out, prompting laughter and cutting through the thick sentimentality in the air. "Women supporting women! Girl power! Yasssss!"

Liz and Victoria disentangled their limbs and sat back down, still beaming at each other. Liz basked in the moment, letting herself enjoy the glory of feeling like she finally had a friend with whom she could be open and honest, who saw her for who she was and loved her for it—or loved her anyway. "Do you have a name picked out?" Annalise asked Victoria, tucking into a rosé-colored macaron. Waiters were carrying out platters of cakes, éclairs, and jewellike truffles.

"We want to give the baby a name that starts with an *M* in honor of Ace's mom," Victoria said. "Jews often name their children after a relative who has passed, and if it's the opposite sex, they use the first initial. Her name was Mildred."

"Thank God you're not having a girl!" Harper said.

"We're naming our boy Leo Grayson!" one of the women called out. "Dibs on Leo Grayson!"

Other women began revealing—and securing ownership over—their future children's names, and Liz realized that no matter the gender, she was probably going to have a Brady, Jordan, or Kobe . . . unless it was a William, George, Charlotte, or Louis. Liz didn't have a family member she wanted to honor by naming her offspring after them, but having a child named for a sports star or a member of the royal family wasn't an appealing prospect either. She was mulling over how best to present her case to Preston and deciding between an apple tartlet and a sliver of carrot cake when there was a flurry of movement, the guests' attention shifting to the door.

"I love this part," Annalise said.

"My husband brought balloons instead of flowers to my shower," Ellen griped.

"Mine better show up with a Cartier box," one of the women from Dawn's class said.

Liz craned her neck to get a glimpse of Ace as he carried out the time-honored ritual of showing up towards the end of the baby shower, bouquet in hand, to honor his pregnant wife. She couldn't believe she was finally meeting Victoria's husband for the first time at her baby shower. It was with no small amount of anticipation that Liz twisted forward in her seat until Ace's frame came into view.

Then the crowd shifted, and as Liz's gaze glommed on to Ace's features, the world as she had known it tilted on its axis and fell away. Liz staggered to her feet to get a better, unobstructed view of his face and felt the color drain from hers. Liz stared and stared at Victoria's husband, her heart pounding against her rib cage like a drum.

"Dad?" she said.

15

—

Victoria

33 WEEKS: PINEAPPLE

"What?" Victoria stared at Liz, who was staring at Ace. Liz remained rooted in place, slack-jawed, as a portentous hush settled over the terrace. Victoria switched her attention from her best friend to her husband. She observed, with an almost morbid fascination, as the blank expression on Ace's face rearranged itself to include confusion, surprise, and the cosmic specter of possibility. Ace's brow furrowed, his mouth twisted in consideration, and he blinked once with disbelief, but then his eyes shone with something resembling stunned clarity. And Victoria knew that nothing would ever be the same.

"Sage?" Ace finally said. There it was.

Victoria couldn't speak, couldn't move, couldn't think. Beside her, Liz gasped, her gulp echoing in the now-dead-silent air. No one seemed to know what to do. Ace looked like he could have a stroke. Liz's face was ashen. And then she ran out as fast as she could manage with her pregnant frame. Ace's gaze shot to Victoria, his eyes connecting with hers, his face awash with shock.

"Umm . . ." Harper said. "What just happened?"

Victoria sat there, a vertiginous sense of confusion crashing over her. She looked at her husband's lips as if they still held the name he had uttered: Sage. A single syllable that had just cratered their lives. And though Victoria would love to believe there was a simple, silly explanation for what had just happened, her intuition told her otherwise. Even if it didn't, she could read the confirmation on Ace's panic-stricken face.

Victoria abruptly stood. She didn't know where she was going, but she knew she couldn't stay there for one minute longer. She strode into the garden, beside herself with the shocking outlandishness of what had occurred.

"Victoria," Ace called after her. He caught up and grabbed her lightly by the elbow. Victoria dramatically yanked her arm away. "Please don't run away from me," Ace begged.

"What the fuck, Ace?!"

"I know—I know," Ace said.

"*What?*" Victoria hissed. "What do you know?"

"Sage—or Liz—" Ace began. Victoria shook her head.

"Stop. I don't want to hear a word you have to say," Victoria snapped. Around them, birds chirped and a monarch butterfly floated delicately in the air. It was absurd. Victoria fumed, so livid that she was trembling. A gardener was headed their way, but upon hearing evidence of a domestic scuffle, he made a sharp turn and headed in another direction. "I'm leaving. Do *not* follow me," Victoria commanded.

Victoria walked away from Ace and didn't look back. She didn't return to the terrace to confront the fallout of her spectacularly disastrous baby shower. She didn't care if she never saw her purse or her phone again. Goodbye forever to the life she had known before. That her iPhone and Bottega Veneta clutch were also on the pyre seemed a mere pittance; this was complete and utter destruction, a total loss.

Her legs carried her through the lobby to the restaurant, where Victoria beelined for the bar and claimed a tufted barstool at the

mahogany counter. The bartender, a once-attractive man in his fifties, tactfully slid over a glass of water and offered Victoria a polite
smile without asking if she was okay or commenting on her ravaged
countenance. Victoria thought he probably had seen a lot worse,
but actually, could any salacious dalliances or sensational scandals
compare to this? *This*, this unbelievable insanity, was straight out
of the tawdry pages of the *Daily Mail*. It was the stuff of a daytime
soap. Victoria couldn't believe it was her life.

"What can I get you?" the bartender asked.

"I don't have my wallet," Victoria answered.

"On the house," he said.

"That's very kind . . ." Victoria hesitated and looked down at her
stomach, which was the size of a regulation basketball. "European
women drink during their pregnancies, right?"

"American too," the bartender said. "From what I've seen, anyway."

"One glass is fine," Victoria said, more to herself than to the bartender. Her doctor had told her the same, though she hadn't felt the
urge until now. "I would love a glass of white wine."

"Sancerre?" the bartender asked.

He was good at his job. Victoria nodded gratefully, and in short order,
she had a crisp glass of chilled French white in her hand. She tasted it. The
tannins tingled on her tongue after she swallowed. Victoria took another
sip and stared at the multicolored array of bottles behind the bar, at the
little jars of blue cheese–stuffed olives and cherries and other garnishes, at
the tidy stack of thick, embossed napkins boasting the hotel's name. She
sat there and nursed her glass of wine until the last spangles of afternoon
light slid downwards and dusk crept in at the corners of the room. The
bartender gave her a bowl of nuts and she ate them even though she wasn't
hungry. Victoria doubted she'd ever be hungry or feel normal again.

Finally, as smartly dressed people with dinner reservations and
carefree expressions began filing in, Victoria recognized that she

would have to determine her next move. Staying there forever was unfortunately not a viable option. She couldn't collect her car from the valet without her ticket, which was in her abandoned purse, and she couldn't order an Uber without her phone, which was also in said purse. She should probably retrace her steps to the Wetherly Terrace or check with the front desk to see if anyone had turned in her bag, but both of those options required an amount of effort that Victoria couldn't muster. "Hi," came a subdued voice behind her.

Victoria turned and saw Harper, her assistant's features muted with concern. She held up Victoria's purse but maintained a tentative three-foot distance.

"Oh, Harper," Victoria said. "Thank you."

Harper outstretched her hand, with the purse, and Victoria gave her an appreciative smile laced with sorrow. She felt fragile, and like all her nerves were raw, and frayed, and exposed. She was light-headed and out of sorts, tentative in her movements, as if the connective cord between her brain and her body had been compromised. Feeling as though she were moving underwater, Victoria slowly opened her purse, pulled out a hundred-dollar bill, and left it on the bar top before she slid off her stool.

"It was on the house," the bartender protested.

Victoria merely nodded to him in thanks and kept walking out of the restaurant, Harper by her side.

"Do you want to sit somewhere and talk?" Harper asked.

"I'm sure you have places to be," Victoria said. "It's Saturday night. You must have plans."

"It's super early!" Harper said. "Besides, it can wait. C'mon." Harper led Victoria through the lobby bar and over to an empty table, where they sat. "When I found out my college boyfriend cheated on me with my little sister, I thought I was going to throw up and then I broke out in hives all over my body, which was so gross I wanted to die."

"You have a little sister?" Victoria asked.

"In my sorority."

"Right. That's terrible. I'm sorry that happened to you, Harper."

"I do have an older sister—a half sister—but she hates me."

"I'm sure that isn't true," Victoria said, at the same time mentally retrieving some long-ago-filed-away information about her clients, Harper's parents. They had gotten together after Harper's father's messy divorce from his first wife.

"It's true," Harper said. "I haven't seen her in years. Our dad cheated on her mom with the nanny."

"Oh," Victoria said. She hadn't been aware of that detail.

"And then he married her. And then they had me. The nanny was my mom."

"Oh."

"I know, right? They definitely don't, like, advertise that, but you know what? They've been together a really long time and my parents actually seem to still really like each other."

"That's great."

"I guess the point is, all families are messed up. And maybe that's okay?"

Victoria gave her assistant a sad smile.

"You'll figure this out," Harper said.

Victoria wasn't optimistic about that, but she was filled with appreciation for her wise little crop-top-sporting assistant. "You're an amazing young woman, Harper. I mean that. I'm lucky to have you in my life."

"Back at ya," Harper said, grinning proudly.

"What ended up happening with the boyfriend who slept with your sorority sister?"

"I keyed his car and put Nair in her shampoo."

"No!" Victoria laughed, something she didn't think her body was capable of.

"Oh yeah," Harper said nonchalantly. "And your enemies are my enemies, so if you need something, I'm your girl. We can put fire ants in Mark's office."

Victoria had nearly forgotten about how Mark seemed to be succeeding in his efforts to score a coup with Nash Winton, but only because this concern had been supplanted by much bigger issues. Namely, her life imploding. Twenty more minutes in Harper's company effectively lifted Victoria's spirits to a degree, or at least proved sufficient distraction, but as she drove home, Victoria plunged back into a cycle of disbelief, rage, and despair on an endless loop.

Nighttime descended with a moody indigo sky and the moon hung low, as if its swollen bloodless sphere carried too much weight to achieve its usual height. Victoria drove home on autopilot, questioning the logistics of how this could have happened, since the central event itself was beyond comprehension. How was it possible that Ace, her husband, the love of her life, was the same man who had abandoned her best friend? The same man who had told her he had *no children*. The same man who had held her in his arms and thanked her for proving everyone wrong and finally making him a father.

Victoria gripped the wheel tightly. She recognized that it *was* possible—in the details, anyway. Ace's real name was Andrew. His close friends had started calling him Ace a couple decades back due to his ace moves in both poker and business—but professionally and in print he was referred to as Andrew. In print. In Liz's yearly Google search . . . what had she called it? An exercise in self-sabotage? Victoria remembered Liz saying that she had quit the practice a few years ago, after her thirtieth birthday, before any mentions of Victoria and Ace's wedding would have cropped up on the internet. Victoria shook her head. If she or Ace had been on social media . . . If she had been the kind of woman who had a couple's picture on her phone's lock screen . . . If Victoria, Ace, Liz, and Preston had had dinner together instead of repeatedly having to cancel for various reasons at the last minute . . . If, if, if. But on second thought, what did the timing and the way it had transpired matter? That it had taken place in public, at Victoria's baby shower, only made it more cinematic, but the facts themselves were explosive in any capacity.

Victoria approached their house, feeling a kind of apprehension in her chest like she was entering a crime scene. Would she find an emptied-out safe, a shimmering carpet of broken glass, a bludgeoned body, or just the metaphorical cadaver of her previous life? Victoria pressed the button to open the gate to their driveway and pulled in, the trees casting elongated shadows that looked like ghosts on the gravel. She opened her garage door and saw that Ace's car was in his stall. Victoria wasn't ready to face him. She couldn't reconcile the person she married with the kind of person capable of these actions. Someone who could lie to her about the most basic facts of who he was. Someone who could rewrite history in every single conversation that had taken place between them. Someone who could callously abandon his own flesh and blood, his child, Victoria's friend, Liz. For the first time, and with a pang of guilt about this, Victoria's thoughts refracted in scope so she wasn't only focusing on her own pain and betrayal but also thinking about her friend. How lost and destroyed Liz must feel too. While still sitting in the driver's seat, Victoria called her. Liz's phone went straight to voicemail. Victoria tried again with the same result. She left a message asking Liz to call her—there was no need to say any more.

Then Victoria walked into the house. She passed through the mudroom from the garage and into the kitchen, where Ace was waiting for her. He sat at the table, illuminated by the sole light in the room that was on, so he looked like he was in a play, the rest of the set fading into the background. Victoria turned on the lights over the kitchen island and then went around turning on every other light in the vicinity. She would not allow him the privilege of a spotlight. She would not give him anything. No latitude, no grace.

"Please," Ace said, his voice broken. "Please just listen."

Victoria wordlessly marched over to the table, yanked out the chair on the far end, opposite Ace, and sat in it. She glared at him across the expanse between them.

"Start talking."

Ace nodded with the look of a man resigned to his fate.

"Thirty-four years ago, I got someone pregnant—"

"Someone. Angela. Liz's mother."

"Yes."

Victoria knew this was obvious and she was being petty, but she couldn't help herself. She was outraged. She was also irritated: Wasn't this the oldest story in the book—a man is so enthralled with the invitation his penis has received, he forgets what it's capable of?

But the lying idiot—Victoria's husband, love of her life—pressed on. "Angela told me she didn't want a baby and she was going to go to a clinic, then she disappeared. A few months later, she called me asking for money and told me she didn't go through with it. I tried to step up and do what was necessary. I sent money; I flew all over creation to see them. But Angela made it impossible, and what was I supposed to do when she was living in Bali or had a new boyfriend and told me they were better off without me, or changed her phone number so I couldn't find them?"

Through her anger, Victoria felt sadness creep in for everyone involved. But then it passed. Victoria seethed at the man she thought she had known, a man whose twin traits of tenacity and honesty were, in part, what had allowed Ace to become a self-made success. "You can throw every excuse in the book at this and you can try to rationalize the decisions you made three decades ago, but right now, you're talking to your wife. Your wife, who you lied to from the start, and then every day after. You looked me in the face and kept this colossal secret from me for every single second I have known you. How, in the millions of minutes we have spent together, in the countless opportunities you had, could you have not told me?"

"I was ashamed. I felt so guilty that I gave up on her. So I buried it. I decided I didn't have a child. I wasn't a father. I was more like . . . a sperm donor. It was the only way I could go on, the only way I knew how to cope. Otherwise, I would have been flattened by it." Ace put his head in his hands. "Over time, it felt like it had never happened. Like it had happened to a different person."

"But it didn't. And now I feel like I married a different person. I don't know who you are."

Ace flinched, and for the first time, he looked his age, weary and overcome. "I know you said not to apologize, but I'm so sorry, Victoria. You won't believe me now, but when we first started seeing each other, I almost told you. So many times. I tried to find the words. But the longer I waited, the harder it got."

"Here are the words: 'I have a child'!"

"I was scared to lose you, this incredible woman who had made it very clear that she wasn't looking for me—or anything serious—but who I was somehow managing to convince otherwise."

"You didn't convince me. You tricked me! I married someone who lied to me every second of every day we were together."

"I didn't tell you. That's different."

"You said I was making you a father. For the first time!"

"That's how it feels," Ace said haplessly. "It's true to me."

"But it's not *true*."

"I'm sorry I didn't tell you. I'm sorry I couldn't talk about it. I'm sorry I gave up on her. I'm sorry I hurt you. I'm so fucking sorry, for all of it. But you have to know, this was the truth for me. I didn't have a daughter. It was the only way I could go on."

"But Liz *was* your daughter and it did happen, and you didn't tell me. So you want to know what else *is* happening? You're sleeping in the guest room tonight."

Ace hung his head. "I'll give you as much space as you need."

Victoria started to stand up, and as she did, there was a strong karate chop to her gut. The timing was so laughable, and Victoria was caught off guard; she sank back into her chair. She put her hand on her stomach and the baby kicked again.

"Are you okay?" Ace asked. "Of course you're not okay, but . . ."

Victoria summoned her composure, then stood up again, mourning the loss of poignant moments in their past, present, and future. Before, she would have excitedly beckoned Ace over so he could feel their baby move. But that was before. Everything between them had been indelibly fractured.

Like he could sense her thoughts, Ace asked, "Can we fix this? Not right now, of course, but can I earn your trust back, eventually? I love you, Victoria, and I will do anything to make this right."

"You lied to me about *everything*, Ace. Everything. So, I don't know. I don't know anything."

Victoria walked out of the room. Her insides felt like a spaghetti squash that had had its innards scooped out by a fork. The whole time Victoria had doubted whether she would be a good mother to their child, she had never questioned Ace's fitness to be a father. The man she had married was made for the job, however late in life he was taking the role. But Victoria had been spectacularly deceived. Ace had abandoned his child; what did that say about him as a man, as a father, as a person?

Victoria slipped under the covers. She had never felt so small in their bed despite her body being multiplied by pregnancy. She had never felt so alone in her life. Ace was down the hall and Victoria felt his presence like an enemy threat in a Christopher Nolan movie.

She lowered her eye mask, the silk fabric cool against her skin, wondering what Liz was doing and when she'd call her back. Victoria questioned if she'd ever be able to forgive her husband, or look at him without cataloging the following lies: when he had told her that he'd never thought about settling down and having a family until he met her, when he pontificated about all the ways that becoming a father—at long last—might change him, when he thanked her profusely for giving him a child and making him a dad—something his friends had never thought would come to pass.

Except it already had.

Sometime in the wee hours, Victoria finally drifted into a fitful sleep. She awoke in the morning with a start and enjoyed a fleeting moment of mental opacity before the fuzziness receded and she remembered everything that had transpired the day before. It wasn't a bad dream. It was her life. Eager for an outlet to expel her type A energy upon (other than making a laundry list of the specificities of Ace's outrageous betrayal), Victoria almost started getting ready to go to the office before being thwarted with the realization that it was Sunday. She sank back into bed and put her hand on her belly. The baby kicked.

"Hi to you too," she said softly. "Apparently pregnant women aren't supposed to be around funerals or sad things, so I'm sorry about this, but I'm pretty sad right now, and I don't think it can be helped. But I love you, and I don't know if it's going to be okay, but you're going to be okay."

Then she spent the entire morning in bed watching reality TV, which was something Victoria Miller had never done before in her life. As she scrolled through the channels, Victoria saw it: *The Catch.* She binge-watched six straight episodes. Then Victoria understood why it was addictive and also why Cam and the other producers should be arraigned on a count of moral indecency against humanity. Women stabbing one another in the back and throwing themselves at a bunch of cheesy guys who looked like they wouldn't pass an STD check if their lives depended on it? Catfights and lies and booze-soaked tears, tragically over-the-top boob jobs and fake lips and women selling their souls for their chance to get a guy. Victoria couldn't tear her eyes away from the screen, caught up in Kylie's and Kelsie's and Kelly's antics as they fought over Finn, dismayed but also fascinated for the inevitable moment they were all hurtling towards when Allegra would find out that Dylan, the man she was in love with, was gay.

There is always a catch.

Victoria clicked to the next episode and thought about how Ace had been described as "such a catch." How his friends, and especially their wives, had congratulated her as if she'd won at life and nabbed herself the ultimate prize: an attractive, charming, successful man without any of the baggage that someone his age was usually laden with, namely sky-high alimony payments, vengeful ex-wives, and bitter children of divorce ready to wreak havoc on any would-be wicked stepmother who came their way. Ace was too good to be true, Victoria remembered someone exclaiming at their wedding. It was a compliment then; it haunted her now.

Victoria immersed herself in the escapist, trashy nonsense that *The Catch* offered on a gilded platter. She wished she could tell these women that no man was worth any amount of sacrifice to their integrity, that the idea that their happiness and fate hinged upon locking down a guy was a delusion they'd been fed their whole lives.

On-screen, Kelly was pulling Kylie into the confessional and swearing (lying) that she hadn't hooked up with Finn and that she had Kylie's back. Kylie tearfully declared that she loved Finn so much and knew they had something special. Kelly promised (lied) that Kylie didn't look bad when she ugly-cried even though there was makeup running down her face. Kylie told Kelly (still to be revealed as the Judas of reality TV) that they were "sisters for life." Victoria scoffed.

Then she thought about her own best friend. She tried to imagine Liz working for this show. She thought about Liz finally getting the courage to quit. She thought about Liz's face, drained of color, when she had uttered that single, apocalyptic word: *Dad.* She thought about how Liz had run out of the baby shower after the big reveal. Were they in their own demented episode of *The Catch?*

There was a knock on the bedroom door. Victoria's head snapped up and she glowered in the direction of a small piece of paper that slipped under the crack, into the room. She paused the episode, then got out of bed and retrieved it. Ace had written, *There's a tray of food outside. You don't have to see me. I am endlessly, genuinely sorry and I will spend the rest of my life proving it, if you let me.* Victoria discarded the piece of paper, throwing it carelessly over her shoulder. She opened the door, picked up the tray, and retreated to her quarters.

Victoria ate all of it while continuing her marathon of *The Catch.* She would have loved nothing more than to giggle over how terrible this show was with her best friend and have Liz give her the inside scoop. She felt sorry for herself all over again, and kept watching, one thumb on her phone as she scrolled Reddit threads. Maybe reality television, not religion, was the opiate of the masses.

It was only when hunger interrupted her sojourn again, hours later (Allegra still hadn't realized Dylan was gay), that Victoria swung her legs over the side of the bed, got up, and walked downstairs to the kitchen. Her face darkened when she saw Ace standing there, futzing at the stove. He heard her and turned around, a meek, fearful expression on his face that she had never seen before.

"I'm making you some dinner," he said. "I can bring it up on a tray when it's done."

"And then what?" Victoria said. "What happens tomorrow? Or next week? Or next month? Do we go on like this indefinitely, being roommates down the hall?"

"I'm trying to respect your needs and give you a wide berth," Ace said. "I want to fix this. You said you thought you had known sadness, until now. I thought I had known regret, until now." Tears started streaming down Ace's face—big, sloppy, ugly tears. "I'm so sorry, Victoria. I am so, so sorry."

Even though she wasn't done with anger, not by a long shot, Victoria suddenly felt drained. She walked over to a stool at the kitchen island counter and sat on it. They usually had music on in the kitchen, especially when Ace was cooking, and the stark silence seemed voluminous and oppressive. Victoria didn't speak for several minutes. When she did, her voice was low and quiet.

"Maybe I could have understood why you did what you did back then. If you had told me. If you had confided in me and trusted me to understand that you made a hard choice in an impossible situation, and it had tortured you for your entire life. But you didn't give me that option. And I don't think—I just don't see how—I'll ever be able to get past that."

Victoria looked at Ace, at the face she had known so well and loved so much, which now seemed foreign to her. His anguish was spelled out across every inch of his body—in his expression, his posture, his very bearing in the world.

"What are you saying?" Ace asked, gutted. "Are you leaving me?"

"I'm not sure. All I know is that I'm replaying all our conversations through the lens of this giant secret and I'm furious. You're not the person I thought you were."

Ace faced her, bereft, his arms down at his sides; he looked like he was offering himself up to be mounted on a cross. "I'm going to check into a hotel," Victoria said, as if the plan had been previously thought through rather than only now occurring to her.

"You stay," Ace said. "I should be the one to leave."

"I can't be here right now."

"Will you please call me if you need anything? You, or the baby?" Ace asked, his voice cracking. Victoria thought that he looked like he might collapse. It was unbearable. She wanted to comfort him, to seek refuge in his arms for her own pain, but he was the one who had inflicted it.

Victoria offered him the barest minimum of a nod, then started walking out of the kitchen and away from the man she had trusted implicitly who had betrayed her unthinkably.

"I'm here when you're ready to talk. Or scream. Or anything," Ace said. "I love you, Victoria."

Victoria took this in without response, without looking back. When she checked into the Bel-Air an hour later, the site of her ill-fated first meal with Liz, her friend had still not returned her calls. Victoria put her phone on the bedside table in her hotel room, where it would sit all night, silent as a stone.

16

———

Liz

When Liz got home from Victoria's baby shower, Preston took one look at her and asked what was wrong, but Liz said she was having a sciatica flare-up, escaped to the bedroom, powered off her phone, and crawled into bed. To speak the words out loud would make them true. To try to explain it to her boyfriend would be to acknowledge that this was something Liz would eventually have to deal with. And Liz wasn't ready for that. Not by a long shot. Preston came in to check on her and Liz said she was fine—she didn't need Tylenol, she'd sleep it off and be ready in the morning to drive to Orange County and see his family. Preston told her to give a shout if she needed anything, then crept out of the room. Liz face-planted into a pillow. The visit was another reason Liz didn't want to tell Preston about her sordid family drama. She was anxious enough as it was about spending time with the Lancasters; the last thing Liz wanted to do was pile on one more reason for them not to like her. Liz cried while watching *Beaches* and went to sleep at 9 p.m.

In the morning, Liz turned on her phone and saw a voicemail from Victoria, her best friend, who was in fact married to the man who had abandoned her, the man she had yearned for her whole life. Liz deleted the message without listening to it. She couldn't face whatever Victoria had to say. Liz turned off her phone again. She thought maybe she'd even leave it at home and intentionally invite the slippery feeling of walking out into the world without the ever-present appendage of an iPhone. Preston would probably understand that choice even less than the dramatic restructuring of Liz's family tree. He was already awake, hammering out emails even though it was a Sunday morning, his body facing away from Liz so the little tap-tap noises of his finger pads against the screen wouldn't disturb her.

"Morning," Liz said.

"You're up." Preston shifted his body towards her. "How'd you sleep? Is your back feeling better?"

"I think so," Liz said, making a show of stretching out and assessing her phantom sciatica's overnight relief. "I'm going to shower and get ready."

That involved feeling like a moose when Liz studied herself naked in the mirror under the bathroom skylight's bright natural glare and working herself into a panic trying to figure out what to wear to see Preston's family. She knew that Victoria would've been able to suggest the perfect outfit. But that option was lost to Liz now. Her best friend slash maternal figure slash life coach was married to the person who had wanted nothing to do with her. Who said the universe didn't have a sense of humor? Liz bit her bottom lip and stared into a pile of moth-nibbled sweaters. She tried to rid all thoughts of Victoria and Ace from her mind. She told herself: *Just get through this day. Put on your game face and get through this day.*

Luckily, Preston didn't seem to notice that anything was amiss on the drive down to Orange County. He filled Liz in on some workplace shake-ups, fanboyed over a new client, and warned her to avoid the Caesar salad at the club. Preston's father Tripp always told guests to order it, but the anchovies were practically drowning in the creamy garlic dressing, which Preston suspected was from a bottle—or worse, a box bought at Costco. Liz thanked him for the tip and looked out the window as the sun streamed down from a cloudless, robin's-egg-blue sky until the ocean's sparkling horizon came into view. On the right, developments stacked with multimillion-dollar homes rose up on cliffs and crawled across the valleys. Manicured, emerald-green lawns stretched to the borders of pristine sidewalks. It was all so ruthlessly perfect that Liz felt unkempt even though she had put herself together with painstaking precision.

"Ten more minutes," Preston announced.

"Great," Liz said, feigning as much enthusiasm as she could and trying to ignore her mounting anxiety.

They pulled up in front of the club nine minutes later. A gangly valet opened Liz's car door and Preston rattled off his family's membership number to the guy behind the desk. When they walked in, Liz expected to see framed oil paintings of sea bass and flounders decorating glossy wood-paneled rooms for smoking cigars and comparing one's ancestry, but the exclusive club was too WASPy to show off the wealth of its members with opulence; instead, threadbare rugs and worn lemon-yellow couches belied any hints of new money. There were a few nautical touches—some mounted schematics of ships, and a black-and-white photograph of a 1960s surfer.

Liz and Preston walked over to the dining room, a sprawling space overlooking the golf course. The hostess, a perky young thing who seemed a little too thrilled to see Preston again—"Weren't you a senior when my sister was a freshman?" she said coyly—led them over to the table. Liz saw that Preston's parents were already seated and at least one cocktail in. Tripp and Cricket Lancaster waved robotically, like pageant contestants, then stood up.

"Preston, darling," Cricket said, kissing her son on each cheek.

Liz respectfully hung back while Preston greeted his parents.

"How are you, sport?" Tripp asked, then embraced him and clapped Preston on the back.

"Can't complain, sir," Preston said. He turned and held out his hand to Liz. "You remember Liz."

Liz stepped forward and slipped her hand into Preston's palm, grateful to have something to hold on to.

"Well, well, well!" Tripp said. "Look at you."

"How are you feeling, dear?" Cricket said. She stepped closer to Liz and double-kissed the air near her cheeks.

"The first trimester was a little rough, but I'm feeling better now. We're excited," Liz said, sneaking a sideways glance at Preston.

"So excited!" Preston said.

"You must be due soon," Tripp said, taking in Liz's midsection as if it were a volcano that might spew at any second.

Cricket swatted her husband's arm. "Tripp, manners."

"Only a couple more months to go," Preston said.

Both Cricket and Tripp briefly inspected Liz's belly, like they couldn't believe this to be the case. Then Cricket gestured to the table. "Shall we sit?"

"Maker's, rocks, for you?" Tripp asked Preston.

"If that's what you're having," Preston told his father.

Tripp pointed to his empty glass, then flashed two fingers to a waiter who had silently materialized tableside. Cricket discreetly tapped the rim of her glass with her index finger to signal that she'd like another as well. Liz knew that Preston's mom favored vodka and preferred to keep the calories down by avoiding any mixers. Cricket had the kind of physique best described as birdlike, and she considered her slim and slender frame a point of pride. Even though it had been a genetic gift, a birthright along with the deed to her family's summer home in Newport (the other Newport), Cricket had maintained her looks with discipline and thought she deserved credit for this dedication to deprivation. The waiter turned to look at Liz.

"Water for me, thanks."

"Don't worry, dear," Cricket told her. "You'll work it off once the baby's here. Are you sure you wouldn't prefer an Arnold Palmer?"

"Water's perfect. Thank you, though." Liz hoped Cricket wasn't going to dispatch her personal trainer to the delivery room as a baby gift. They all made polite small talk, and then the waiter returned with the drinks. Tripp looked at his watch.

"Piper and Brooks should be here any minute," he said. "But we'll toast again when they arrive." Tripp held up his glass. "To the new member of the family." Liz didn't know whether Tripp was talking about her or the baby, but she held up her water glass and clinked it against everyone's.

Out of the corner of her eye, Liz saw Piper sweeping into the club. Brooks was by her side, dashing as ever with a thicket of wavy brown hair and a gold signet ring on his pinkie finger, which only a man who used *summer* as a verb could pull off. Piper was wearing what she had referred to on her Instagram as equestrian chic. Brooks always looked like he had stepped out of a Ralph Lauren ad and today's popped-collar-and-driving-shoe combo didn't disappoint. The hostess who had hit on Preston directed Piper and Brooks to the table, and Liz averted her eyes before Preston's sister could notice her staring.

"Hello, hello," Piper said as they drew closer. Liz thought that if sterling silver had a sound, it would be the smooth polish of Piper's voice. Everyone stood up from the table. Piper went to embrace Preston first, so she didn't notice Liz—or that she was pregnant.

"You're such a stranger," Piper said to Preston, playfully punching her younger brother on the shoulder. "Have we lost you to the wilds of LA for good?"

"Just been busy," Preston said. "You're looking sharp as ever, Pipes. How do you find the time to get all dolled up when you're so busy bossing everyone around?"

While the siblings continued ribbing each other, Brooks greeted

Cricket and Tripp, then turned to Liz. She watched his eyes pop open in surprise, then become clouded with something—alarm? Liz was about to offer her arms to hug him hello, but Brooks hesitated and shot a nervous look at Piper. As if she could feel something lurking in the shadows, Piper turned slowly.

"Surprise! We're having a baby!" Preston needlessly narrated.

Piper's face folded violently. Then she ran off in the direction of the bathroom. Liz didn't know what to do; none of her feared scenarios had been *this* bad.

"Oh my," Cricket finally said. They all tried to pretend that the other country club members weren't looking over at their table, that it hadn't been a scene.

Brooks cleared his throat uncomfortably and turned to Preston and Liz. "We've been having a hard time getting pregnant."

Liz's heart sank. For fuck's sake! She had shoved her unborn child in front of a woman battling infertility? The one thing Piper couldn't do, Liz had accomplished (mostly) by accident?

"I should check on Piper," Brooks said, then set off after his not-pregnant-but-otherwise-perfect wife.

Cricket and Tripp sat back down, and then Preston, so without knowing what else to do, Liz joined them. Cricket took a sip of her cocktail, then blotted the corners of her mouth with a napkin.

"I'm so sorry," Liz said softly.

The waiter appeared and set down a basket. Tripp dug into it with gusto and pulled out a roll and a pat of butter. Liz could see where Preston had gotten his bearing from; nothing could get the Lancaster men down for too long.

"It's not your fault she waited," Tripp said. "She's practically forty."

Piper was thirty-seven, a good three years shy of the milestone Tripp impugned her with.

"It is a shame, though," Cricket said with a sigh.

"Wait, you knew about this?" Preston asked his parents. Their expressions didn't give anything away, but their lack of denial spoke volumes. "You could've given me a heads-up," Preston said. "I wouldn't have sprung it on her like that."

Cricket took another sip. "We didn't know Piper would react that way."

Liz questioned what other way Cricket thought her daughter possibly would've reacted. With joy and pride that her younger brother had knocked someone up, while she was being crushed by the singular pain of trying and failing to get pregnant?

"I guess she's sensitive about it," Tripp said. *You think?* Liz wanted to say. It was like the Lancasters could mimic the range of normal human emotion but didn't, in fact, feel anything. For so long, Liz had wanted Angela to feign normalcy; now that she was on the receiving end of such a charade, she wasn't sure this was better.

"How long has this been going on?" Preston asked.

"About a year, I suppose. Yes, since the regatta, so about a year," Cricket said. "Don't mention anything when your sister comes back, though. Piper didn't want anyone to know. It's a private matter, after all."

"Did Brooks have his swimmers checked yet?" Tripp asked Cricket under his breath, but also loud enough that the next table over could probably hear.

Cricket silenced him with a splintery look. Or tried to, anyway.

"I know he played water polo at Yale, but still," Tripp said, cocking his head suggestively.

Cricket glanced at Preston and Liz. "Let's focus on more pleasant matters. How is the nursery coming along?"

Cricket offered to send her decorator to Los Angeles, Piper and Brooks came back to the table wordlessly and didn't mention anything, Tripp tried to push the Caesar salad on Liz, they avoided any talk of babies for the rest of the meal, and Piper offered several book recommendations. From what Liz could tell, Piper only read historical fiction set in the equestrian world in which she had spent most of her youth. She loved sweeping epics about racehorses and jockeys overcoming challenges. Liz pretended she'd check out one of Piper's suggestions, with zero intention of ever following through on the story of a horse who had triumphed against all odds.

The afternoon stretched on in the frigidly air-conditioned dining room of the country club, and various friends and golf course foes came over to say hello to the Lancasters. No one mentioned the pregnancy. Liz's bladder was about to burst, but she didn't dare stand up and show off her expectant state. Finally, Preston told his family that he and Liz needed to get going and head back to LA before traffic hit.

Liz excused herself to the bathroom, shuffling off quickly in the hopes that speed would offer a disguise of sorts. They all met at the entrance to the club to say their goodbyes. Liz died a thousand deaths while embracing Piper and trying not to feel where her belly pressed up against Preston's sister's trim frame.

"Congratulations," Piper said crisply, finally acknowledging the pregnancy.

"Thank you," Liz said. "And . . . it was nice to see you again," she finished lamely.

Piper cleared her throat. "Sorry for running off like that and causing a scene." She gestured vaguely behind her, as if the hostess stand represented the past. "Brooks and I are starting IVF."

Liz didn't know whether to offer condolences or good luck. This was one of the shortest and hardest conversations of her life. "I hope it goes well," Liz said.

"Thank you. So you see, pregnancy is on my mind. And I was a bit surprised—" Piper motioned to Liz. "I didn't know you and my brother were that serious."

Liz blurted out, "We didn't either!" Piper gave her a strange look, which Liz returned with a silly one, to suggest that she was kidding.

"Anyway, safe drive back," Piper said breezily. "We should do this again soon."

There was nothing in Piper's voice to suggest sincerity. Liz decided it wouldn't be a good time to bring up the baby shower. Maybe she would read the horse book after all. She could use a crowd-pleasing David and Goliath tale.

———

Liz didn't turn her phone back on until halfway into Monday, when she was about to depart for her daily trip to the coffee shop. She wanted to keep the phone off and avoid any more of Victoria's attempts to contact her, but she also couldn't risk missing an unlikely but much desired call from a potential employer responding to her application. Liz saw, with dismay, that she had six more voicemails and texts from Victoria. They ranged from sad—*I'm devastated too. Please call me back*—to confused—*I don't understand why you're shutting me out*—to mildly indignant—*I'm as surprised as you are, so please don't take it out on me. It's not fair, Liz. I didn't know Ace had a child. We need to talk.*

Liz slipped her computer into her tote bag and considered whether it was fair, not that it mattered. Why did Victoria think she was owed fairness, of all things? Even if what Victoria was saying was true, that she hadn't known about Ace's secret love child and hadn't knowingly married a man who'd abandoned his daughter, Liz still couldn't be friends with her. Liz couldn't hang out with the wife of the man who hadn't wanted anything to do with her, the person who had carved a hole in her childhood, who happened to be expecting her half brother at the exact same time she was having their grandchild. Liz fired off a text to Victoria: *I don't want to talk to you. Please stop texting me.*

Liz put her phone back into her pocket, hoping maybe that would be that, even though she suspected Victoria wouldn't give up so easily. Victoria was someone who had mettle and persistence in spades, like she stocked these qualities alongside the sea of Manolos in her closet. So Liz wouldn't have been surprised if Victoria had shown up at the coffee shop. She didn't, though. Several hours later, when Liz closed her computer, said goodbye to her favorite barista, and drove home down Sunset, she thought she was in the clear. Liz wasn't expecting what awaited her when she pulled into the driveway: Ace sitting on the front step.

Liz hit the brakes too hard and the car jolted to a stop. No part of her wanted to deal with this, but she was trapped. Liz turned off the ignition and thought about the irony of her father figuring out a way to get her address when he hadn't been interested in her whereabouts for decades. Then she stepped out of the car to confront him.

"You have some nerve," Liz said, knitting her brows together.

"If you never want to see me again after this, that's fine. But please—ten minutes. There's never one version of the truth, Liz, and you deserve to know all the sides."

Liz hesitated, then looked at her father's face. He had a strong jawline, slightly hooded chocolate-brown eyes, and salt-and-pepper hair. People probably called him youthful and distinguished. Liz didn't want to notice this, but they had the same chin and face shape.

"Fine. Ten minutes. We can go around back."

Liz marched to the side gate and around the house to the backyard, then sat down in a chair by the firepit. Ace took a chair across from her. Liz looked at him again and thought how bizarre it was to be in the company of a person she had wept for, then shuttled to the side of her thoughts and resigned herself to never know.

"It was summertime, and I met your mom when we were out one night," Ace began.

"You can call her Angela. I do."

"Okay. Angela was in town for a few months and she was fun and wild and carefree," Ace said.

"Interesting rebrand of a loose cannon, but go on," Liz said dryly.

"I had just lost my mother. I barely had a penny to my name, and I met this girl who was full of life and passion, who didn't give a damn about answering to convention. I don't know if I wanted to be like her or be with her, but it was intoxicating."

"Until it wasn't, I'm guessing."

"I admired what a free spirit she was, but ultimately I wasn't built the same. I was an orphan—no fallbacks, no safety net, desperate to make a name for myself and do something with my life."

"So you tried to end it and she got herself pregnant?"

"No," Ace said. "As far as I know, your mother didn't do it intentionally." Liz felt her throat go dry. She wasn't sure if she was imagining a flash of judgment on her father's face: *What sort of person would trap a man like that?*

"I'm going to be completely honest with you, even though no one likes radical transparency. They might say they do, but no one actually likes the truth," Ace said.

"Easier to live in a fantasy," Liz muttered.

"It is, and there are truths we shield the people we love from."

"Are you making a case for honesty or against it?" Liz asked.

Ace smiled mournfully. "I'm starting to realize that even if they're hard to hear, there are some truths that need to be brought to light."

"I can take it." Liz squared off like a boxer in the ring, ready to take her blows.

"Neither of us was ready for a baby. Angela wanted to travel the world, not be tied down. She told me she was going to terminate the pregnancy."

Liz swallowed hard. She wasn't surprised. After all, she had often wondered why Angela hadn't opted out, but Ace was right—the bare-faced truth was still a bitter pill.

"I said what you're supposed to in that situation, and also what I believed: that it was Angela's choice and I'd support her in whatever she decided," Ace said. "I gave her money for the procedure and offered to take her, but she said a friend was going to. Then she disappeared."

"Sounds about right," Liz said with a forced bravado.

"She called me months later and said she had changed her mind and was due with our child in a few months. She told me that when she went to see her parents, they gave her a choice: leave and don't come back, or let them raise her baby."

Liz listened, rapt. She'd never met her grandparents. Angela had never offered any explanation and always became annoyed whenever Liz asked about them. Finally, one day, Angela told Liz they were dead. Unless Liz wanted to visit them six feet under, she should stop bothering her.

"Angela went to crash with some friends in the city and called me from a street corner on the Lower East Side, asking for money. I sent as much as I could. When you were born, I flew across the country to meet you."

"You did?" Liz asked.

"I held you in my arms and I was absolutely terrified, but you were also the most miraculous thing I had ever seen, and I was prepared to step up and do what was necessary."

Liz considered this, unable to digest this information that went against everything she had known. "I don't understand. She always told me you didn't want anything to do with us, and we were better off without you."

Ace sighed. "She told me that second part too."

"She lied? She kept you from me?"

"No," Ace said, his face creasing with the difficulty of this admission. "Not exactly. I told Angela I wanted to be part of your life as much as I could. That said, I couldn't move across the country. Professionally, I was finally starting to make headway in LA, and Angela said she wasn't going to stay in New York anyway. She wasn't going to stay anywhere too long."

There was a light breeze, but Liz felt like she was suffocating under a blanket of stagnant air. She wanted every detail, but she also wanted it to be over.

"We made it work, for a while. Angela sent pictures when she remembered. I sent money when I had it. I flew back and forth every few months, to wherever you two were living. Over time, Angela got tougher to deal with. She wouldn't answer my calls for weeks. I didn't know where you were. If I said anything about the situation, Angela would fly off the handle, furious that I was criticizing her parenting. What did I know? I flitted in and out of your life. I wasn't responsible for taking care of you day and night."

"And then what?" Liz said.

"I went to see you in Woodstock for Thanksgiving. You were almost four and Angela was smoking a joint around you. We got into a screaming match. She told me that having a father who was half in, half out wasn't good for her daughter—not ours, *hers*. She said she was dating someone and it was getting confusing for you. She had found you a new dad and you were better off without me in your life."

"And you believed her?" Liz asked, dismayed. Who would value Angela's opinion above their own good sense? "You handed me over to one of her boyfriends? One of the guys who lasted as long as a carton of milk? You just . . . gave up on me?"

"Not right away. I did fight to be part of your life. Angela changed her phone number, so I didn't have a way of contacting her. I flew back to Woodstock, but you were in the wind." Ace paused and his face filled with sorrow. From the neighboring backyard, the distinctive intro of Bruce Springsteen's "Thunder Road" emanated. "I should have kept trying. I should have done whatever it took. I tried to convince myself that Angela was right and you were better off without me. But there's no excuse. There's never a justifiable reason for a parent abandoning their child. I'm sorry, Liz. I am so sorry I failed you."

"I never even knew you met me," she said somberly.

Ace's expression deepened with the imprints of regret. "I'm so sorry," he repeated. "For all of it." He wrung his hands, and the way he looked at Liz cut her. And even though Liz couldn't absolve her father of his sins, she now knew that the narrative she'd been spoon-fed her whole life wasn't the full story. Like Victoria had said, nothing was black and white. Still, it was overwhelming to confront the expanse of gray.

Liz was flooded with questions: Would Ace have ever found her if they hadn't been reunited by sheer coincidence? Would Angela admit to her wrongdoing? Was Liz, keeper of secrets, loser (or winner) of birth-control roulette, able to claim the moral high ground over her father? Was a predilection for making messy life decisions an inherited trait?

Liz looked at her father. "I knew your name so I used to look you up online when I was younger. I would fantasize about you coming to find me. But that wouldn't have happened, would it? We wouldn't have met if this hadn't happened."

Ace startled for a moment, as if this hadn't occurred to him. "I don't know," he said finally.

"Thanks for your honesty, at least," Liz said. She stood up. Her wrists ached, her bladder was screaming, and her head was pounding. She needed to hibernate like a bear and emerge from her cave into an alternate reality where she had an upstanding nuclear family and a Maltipoo.

"I'm sorry I wasn't a part of your life," Ace said. "I'm sorry I wasn't your dad. I can never make up for the past, but maybe we can have something different, going forward," Ace said. He reached into his pocket and handed her a piece of paper with his phone number written on it. "When you're ready. If you're ready. Call me anytime, day or night."

Liz looked at Ace dolefully. Then he turned and left.

Long after the father Liz had never known walked out of the backyard, she stared into the charcoal nubs in the firepit and wondered if there was a world in which she could forgive him so this exit would not mean that he was walking out of her life once again.

17

Victoria

Victoria sat at her desk, scrolling through all her unanswered texts to Liz until she reached the response Liz had finally sent, reading the words yet again, as if the hundredth time might lead to a different interpretation of *I don't want to talk to you. Please stop texting me.* Victoria couldn't comprehend why Liz was villainizing her—Victoria wasn't the perpetrator; she was another victim, a bystander, a casualty. When Victoria looked up, she saw Ellen, Deborah, and Annalise walking towards the office kitchen. Victoria stood and followed them down the hall. As she did, Harper's head rose over her cubicle wall, her eyes monitoring Victoria's path like a gambler at a racetrack. "You okay?" Harper mouthed.

Not even a little. But Victoria nodded. She had exchanged "good mornings" with Mark earlier without spitting in his face, so she was arguably fine, wasn't she?

Victoria entered the kitchen. Ellen, Deborah, and Annalise turned, their faces bathed in compassion.

"Victoria," Ellen said gently. "How are you?"

"Embarrassed," Victoria said. "I owe you all a proper apology. It's incredibly overdue. I'm sorry the shower you threw for me ended so dramatically. It was perfect until . . ." Victoria gestured—*you know.*

"There's no need to be embarrassed or sorry," Deborah said.

"These things happen," Annalise said.

"Do they?" Victoria said.

"Well, *things* happen," Ellen said.

"At my shower, my sister threw a fit because there weren't any vegan options on the menu and she was furious we didn't take her lifestyle seriously," Annalise said.

"Two of my friends weren't speaking to each other when I had a sprinkle for my second," Ellen said. "But I had baby brain and I accidentally seated them next to each other. Funny enough, though, I didn't remember that until now. I guess you try to block out the bad stuff and hold on to the good."

Victoria nodded. Had Ellen just delivered a sound philosophy to apply to life in general?

"How are you doing?" Deborah asked. It was said with such kindness, Victoria made a mental note not to impugn her for her troll collection again; everyone had layers.

"I've been better," Victoria admitted.

"Tea?" Ellen asked, pointing to the selection of sachets on the counter at the same time Annalise asked, "Do you want to talk about it?"

Victoria considered. Did she? She had been so accustomed to dealing with everything on her own, and then with Ace as her sounding board and confidant, but then she had Liz, and the benefits of a true friendship had opened up to her. It was like her stamina and ability to function on her own had atrophied with disuse. "Okay . . ." Victoria said. "Yes. Thank you."

Victoria sat down with Ellen, Deborah, and Annalise and they proceeded to lend a thoughtful, compassionate ear as Victoria told them she didn't know what she was more troubled by: her husband's unfathomable betrayal or her best friend's refusal to talk to her.

Ellen tsk-tsked. "This is all so hard, and you're pregnant, so everything's heightened. The hormones take everything up at least ten notches."

Annalise nodded. "When I was pregnant, I used to cry over the littlest things. Puppies, cute memes, reruns of *Friends*—you name it! And obviously, this is *not* a little thing."

"No," Victoria said. "It's not."

"Men are men and we love them, but we're also not totally surprised when they make the mistakes that men make," Deborah mused. "When you're hurt by a woman, it's a million times worse, because we're supposed to know better."

Victoria, Ellen, and Annalise all paused and exchanged looks as they pondered the wisdom Deborah had proffered.

"I was surprised, though," Victoria said. "I was completely blindsided by what my husband did. And I feel so stupid. I thought I had married this great guy. I thought we had a beautiful life."

"It doesn't mean those things aren't true," Ellen said.

Victoria shook her head. "I should have known better. How many stories have we heard about men having second families? How many clients have been hiding gambling problems or massive debts from their spouses? How many affairs and love children and secrets do I have to be privy to before realizing I'm a sanctimonious idiot?"

The women looked at her compassionately, and Victoria realized that maybe if she had possessed a coven like this before, when she had begun dating Ace, she wouldn't be in her current situation. If Victoria had had friends who asked, *What sixty-year-old man has no baggage? He really never got married and had kids? Why?* If they had pressed and Victoria had probed. But she hadn't. Victoria had taken what Ace presented to her at face value.

Victoria knew she couldn't live in the past, dwelling on the could-haves and should-haves, but the here and now was unthinkable and the future was entirely undefined. She manufactured a work meeting, telling Deborah, Ellen, and Annalise that she had to go, and they said to ping them anytime she was in the mood for another kitchen meetup. Victoria thanked them profusely, then collected her purse from her office and told Harper she was running out for a coffee—never mind the fact that she had emerged from the kitchen, which housed no fewer than three varieties of coffee.

"I can go get one for you!" Harper said.

"I want to stretch my legs," Victoria said. "Text me if you'd like something." Victoria saw Harper blush with pleasure.

"Okay, I'll text ya!" Harper said.

Victoria drove to the coffee shop on a mission, aware that she was blatantly ignoring Liz's demand, but also figuring that if Liz really didn't want to see her, she would have changed her routine and picked another coffee shop. If Liz was there, a tacit invitation of sorts could almost be construed.

Victoria strode into the coffee shop and saw her immediately, like Liz was a beacon. She was huddled over her computer with a drawn, maudlin expression, the carcass of what was once a blueberry-oat muffin sitting on a slightly chipped puce ceramic plate in front of her.

"Hi," Victoria said. A Miley Cyrus song was playing in the background and Victoria remembered how they had raised the volume and Liz had belted it out when they drove to Fresno together. Now, Liz looked up at Victoria with dread, her face darkening like a sky in the Carolinas with a tropical storm approaching, and the smoky pop song provided the wrong soundtrack for this moment.

"Ambushing me in public? That's like a guy breaking up with you at a fancy restaurant so it can't get too ugly."

"We can go wherever you want," Victoria said. "You have to talk to me at some point." She slid the chair away from the table and sat down in it so she and Liz were at the same eyeline. "We're going to see each other again at Dawn's class anyway," Victoria reminded her.

"Maybe," Liz said, with a disinterested shrug. She fingered the discarded wrapper of the muffin and refused to meet Victoria's gaze. Victoria noticed the sallow circles under Liz's puffy eyes that spoke to sleepless nights. She could relate.

"I'm hurting too," Victoria said. "I lost my husband and my best friend, all in one moment. My entire world was shattered too."

Liz finally looked up at Victoria. "What do you mean you lost him?"

"You don't think I had any idea, do you?"

Liz hesitated but then shook her head.

"I'm staying at a hotel. I'm pregnant and heartbroken and alone and I understand that you're reeling, Liz, but I am too, and I don't understand why we can't be suffering together. Why are you putting me in the same camp as Ace when my only crime was ignorance?"

"You're my stepmom," she said. "You're married to the man who abandoned me. When I told you about Googling my dad, I didn't think you were married to him! It's all too weird and I don't know how to deal with any of this. I just—can't. I can't do this."

"There isn't a playbook and I don't have the answers either. But don't you think we'd navigate it better together?"

"You're married to him," Liz said. "That's always going to come first. That's how it works."

"I'm not even speaking to him right now."

"You gave him my address!"

Victoria let out a small, rueful laugh. "No, I didn't."

"Well, he showed up at my house."

Victoria took this in, stunned for a moment. "I had no part in that." Now that she knew, Victoria wasn't surprised. Ace was the kind of guy who would anonymously and generously donate to a tragedy-stricken stranger's GoFundMe, who would leave a steaming vat of chicken noodle soup on a sick friend's doorstep, who would lend an ear, or a dollar, or a word of advice to anyone who needed it. He was the kind of guy intent upon doing the right thing. Which made it hard for Victoria to reconcile *that* person with the same man who had concealed his participation in creating a living, breathing human who was an infant, and then a toddler, and then a child, and now an adult, sitting before her.

"I miss you," Victoria said. "I want to know how you're feeling—with the baby—and how it went with Preston's family . . . all of it. It's so hard to go from having you be such an important part of my life to not having you in it."

Liz looked at Victoria sadly. The hubbub of the coffee shop faded into the background, and Victoria didn't notice the other customers or what music was playing or the locomotive-style steam releases of the espresso machines behind the counter.

"I miss you too," Liz said, and for a moment, Victoria was hopeful. "But everything is different now. It's too weird."

Liz lowered her head. Victoria wanted to grab her by the shoulders and shake some sense into her and scream, *Snap out of it! It's not that hard, it's simple! I'm not to blame!* But Victoria couldn't force someone to see things her way any more than she could coerce Liz into being friends with her. Victoria surrendered in defeat, sliding her seat out from the table to give her pregnant stomach ample berth. "If you change your mind, or you ever need anything, you know where to find me," she said.

Liz stared at the deconstructed muffin, noncommittal. With great effort, Victoria finally turned away. She drove back to her office and only realized after she had parked that she hadn't checked to see if Harper wanted anything. Victoria stopped by the kiosk in the lobby, and though the baked goods were largely picked over by this time in the afternoon, Victoria selected what she could—an assortment of mangy frosted crullers and misshapen scones—and added a hot chocolate because anything with whipped cream seemed like it would be up Harper's alley.

"The PSLs are going to be everywhere soon," the middle-aged woman behind the counter said flatly.

"Pardon?" Victoria said, her mind automatically going to P&Ls.

"Pumpkin spice lattes," the coffee shop clerk explained.

"Right," Victoria said.

It seemed like every year, the autumnal trends were ferried out earlier and earlier, with holiday-themed everything stepping on the heels of the multicolored autumn leaves. Victoria collected the hot chocolate and the pastries, trying not to think about the future, or what the holidays might look like for her fractured family.

"Thanks. Have a good afternoon." It was taking extreme effort to function as a normal human.

When the elevator opened on her office floor, Mark was in the lobby, waiting to go down.

"Victoria," he said, looking like a cat that had just swallowed a goldfish. She supposed he had, if Mark was making headway signing Nash Winton as a client. Victoria tried to evacuate the annoyed frown forming on her face.

"Hey, Mark," she said.

"Looks like it's almost game time. You ready?"

"Is anyone ever ready?" she asked.

Mark laughed, even though Victoria hadn't meant it as a joke. Victoria felt sorry for Mark's sons, three boys all named after dead presidents. Mark seemed like the kind of father who would fall into the trap of perceiving his kids' successes and failings as a direct indication of his own parental report card.

"How are the boys?" Victoria asked politely.

"Great," Mark said. "Reagan's reading already!"

"How wonderful," Victoria said. She started walking, not waiting for Mark to expound on any more of his little superstars. "See you later, Mark."

She tried to shed the image of Mark boasting about Nash to his sons from her mind. It seemed like an exceptional amount for her to have to endure—Ace's deception, Liz's rejection, Mark's entire existence. She needed to assert herself, even momentarily, if only to serve as a reminder of what she was made of.

Victoria found Harper scrolling through videos on TikTok, cackling with pleasure. She was thrilled with the hot chocolate and grateful for the assortment of pastries, but her face fell when Victoria asked her to step into her office.

"Did I do something wrong?" Harper asked anxiously. "I was only taking a two-second TikTok break! And I can still hear when the real phone rings."

"Not at all," Victoria assured her.

Harper stood up and nervously followed Victoria into her office. Victoria shut the glass door behind them and gestured for Harper to take a seat on the couch. Victoria had failed to repair the rift with Liz and her own life was inarguably a dumpster fire, but there were still some things Victoria was good at. She offered Harper a warm smile, but Harper peered at her across the coffee table like she had knocked over a beehive and the attack was imminent.

"I promise, Harper, you didn't do anything wrong."

"*Okaaaay*," Harper said, drawing out the word like it had ten vowels. "But am I getting fired? Just tell me. Wait, no, don't tell me! Okay, tell me. Is this a sorry-I'm-firing-you hot chocolate?" Harper held up the drink. Her pink lipstick had already left a mark on the white plastic top.

"Actually—yes. But only because I care about you."

"I don't get it," Harper said, crushed.

"Harper, you're one of the worst assistants I've ever had, and also my absolute favorite."

"Really?" Harper said, brightening like she had exclusively glommed on to the positive, latter half of Victoria's declaration.

"Yes. I've been thinking about this for a while. I could keep you on indefinitely, and enjoy having you as my assistant, but it would be selfish of me. This isn't what you want to be doing."

Harper tilted her head in thought. "I like working for you. It's not *not* what I want to be doing."

"I appreciate that, but that's not the same thing. 'Not bad' doesn't make something good. 'Not no' isn't a yes. And 'almost' isn't enough. What *do* you want to be doing?"

"I have no clue," Harper said. "My parents just wanted me to have a job after I graduated. They said they'd pay my rent and half of my credit card bill as long as I had a job."

"That's important. But building a future for yourself out of something you're passionate about is more important."

"How do you figure out your passion?" Harper asked. She radiated an innocence that almost made Victoria nostalgic, except Victoria had never possessed such a quality. Life had intervened in a way that negated this possibility.

"In some cases, trial and error," Victoria told Harper. "But you should also think about what interests you. What do you do when you're not at work? Or, when you are at work?" Victoria flashed Harper a knowing look. "What are you looking at all day on your phone?"

"Not all day!" Harper giggled. "But—Betches and Deuxmoi and Who What Wear and TikTok, obviously, so I can stay up-to-date on current events. Stuff like that."

"You love fashion and pop culture. Not finance."

"I think it's cool that you do, though!" Harper said. "I've just never been good with numbers. I suck at math and I wish I could care about hedge funds, and I try—I do!"

"I know you do," Victoria said, wondering if Harper thought she worked for a hedge fund. This was a distinct possibility.

"It's just so boring and confusing to me," Harper said apologetically.

"Finance doesn't have to be your thing. Look at you."

Harper looked down at her asymmetrical lilac miniskirt, cutout button-down, and stacked heels. She smiled with satisfaction, like she had aced the GMAT. "I'm kinda serving up a look today," she said.

"You always do," Victoria said. "Which is why you should be working in fashion, or PR, or marketing, or maybe some combination thereof. You have style and you're great with people, and while I appreciate you learning orchid maintenance tips and doting over me, your talents are being wasted here. I want to see you flourish."

Harper fluttered her hand in front of her eyes. "Boss! You're going to make me cry!"

Victoria thought she had been kind, yes, but she hadn't necessarily said anything to elicit this intense of an emotional reaction, until Harper said what she did next. "No one has ever told me I'm talented before."

"That can't be true."

"It is. I've been called pretty and fun and stuff like that, but no one has ever told me I'm good at anything. You really think I'm good with people?" Harper asked shyly, like a girl confirming a boy had pushed her in the sandbox because he had a crush.

"I know you are," Victoria said. "You've taken on someone who isn't—me—and carried me, especially these last couple months. I'm grateful for you, Harper, and I don't know what I'm going to do without you, but I know I have to figure it out. For your sake, I have to let you go."

"I'm going to miss you so much!" Harper said.

"We'll see each other," Victoria said. "We'll still be part of each other's lives."

Harper made a show of exhaling in relief. She and Victoria smiled at each other, and then Harper's eyes flared with alarm. "My parents are going to be so mad."

"I'll talk to them," Victoria said. "Or you can quit, but it's better this way, for severance. Insurance and unemployment—all of that."

"I don't know what any of that means. Adult stuff is so complicated," Harper said.

"It is," Victoria said. Harper likely wouldn't know the half of it for years to come, if she was lucky. The wisdom accrued from experience didn't always nullify how complex life could be, how clarity gained could be an elusive prize. "It really is," Victoria repeated, "but you're going to figure it out."

Harper beamed. "Because I'm more than a pretty girl with my parents' platinum card."

"You're a lot more than that."

"I didn't feel that way, until I met you," Harper said. "And just so you know, you said that I've been taking care of you, but it goes both ways. There are a lot of times I've thought, 'Wow, Victoria knows me better than my own mom.'"

Later, Victoria went back to her suite at the Bel-Air and replayed those words in her mind. She wasn't speaking to her husband, her best friend didn't want anything to do with her, maternity leave and its unavoidable consequences loomed before her, and the plunge into the great unknown awaited her in mere weeks, with all its uncertainties. Victoria knew this was why people nested—so they could latch on to some semblance of control before their lives were knocked off-kilter for the indefinite future, so they could tell themselves that preparation would serve them well, as if they were outfitting their kit at REI for a wilderness trek. But parenthood was a summit that one could never adequately equip themselves for. Despite the terror this presented, and the laughable precariousness of the current state of her life, Victoria held on to Harper's words like a talisman. As she ordered room service, cued up *The Catch*, and wrapped herself in a fluffy bathrobe, ready to lose herself in Kylie's and Kelsie's and Kelly's capers, Victoria thought, *I can do this. No matter what, regardless of what our family looks like, it will be okay. I'll put my son first. I'm going to be a good mom.*

A few days later, Victoria walked into Dawn's class, remembering why she had signed up for it in the first place—not solely for the tips and tricks of the trade, but for the village that everyone told Victoria she would need to support her. The women filtered in, murmuring hellos to each other, gravitating towards their usual spots on the Crayola-hued rug, and offering jittery smiles to Victoria without letting their gazes linger too long. Victoria waited, one eye peeled on the doorway, but Liz never showed. The person-sized space where she usually sat remained between Victoria and the next woman for the whole class, like the hole in a child's mouth after they had lost their first tooth—an awkward void. Liz's absence distracted her so intensely that Victoria couldn't have said what the topic was that had been covered. Her only answer would have been: loss.

18

Liz

36 WEEKS: THROW PILLOW

When Liz called Angela, her mother didn't seem particularly impressed when Liz said she needed to talk to her about something important. In fact, it was like she hadn't heard it at all, which was typical—but Angela did tell Liz that the timing was uncanny. She was in town! The art fair in Taos had been a bust, filled with tourists with no taste, all turquoise jewelry and Pendleton shirts. Angela was done peddling her wares to collectors with no class; she was focusing on her craft for art's sake alone. Liz tried to interrupt this diatribe, thinking that she could probably recite her mother's monologue from memory at this point. Finally, Liz demanded the address for the Yellow House Foundation, the artists' colony where her mother was staying in Topanga.

"Why?" Angela asked. "Are you finally going to come see my goddess series? This is a highly coveted residency, you know."

Liz stifled a primal scream. "I just told you I need to talk to you about something important," she said.

Angela eventually rattled off the address, which Liz scribbled down on a scrap of paper. Of course Angela was staying at some so-called artists' colony. It probably had signs: "Failed artists unite!" and "Dying dreams fade away here!"

Liz stomped to her car, put the address into Waze, then blazed a path of fury through the canyon roads, barely noticing the serpentine twists that were dotted with fresh farm stands, funky vintage shops, and markers noting that day's wildfire risk. Smokey Bear said it was high. No kidding. Liz was about to go scorched earth. She was filled with a rage that bordered on delirium right up to the second she parked in a dirt patch in front of a bunch of yurts decorated with dream catchers and wind chimes.

"Where's Angela?" Liz asked the first person she saw, a guy in his sixties with tanned skin and huarache sandals who looked like he enjoyed stained glass and acid trips. He pointed, unbothered by Liz's lack of pleasantries. Liz strode over to one of the yurts. "Angela!" she shouted through the door. Liz didn't care enough to peer inside and get a glimpse of the setup at this world-famous artists' colony. A dead fly was trapped in the doorframe, its green-black wings glinting in the sunlight.

"Angela!" Liz yelled again.

Her mother ambled out with barely concealed annoyance, as if she were a great master who had been interrupted during the creation of something that would soon hang on the walls at MoMA. The cheap plywood door banged shut in the frame behind her.

"Why are you shouting? This is quiet creation hour," Angela said.

"How could you tell me that my father didn't want anything to do with me? How could you let me think that all these years?" Liz watched Angela's face harden in the sun, which was beating down on them, but it didn't betray any guilt.

"Who told you that?"

"He did!"

"He who?

"My father!" Liz thundered. "He found me. Or I found him. Accidentally. It doesn't matter. What does is that you lied to me."

Angela thrust a hand on her hip. "What was a lie? That we got to travel all over the world together, and live in Ubud and Marfa and Nosara? You met Osho! And Ed Ruscha! You had seen the Taj Mahal and Angkor Wat by the time you were ten. What other child could say that?"

"That isn't the point. You changed your phone number and told him I was better off without him," Liz said, not to be deterred.

"Will you stop screaming?" Angela gestured around. A tumbleweed blew across the dirt and the faint scent of palo santo wafted through the air. Liz noticed a smear of orange paint on her mother's forehead.

"Who are you worried about hearing us?" Liz asked. "Some stoned potter with delusions of grandeur? Artists at work. Better alert the Met!"

"You are so high and mighty," Angela sniped. "Just because you could never grasp the life of a creative spirit, you want me to apologize for not being the kind of mother who lives for a bake sale? I don't aspire to mediocrity, Elizabeth. And boo-fucking-hoo for you that you grew up around different kinds of interesting people, having adventures, seeing this world instead of being stuck in one tiny pocket of it, collecting Girl Scout badges like a feeble little mouse. What a terribly deprived childhood you had."

Liz started trembling with anger. "You don't get it."

"What? Tell me what I'm missing, since you suddenly seem to have all the answers."

"All I ever wanted was the tiniest amount of stability. A house with four walls that we'd stay in long enough for me to remember where the bathroom was if I woke up in the middle of the night. People I could count on. Some kind of family."

"We were a family. You and me. We didn't need anyone else."

"I did!" Liz cried. She thought she saw Angela flinch, but she plunged ahead. "I needed someone who was a constant, even a few times a year, instead of a commune sister named Poet I'd never see again or a boyfriend or girlfriend you'd be really into for three to six months and then really not into, just as quickly." Liz paused briefly and looked Angela straight in the eye. "I needed my dad, who wanted to be part of my life."

"Easy for him to say that now," Angela said. "How about when I was pregnant and alone? Where was he then?"

"Trying to be there!"

"Really?" Angela said, her voice suddenly becoming rattled by something that sounded like sadness. "Sending money isn't the same as being there. Saying that you're ready to do the right thing isn't the same thing as being a father."

Liz took this in. Angela deflated further, a blow-up mattress unplugged from its power source. "Every time he flew in, I saw that we were holding him back. That we were a duty to be fulfilled in the name of doing the right thing. I didn't want to be an obligation, and it's the last thing I wanted for you. I wanted you to be loved. Not because someone felt they had to, but because they chose to. Actually—no, because they *didn't* have a choice about it. Because loving you wasn't even a question."

Liz felt knocked sideways. Had Angela really made the decisions she did for Liz's benefit?

Liz pictured her mother, practically a child herself, cast out by her own parents, with no one to lean on, still making the bold and brave choice to do it alone. To shield her child from the insufficient and subpar involvement of a Disneyland dad who popped in from time to time bearing a Barbie or jumbo-sized Hershey's bar. That wasn't parenting—that was visiting. And yet, even though Liz yearned to embrace this vindication of Angela's actions, she couldn't fully endorse this rendition of events. It was like trying to believe in the stories of the Bible but bumping up against the facts: How exactly did the Red Sea part? Was it God or just the tides?

Liz said, "You didn't even tell me that he had met me. You let me think that he was never part of the picture. You just wiped him out of existence and left me feeling . . ."

"Loved. Inspired. Lucky."

"A lot of other things too," Liz said, fighting as always against Angela's inability to contemplate a narrative other than her own. "I should have at least known he tried. It wasn't your place to deny me that."

"Then whose was it? Besides, I'd say Osho and Nosara were a better trade."

"Why can't you ever admit you've done something wrong?"

"Because I haven't," Angela said.

"You are TOXIC!" Liz screamed, years of pent-up frustrations and resentments that had been snowballing abruptly finding expression in a blizzard of rage. "I'm done with you, Angela. I am *done*. I don't want me or my baby around your narcissistic bullshit." Angela opened her mouth to respond, but Liz cut her off. "I mean it. Don't text my boyfriend, don't call me, don't break into our house. Stay away."

Liz turned and walked to her car without looking back. When she got into the old Audi and sank into the driver's seat, which was practically molded to the shape of her body, Liz took a deep breath. On some level, Liz recognized that this had been brewing for a long time, and that she had finally expressed so many things she'd been keeping a lid on for years. Jayne would be proud. Jayne, the therapist whose calls Liz was ducking because she was running out of reasons to keep skipping and rescheduling appointments. Jayne, whose job it was to tease out irregularities in Liz's demeanor so she couldn't get anything past her, the way Liz could with Preston, or Cara and Madison and Freya, or her favorite barista at the coffee shop. Liz knew she'd have to confess everything to Jayne soon. Liz also realized that even though she had technically regained a father, without having him or Angela or Victoria in her life anymore, she had essentially orphaned herself. Liz was truly alone.

Angela stayed away, Victoria stayed away, Ace stayed away. Liz's body continued to expand, seemingly by the minute, and she could not only feel, but also see her baby's movements—a sharp jab of an elbow or a knee that caused a ripple of movement beneath her skin. Liz observed it with fascination even though her back ached constantly and she dripped with fatigue. She ate muffins and ordered diapers. She test-drove strollers with Preston. She skipped Dawn's class to avoid Victoria. She wrote back to the group text with Cara, Madison, and Freya, who were busy putting the finishing touches on her baby shower, not that Liz cared what color flowers they chose or if the "Oh Baby" cake was from SusieCakes or Magnolia Bakery. She texted her friends that the final guest count was up in the air, lying that Victoria might have to attend a work conference and saying that Angela was always unreliable, so who knew if she'd show?

Liz still couldn't bring herself to tell Preston what had happened at Victoria's shower. The longer she waited, the harder it got, because she'd also have to explain the delay. It was easier to pretend things were fine than to detail all the ways they weren't. Liz didn't want to explain why she'd excommunicated her parents and best friend; she didn't want to have to defend her choices.

One morning, after a night interrupted by at least four bathroom visits, Liz was lying in bed, her computer propped on her belly-desk, when she got the email. She sat up so quickly, the laptop slid off her body and careened into the comforter. Liz dug it out and reread the email in wonder. A female indie filmmaker wanted to schedule an interview with her. Preston's coworker had passed along Liz's information and résumé, and she wanted to follow up directly. Liz was so thrilled that her third-trimester fatigue lifted like a curtain. She shucked off the linen sheets and leapt out of bed—as much as a very pregnant person could leap. It was more of a slow roll to an upright position. Liz went into the bathroom and splashed her face with cold water and brushed her teeth, then pulled on a stretchy sundress before she replied to the email, as if her appearance could be detected over the ethernet highways. Yes, she was available. Yes, she was interested in the project.

As Liz was telling herself not to get her hopes up, at the same time vowing that she'd figure out childcare and do whatever it took to make this situation work if the opportunity did come about, Liz got a response from the filmmaker, asking if she wanted to hop on a quick Zoom and get to know each other. Liz briefly considered the wisdom of playing it cool—was this like dating, when you weren't supposed to be available last minute, unless you were only in the market for a one-night stand? Liz decided that even if that were the case, she was far past the point of playing anything cool. She wrote back that she'd love to, swiped a hairbrush through her tangles, smeared blush on her cheeks, and tried to figure out how to turn on the enhancing filter on her Zoom app.

Ten minutes later, Liz was having a surprisingly great conversation with Noora Khan, a filmmaker whose documentary short about her heritage had sparked conversation and interest at Sundance. Noora had signed with Preston's agency and the indie finance team helped her get funding for her first scripted feature. Liz raved about Noora's short and said she knew how hard it was for anyone to get a movie off the ground, not to mention a female writer-director. Liz was struck by Noora's focused passion for her film, and she found herself developing a girl crush in record time.

"Straight up, I don't have room in my life for bullshit," Noora told her. "The budget on this is supertight and so's my crew—everyone has to get along and pull their own weight."

"After my last job, I think I've used up enough energy petting egos for a lifetime," Liz said. Then she chastised herself for bringing up *The Catch*, even though Noora had her résumé.

"Yeah, what was it like working on that show?" Noora asked.

"Horrible," Liz said. "I'm surprised you still wanted to meet me, with that on my résumé."

"My girlfriend is obsessed with *The Catch*. Which is obviously a glaring character flaw. But I'm more interested in why you left."

Liz thought about forming a carefully worded, polite response. Then she left that idea in the rearview. "*The Catch* is toxic. I was sick of being part of it. I want to do something I'll be proud to show my child one day. I'd love to do something that makes a positive difference in the world, but I'll settle for not being part of the problem."

Noora smiled at Liz across the pixelated screen. "I heard about the email," she said.

Liz started. "I thought the show's lawyers had buried it."

"Nothing that good stays dead," Noora said. "It was leaked all over the internet. Anonymously, of course. But it was one of the reasons I wanted to meet you."

"And they say to use LinkedIn."

Noora laughed, then got down to brass tacks. "I work hard, I work fast, and I also work on instinct because it's always served me well. I like you, Liz. Are you in?"

Liz flushed with pleasure. "Yes. Absolutely."

They discussed the shoot schedule, Noora's time frame for editing, and how Liz's pregnancy, which would by then be a baby, might affect her ability to work on the project. Liz said that while she couldn't honestly tell Noora what postpartum life would look like, she was as dedicated to this project as she was to her unborn child; Liz was determined to take advantage of this opportunity and prove herself. This was good enough for Noora, who told Liz she'd send her the script and storyboards. They signed off Zoom with plans to touch base again soon, then Liz shrieked with excitement.

She wandered around the house, buzzing with joy and checking on the crib that Preston had put together over the weekend. A bit later, still filled with newfound energy, Liz set off on a walk around the neighborhood. It was the most physical movement she had asked of her body in weeks. Liz panted as she tackled the street's incline, but she also waddled with purpose. She admired the houses and gave a neighborly wave to two women power walking past her in visors and ankle weights. Liz breathed in the crisp, perfect, eighty-degrees-in-September air; this was one of the reasons why people moved to Los Angeles. Liz reveled in how lucky she was to live in this city, and to be herself, in this moment. She also recognized that soon she would be pushing a stroller on this very walk.

When Liz got home, her feet ached when she removed them from her sneakers, and she noticed that her entire body was swollen, but she chalked it up to the shock of exertion. Plus, maybe it had been warmer outside than she had realized and she was dehydrated. Liz chugged a bottle of Preston's electrolyte-enhanced water, but she didn't deflate. Still, she wasn't concerned until she sat down and crossed one leg over her other calf for a minute. When Liz removed it, there was a two-inch indent in her leg. That didn't seem right. But Liz didn't start freaking out until she opened her computer, Googled her symptoms: "fat feet + very swollen + pregnancy" and scrolled through some of the potential causes for edema. She called Dr. Rosenblatt's office and described what was going on, expecting the nurse to say they'd call her back, or to tell Liz that she was overreacting. Instead, the nurse put her on a hold that was so brief it filled Liz with fear. Normally, she could expect a wait time as long as the cable company's.

"Liz?" The nurse's voice crackled back on the line.

"Yes?"

"Dr. Rosenblatt would like to see you as soon as possible. Can you come in right now?"

Liz's skin immediately broke out in pinpricks and an icy sheen of sweat, like when she had gotten food poisoning from a shady street-meat cart outside an even shadier club in Hollywood that Cara had taken them to one night in their twenties. Liz remembered that Madison had gone home that night with a B-list actor from a '90s sitcom who asked her to sign an NDA before they hooked up. And Liz had thrown up—for three days.

"Is it bad?" Liz asked the nurse.

"Dr. Rosenblatt wants to examine you. We'll see you soon?"

Liz managed a strangled yes, then hung up the phone, shoved her grotesquely inflated feet into flip-flops—the only footwear that could handle their girth—and grabbed her car keys. She didn't want to call Preston and worry him for no reason. It was probably nothing, she told herself. Even though the internet hadn't listed the thrill of employment as one of the causes of edema, it wasn't like the internet knew everything. Liz drove down Sunset, its glittery billboards showcasing Florence Pugh's Tiffany & Co. ad, Sofia Richie Grainge's K18 hair care routine, and Gigi Hadid's supermodel-endorsed knit-wear line. Liz was surrounded by glamour and beauty and elegance—what could be wrong?

She soon found out. Rather than being allowed to linger in the waiting room at the doctor's office long enough to flip through old issues of *People* magazine, Liz was ushered right back. The nurse weighed her and Liz saw her try to maintain a neutral expression while she wrote down the number. Liz leaned over to peek, then gasped. She had gained ten pounds since her last weigh-in, which had taken place at her routine appointment the week before. Ten pounds in one week seemed . . . not okay.

"Try to stay calm," the nurse encouraged, strapping on a blood pressure cuff. Liz tried not to tense up as it encircled her arm, growing tighter and tighter and—was it cutting off her arm? Liz held back a hiccup of discomfort. Finally, the cuff released, Liz expelling air along with it. The nurse removed the cuff and Liz rubbed her arm.

"I'll have you provide a urine sample and then we'll get you into an exam room so Dr. Rosenblatt can see you," the nurse told her.

"How worried should I be?" Liz asked.

"Try to stay calm," the nurse repeated, which, Liz thought, had to be the worst possible thing to say to someone who wasn't calm to begin with, and who was venturing further and further away from its shores with every suggestion to remain there.

Liz's heart felt speedy, like after Cara had dosed her with molly water at Coachella, and she was a little lightheaded as she went into the bathroom, wrote her name and birth date on a sticker with a purple Sharpie, put it on a plastic cup, and crouched over the toilet, trying not to get any pee on her hand. She failed, screwed the cap on the cup, placed her sample in the two-sided cubby in the wall, and scrubbed her hands furiously—at least three renditions of "Happy Birthday," as the poster on the wall advised. The same nurse was waiting for Liz when she walked out of the bathroom.

"Was my blood pressure high?" Liz asked, then thought she'd need to try a different approach. This nurse wasn't giving her anything. "Okay—I know it was high," Liz said, as if they were both in on a fun secret. "But how high was it?"

The nurse showed her into an exam room and flipped the switch next to the door to show that the room was occupied. "Dr. Rosenblatt will review your levels. He'll be in soon."

Liz knew that stressing about her blood pressure would only cause it to rise even more, but really, what choice did she have? Liz changed into the blue paper gown and sat on the exam table, feeling her blood pressure skyrocket. When Dr. Rosenblatt knocked tersely on the door a few minutes later and opened it without waiting for a response, Liz was already immersed in a full-fledged panic.

"Am I okay? Is my baby okay?" she asked as soon as he stepped inside.

"We are going to take steps to ensure that," Dr. Rosenblatt said, and Liz's heart seized in terror. That was not a yes.

"The symptoms you're presenting with—edema, sudden weight gain, elevated blood pressure, and protein in your urine—indicate preeclampsia," Dr. Rosenblatt said.

"Preeclampsia? That's bad, right?" Liz asked, the blood in her veins suddenly feeling ice cold, and how was that possible at the same time her pressure was so high? Shouldn't it feel warmer? It was difficult to breathe.

"You're going to have your baby, Liz."

"I know, at some point," Liz said. "But what do we do now?"

"We deliver the baby. Today."

"But—it's too soon."

"You're thirty-six weeks," Dr. Rosenblatt said. "We may decide to administer a steroid shot at the hospital for the baby's lung development, but I assure you, he or she is fully cooked."

Dr. Rosenblatt waited for this to sink in. Liz didn't appreciate the Food Network lingo or her doctor's serious expression.

"Okay . . . I didn't bring my hospital bag. Should I go get it?" She also hadn't fully packed it, but Liz figured she could throw in nursing bras and toiletries pretty quickly.

"No," Dr. Rosenblatt said, with no room for misinterpretation. "My office already called over to the hospital. Let's go have a baby, Liz."

"Right now?" She really wasn't trying to be an idiot; it just wasn't computing.

"Yes," Dr. Rosenblatt said. "It would be faster if your partner met us at the hospital."

Liz mumbled something about calling him, and then, when Liz

was in the back of the ambulance, a fetal heart rate monitor strapped to her belly and a collection of sensors analyzing her own stats, one of the paramedics helped dig Liz's phone out of her purse so she could call Preston. Even though she was half naked, sweating, and so puffy it was like she had spent a few minutes rotating in a microwave tray on high, and even though there was a real medical emergency going on, Liz was still embarrassed when her three calls to her boyfriend's cell phone went unanswered.

"He must be in a meeting," Liz told the paramedic, who looked like she could nab a role in a Dick Wolf procedural. "Or a bad cell zone."

"Do you want to text him that it's important?" the paramedic asked. "Or is there another number you can call?"

"I can try his office," Liz said, realizing that she never called Preston at work. The view through the windows of the ambulance looked like it was being reflected by a fun house mirror at a carnival. Liz was about to dictate the agency's name so the paramedic could help her sift through her contacts, but then they were pulling into the ambulance bay at Cedars and there was no time.

Everything moved quickly after that. Liz was whisked into the hospital on a stretcher and admitted with a plastic bracelet on her wrist to prove it, then poked and prodded by hands—so many hands—before she was wheeled into a room on the third floor, in the maternity ward. Liz flinched each time a nurse tried to insert a needle into her vein for an IV.

"I'm sorry," the nurse said. "Let's try the other arm."

Liz looked down and saw that her arms were so swollen, they were deflecting the needle's path like they were made of rubber. Her left arm bore the evidence of the failed attempts, little circles of blood sprouting up in a pointillist pattern. Finally, the nurse was able to get the IV started on her right arm, and then Dr. Rosenblatt appeared, now outfitted in scrubs, to explain Liz's options: They could induce labor or schedule an emergency C-section. He detailed the pros and cons of each, but stressed the urgency of getting the baby out as soon as possible, to protect both the baby's health and her own. Liz listened carefully to the medical jargon, and then she burst into tears.

"You're going to be all right, Liz," Dr. Rosenblatt said. "I'm in the business of bringing people into this world, not allowing them to slip out of it." He gave her a sturdy nod, then told Liz he'd give her a few minutes to think about it and stepped out of the room.

The nurse rubbed Liz's shoulder with a caring, maternal air, which only made Liz cry harder. This scenario hadn't been covered in Dawn's class, or if it had, Liz had unwisely skipped that lesson. What if, in attempting to avoid Victoria, Liz had contributed to her own doom? The nurse retrieved her phone, and Liz tried calling Preston again, but he still wasn't answering his cell. When she called the office, Liz reached his assistant, who told her that Preston was off-site for the agency-sponsored US Open viewing event. Liz had forgotten about that. "Do you want me to leave word?" Preston's assistant asked robotically. Liz asked her to tell Preston to call her as soon as possible. She wondered if she should've gone into detail, but she couldn't handle the thought of Preston's assistant transcribing a message about his girlfriend blowing up to the size of a sumo wrestler, and being diagnosed with a life-threatening complication, and facing the task of making a critical decision about how she was going to bring their child into the world.

"Have a nice day," Preston's assistant told her, and Liz almost laughed.

She hung up, and the nurse asked Liz if there was anyone else she could call. Liz's eyes danced around the room frantically. She hesitated for a second, but then she reached for the phone.

19

Victoria

36 WEEKS: SWISS CHARD

Victoria burst from the North Tower elevator onto the third floor. She frantically scanned the signs on the wall outside the elevator bank that indicated where Labor & Delivery was located in the sprawling medical complex, then barreled down the hallway.

"Ma'am, are you in active labor?"

"Let's get you admitted, ma'am!"

Victoria impatiently explained that she was not there to have her baby, she was there to visit someone, and she needed Liz Reynolds's room information. Finally, after she managed to convince everyone that she was not, in fact, in the throes of labor, one of the women at the desk offered Victoria a pleasant smile.

"I'm family," Victoria said firmly.

"It's not the ICU!" the woman replied sunnily. "You don't have to be a family member to visit."

Victoria recited Liz's name once more and waited while the woman typed, her sparkly fuchsia nails echoing against the keyboard in staccato pings. The beeping of the machines in the maternity ward was interrupted every now and then by an infant's sharp peal. After receiving Liz's room number, Victoria located it and flung open the door. Her eyes shot over to the bed.

"Liz."

Liz's face rose to meet Victoria's, reflecting a mask of abject terror. Victoria saw that Liz was swollen to an alarming level. She looked like a deformed version of herself, so distorted that even her face looked misshaped, like it had been formed out of putty. Victoria tried to control her eyes from flying open in alarm.

"Thanks for coming," Liz croaked, and bit her bottom lip. Victoria rushed over to Liz's bedside. Her heart burned at the look of pure panic on Liz's face. Liz was literally so large and yet her expression made her appear small in the regulation-sized hospital bed.

"Of course," Victoria said. "Of course I'm here. We're going to get through this. You and the baby are going to be fine."

Liz whimpered gratefully and Victoria took her hand—the one that wasn't tethered to an IV like a phone plugged into a charging cord—noticing that it was mottled with bruises and, also, that it felt like a clammy, overstuffed burrito, which was disconcerting. Victoria knew she needed to remain calm, and in control—or at least, she had to maintain the appearance of her conviction that everything would be fine, even if internally she was racked with worry. Victoria peered at the name tag on the nurse's pocket without breaking her clasp on Liz's hand.

"Excuse me, Gayle? May I ask, what's the plan?"

The nurse turned with a ready smile. "I'll have the doctor come in and speak with you both." Gayle looked and Liz and said, "Right now, we're doing just fine, aren't we?" She came over and gave Liz an affectionate pat on the shoulder before leaving the room. Victoria and Liz hadn't been alone since the last time they had seen each other, in the coffee shop, when Liz had told Victoria that she wanted nothing to do with her.

"How are you feeling?" Victoria asked, searching Liz's distended face.

"I—I don't know. Not good. It's bad," Liz said. "I couldn't reach Preston—and—I don't—I mean—I have to choose—I don't know what to do."

"We'll figure it out, I promise."

Liz still hadn't let go of Victoria's hand; she was clutching it like it was a lifeline. With her free hand, Victoria took out her phone. "My doctor delivers at Cedars too. I'm going to ask her to come in and give us a second opinion."

"You don't—okay."

"I'm sure your doctor is great, but it's always good to get another opinion."

"Thank you," Liz whispered.

"No need," Victoria said, lifting her phone to her ear and issuing the request to have her doctor paged to the hospital. When Victoria hung up, Liz's doctor was walking in, flanked by several young but cocky doctors who screamed "resident."

"What do we have here, a two-for-one special?" one of them joked.

He was immediately silenced by a reproving look from Liz's doctor, which Victoria appreciated. Then Dr. Rosenblatt introduced himself and shook Victoria's hand. He didn't ask Victoria how far along she was or even mention her pregnancy, which Victoria also approved of. Dr. Rosenblatt laid out the situation in a levelheaded, comprehensive manner, explaining that they would need to decide whether to proceed with an emergency C-section or to induce labor. He mentioned that while they were monitoring Liz's vitals and the fetal heartbeat, and both were currently stable, time was still of the essence. Liz's blood pressure was elevated, and with preeclampsia, delivery was the only remedy.

"Do you have a preference—induction or C-section?" Victoria asked Liz. She watched her friend's eyes dance wildly around the room—a caged animal with no escape in sight. The residents standing in a line behind Dr. Rosenblatt, like a troupe of backup dancers supporting the main act, waited on Liz's answer, staring at her unabashedly. Victoria saw Liz shrink into herself, or try to anyway, then shoot an uncomfortable look at the unfamiliar faces in the room. The presence of strangers was not helping this situation. Liz's eyes bounced to Victoria and seemed to shout, *Help!*

Victoria turned briskly to the viewing audience. "Could we have another moment alone? I understand this is time sensitive. We won't take long."

Dr. Rosenblatt nodded. "Of course."

Two of the residents looked disappointed, like they'd be missing out on the action. When they didn't heed Dr. Rosenblatt's exit soon enough, he snapped his fingers, and they all heeled like spaniels, trotting out behind their boss.

Victoria turned to Liz again. "You were planning on natural labor, right?"

"Not *natural* natural—drugs and an epidural, but not a C-section."

"Drugs seem natural to me," Victoria said, eliciting a faint smirk. "But I meant vaginal birth. So, if you choose to induce, it's not that different from your birth plan."

"But what about that woman from Dawn's class who told us the horror story about her friend who had to be induced and she was in labor for three days and the epidural didn't work, and she wasn't dilating, and then she had to have a C-section anyway? She said it was the worst of both worlds, and beyond brutal."

"Didn't she also say that about the traffic on the 405 getting to class one day?" Victoria pointed out.

Liz nodded.

"If you don't want to induce, though, plenty of women have C-sections."

Liz's face went slack. "It's just—the idea of being cut open? I've never even had surgery. They take out your organs and put them on the operating table and put them back in? That really freaks me out. I want my organs inside. What if they don't replace them correctly?"

Victoria smiled affectionately. "You know I'm having a scheduled C," Victoria said, "And that shouldn't sway you, but I did do a lot of research and it's a controlled, safe procedure. They don't actually remove your organs and put them anywhere. You're awake and conscious throughout the whole thing; you just can't feel anything from the waist down."

Victoria watched Liz consider this with shaky, panicked breaths. She needed to calm Liz down, and they also had to come to a decision. There was one window in the room with a surprisingly prime view of West Hollywood; a cloud passed over the sun, momentarily obscuring the light filtering in and casting a gloomy filter over the room. The monitors kept beeping, like a metronome keeping time.

"This is entirely your choice. Either way, whichever you prefer, you're going to have your baby today, and you will be okay, no matter what you decide."

"But I'm not ready!" Liz said, her face twisting up with angst. "I can't believe this is happening."

"I know," Victoria said soothingly. "Do you want to try calling Preston again?"

"No," Liz said miserably. "He's at an off-site and not picking up." She looked at Victoria beseechingly. "Tell me what to do. I don't know what to choose."

Victoria froze, simultaneously honored by the tremendous import in her opinion that Liz was placing on her and also felled by its pressure. How could she make this decision? What if something went wrong? Victoria would never forgive herself. She pulled out her phone again and texted while talking.

"I'm going to see where my doctor is. If she isn't here in five minutes, I'll make the call."

It wasn't a definitive answer, but it was a plan, which seemed to mollify Liz. Her breathing abated to an almost normal pace. Victoria's doctor texted her back, saying that she would be there in two minutes. "She's almost here." Liz whimpered in relief that Victoria felt too.

Dr. Waldman entered the room minutes later, looked through Liz's chart to assess the situation, and conferred with Dr. Rosenblatt, who didn't seem thrilled to have to contend with an interloper, as if his professional acumen were being called into question, but Victoria assured him that there was no doubt as to his competency. Victoria assumed he had also never dealt with two pregnant ladies in a room, one on the verge of a hysterical collapse, and the other with a demeanor that said, *Try to question me and I will have my water break on command, and then where will we be?*

In the end, though, no one made the decision. A monitor flared with alarm, beeping with the urgency of a smoke detector going off, and both doctors whipped into action. Victoria watched them exchange a fleeting but undeniable look as Dr. Rosenblatt checked the baby's heart rate on the fetal monitor and Dr. Waldman measured Liz's blood pressure.

"Liz, your baby is in distress," Dr. Rosenblatt said. "At this point, inducing is no longer an option. We're going to prep the OR for an emergency cesarean."

"Oh God!" Liz said, her chin wobbling.

"Liz, look at me," Victoria commanded. "You are going to be okay. Your baby is going to be okay. I'll be right by your side, every step of the way." Victoria said this, assuming she could go into the OR, without getting official confirmation, but she would break down the doors if need be. Victoria took her eyes away from Liz for a second to direct her attention to Dr. Rosenblatt. "I am allowed to go in with her, right?"

"She has to!" Liz screeched.

"I'll have the nurses help you get geared up."

"Just don't go into labor," Dr. Waldman said to Victoria with a smile, then turned to Liz. "Dr. Rosenblatt is extremely experienced and I agree with his assessment entirely. I'll stick around in case either of you need anything, but I'm not at all worried. Congratulations, Liz, you're having your baby."

"Thank you so much," Victoria said to her doctor, and then the nurse, Gayle, came in with a set of scrubs for Victoria and a surgical cap that looked like the kind of hairnets worn by cafeteria workers. Gayle looked between Liz and Victoria, amusement dancing on her lips.

"I've been doing this a long time," Gayle said. "And this is a new one. What was that movie about the mom and daughter giving birth at the same time?"

Victoria and Liz stole a look at each other, but neither filled in Gayle on the familial twist. Their situation was more like the exaggerated drama of a movie than Gayle knew.

The anesthesiologist, a man in his fifties with a shiny, bald dome of a head, came in and asked Liz if she was allergic to anything, described his involvement in the procedure, and wanted to know if she had any questions. Liz looked like *all* she had was questions, but she shook her head mutely. Then Dr. Rosenblatt returned, minus his entourage of residents. He instructed Gayle to unhook some of the monitors and then they told Liz they were going to roll her down the hall to the OR. It was time.

"Don't leave me," Liz said to Victoria, frantically squeezing her hand.

"I'm not going anywhere. Let's go meet your baby."

The OR was smaller than Victoria expected, sterile but not unpleasant in its asceticism, and filled with a small army of doctors and nurses whose movements were purposeful, which imbued Victoria, and she hoped Liz, with confidence. Victoria looked at her friend, but no—Liz's face was still bathed in terror.

The anesthesiologist asked Liz to sit up, then started the process of numbing Liz's lower half. Victoria nodded encouragingly.

"You're doing great."

"I'm freaking out!" Liz said. "What if something goes wrong?"

"It won't," the anesthesiologist said.

"It won't," Victoria reiterated.

"What if it does?" Liz said, a tinge of irritation creeping into her voice, and Victoria realized she was wrong to discount the possibility, to suggest that it didn't exist. There was risk inherent in everything in life, and to pretend otherwise was to peddle in denial at a time when it was crucial to do otherwise.

"If something happens, we'll deal with it. You have an excellent team of doctors," Victoria said, pointing around the room at said team. "And you have me, and I'm right here. There is nothing we can't handle together." Wasn't that the Faustian bargain that life made? Throwing shit at you but also equipping you to handle it?

Liz didn't seem comforted, however. She looked at Victoria as if she were going into brain surgery and might not make it through to the other side.

"If something . . . happens . . . make sure my baby is okay." Victoria opened her mouth, but Liz pressed on urgently. "Promise me. I know this is like a scene from *Beaches*, but please. Promise."

"Of course I will. But nothing is going to happen to you. You're going to be taking your baby to the coffee shop in one of those twee carriers because you're going to be one of those moms who wear their babies strapped to their chest. And I'm going to make fun of you and you're going to tell me to leave you alone, and I'm not going to listen this time because I don't care if you don't want to talk to me or if the situation is weird, you're stuck with me, and that's all there is to it."

"I won't tell you that again."

Victoria smiled at her friend, with whom she had formed a connection as unlikely as it was irreplaceable.

"Can you feel this?" the anesthesiologist asked, pressing on Liz's lower back.

"No," she said.

"Good, how about this?" he asked, pressing on a different spot.

Liz shook her head, then looked at Victoria.

Their eyes met, and a silent moment of understanding transpired between them that was interrupted by a nurse asking Liz if she wanted to watch, or if she'd prefer them to hang a curtain.

"Watch?! My body being cut open? No!"

"We'd like the curtain, please," Victoria said.

"You got it," the nurse chirped, and began erecting a piece of fabric that was hung from two metal poles, no sturdier or more substantial than a curtain at a slipshod theater production.

"Whatever you do, don't look," Liz begged Victoria. "I don't want you to see my guts."

"We're starting now, Liz," Dr. Rosenblatt said from the other side of the curtain. "You might feel a slight pressure, but this shouldn't hurt at all."

A nurse stood at Liz's shoulder. "You're doing great, mama."

Victoria realized that this would be the start of other women addressing them as *mama* instead of *lady*, *girl*, *babe*, or even *bitch* in the colloquial *Hey, bitch!* kind of way. Not that anyone had ever called Victoria that, but still. It had been a challenge to graduate from *miss* to *ma'am*, and she dreaded the late-in-life *dear* that would someday announce her entrance into old age, but *mama*—that would take some getting used to. *Mama* implied a status, a vocation, a complete subsuming of identity. Once you were a mother, you could still be a wife, and a career woman, or a book lover or oenophile or home chef or professor or recluse, but you could never *not* be a mother again. You would always be a mother first.

Without intending to, Victoria snuck a peek over the curtain.

"Don't look!" Liz shouted.

"It's not gross," Victoria said. "I promise." It wasn't. It was surprisingly tidy and bloodless. Contrary to the rumors and myths, there was no spleen or lower intestines laid out on the surgical tray awaiting redelivery back into the body like a FedEx package that had to be rescheduled because it needed a signature. Victoria saw that there was an oblong ring of plastic, almost like a basin, lining the opening in Liz's lower body, stretching her from where the horizontal incision had been placed, several inches below her belly button.

"I know you're going to say no," Victoria said, shifting her face back to Liz, "but I really think you're going to want photos of this."

"NO!" Liz roared.

"What about Preston? This is the moment his child is coming into the world."

Privately, Victoria thought that if he was missing this for a sports game, or a signing meeting, or whatever he was so consumed with that he wasn't answering his phone, Preston deserved whatever reckoning was coming to him, but that wasn't Victoria's place to say, and she also didn't know the circumstances leading to his absence. Maybe he was blamelessly dead in a ditch and that was why he couldn't be present at the birth of his child.

"I don't want Preston to see my insides!" Liz said.

Dr. Rosenblatt's voice rang out from over the other side of the curtain. "You're going to feel some pressure, Liz, and then a big push."

Victoria took out her phone, and at the precise moment that Liz's doctor broke the amniotic sac and pulled Liz's baby into the world from her placenta, Victoria captured the moment. She saw a tuft of dark hair, matted with fluid, and a red, disgruntled little face. A high-pitched cry pierced the room and Victoria thought she had never heard a more beautiful sound.

"Baby's out!" announced Dr. Rosenblatt.

"You did it," Victoria said, forcing herself to tear her eyes away from the screaming new infant being taken for the Apgar test. She smiled at Liz through awe and adrenaline.

"Is my baby okay?" Liz asked, still panicked.

Another nurse came over. "You have a healthy baby boy. Congratulations, mama."

Liz exhaled with relief. Then her whole body started shaking, the convulsions rocking her like she was having a seizure.

Victoria shot a worried look at the other nurse, by Liz's shoulder.

"The shaking is normal," the nurse said. "It's a side effect of the medication, but it's nothing to worry about. They're cleaning off and measuring and weighing your baby, and then we'll bring him over."

"Him," Liz said in wonder, her teeth clacking against each other. And then he was there. A nurse carried over a tiny bundle wrapped in a muslin blanket who was still screaming in protest about being wrenched from his cozy nook. The nurse announced that he weighed six pounds, two ounces, and had measured an even eighteen inches.

"Hi," Liz whispered to her baby in wonder.

"He's perfect," Victoria said, her breath catching in her throat. She watched Liz's eyes trace the contours of her baby's face. Thirty-six weeks of wondering what this little person would look like had led to this reveal, a mystery unraveled in one transcendent, indescribable moment.

"He is, isn't he?" Liz said, looking up at Victoria in awe. "Can my friend hold him?" she asked the nurse.

"Of course."

"Really?" Victoria said, somehow more stunned by this than when she had gotten the unexpected, urgent call from Liz only several hours earlier.

"I'm shaking too hard," Liz said. The nurse passed Liz's minutes-old infant into Victoria's waiting arms. Victoria allowed instinct to take over, and her body knew without needing instruction how to mold itself to accommodate a newborn. She stared down at his tiny face like the magic of the universe was unfurling before her. *This is life*, Victoria thought. And then she wept. She cried with relief that Liz and the baby were okay. She cried with gratitude that Liz had relented and asked for her. She cried with reverence, having witnessed the miracle of all miracles. She cried with joy, which was spiraling through her body in ribbons and emanating through every ounce of her. As she did, Victoria was keenly aware that it would forever be one of the most mesmerizing, defining moments of her life.

20

Liz

ONE WEEK OLD

While Liz finished nursing the baby, who would only latch after she tried to coax him into it for at least twenty minutes, Preston opened the door for Cara, Madison, and Freya, who came flooding into the baby's room, their arms laden with gift bags.

"Oh my gosh," Cara whisper-screamed.

"Lizzzzzz," Madison said, putting her hand over her heart as she looked at Liz and baby Charlie.

"Nice tits," Freya said.

Preston listened to the women gush over Charlie and fuss over Liz, telling her how great she looked. Only she didn't. Liz hadn't slept more than two hours at a time before she was woken by her human alarm clock, and she'd developed such huge, dark circles under her eyes that she looked like a raccoon. The breasts that Freya had complimented were 50 percent larger than usual, but they were also engorged with cement—throbbing and hard as rocks. Liz had definitely maybe remembered to brush her teeth that morning, but the last time she had put a comb through her hair was anyone's guess. Maybe since the hospital. Liz had stayed for four days while she was monitored and given a magnesium drip for the preeclampsia. Then she was discharged into the wild without any nurses to administer pain meds or help her execute a swaddle. Liz had thought pregnancy was a gauntlet, but it turned out that postpartum was a civil war.

"Do you girls need anything?" Preston asked. *Sleep. Sanity. No mirrors anywhere.*

Liz shook her head. "No. Thanks, though."

"Then I'll let you ladies do your thing," Preston said, and went off to the kitchen, where he had set up a temporary desk while he was on paternity leave. Though Preston would take the six weeks contractually available, there wasn't a world in which he wouldn't work. He would simply tend to business from home instead of reporting to the office and call it paternity leave. After the past three days listening to him boisterously roll calls and thank colleagues and clients for the Dodgers onesies and baby Nikes they had sent over, Liz had encouraged Preston to go back to the office, telling him that she and the baby would be fine and he didn't need to play out the entirety of his paternity leave at home, but Preston resisted. He *wanted* to be there.

"We come bearing gifts," Freya said. "But I come with the good stuff." She grinned and took a white box out of a shopping bag—Sugarfish's signature Trust Me omakase to go—and then, with the other hand, lifted a bottle of white wine above her head like it was Simba in *The Lion King.* "Sushi and booze, baby."

"Bless you," Liz said.

"It was my first meal after I pushed out the twins," Madison said, sitting down on the bed next to Liz so she could get a better view of the baby. Liz and Preston hadn't had time to move the queen-sized bed out of the room, completing the conversion from guest room to baby's room before their son's early arrival. Now, though, Liz had been sleeping there to shorten her commute to the crib. Charlie could sense the second Liz had fallen asleep and would start wailing like one of those tornado alarms in Kansas, instantly snapping her out of it. Freya plucked a salmon roll from the Sugarfish container and held it up to Liz's mouth so she could eat it even though her arms were full of baby. Liz moaned in pleasure.

"Thank you," she said.

"We're so glad you're okay," Cara said. "That was really scary."

"Don't worry about your shower," Madison said. "I knew it was scheduled too close to your due date! We'll change it to a sip and see when you're ready."

Liz thought she'd never be ready for an event with a name like that, but she nodded agreeably, too tired and hungry to get into it. Freya held up a crab roll and Liz opened her mouth like a baby bird, then swallowed it in three delicious bites.

"How's he sleeping?" Cara asked, looking at Charlie's little face.

"Great. For two minutes at a time," Liz said. "Am I going to be this tired forever?"

"No," Cara said at the same time Madison said, "Yes."

Freya shrugged. "I have three nannies."

"I remember feeling like your baby is never going to sleep through the night and you're going to be this zombie cow who's changing diapers and nursing and burping your baby forever, but it does change," Cara said. "And then you actually miss this time."

"Cara's right," Madison said. "I'm always tired, but I have twins, so don't listen to me."

They all looked down at Charlie, who was nestled in Liz's arms, sleeping peacefully for once. Like an angel who wanted to cast doubt on his mother's claims that he fought the activity at all costs. The Hatch sound machine was on and a humidifier hummed in the corner; the smell of baby lotion clung to the air, while a sheep mobile from RH Baby & Child that Preston's mother had sent twirled lazily over the crib. It was all very serene and soothing and Liz wished she felt, inside, a fraction of the peace that was all around them.

"He's adorable," Madison said. "And I love the name. Charlie Lancaster is so cute."

Liz thought so too, which was why she had agreed to Charlie from the short list of names she and Preston had been tossing around. She was equally glad that she had succeeded in making Charlie the official name, not the nickname, instead of Charles. If Preston had been disappointed that Liz refused to give their son the name of England's reigning monarch, he'd handled it well, agreeing to compromise on Charlie. And if Preston wanted to address their child as his little king, in private, that was his choice.

Freya opened the bottle of wine she had brought—Liz wondered if Freya went everywhere with a wine opener—and poured a generous amount into a plastic cup that had also appeared out of nowhere. Freya handed it to Liz, then poured the rest of the bottle into three more cups, keeping the largest for herself. "Cheers! You did it. And you had a C-section, so you'll still be tight down there," Freya said with a wink.

"Not that you're probably thinking about that yet," Madison said.

Liz shook her head. She was not. The thought hadn't crossed her mind once, even though she had worried about Preston's voluntary abstinence throughout her pregnancy. Now that Liz considered it, though, she could confirm that she had never felt less sexy, or more uninterested in the act.

"You probably have, what, six more weeks until you can have sex, anyway?" Cara asked.

"Something like that," Liz said. When she was being discharged, Dr. Rosenblatt had rattled off guidelines for when Liz could drive, exercise, and have sex again. Liz was only eager to do one of those activities. She lifted the cup of wine and drank greedily. *Am I becoming a wine mom already?* Liz thought. She was only one week in. That couldn't be a good sign.

Charlie woke up and Cara and Madison doused themselves in hand sanitizer and took turns holding a calm, sweet infant whom Liz had never met before. Freya declined, saying she wasn't a baby person, but when Charlie was ready for his fake ID, she was the gal to call. Just when Liz was beginning to relax, the wine warming her body and thickening her tongue in a pleasant way, Cara asked if there was an update on Victoria and Ace. Had Liz forgiven her father? Had she spoken to her friend? And wasn't Victoria due soon too?

Liz's entire body stiffened. With effort, she cleared her throat and said no, yes, and yes. She hoped her short answers would shut down the subject fast. Preston was in earshot, and with the chaos of her emergency hospitalization and the nonstop pace of mothering a newborn that had followed it, Liz still hadn't told him that Victoria's husband was her father. Preston and Victoria had finally met in the hospital, her friend was back in her life and visiting every day, and Preston hadn't noticed that anything had ever been off between them, which made it easier for Liz to keep delaying.

"What are you going to do about your dad?" Madison asked.

"I don't know," Liz said, suddenly more tired than ever. "Victoria's still living at a hotel, so there's no pressure there to see him or anything."

"Do you think they'll split up?" Cara asked.

"I'm not sure," Liz said. She really wasn't, but it also wasn't her place to conjecture about Victoria and Ace's future. Liz didn't tell Cara, Madison, and Freya that Victoria's dilemma was similar to her own. Part of Liz wondered if she could get over the past—the murky outlines of its truth, something she'd never be able to really decipher—and work towards a future with her father. Another part of her thought it was too late; she couldn't start a relationship with a stranger at this point just because they had the same large hands and defined chin.

Charlie started fussing and Madison passed him back to Liz. As her friends tried to talk over his shrieks, Liz felt satisfaction in the proof that she hadn't exaggerated. Her baby wasn't the angel they'd witnessed so far; he was . . . *this*. Freya unsubtly looked at her watch while Liz tried and failed to get Charlie to latch and her baby resisted all the tips that Cara and Madison offered.

Finally, Freya said, "Maybe he needs privacy," and shot a look at Cara and Madison, who got the hint.

"Call us if you need anything," Cara said.

"Like booze," Freya said, and Liz thought, *Yes.*

Charlie continued complaining after they left, and then Preston appeared in the doorway, an expression on his face that Liz had never seen before. He looked at her for several long, loaded minutes. Liz didn't know what was coming, but she felt herself holding her breath.

"Do you have something to tell me?" Liz thought Preston said, but she couldn't be sure, because Charlie's cries were growing even more operatic.

"What?" she said, her voice raised over the baby's wails.

"Do you have something to tell me?" Preston said, louder. "About your father?"

Liz felt her face drain of color. "Were you eavesdropping?"

"We live in the same house, Liz. I couldn't help but hear your friends talking about your long-lost father like they knew something that I definitely don't." Preston lobbed a hurt look at her.

Charlie let out one last angry scream, his loudest yet, then finally latched. The silence that followed still seemed to contain his shrieks, and for once, Liz would have welcomed her baby screeching his head off so she and Preston wouldn't be able to have this conversation. Preston looked at her, his eyes darkening to a slate gray. Liz swallowed hard.

"I've been meaning to tell you."

"You've been meaning to tell me?" Preston repeated. "Then why haven't you?"

"I've been a little busy, if you haven't noticed." Liz gestured around the room like *Hello, I have a newborn to take care of.*

"I've been helping and that's a paper-thin excuse if I've ever heard one."

It was, and Preston had been proving himself to be a hands-on dad—whenever he could be, anyway. Preston had suggested they alternate the night shifts, but this plan fell through when Preston demonstrated an ungodly ability to sleep through anything, even the primal screams of their child. But hey, it wasn't his fault that Liz was a light sleeper and Preston excelled at taking selfies with baby Charlie resting on his chest, so Liz bore the brunt of caregiving while Preston received all the glory of Instagram.

"You told me your dad left when you were young and you never heard from him again," Preston said. "When did he come back into the picture? And why—seriously, *why*—didn't you tell me?" He looked at Liz uncomprehendingly, practically begging her to conjure up a legitimate explanation for her wrongdoings.

Liz sighed. She wished she could close her eyes and pretend this wasn't happening. She wished she could go to sleep and wake up when it was over. She wished she could sleep, period. "At Victoria's baby shower. He's her husband."

Preston's eyes widened as he dramatically shook his head back and forth. "*What?*" He spat out the word, incredulous.

"I should've told you sooner, and I was going to, but it was a lot for me to process, much less try to explain to someone else."

Preston took this in. "But I'm not just someone else," Preston said, his forehead cratering in.

"Okay. But . . . who are you?" Liz finally said. It was, obviously, the wrong response.

"What the hell, Liz?" Preston said, his face stormy. "Who am I? What does that mean?"

"I don't know," Liz said. "Does anyone really know the person they're with? They only know what the other person shows them. I'm sure there are a lot of things about you that I don't know."

"You know my parents!" Preston said. "You know all the major things. And if I had a relative come back into my life out of nowhere, you'd know about it." Preston started pacing back and forth. "We have a baby together! We're supposed to tell each other things and it's like, yo, dude, your fucking dad came back into the picture and you, what, forgot to mention it?"

Liz realized that she and Preston were having their first real fight with their baby attached to her breast. Also, that Preston had just addressed her as *dude*. Neither was ideal.

Liz cleared her throat. Even though Preston was right—of course he was right—her mood was so foul that this only served to make her more annoyed. "What do you tell me? About work? That LeBron is crushing this season? Not to order the Caesar salad at the club when we visit your parents?"

Liz watched Preston's face refract with surprise. She had never talked to him like this before. He probably didn't think she was capable of it. It came as a bit of a shock to Liz too, but the dam had been broken, as if her roiling hormones had attacked the barrier and now all her emotions were spilling forth. "Instead of salad recommendations, how about telling me how you feel, I don't know—about anything? We don't talk about anything real. Do you even want this—you and me, our baby, us playing house together—or is it just something that happened that you went along with?"

Preston regarded her nervously, like Liz was a pipe bomb that might detonate at any moment. "Of course I want this. My family just—they're not the touchy-feely types. I'm sorry if I don't talk about my feelings more. I can work on that."

Preston's acquiescence made Liz feel even worse.

"I'm sorry too," she said. "I should have told you about my father sooner."

"Do you really think we don't talk about important things?" Preston asked.

"Well . . . yeah. We've never talked about how you feel about us. We've never talked about if you want to get married someday or if becoming a dad was something you wanted. We've never talked about how bad it made me feel that you didn't want to have sex when I was pregnant. We've never talked about how annoying it is that you adore Angela and you don't see how she drives me crazy."

"Okay," Preston said, shifting on his feet. "But how could I know you wanted to talk about that stuff if you didn't say anything? Why didn't you bring up any of that until right now?"

It was a good question, and one that Liz wasn't prepared to answer. "I guess I was scared," she said finally.

"That's why you didn't tell me about your dad? You were scared?"

"No!" Liz looked at Preston. How was he still stuck on that when this had become a much bigger conversation? "I didn't tell you because it was easier not to have to think and talk about it. And because, like we've just established, that's how you and I are with each other."

Charlie spit out her nipple and started wailing again. Liz tried to switch the baby to the other side, wondering how long Charlie would reject her left breast, like a hotel guest objecting to the location and layout of his room and harassing the manager for an upgrade before finally accepting defeat and surrendering to the only accommodations that were available. Preston watched her try to tend to their child, the wheels turning.

"Wait . . . You told me that Angela is at a silent retreat in upstate New York and that's why she hasn't texted or been here. She's not really at a silent retreat, is she?"

"No," Liz said. "For all I know, she's still doing fire-spinning workshops in Topanga."

"She's in Topanga?" Preston looked as crestfallen as a six-year-old learning that parents were the ones who snuck dollars under pillows rather than a small roving fairy who traveled the world collecting baby teeth.

"After I found out that she kept my dad from me, I said I didn't want anything to do with her and told her not to contact either one of us. That's why she hasn't been here. That's why she hasn't met the baby."

"You *lied?*" The disappointment on Preston's face made Liz's stomach turn.

"I guess we're even now," Liz said.

Preston's face hardened. "What are you talking about?"

"You weren't there when our son was born! I called you over and over again and you didn't pick up!"

"I was with clients so I wasn't looking at my phone. I've apologized a million times!" Preston said. "Don't you think I'll regret missing the birth of my son forever? And why are you throwing it in my face when you said you forgave me?"

"Maybe that was another lie. Maybe I was lying to myself," Liz said. "Because I don't really understand how someone who's permanently attached to his phone like it's superglued to his hands, who knows his girlfriend is eight months pregnant and could go into labor at any second, how does that guy not check his phone for three *hours?*"

"I was working," Preston boomed. "I was entertaining clients and it would have been rude for me to be on my phone and I'm sorry, but it wasn't intentional. You choosing to keep something from me and lying to me for *weeks?* That's not the same thing."

Liz mulled this over silently.

"Do you not believe me that I was working?" Preston asked.

Liz met his eye. "I believe you." And she did. Liz didn't think Preston was off at a hotel cheating on her with some young, thirsty assistant while she had been frantically trying to reach him. She trusted that he was where he said he was, doing exactly what he claimed. Preston had been doing his thing. But his thing didn't include thinking about his pregnant girlfriend, and wasn't that a problem? They looked at each other unhappily.

"Maybe we both need to cool off," Preston said. "We'll circle back to this," he added, like it was a deal point that needed adjusting, and walked out of the room. Liz soon heard the robust sound of Preston's Zoom voice echoing through the house.

Grim, she looked down at baby Charlie. "That didn't go well," she said. Charlie sucked harder and Liz's nipple twinged with pain, then he released it with a sour look on his little face, as if he had lofty expectations and Liz had come up short. "Join the club," she told her son. Liz picked up Charlie from the My Brest Friend nursing pillow and tried to adjust a burp cloth over her shoulder. But Charlie didn't wait until he was in position to spit up all over her. The chalky white liquid dribbled down Liz's chest and soaked her shirt. Liz looked at Charlie and she could've sworn he looked pleased with himself.

The afternoon stretched on in the same way, the hours blending together in an endless cycle of tasks repeated ad nauseum. By the time Victoria stopped by after work, Liz was in a foul mood. She tried to pretend otherwise, pasting on what she thought was a plucky smile, but Victoria saw right through her. Liz quickly folded and told Victoria what had happened with Preston.

"The real issue, which I think you already know, is *why* you didn't want to tell him about these huge things going on in your life," Victoria said.

"I know," Liz said miserably.

Charlie started crying in his bassinet and Liz looked over, dread gripping her insides as her focus shifted, but not by choice. "I just fed, changed, and burped him." Liz had thought her long history of not knowing what a guy wanted from her might change with the arrival of her own son, but no.

"May I?" Victoria asked, gesturing towards the baby.

Liz nodded and Victoria picked up Charlie, cradling him in her arms and shushing him like she had done this a million times. Like she was a natural. Like she was the kind of mother Liz had thought she'd be. Charlie instantly quieted and mewed like a kitten.

"I swear, he'll only do that for other people," Liz said. "He hates me."

"He does not. You're exhausted," Victoria said. "You haven't slept in days and you just had this major confrontation with Preston, so now you're emotionally drained on top of everything else. Why don't you go lie down and I'll watch Charlie for a while?"

Victoria didn't wait for Liz to answer; she nestled into the rocking chair and rested Charlie on her baby bump, which was now large enough to signal that it was nearing the end of its tenure, but still small enough that it could provoke the wrath of every woman who gained more than thirty pounds when she was pregnant. Charlie cooed happily and Liz watched Victoria smile into his adorable, traitorous face.

"Your baby will be here soon too," Liz said. Victoria's C-section was planned for the following week.

Victoria nodded. "I never thought I'd be bringing him into the world under these circumstances . . ." She trailed off and Liz felt a stab of anger at her father for everything he had done to make such a mess of things and hurt so many people along the way. But with this thought came another one, which was that he wasn't solely to blame. Angela had done her fair share, agent of chaos that she was, to create and contribute to the situation. Liz stewed on it, and Victoria looked up before she could wipe the look of unhappiness from her face.

"Go rest. I promise, you'll feel better if you sleep a little."

Liz rose to her feet. "I'll try. Thank you."

She went into the bedroom and slipped under the covers, but it was like she had lost the ability to sleep. Liz tossed and turned, aching with fatigue, trying everything—an eye mask, a sound machine app on her phone—but nothing worked. She couldn't get comfortable. Nothing would silence her negative thoughts and release her into slumber. After forty-five minutes, Liz gave up and returned to Charlie's room, where Victoria and the baby were sitting in the same contented position.

"You couldn't sleep?" Victoria said.

Liz shook her head and collapsed onto the bed. "This isn't what I thought it would be like."

"Liz, you need to give yourself a break," Victoria said. "You have so many hormones flooding through you right now. Your body just did something miraculous. You made a life and now you're sustaining that life—you alone."

"Don't forget about the twenty Dodgers onesies we own now," Liz said. Victoria observed her thoughtfully for a moment. Liz was past caring about how feral she looked. She was more concerned about how she felt. Because she felt as though she was irretrievably set on a course of failure. Liz was failing to rise to the occasion of motherhood. She was failing to be imbued with the sense of fulfillment she thought she would be. She was failing to love her child properly.

"You really need to sleep," Victoria said. "Being depleted like this isn't good for anyone—you or Charlie. I didn't get you a baby gift yet, so I'm getting you one now. I'm giving you a night nurse."

"That's too much," Liz said. "I can't let you do that."

"You don't have a choice. It's a gift."

"I know how much night nurses cost."

"There's no point in having money except to put it to good use," Victoria said. "I've seen money tear families and marriages apart. I've seen it bring momentary satisfaction. Sometimes, even, the illusion of happiness. But honestly? Money only has real value when it can do something useful."

Liz considered Victoria's words, then said somberly, "I wanted to be good at this."

"It doesn't mean you're not. There's no shame in accepting help," Victoria said. They were both quiet for a moment. Liz looked at her friend as the setting sun sent shards of light crashing into the room through the slatted blinds. "I used to think there was honor in doing everything alone," Victoria said. "But who's handing out trophies for that? And who really wants a prize for being great at being alone?"

"I don't know," Liz said. "What about all those sayings about how we come into this world alone and we go out alone?"

"That's about being okay with who you are. While we're here, we're not meant to be alone. We're supposed to fill up our lives with people to love and with the stuff that gives us meaning."

Slowly, Liz nodded at the friend she loved who had given her life so much meaning and hoped that this small moment of gratitude would be followed by others, that they would flow naturally rather than having to be excavated from a mine. Liz fervently wished, as she had so many times in her life, that she could be a stronger, faster, better version of herself. But now this hope was amplified. Liz glanced at her baby. Now, her faults and inadequacies didn't just affect her. There was so much more at stake. She turned her gaze to Victoria. She also had so much more in her corner.

21
———

Victoria

38 WEEKS: MINI WATERMELON

Victoria entered the ballroom with such dread, she almost wished she could go into early labor and recuse herself from the charity gala at which her firm had bought a table, thus mandating her presence. She had no stomach for these things under the best of circumstances, but now, to have to go alone, without being able to enlist Ace as a social buffer, Victoria felt nearly as miserable as Liz had seemed in the weeks since she'd had Charlie. Victoria's eyes swept over the room: Gargantuan floral arrangements stood sentry in the middle of each table and an orgy of pretzel rolls filled bread baskets. Gold-rimmed plates sat atop chargers and would soon host barely edible entrées. The quality of food at these things seemed to plummet in direct disproportion to the cost of a seat. Victoria reminded herself that it was for a good cause and that this was her last obligation requiring heels, facial gymnastics, and rubbery chicken paillard before she went on maternity leave.

Any positive feelings instantly evaporated when Victoria arrived at her table and found Mark leaning against his velvet slipcovered chair with an air of arrogance that would make Napoleon seem humble. Mark's blandly sweet but forgettable wife was sipping a glass of white wine on one side of him. Nash Winton stood on the other.

Victoria swallowed a bite of air. Nash turned to her, so she recovered as quickly as possible and offered everyone a polite wave.

"Victoria, I didn't know you'd be here," Nash said with a grin. "Mark mentioned that you were due any second."

"How sweet of him to keep tabs on my uterus," Victoria replied evenly.

"You look amazing!" Mark's wife gushed. She apparently hadn't gotten the memo that her husband and Victoria were engaged in the silent subterfuge of a cold war, and this compliment had been lobbed across enemy lines.

"Thank you," Victoria said. "Shall we sit?" She did without waiting for anyone else, availing herself of one of the benefits of pregnancy. Nash sat down next to her.

"All right if I keep his seat warm?"

Nash gestured to the place card. It took a moment for Victoria to register her husband's name on it. She thought she had changed the RSVP to reflect that she would be attending on her own, but apparently this task had slipped through the cracks. As a result, Victoria was being confronted with the uncertain status of their relationship by Nash Winton, of all people, in front of Mark Berg, *really* of all people.

"Ace actually can't make it," Victoria said.

"Lucky me," Nash boomed. Did Victoria imagine the genuine pleasure on the billionaire's face, and its exact opposite spreading across Mark's like a rash?

They all turned their attention to the stage as the program began, a celebrity emcee trotting out jokes before urging the crowd of deep-pocketed attendees to dig even deeper during the live auction, which would follow the appetizer course. Waiters appeared with salmon crostini and Victoria had an unfortunate flashback to the smoked-salmon-induced conference room incident. She and Nash looked at each other at the same time. He raised an amused eyebrow, turned to the waiter, and waved off the appetizer. "For neither of us, thanks." Then he winked at Victoria. "We should probably get some air, to be safe."

Victoria was past the food-provoked-nausea phase of her pregnancy but couldn't turn down the petulance that a tête-à-tête with Nash would bring about in Mark.

"Probably best," she agreed, and Victoria and Nash stood and politely excused themselves.

"Mark is going to be breathing fire," Victoria told Nash when they reached the atrium and sat down in a set of chairs nestled in the foliage. "Unless you already signed with him?"

Nash threw his head back in a hearty guffaw. "Why would I ever do that?"

"Then why have you been meeting with him?" Victoria asked.

"Doctor's orders. I've had to stay off the court since I pulled a ligament," Nash said. He met Victoria's confused glance with a mischievous expression dancing in his eyes. "I need to get my fun in somehow."

"You've been toying with him?"

"It's almost too easy," Nash said. "You should see him running in circles to impress me." Nash squared to look at Victoria. "Did you really think I would sign with Mark Berg?"

"I was once pretty sure you were going to sign with me," Victoria said pointedly. "Until my pregnancy disqualified me."

"Why would it do that?" Nash replied.

"Then why?"

"You apologized once," Nash said. "Then I didn't hear from you. Mark was on my call sheet day after day. I thought you passed me off to him."

"Never," Victoria said, horrified.

Nash looked her in the eye. "If I gave you my business, would you pursue every deal with the same ferocity with which you once went after me?"

"Yes," Victoria said unequivocally.

At that exact moment, Mark burst into the atrium, looking at them as if he had caught them naked, fornicating in the bushes. "The live auction is about to start," he said.

"We don't want to miss that," Nash replied.

"Thanks so much, Mark," Victoria said as she walked past him, back into the ballroom, relishing the pout on his face—Mark had really thought he'd had a shot at prom king.

Two nights after the charity gala and several emails from Nash later, in which they were starting to hammer out the details of their business, Victoria pulled into the driveway of the Bel-Air and stepped out of her car. The valet attendants opened her door and welcomed her back by name. She wondered what the staff thought of this extremely pregnant woman who had decamped to a hotel on her own. Her room wasn't equipped to welcome a baby, much less to accommodate Magda, the baby nurse she and Ace had hired months ago. During the tense few moments when Victoria and Ace had been alone together at her last doctor's appointment, before Dr. Waldman came into the room, Ace told Victoria he would move out so she and the baby could be at home, where they belonged. This arrangement made the most sense, but Victoria had told Ace that she was comfortable at the hotel and would stay there until her C-section. The truth was, Victoria wasn't ready to see or step foot in their house again, the house in which she and Ace had been deliriously happy, the house in which she had been blissfully ignorant and cruelly deceived, the house that was fraught with memories that were now tarnished because in their beauty they also contained Victoria's stunning ignorance.

Victoria walked into the interior of the hotel, pulling out her phone to check her schedule for the next day to see when she could duck out to visit Liz and Charlie. She noted that her new assistant, Edward, who had taken over for Harper a couple weeks earlier, possessed a militant command over Outlook (and a degree from HBS), if not any of his predecessor's charm. Victoria texted Harper to see how her job interviews were going, then fired off an email to Edward asking him to cancel her lunch the next day so she'd have time to see Liz and Charlie.

Victoria only looked up from her phone as she entered the intimate hotel bar to order a quick dinner before retiring to her room. When she did, she saw her husband sitting there.

Waiting for her.

Victoria was so taken aback that she halted in her tracks. Ace looked at her apologetically. He mouthed, "I'm sorry, but . . . ," then held up his hands helplessly, palms to the ceiling. Victoria took him in; there was a force field of mournfulness around him. Victoria had avoided looking directly at Ace when he had come to her recent doctor's appointments, but now that she did, she saw that he had aged what looked like decades in weeks. His face sagged and the laugh lines Victoria had loved so much now just looked like wrinkles. His dimples had vanished.

Victoria forced her feet to move closer to him but stopped to allow a three-foot gap between them: near enough so they could talk without shouting, far enough to preclude the possibility of touching.

"I couldn't take it anymore. I had to see you. I had to talk to you," Ace said.

Victoria could no longer put this off. She motioned to a discreet nook in the corner and Ace followed her there. They sat down in the cozy velvet chairs across from each other. It was dark in the bar, the dimness of the place an intentional choice to flatter its guests, muting any imperfections and disguising what a killer martini would further help to erase. It was still early, and the room was empty except for a few men sitting across the room, nursing old-fashioneds. Victoria drew her eyes away from them, from their unbothered, carefree cocktail hour, and fixed her gaze on her husband.

"I'm dying without you," Ace said.

"That's some opener," Victoria said.

"All I do is torture myself with the idea that the biggest mistake of my life could cost me everything. I think about a future without you and . . ." Ace shrugged, his shoulders slumping in defeat. "I don't have any interest in that. I do not want a future unless it has you in it," he said, his eyes growing glassy. "I know I caused this mess and I have no right to pity myself or talk about how terrible I feel, but I miss you so much. I'm sick with guilt and grief. I'm paralyzed with the fear that you're done with me. I am so, so sorry I did this to us."

"I know you are," Victoria said. Their eyes met. Between them transpired the natural question that followed: *But is sorry enough?* Victoria drew in a ragged breath. "The first few weeks after I found out, I was consumed with anger. I just burned with rage. I was so mad at you for betraying me like this. For blowing up our lives. For not being the man I thought you were."

"Trust me, I hate myself for that. For all of it."

"But then I realized, as good—no, as necessary—as it felt to sit in that anger, to seethe and rage, it would only serve me for so long. Anger won't rewrite the past. It isn't going to help me decide what to do going forward."

"I wish it were as simple as you decking me in the face and us getting on with it," Ace said.

"I do too."

A busboy delivered water glasses, and Ace and Victoria looked at each other silently until he went away as unobtrusively as he had come.

"I miss you so much," Ace said, his voice hardly over a whisper.

"I do too. I miss what I thought we were."

"Do you think we can ever get back to that? Would you be willing to try?" Ace asked, and he winced, as if it hurt to voice the question because he was so terrified of Victoria's answer.

"I don't think so," Victoria said, and Ace's face collapsed again. "What I mean is, we can't go back. We can't ever be that couple again, two people who never had a massive secret come between them. I don't know about the rest, but I know that's not possible."

"Right," Ace said, his voice assuming the laborious control of a jeweler placing a precious gem in an intricate setting. "But can we find a way forward?"

A waiter came over, and Victoria and Ace paused for her to order sliders and a side of truffle fries. Despite the import of the conversation, Victoria's stomach was growling and she couldn't ignore its persistent complaints. Ace shook his head at the waiter, like he couldn't even contemplate food or drink given the gravity of what he was dealing with, and the waiter quickly went off.

Ace leaned forward intently, both of his hands resting on the table before them. "I can't and won't give you up easily, Victoria. If you tell me there's no hope, and you absolutely don't want anything to do with me ever again—"

"We're having a child together," Victoria interrupted to point out. "That's not exactly an option. We're tied to each other for life."

"Of course," Ace said. "But I'm talking about you and me. If you can see no way forward for us, I guess I'll be forced to accept that. Maybe. Someday. But I'm not going down without a fight. Real love isn't watching the sunset in a hot-air balloon over Cappadocia and not being able to keep our hands off each other or stomping on a glass in front of two hundred people after saying our vows or skinny-dipping at that hotel in Big Sur at six in the morning."

"Those were great times, though," Victoria said. "And I thought they were real."

"They were real," Ace said. "But that's love in the beginning, when it's easy. Anyone can look at one of the wonders of the world with a beautiful woman they're falling head over heels for and think, 'This is the good stuff. This is what life's all about.'"

"So, what is it all about? If not that, what?"

"Everything that comes after. The stuff that's usually shoved out of the frame. The mess. Your woeful insufficiencies as a man, a husband, a father, and a human coming to light. It's hoping that I am more than the sum total of my worst mistakes and biggest regrets. It's praying that you can look into my eyes and still see the man you married." Ace looked beseechingly at Victoria. "I'll be the first to admit that I don't deserve you. I let you down, profoundly. But I'm still all the good things too. I'm still the person you said yes to. That person was real. We were real."

Ace paused to catch his breath. Victoria couldn't help holding hers. "I beg you. Remember everything that was wonderful too. I know we're stronger and greater than what could break us. Please, fight with me because we're worth fighting for. I'll do anything to win you back. I will spend every day trying to rebuild this, and to be worthy of you."

Ace's eyes were endless pools of emotion. Victoria hadn't known what she wanted, she hadn't known what she would decide, or what she was capable of, until that moment. She slipped her hand across the table towards Ace's, and for the first time in what felt like an eternity, she reached out for her husband. Her fingertips grazed his skin. The sensation was deeply familiar instead of jarring; her hand fit neatly into its usual spot in Ace's. Perceiving her gesture as an auspicious overture, Ace squeezed Victoria's hand like he would be unwilling to ever let it go.

"I don't know how to do this," Victoria said. "I don't know how to look at you and not think about the millions of tiny lies you told me over the course of our relationship, in service of the big one. I don't know how to rebuild something that feels like it's irrevocably damaged, if not broken beyond repair. But I hope it's not. Because I do love you, Ace, despite it all, and hopefully always. So, I'm willing to try."

Ace bent over the table in relief, his shoulders heaving, at the same time the waiter approached with Victoria's sliders and fries. The waiter hesitated in deference to the weeping man, but Victoria ushered him over.

"He's okay," Victoria told the waiter, gesturing to the baby she was incubating. "Just a little emotional about the fries." The waiter smiled at her and asked if they needed anything else. Victoria politely declined and thanked him for his help. The smell from the trio of perfectly cooked sliders wafted up to her nose and Victoria couldn't wait any longer. She lifted one to her mouth. Ace raised his head.

"Sorry, I know this is a big moment, but I'm starving."

Ace smiled at her. "I love you, Victoria Miller. I love you so much."

Victoria bit into her burger and looked into her husband's eyes, her husband who, it turned out, was already a father but would soon be a father again, thirty-some years separating the incidents marking his entry into fatherhood. And then something occurred to her.

"You're a grandfather, by the way," Victoria said. Ace looked at her quizzically, like he couldn't comprehend the words she had spoken. "Liz had her baby. He came early, and it was pretty scary for a minute, but they're both okay."

"A grandson," Ace said, awash with wonder and trepidation.

"They named him Charlie."

"Charlie," Ace echoed as Victoria polished off the first slider and moved on to the next. "I wonder if she'll let me see him. I wonder if she'll let me see her," Ace said.

"Liz took me back," Victoria said. "And I took you back—on a temporary basis pending parole, good behavior, couples counseling, the works—"

"Yes to all of it," Ace said.

"So, there's hope yet," she said.

Victoria offered Ace a fry and he accepted it, then nibbled it cautiously like food might prove a shock to his system. "Can I take you home tonight?" Ace asked. "Are you ready?"

Victoria slowly nodded. "After I finish this," she said, pointing to her plate and gathering another handful of fries.

"I would never dream of coming between a lady and her fries," Ace said. "And I will never let anything come between us ever again. You have my word."

Intensity radiated from Ace's face and Victoria could tell he meant this with every ounce of sincerity. Ace couldn't promise that he wouldn't hurt her again, or that they would never encounter another hardship, any more than he could promise to lasso the sun into submission so Victoria would never have to experience another cloudy day. But her husband could—and he had—pledged his commitment to work not just on their relationship, but on himself. To figure out why he had lied and concealed the truth for so long. To tease out the reasons for his flaws. To atone. To change. To set them all on a path to healing. And Victoria thought that Ace was right—this vow he had made to her in the hotel bar was perhaps more meaningful than the earnest and poetic words he had spoken at their wedding in front of their tearful guests. It was easy to fling promises into the wind in the beginning of a relationship when lust and infatuation hadn't yet started their slow but inevitable decline. When nothing had happened that would pose a threat or a danger to a relationship, when incompatibilities hadn't yet been discovered, when secrets hadn't been unearthed.

As Victoria settled into resolve, rejoicing in its familiarity rather than struggling with the unfamiliar contours of indecision as she had been these past weeks, Victoria felt a poke to her abdomen. She looked at Ace. "He's moving around a lot right now. Do you want to feel him?"

Ace's face lit up with a joy that almost hurt to look at because it was so pure and fragile; it was evident that Ace had feared he would never feel such a sensation again.

"Can I?" he asked, pointing to Victoria's side of the table. She nodded and Ace came around to sit beside her in the low, plush chair, which was large enough to comfortably house two people, or in this case three. Ace put his hand on Victoria's stomach, next to hers, and they both felt their son kick and turn within her body like he was completing a tumbling routine.

"I wonder if he's saying he's ready to come out and meet us," Ace said.

"Are you?" Victoria asked. "Ready to meet him?"

"Yes," Ace said. "I am." He moved his hand so that it rested on top of Victoria's. "I know we have a lot of work to do between us, and a long way to go, but I am."

Victoria nodded and interlaced her fingers with her husband's. They sat like that for a few more minutes and then Victoria said, "Let's go home."

And then, as Ace scanned the room for their waiter to ask for the check, Victoria's water broke.

Contrary to popular notion, it wasn't a sudden gush of liquid that soaked her chair. There was no exaggerated splash requiring raincoats and wellies. There was simply a slow but steady circle of liquid darkening Victoria's dress, which was accompanied by a sudden, unholy cramping sensation that told Victoria that things were about to deviate far from the plan. Her eyes shot to Ace.

"I think my water just broke."

"What?" Ace jumped up. "What do we do?"

"I'm pretty sure I'm having contractions too. We should get the check," Victoria said.

"The check? We should get the car!" Ace extended his hand and helped hoist Victoria to her feet. "We'll settle the bill later."

Victoria thought about protesting, but ten minutes later, when the car was barreling down Sunset Boulevard and contractions were slicing through her body, she was glad she hadn't. She lay in the back seat, gritting her teeth through unimaginable pain, regretting that she had zoned out during Dawn's lesson on breathing techniques. She hadn't thought she would need them. "How are you doing?" Ace asked, darting a nervous glance in the rearview mirror.

"NOT GOOD!" Victoria bellowed as another contraction ripped through her.

"Fuck! These seem really close together. How is it happening this fast?"

"I don't know! This isn't supposed to happen to first-time moms!"

"Can you tell how dilated you are?" Ace asked, running a yellow light.

"How? No, I can't tell! I'm not a doctor."

"Let me see," Ace said, stopping at the next light. He turned and craned his neck while Victoria shifted her body and pulled up her dress so Ace could try to take a peek. "Oh God." Ace's face went white.

"What?" Victoria demanded, then screamed through another contraction.

"I see hair," Ace said, turning back around and flooring the gas the instant the light turned green.

"Mine or the baby's?" Victoria asked.

"Well, since you lasered off all of yours . . ."

"FUCK! I'm not having my baby on Sunset!"

"We are not having a car baby," Ace said, speeding through a windy portion of the road. "I'm going to get us there in time. Just breathe. And maybe . . . try to hold him in."

"HOLD HIM IN?"

"Sorry, sorry. That was stupid."

Nevertheless, Victoria tried. Ace drove as recklessly as he could without risking an accident. And by the time they pulled up with a screech in front of Cedars, Victoria and Ace were both screaming and the baby was crowning, but they had succeeded in seeing to it that their child would not be brought into the world in an automobile.

22

—

Liz

TWO WEEKS OLD

Liz watched Preston dote on baby Charlie, babbling to him about how cute he looked in his Lakers onesie as he picked him up for yet another father-son selfie. Liz counted the number of times Preston kissed their son: one, two, three, four . . . definitely more in a five-minute span than Preston had ever kissed her. And then Liz felt like a husk of a person who was missing the right equipment. Namely, a heart. What kind of mother was jealous of her own baby? What kind of woman expected to be kissed and adored more—or as much—as a helpless newborn? Liz felt her skin grow hot with shame. She was the woman in that movie about a prostitute turned serial killer that Charlize Theron had gained weight, looked ugly, and won an Oscar for. Because Liz was a monster.

Liz had thought she would immediately be flooded with an all-consuming love for her child. That was the expectation. That's what all the other mothers in Dawn's class reported via the group chat. The more Liz sifted through their gushing messages about the sublime nature of motherhood, the worse Liz felt about herself. *My whole entire heart. I didn't know I could love like this.* In the hospital, Liz had felt like she was being introduced to a stranger who had just so happened to be living in her body for thirty-six weeks and then had stepped out of the door red-faced and furious over his eviction, which was rich given that he had absolutely destroyed the place. When would she feel like her baby was the most beautiful, precious thing she had ever laid eyes upon? Liz was pretty sure he looked like a potato.

"Is it okay if I take a shower?" Liz said.

Preston turned. "Yeah, of course. I got him."

"Thanks."

"Don't I, buddy?" Preston said to Charlie. "We're great, aren't we, pal?"

Liz headed to the bathroom even though no amount of soap and water could fully wash away the smell of leaked breast milk. Still, she took off her clothes, avoided looking at her still sore, puffy, and lumpy reflection in the mirror, and stood under the showerhead, letting the water crash down over her body.

Liz and Preston still hadn't talked about their fight. Despite Preston's suggestion that they "circle back to it," both of them had been nimbly avoiding a discussion of how Liz had concealed the news about her father. Preston had been acting like everything was normal, checking to see what Liz wanted to Postmate for dinner, chatting up Gloria, the saint of a baby nurse Victoria had hired for them, and asking if Charlie looked like he had bicep muscles already. Because Preston could've sworn he could detect some muscle definition, and he knew their son was going to be an athlete. Liz had half-heartedly muttered something in the neighborhood of agreement and wondered if she had hallucinated the entire heated exchange between them.

Liz forced herself to get out of the shower, dried herself off, and went into her closet. She picked up a pair of sweatpants from the floor—she was rotating between three pairs—and tugged them on, hoping they were relatively clean. She strapped on a nursing bra, the least sexy piece of lingerie imaginable, and threw on a button-down shirt, which she had discovered allowed the easiest access for breast-feeding and had the added benefit of her not having to lift her shirt and expose the roll of flesh that hung over her waistband. It wasn't helping Liz's mental state that she still looked five months pregnant. No one was talking about that on the group chat. She was about to put on some perfume, a last-ditch attempt to feel halfway human, when she remembered that women were supposed to avoid fragrances when they were nursing. Liz applied some mascara instead, marking the first time she had put on makeup in weeks.

"You look nice!" Preston said when she walked back into Charlie's room. "Going somewhere?"

"The hospital. To see Victoria, remember?"

Liz had told Preston at least three times that Victoria's water had broken the night before, and rather than having a scheduled C-section on the appointed day, Victoria had nearly had her baby in the car on the way to the hospital.

"Oh yeah, of course," Preston said.

Liz tried to decide whether Preston really was being irritating, or if everything he did would annoy her until he stopped avoiding the follow-up conversation they needed to have. Surely they couldn't go on like this forever?

"It's nice of Victoria to invite you to come to the hospital right away."

"She's my best friend," Liz said. "And also my stepmom." Liz watched Preston's reaction closely. She had brought up the loaded topic that had started everything to begin with and wondered if this would shake something loose.

"Right," Preston said, which was the equivalent of saying nothing.

"My dad's going to be there too," Liz said. "They're trying to make things work."

"Oh. Are you . . . cool with that?"

"I can't avoid it forever," Liz said. "If Victoria's going to be in my life, then he is too, and maybe that's not the worst thing in the world. Maybe it could even be good to get to know my dad."

"Yeah, totally." Preston bounced Charlie on his knee, prompting a contented sound from their newborn that sounded like a baby goat. Preston was a natural with babies—who would have thought? Then again, an infant didn't require meaningful conversation.

"I should try to feed him," Liz said. She and Preston should also talk, but maybe it would go better when he was ready (would he ever be ready?) or after Liz had gotten a few more decent nights of sleep thanks to Gloria. So, she didn't push it. She unbuttoned her shirt, then held out her arms for baby Charlie, who immediately began screaming in protest about the handoff. Preston looked away, as if she were a stranger, as if Liz needed privacy, as if he had never seen her breasts before, as if they had gotten pregnant by having sex through a sheet.

When Gloria arrived, Liz felt guilty about how relieved she was to leave Charlie in her capable hands, and how thrilled she was in general to be away from her baby's cries and needs. The Uber ride to the hospital practically felt like a vacation. Liz was still wearing sweatpants in public, but you couldn't have everything. At least she had showered that day and had made a reasonable effort with her appearance. Liz stopped in the gift shop of Cedars to pick up some flowers for Victoria, wishing she had thought of it earlier so she could've gone to a nice florist's shop or had come up with something better and more meaningful to bring.

Liz took the elevator up to the third floor, thinking that it was much nicer to enter Labor & Delivery on foot rather than on a stretcher. A tour of expectant parents in various states of awe and glee walked through the facility, clutching brochures and listening to the guide describe the NICU's capabilities—although hopefully they would not need those, Liz overheard her say. Liz waited behind a pregnant woman and her wife, who were checking in at the front desk. They were lit up with anticipation and showed no signs of anxiety or fear, which was astounding to Liz. When the pregnant woman was admitted and she and her wife moved off to their assigned room to wait for her contractions to increase in frequency, Liz stepped forward and gave her name.

"I was just here," she told the woman behind the desk. "As a patient. It's a little different to be a guest." Liz had no idea why she was saying these things or why the woman would care.

"Congratulations!" the woman behind the desk said. "How's your baby?"

A traitorous little fucker, Liz thought.

The woman's eyes widened and she looked at Liz cautiously, as if she might need to press the red alarm button hidden underneath her desk and summon security guards to place Liz on a 5150 hold. It took a few seconds, but then Liz realized she had said this out loud. *Shit.*

"Kidding!" Liz said, exaggerating her playful tone. "He's adorable. He's so sweet. It's hard to even be away from him for a little while to visit my friend." The woman nodded with relief—crisis averted—and Liz thought that at least she knew the right thing to say, even if it was a complete load of crap.

"Which room?" Liz asked, and the woman directed her to the correct hallway. As Liz was walking to Victoria's room, she saw Ace emerge and turn Liz's way so he was headed directly for her. Liz mustered a smile and kept walking towards her father.

"Liz," her dad said. Ace started to reach out his arms for a hug, but then he seemed to think better of it and pulled them back; Liz saw herself in this gesture. It was bizarre how you could not know someone at all and still be able to detect the strong throughline of genetics, how you could see parts of yourself in someone without knowing what made them tick, or what they thought about the most basic things.

"How's Victoria?" Liz asked.

"She's a champion. Humans would cease to exist if it were left up to men." Ace gave her a kind, fatherly smile. "I was glad to hear you were okay, Liz. I'd like to be a part of your life, but if that isn't something you're open to, I'll make myself scarce when you and Victoria spend time together. I don't want to come between you two again. I know how important your friendship is to her."

"To me too," Liz said. "And that's nice of you to offer. But I think this is an all-or-nothing kind of situation. We're either all going to know each other and see each other, or we're not. You can't sneak out of the house when Charlie and I come over. I can't pretend that you don't exist. And you can't pretend I don't either. Not anymore."

"I don't want to," Ace said, letting this sit between them for a moment.

"So, I guess we're all in this together," Liz said.

"I want to know you, Liz. I can't wait to get to know you."

Liz thought about all the times she had fantasized about her father when she was a child. In her mind, he was a dashing figure sweeping up to the front door of the elementary school in a limo and whisking her off to somewhere fabulous (and taking out Angela and her deranged anti-DARE protest in the process). He was a fan on the sidelines of the soccer field, cheering ferociously for her. He was a fellow hater of onions. He was a stranger, a shadowy mystery, full of possibilities for Liz to dream up and long for. But now her father wasn't a question mark. He was real, and standing before her, with all the flaws that this involved, and he was offering Liz the chance to find out the answers to the questions she had held her whole life.

"I want to know you too," Liz said. She and Ace smiled shyly at each other, and a world full of potential was contained in their shared gaze. The possibilities were like the stars, twinkling and bountiful. Liz and Ace had missed out on more than thirty years, but all was not lost. They had now. And tomorrow. And all the days after that.

"First, would you like to meet your half brother?" Ace asked, and gestured towards Victoria's room.

"That is so weird," Liz said, and they both laughed.

"Maybe we won't say that too much," Ace said. "We'll just refer to him as Miles."

"For your mother?" Liz asked, remembering that he and Victoria had been planning on naming their son after Ace's mother.

"Yes," Ace said reverently. "Your grandmother. She was a wonderful woman." Liz watched Ace grow reflective. "Sometimes I think this would have gone a lot differently if she had been there."

Liz wondered if her grandmother would have seen to it that Ace scoured the ends of the earth before allowing himself to lose the scent of his daughter's trail. Would anyone's wisdom or wrath have been a match for Angela's stubbornness? Would one stroke of fate, one missing piece, one tweak in history, have made a difference, or was it all going to play out this way anyway, leading them here?

"I guess we'll never know," Liz said.

"But we can control what's next," Ace said, finishing her thought.

Liz smiled at him, then walked to Victoria's room and saw that Victoria had upgraded to the suite where celebrities welcomed their babies. The space was the size of a penthouse in a luxury hotel and was situated on the corner of the floor, so it boasted two walls of windows showcasing the impressive view. Sunlight streamed in and classical music played softly from a portable Bose speaker set up on the coffee table in front of the couch. Stunning bouquets dotted the room—Liz saw cards from the women who had thrown Victoria's baby shower—and a bottle of Dom Pérignon sat on the windowsill. Victoria was resting in bed, her phone in her hand, her baby sleeping in the bassinet next to her.

"Well, well, well. There are babies who sleep?" Liz said.

Victoria's face lit up. "You're here."

"Of course. I even brought ugly flowers." Liz held up the token bouquet.

"You shouldn't have."

"I honestly probably shouldn't have," Liz said, looking at the tacky blooms and then at their competition. Liz dropped them on the table and approached the bassinet.

"He's beautiful."

Victoria grinned. "Not bad, right? I think I'll keep him."

"Hi, Miles," Liz said to the baby. "I'm your mom's best friend, and your half sister, and the mother of your best friend, whether you and Charlie like it or not."

"They have no choice in the matter," Victoria confirmed.

Liz pulled a chair over to Victoria's bedside and sat down. "How are you feeling?"

"All right!" Victoria said cheerfully. "Especially given that I almost had my baby on Sunset Boulevard."

"I can't believe that happened."

"Me neither." Victoria gave her newborn an affectionate glance. "If his entry is setting the tone, we're in for a wild ride."

"Then again, your baby is *quiet* and sleeps. Bitch."

Victoria laughed. "I'd offer to trade you, but I think that's the only thing that could make our situation any weirder."

"Good idea. Let's *Parent Trap* the hell out of this and see if anyone notices."

Victoria smiled. "Are you getting some sleep? How are you?" she asked.

"I'm okay." Victoria searched her face and Liz looked away. "I don't know why I'm not as happy as I should be," Liz said, studying the floor. "I have what I always wanted. I live with a great guy and our cute baby in a nice house with his-and-hers closets—in the Bird Streets, no less!"

Victoria took her in and then carefully asked, "But what if that's not what you want?"

"What do you mean? Of course I want those things."

"If you don't, it's okay," Victoria said. "Sometimes we get what we thought we wanted only to realize we want something else. Or sometimes we *think* we got what we wanted, but it's not the real thing."

"I can't exactly return my baby because we're not bonding like I thought we would."

"I'm not talking about Charlie," Victoria said.

Liz felt herself getting defensive. "I knew it. You don't like Preston. I could tell."

"Preston is perfectly likable," Victoria said. "And it's your life, Liz, but . . ."

Liz crossed her arms over her chest. "Not everyone gets a romance like it's out of a Nicholas Sparks novel."

"Trust me, I know," Victoria said wryly. "I'm not saying everything should be perfect, or even that perfection exists."

"Then what are you saying?"

When Victoria spoke next, she did so slowly and tenderly. "You don't have to stay with Preston because you have a baby together." Liz fought the childish temptation to put her hands over her ears and block out Victoria's words. "You deserve someone who acts like you hung the damn moon, Liz."

"He does!" Liz insisted.

"Does he, though?" Victoria said, and though Liz was silent for a minute, she felt something treacherous bubbling up beneath her skin.

"At least the guy I'm with didn't lie to me for years," Liz said.

Victoria pressed her lips together but took this calmly, without even a hint of outrage.

"You're right. That is something. But is it everything? Is it enough?" Victoria studied Liz, who was refusing to meet her eye. "You aren't Angela," she said gently. "You wouldn't be turning into her if you chose not to be with Preston. You'd be choosing yourself."

Liz glared at Victoria. "Must be nice. You've had your life figured out for a whole twenty-four hours and you're already telling everyone else what to do."

"I'm offering my perspective, not trying to force my opinions on you," Victoria said.

"Things are fine—they're good!" Liz said. "So what if we had a fight? Everyone fights. Preston asked me to move in with him. He has a good job and he's a nice guy and a great father. And fine, our relationship isn't some crazy, passionate love affair that people are going to make movies about, but you know what? Not everyone gets that. It's not realistic."

"Are you actually making a case for average?"

Liz refused to look at her, turning away from Victoria and focusing on Miles instead. He was still sleeping peacefully, which shouldn't have further enraged her, but it did.

"I wish you could see yourself how I see you," Victoria said. "I wish you could see how funny and smart and beautiful and strong you are. Because if you did, you would know that you don't have to settle for an approximation of the real thing."

Liz swallowed the lump in her throat and stood up abruptly. "I'm sure you think you're trying to help, but acting like you know what's best for everyone and pushing your opinions on me—that's not helping."

"I hear you. I said my piece. I won't mention it again."

Except Liz would know she was thinking it. Every time she looked at Victoria, she would remember the words Victoria had just said aloud—scary, alluring, dangerous words. Victoria held out her hand to Liz, but Liz refused it. She needed to withhold any confirmation that Victoria was onto something; she needed to try to banish this conversation from her mind.

"I'm happy," Liz said. "What we have is good." Liz didn't say what she was really thinking, which was that it was *good enough*. And rather than striving towards an unattainable goal, wasn't it better to accept and appreciate what she had?

Victoria nodded and started to talk about when the nurse had come to administer a hearing test on baby Miles, but Liz was so discomfited that she conjured an excuse to leave, congratulated Victoria again, and scuttled out of the room. Liz walked down the long hallway, past all the new parents rejoicing over their babies and making plans for the glorious futures they would share together. She told herself that this was the case for her and Preston too.

23

Victoria

THREE WEEKS OLD

Victoria walked into the nursery and saw Ace leaning over the crib, watching their baby sleep. She paused in the doorway, before he could notice her, and observed him like he was a stranger. Because in a way, he was. This was an entirely new and different man from whom Victoria had known. That Ace had been reduced to rubble. This Ace was a father who had been transformed twice in recent days: first, at the chance to forge a relationship with his adult daughter, and second, with the singular and surreal experience of seeing his son come into the world. Ever since that moment, Ace had been glued to Miles's side. The way Ace looked at their infant made Victoria feel a sensation she hadn't experienced since she rewatched *The Notebook* on a red-eye to New York. Everything hit differently at thirty-thousand feet. But this. *This.* This was something else. Despite, or because of, everything that had preceded these moments, Victoria was filled with extra gratitude for them.

"How long have you been standing there?" Victoria asked, walking into the room.

Ace looked up from the crib with a guilty expression, as if he had been caught illicitly browsing porn on his iPad instead of researching the city's tax incentive for replacing real grass with artificial turf. "Half hour, give or take?"

"So, two hours?" Victoria said with a smile and went over to stand by his side. Ace put his arm around her and they stood there together, admiring the life they had created.

"I told Magda to take a break," Ace said.

Victoria nodded, having assumed as much. Before Miles's arrival, they had intended to be hands-on with their son; now that he was here, they found themselves bordering on the maniacally micromanage-y. But as Victoria's delivery experience had reinforced, what was parenthood if not a set of theoretical and best-laid plans that were swiftly upended by reality? Miles moved almost imperceptibly in his swaddle and Ace leaned forward as if to improve his already unimpeded view. Victoria watched him soak it in.

"God, he's beautiful," Ace said.

"He's perfect."

"He's lucky he got your bone structure," Ace said.

"He's three weeks old!" Victoria said. "You can't tell that yet."

"I'm sure of it, and you can't convince me otherwise," Ace said. A grin blossomed on Ace's face and stayed there like it had planted roots. "Should we bring our dinner in here and eat it while we watch him?"

"Like dinner theater?" Victoria said, with a laugh.

"I guess we could go into the kitchen," Ace said, pulling out his phone and tapping the monitor app to bring up the live feed of Miles sleeping. Victoria had caught Ace checking it obsessively any time he wasn't in Miles's direct vicinity. Once, even, when Ace was on his way to the bathroom, and she had said they really needed to draw a line.

They went downstairs to the kitchen and propped up their phones alongside each other on the counter, both displaying video of the monitor.

"In case one fails us," Ace said, like this made perfect sense.

"We are completely unhinged," Victoria said.

But she wouldn't have it any other way. This was what she had been too naive to even know to hope for before everything had happened that almost broke her and Ace apart—before everything he had done. That these blissful, graceful early days, together with their son, were even happening sometimes took Victoria's breath away.

"Salmon and Moroccan couscous?" Ace asked, drawing her back to the present and the pressing need of her appetite, which had grown from spirited to insatiable in the days since Victoria's body had stopped sharing one with her baby but provided sustenance for him just the same.

"Sounds good," Victoria said. "I'll text Magda and see if she wants some." Victoria picked up her phone and minimized the monitor app to do this while Ace pulled out the fillets from the fridge and gathered the necessary seasonings from the pantry. She watched him move about the kitchen, thinking that no matter how many times she had done this, it never lost its appeal. She sat at the counter, watching him cook, the faint buzz of the sound machine in Miles's room emanating from the twin app feeds on their phones.

"I'm so happy," Victoria said. She gave Ace a slightly goofy grin, as if she were surprised that this had come out of her mouth. As if statements like this were reserved for simple, less serious people. As if happiness were a silly pursuit and not actually the goal.

"Me too," Ace said. He paused to look at her, and while with most people it stopped there, Ace saw her. "It's bothering you, though, isn't it?"

"Liz? Yes." Victoria sighed. Since the hospital, when Victoria had voiced her concerns about Preston, Liz had been distant.

"Give her some time," Ace said. "She'll come around."

"I don't know," Victoria said. "I shouldn't have pushed."

"You were trying to help."

"Because what every new mom wants to hear is *You could do better.*"

"Is this guy a tool or what?" Ace asked.

Victoria smirked at the protective-dad persona that Ace had immediately assumed. He looked up to catch a glimpse of her expression.

"Because I will grab my shotgun!" Ace said, veering into the dramatic for the sake of the joke.

Victoria smirked, then thought about Ace's question. "Preston isn't a bad guy. I just think he and Liz are the wrong people for each other." Victoria watched Ace fuss with the couscous, adding a dusting of cumin.

"Is this because of me? Does she choose the wrong men because she was abandoned as a child?"

Victoria's face turned down at the plaintive, guilty expression on her husband's. "I don't know," she said quietly.

"Textbook daddy issues rearing their ugly head."

"Don't do that," Victoria said. "You'll drive yourself crazy, and the truth is, we'll never be able to figure out all the reasons why Liz is who she is."

"But that's how life works: action, consequence. I left my daughter and it messed her up," Ace said.

"It could be worse," Victoria replied. "She didn't join a sex cult. She chose a nice guy who might not be right for her, but she's not shacked up with a convicted felon or recruiting runaways to harvest their organs."

"Damn," Ace said. "Where did you even come up with that?"

"Do you feel better now?"

"I think?" Ace said, and they shared a laugh. Then he turned serious again. "I know parents mess up their kids. Sometimes in small ways, sometimes in big ways. And I know I screwed up in the biggest way possible. But I hope I can have a relationship with Liz. I hope I only mess up Miles in the little ways. I hope there's still time for me to be a good dad. To both of them."

"Me too," Victoria said, and raised her glass. "To only messing up in the little ways."

"To us," Ace said.

Us.

Victoria never thought the word would mean so much, but she clung to it for the rest of the night, throughout the lovely dinner Ace had cooked them that they shared with Magda, and during Miles's nighttime feeds, each spaced several hours apart, which left her weary in the morning, almost jet-lagged with the disoriented sense of things being jolted out of their usual routine, but Victoria's fatigue was also steeped with the sweetness of satisfaction.

———

The next day, Harper arrived with an armful of beauty products. "Before you thank me," she said, stepping into the herringbone-tiled foyer, "they were free from my new JOB!" She pushed the box towards Victoria so she could make jazz hands. Light bounced off the chunky gold rings decorating at least six of Harper's fingers.

"Harper, that's amazing!" Victoria said. "And I'll thank you anyway. Come in." Victoria ushered her inside and directed Harper towards the living room. Harper sat down and remained practically motionless, as if she were in a museum and even breathing could damage the fifteenth-century artifacts.

"Is it weird to be in my house?" Victoria asked.

"Not at all!" Harper said.

"Relax. We're friends, Harper." Her former assistant's face looked like a flower opening as this statement found its mark. "Tell me about this new job before the baby wakes up and I can introduce him to his future favorite babysitter." Harper's eyes flew open. "No pressure there," Victoria said. "You can just be a fun friend."

"I know negative zero about babies," Harper said. "They scare me."

"I felt the same way. You have a lot of time before you have to worry about that, though."

"My parents have always told me, 'Get a job, don't get pregnant,'" Harper said. "So I guess I'm totally winning right now." She beamed at Victoria, who chuckled. "Plus, I'm not going to make a sex tape and use it to try to become an influencer, so they can relax and maybe just, like, try being proud of me?"

"I'm sure they are," Victoria said.

"They actually seemed surprised that I was into my new job and I told them, 'Thanks for hooking me up with a gig in finance but that's so not me, and Victoria says it's not about having a job for the hell of it. It's about finding one you like and maybe even love.' Which—funny enough!—is kinda the same thing I think every time I go home with a guy. Will I like him? Will I maybe even love him? Or will I delete my number from his phone while he's sleeping and ghost the hell out of him?"

Harper looked at Victoria. "Don't worry! It's not like I do that every weekend."

"I am so old," Victoria said with a laugh.

"Nah," Harper said. "You're just a mom now—in a good way! Whatever you do, don't watch *Euphoria*."

Victoria and Harper both looked up as Magda entered the room holding Miles, who had woken up for his midafternoon feeding. Victoria thought it would put Harper over the edge if she were to lift up her sweater and expose even a sliver of breast, so she asked Magda to grab a bottle from the fridge, then asked Harper if she wanted to feed the baby.

"Omigod, so honored that you'd trust me not to break him, but I'd be too nervous."

Harper filled Victoria in on the cast of characters at her new workplace and thanked her, once again, for being such an important person in her life. Victoria tried to wave this off—she hadn't done *that* much, she had done what anyone in her position would—but Harper insisted. She told Victoria that most people wouldn't have noticed her. Most bosses would have kept ordering their coffees and their lunches and not taken an interest in the person who was bringing it to them. They wouldn't have cared enough to try to figure out what Harper should have been doing with her life instead of being an assistant in a field she knew nothing about.

"But do I meddle too much?" Victoria asked. "I meddle too much," she said, answering her own question.

"No! What do you mean?"

Victoria explained how she had offered Liz unsolicited advice on her relationship. "I need to stop inserting myself so much into people's lives."

"No," Harper said, shaking her head. "That's not true. You're a real friend. The kind who's going to tell you when you have food stuck in your teeth or an outfit looks terrible or you need to make a life change. I don't know Liz, but it sounds like there's some truth you dropped that she needs to deal with."

Victoria ruminated on this.

"This is who you are," Harper said. "It's how you show up for people. It's what makes you *you* and it's what makes me want to be like you."

Later, Harper skipped down the front path towards her car, then turned around to give Victoria an affectionate wave. The genuine joy Victoria felt from having forged this bond was like the thrill she derived from closing a deal, signing a new client, or making an unspeakably large amount of money. But as she watched Harper pull out of the driveway, Victoria realized that previously she had only assigned this sensation to events in her professional life. She was genuinely as glad to have Harper in her circle as she was to have Nash Winton on her client roster.

After Harper left, Victoria went into the kitchen and pulled out her laptop. Even though she was technically on maternity leave, she still checked emails and worked a few hours every day. Victoria sat at the table and checked the necessary tasks off her list, the room wrapped in light coming in from the large bay windows. Outside, a hummingbird hovered delicately over the bougainvillea bushes, whose magenta blooms danced gently in the soft breeze.

Then she went upstairs to do tummy time with Miles, realizing that Ace wasn't home yet. He had left earlier for his thrice-weekly four-mile run on the grassy median separating traffic down San Vicente Boulevard. Victoria admired his love of running even though she shared no desire to emulate it unless she were escaping a bee. Victoria looked at her watch; tummy time had become a sacred occasion, and Ace never missed the part of the afternoon where they put Miles on a soft blanket and encouraged him to pick up his head, even though his muscles would not be developed enough to accomplish the task for some weeks.

Victoria called Ace, but he didn't answer. The afternoon was stretching to its conclusion, the light outside glowing gold with the setting sun, and Victoria started to grow concerned.

And then her phone rang. Victoria looked at the screen and saw that it was displaying an unknown number. Combined with a bone-chilling sense of premonition, this was enough to still her breath. She walked out of Miles's nursery, into the hallway, and picked up the call with trembling hands. Once she heard the news that awaited her on the other end, Victoria dropped the phone, which went crashing to the ground with a gunshot echo of glass and metal hitting wood. Victoria followed it, falling to the floor as if she had been bludgeoned by the words she had heard and would never, ever recover.

24

Liz

FIVE WEEKS OLD

Liz started to head home from her walk, if moving her body twenty feet down the street and parking herself on the front step of an empty house for sale could be called a walk. But Preston didn't need to know about that. No one needed to know that Liz had stared blankly into space for an hour, not even looking at her phone, dreading when the timer she had set would go off letting her know that she should probably return to her boyfriend and baby. Which was something that should fill her with joy but still didn't. *Please let my maternal instinct kick in,* Liz begged someone, anyone, the universe, God? Liz had tried to reassure herself that it would happen. Maybe she was just operating on a delay, like when the audio feedback was a few seconds off. She wanted to discuss her concern with Victoria, but after the conversation in the hospital, Liz was also reluctant to admit that anything was amiss.

Liz stopped in front of Preston's house before opening the door. She'd given up on trying to consider it their house. She lived there, but it would always be Preston's house. Liz tried to practice putting a smile on her face so she'd seem happy, excited, thrilled to be back!

Then she pushed open the door and was surprised to see Preston waiting on the other side of it with a grin on his face—one that, unlike hers, didn't appear forced.

"Hi?" Liz said, her voice rising to imply *What's going on here?* Something was obviously happening. But what? Preston looked too pleased with himself for it to be an intervention.

"I have a surprise for you," Preston said.

"Okay," Liz said cautiously. She thought, *Oh my God, is he proposing?* Her stomach twisted into knots at the idea, which was weird because not that long ago, it was all Liz had wanted. A ring sparkling on *that* finger. The title of *Mrs.* in front of her name. The promise, or at least the illusion, of someone promising to love her forever.

"You've seemed a little down lately," Preston said. "I know it's a lot, having a newborn, and we've been going through some stuff, so I wanted to do something to cheer you up."

Preston took both of Liz's hands and ceremoniously tugged her inside. This felt like something that someone might do before they dropped to one knee and pulled out a ring, and Liz suddenly felt as if she might throw up, or start shaking like after her emergency C-section from the effects of the anesthesia.

"Where's Charlie?" she asked to delay and give her a second to think.

"In his crib, sleeping. He's fine!" Preston said.

"He's been asleep this whole time?" Liz asked, even though she knew that the answer was probably yes, because Charlie only chose to unleash his bloodcurdling cries when Liz was around.

"Yeah! He's such a great baby," Preston said in the same tone of voice he used when he was bragging about a star client. "Now close your eyes," Preston instructed. Liz did. "And don't peek!" She wasn't going to, but Liz sensed Preston standing there to make sure.

"I won't," she said to reassure him.

"I'll be right back," Preston said.

Liz heard his footsteps retreating, and then the sound of the bedroom door opening, and then the jingle of something in Preston's hands as he returned.

"Okay!" he said with the showmanship of Vanna White on *Wheel of Fortune*. "You can open your eyes!"

Liz peeled her eyes open and blinked three times, dumbfounded by what was in front of them.

"Surprise!" Preston said with a huge, white-toothed smile on his stupidly happy face, which was so proud of what was in his arms: a small white-and-brown corgi puppy. It cocked its head, its ears sticking up at attention, and stuck its tongue out at Liz in what looked like a matching smile to Preston's.

"You got me a puppy?"

"Isn't he cute?"

"You got me a puppy?" Liz repeated. The smile started to slide off Preston's face.

"I thought you'd like him. And studies have shown it's great for babies to grow up with dogs."

"What studies?" Liz said, her teeth gritted together. "Have those studies also looked at how the mother feels about taking care of one more thing that needs constant attention? One more thing that needs to be fed and watered and walked? One more thing that's probably going to pee on her and keep her up all night? Did the studies show that the last thing a new mom needs—the absolute last fucking thing—is something else to take care of?"

Preston's eyebrows shot up in an *oh shit* sort of way and he held the puppy closer to his body, as if to protect the poor canine from the unhinged female it had been unlucky enough to cross paths with.

"What possibly could have made you think I wanted a dog?" Liz said. She held out a faint, vague hope that Preston would say he remembered how she'd always wanted a pet when she was younger but she could never have one because she and Angela moved around so much.

"I—um—who doesn't love puppies?" Preston said.

"A NEW MOTHER!"

"I'm sorry. I'll take him back."

"A puppy isn't an Amazon order you can return at the nearest Whole Foods kiosk," Liz said. "It's a living thing."

"I was trying to do something nice," Preston said, hurt in his blue-gray eyes, which made Liz feel bad, but she still couldn't manage to calm herself down. "I thought you'd like him," Preston said.

"Why? Because *I'm* the one who's obsessed with the royals? Because I've ever once said I loved corgis? Because I look like I want to carry a stupid, useless little purse that isn't big enough to hold anything like Queen Elizabeth—and don't you dare say 'God rest her soul' or I swear, I will lose it."

Preston looked at Liz like she was already in the process of losing it, or worse, had already lost it, which was fair enough. "I'm sorry. I didn't mean to upset you. I really thought it would be a nice surprise."

Liz's face fell. She looked down at the ground. "I know you did. I'm sorry. I'm an asshole," she said to the wood floor. But where to go from here? Because Liz could no longer ignore what was staring her in the face, what she had gotten so angry at Victoria for pointing out, mainly because she didn't want to admit it. It was what Liz had known, deep down, for a while probably, but she didn't want it to be true. Liz was so focused on being chosen that she had forgotten about doing the choosing too. Liz had been so grateful to be picked by Preston that she hadn't bothered to dig deeper and figure out whether he was a great guy for her, if they made each other better, or if they wanted the same things. All the warning signs had been there too. Liz had waved at them. She had marched defiantly past a sea of red flags . . . only to arrive here. With a fluffy purse dog.

"Preston . . . we shouldn't be together," she said.

Preston's face spasmed like he had been slapped out of nowhere and he couldn't believe someone had the audacity to treat him that way. "What?" he said. The word sounded like water sizzling on a hot pan.

"Maybe we should sit down and talk?" Liz suggested.

"I don't want to sit," Preston said tightly. "What are you saying right now?"

"Please?" Liz asked again. "I'm tired from my walk." From her non-walk, but still, Liz was bone-weary in a way that had nothing to do with exercise.

"Fine," Preston said coolly, and followed her to the kitchen. They sat down at the table, several seats apart from each other, the puppy nestled contentedly in Preston's arms. Miraculously, Charlie was still sleeping, and Liz wondered if he would give his parents the gift of not starting to wail in the middle of their breakup.

"I care about you, Preston, and I think—no, I know—you care about me, but if we're really being honest with each other, and ourselves, in the way that counts, I think we can both admit that we don't make sense together. We're not going to make each other happy, in the long run."

"How do you know that?"

"We don't want the same things," Liz said.

"But we do. We want a family. We *have* a family."

"Maybe we want the same big thing. But all the other things, all the little ways of being that family? Of being together? They don't line up. And all the little ways—those are everything."

"I don't get it," Preston said. "Where's this coming from? Is this because I didn't want to have sex when you were pregnant? Because I told you it wasn't about you."

"That didn't help, but no. I hate sports and vegan food and counting macros, but even more than that, I don't like who I am in this relationship. I'm always pretending to be a better, different version of myself so you'll like me. I tamp down who I am and try to curate this other person and I can't do it anymore."

"That's what everyone does in the beginning of a relationship. We haven't been together that long. You have to give it time," Preston said, like he was revealing the answer to one of the mysteries of the universe. And maybe this was true, to various degrees, for everyone. Maybe Preston was right. But it wasn't enough.

"I'm afraid I'd be doing it forever," Liz said quietly. The puppy made a noise in its sleep and they both looked at it. Preston put his hand on the corgi's head. Liz was breaking up with a guy who was good with dogs and babies. He was everything Liz thought she had wanted and tried, for so long, to hold on to. He was a good guy. He just wasn't *her* guy.

"I don't make you watch sports. Or eat tofu," Preston said.

"We can be friends, Preston," Liz said. "We'll coparent. But we don't have to be together because we have a child."

This sat in the air as Preston digested it. Finally, he said, "Are you sure about this? I thought things were pretty good."

Liz knew this was true; Preston didn't need or want anything too deep. He could coast indefinitely with a woman who tolerated his obsessive sports viewing and constant phone habits, attended the requisite work events and made polite small talk with his coworkers, and matched his unruffled disposition with an even-keeled, undemanding personality of her own. It was a perfectly pleasant life that Preston offered, full of consistency and stability.

Liz nodded.

"I want to be with someone who understands me, who's passionate about me, who loves me in the way I want to be loved. Maybe I'll never find that. Maybe I won't meet that guy. Maybe I'll never choose someone who chooses me back. But I have to start choosing myself."

Preston swallowed hard. "How is this going to work?"

"I don't know yet," Liz said. She hadn't thought about the logistics and was suddenly overwhelmed by them. She'd need to find her own place, one that was big enough to fit her and Charlie. She and Preston would have to figure out some sort of schedule. She'd need to map out childcare for when she went back to work editing Noora's film, which had started filming.

"Obviously, stay here as long as you like," Preston said. "We're a team even if we're not boyfriend and girlfriend."

"Thank you," Liz said. "Seriously, Preston. I know you mean it and—thank you."

Preston nodded, forlorn. "Whenever any celebrity couple splits up, they always say they're going to stay on good terms for the sake of the kids, and then it immediately gets nasty and they're ripping each other apart in the press," he said.

Liz looked him in the eye. "I promise never to rip you apart in the press."

"I promise to always say nice things about you to TMZ," Preston said.

"These sound like vows. But instead of wedding vows . . . *unwedding* vows."

Preston stood up and faced Liz, who rose to her feet as well. They regarded each other as if they were standing at an altar.

"I solemnly swear to be the best ex-boyfriend I can be, in sickness and in health," Preston said.

"I solemnly swear to be the best ex-girlfriend I can be, in sickness and in health," Liz said.

"I vow to coparent well with you."

"I vow to always put our family first."

"I vow that things will always be cool between us," Preston said.

"I vow to always want the best for you," Liz said.

"I promise I'll always be here for you. I'll always be your friend."

"I promise if I come across a cute girl who loves baseball and intermittent fasting and Buckingham Palace, I'll send her your way," Liz said. They grinned at each other.

"Best unwedding vows ever," Preston said.

Liz held her arms out and they hugged, the puppy between them. As they embraced, Charlie woke up and started to cry, but not with the high-pitched frenzy of a smoke alarm like usual. It was just the annoyed mewing of a tiny human demanding attention.

"Should we go introduce him to his new pet?" Liz asked.

"You think I'm keeping this bad idea on my own?"

"Now it seems like a bad idea, once you're the one who has to take care of it?"

"Obviously," Preston joked.

"You know what?" Liz said, looking at the furry little ears standing at attention and the black button nose. "I think you should keep it . . . Him? Her?"

"Him. We're a boy family, aren't we?" Preston said, lifting up the corgi and giving him an affectionate glance. They looked like they belonged together, like there was no other owner in the world that would be as perfect for this royal-endorsed breed of pup than Preston Lancaster.

"You definitely should keep him," Liz said.

"I think I might. If the boss agrees," Preston said, motioning with his thumb towards Charlie's room. The baby's cries were growing more persistent, so Liz and Preston exchanged a wordless look and walked into their son's room.

Liz picked up Charlie, who for the first time quieted instantly and settled into her, resting his little head against her chest. Liz felt tears of relief spring to her eyes.

"Well, buddy," Preston said, addressing Charlie. "The bad news is, your parents split up. The good news is, you got a puppy." He picked up the dog to meet the baby. Charlie remained indifferent, but unopposed. The puppy wiggled in Preston's hands and stretched out to lick Charlie on the cheek.

"It's official!" Preston proclaimed. "Did you see that?"

Liz smiled and thought that their breakup had outshined many of their so-called happy times together as a couple. Her phone rang in her pocket and she ignored it. She wanted to stay present in this moment and experience all of it fully so she could file away the details for future reference: the flood of warmth she'd felt at having her baby nestle against her; the soft, spectral light in the nursery; the quiet white noise of the sound machine; the kindhearted ex-boyfriend and the absurdly cute puppy beside her.

"Do you want me to get that for you?" Preston asked, pointing to Liz's phone.

"It's okay," Liz said, shaking her head. But when the phone rang again, Preston reached into her pocket and fished it out for her. He held it up so Liz could see the display: Victoria.

"I'll call her back," Liz said.

Liz was about to ask Preston to text Victoria to tell her that, but a message came through from Victoria first: *Ace had a heart attack. We're in the ICU.*

Liz stared at the words on her phone.

"What happened? What's wrong?" Preston asked.

Liz couldn't manage to speak. Something cried out. It was only after a few seconds that she realized the strangled, inhuman noise had come out of her own mouth and not from an animal howling its despair into the pale, pockmarked face of the moon.

25

Victoria

THREE WEEKS OLD

Victoria stared at Ace. Tubes and wires spiderwebbed from his body, connecting him to monitors and IVs and the ghastly breathing tube that plunged down his throat, supplying oxygen to his lungs. Victoria couldn't make sense of the fact that the person in front of her was her husband. Ace looked like the Madame Tussauds wax figure version of himself, or the fake food in the display case of a Starbucks—it almost resembled the real thing, but upon closer inspection, it was cardboard and plastic. *This couldn't be real.*

"Come back. Come back to me," she pleaded, her voice a hoarse whisper. Ace didn't move. He hadn't opened his eyes since the quadruple-bypass surgery that had followed the massive heart attack that had sent him toppling over into the grassy median separating the lanes of traffic on San Vicente. If a fellow jogger hadn't seen Ace keel over and had the good sense to call 911 and perform CPR, they might not even be in this position. There might be no hope at all. Victoria tried to keep this in mind, but fear and abject terror did not create fertile ground for perspective and gratitude. All Victoria could think about was her unfathomable reality and the unbearable potential that the future might hold. To make it worse, Victoria was powerless in her suffering. She could do nothing but wait, which was agony. She now understood why people looked to religion and appealed to a higher power. But having discounted religion long ago, Ace, her unconscious husband, was the only person she could direct her pleas toward.

"We need you," Victoria said. "You have a wife and two kids and a grandson who need you. You might think I would be fine—and yes, I would take care of Miles, I would make sure Liz was okay—but I wouldn't be, Ace. I would be destroyed without you." Victoria's body was racked by sobs.

"You're everything to me," she said between tears. "And I can't do this. You told me you didn't want to live without me. Now I'm telling you the same. You told me you'd fight for me. You said you'd do whatever it took to get me back. You'd spend your entire life fighting . . . I need you to fight. *Fight*, damn it, fight and come back to me."

Victoria let her head fall into her hands and expelled angry, violent tears that came in torrents.

"Please, Ace. *Please*," she begged.

The only response Victoria received was the sound of her own stomach gurgling with a buildup of acid. It was as if every organ were furious about its futility. The doctors couldn't even give Victoria the odds of Ace's survival with any kind of reliable accuracy. The unbearable truth was that the human body remained largely a mystery and the medical field was peppered with question marks and trial and error. Victoria was indebted to the paramedics and the doctors and the surgeons who had worked valiantly to save her husband, but she could not look to them for any more aid or answers. No one knew what would happen next.

Her stomach made its loudest, angriest noise yet. Victoria's body was rebelling against her own neglect: Her head was pounding and her breasts were aching because she hadn't fed Miles in hours. There was plenty of milk that she had pumped in the fridge at home, and she knew that Miles was being well cared for by Magda, but Victoria craved the sight and touch of her baby in a cellular way. Despite being leveled by grief to a degree that should preclude the ability to function, the world was still spinning madly on its axis and it was demanding things of her—namely, that Victoria express her milk or suffer the consequences. She forced herself to her feet and walked on spindly legs to the nurse's station, which was located on the other side of the cluster of three curtained-off areas—they couldn't really be called rooms— one of which Ace was occupying.

"How are we doing?" the nurse asked kindly, looking up from her computer. She had strawberry-blonde hair and a no-nonsense but up-beat demeanor, admirable given the bleak setting where she spent her working hours. Victoria checked her name tag even though the nurse had introduced herself several times. Victoria's mind was like a sieve and facts were grains of sand slipping through.

"Janine," the nurse said, seeing Victoria searching for her name tag.

"I'm sorry," Victoria said. "I knew that."

"That's the last thing you should be worrying about," Janine said. "Do you need anything? Water? Something to eat? More blankets?"

"I ran out without my breast pump. I don't want to leave my husband to go home and get it . . ."

"I'll find one for you," Janine said.

"Thank you so much."

"Of course," Janine said, picking up the phone. "But, Victoria, if I may—sometimes being in the ICU is a marathon, not a sprint. You have to take care of yourself too."

Victoria nodded.

"Maybe you can take a break and go see your son?" Janine suggested.

"Maybe," Victoria said, but as much as she was tempted, and wanted so badly to feel the smooth velvet of Miles's skin underneath her fingertips and kiss the soft, downy fur of the baby hair coating his head, she knew she wouldn't. She couldn't imagine leaving Ace. If he woke up or worse—the alternative—and Victoria wasn't there, she would never forgive herself.

Victoria went back to Ace's bedside and sat vigil. She tried not to let her mind go to the scary places, but Victoria couldn't help but plummet into the depths of her despair. What would she do if Ace didn't survive this? Was she about to become a single mother? Did she and Ace come back together only to have him cruelly snatched away? Why had this happened to him? To her? Why? Victoria knew that was a preposterous question, and one that didn't have an answer, but she couldn't help asking it anyway. Ace was the fittest sixty-year-old imaginable. He ran more than ten miles a week, he never smoked, and he had received a squeaky-clean bill of health at his last physical. *Why?*

Victoria listened to the whirring of the breathing tube—the rhythmic intake of air being pushed through Ace's lungs and then expelled. She took his great big hand in hers and almost expected it to be cold because it was so lifeless. But it was warm and like holding a brick. Thinking back to all the times she had slipped her hand in his and they had walked together, hand in hand—whether it was through the farmers market or a neighborhood in a new city they were exploring together—Victoria was hit with another wave of sorrow. Would Ace ever hold her hand again? Would Ace witness his son's first steps? Would he meet his grandson? Would he see Miles and Charlie grow up?

The questions were so harrowing that Victoria bent over in the chair, keening. She felt milk leak through her nursing bra, blooming in wet spots on her shirt. She kept staring at her husband, but nothing changed. Ace was somewhere else, a place unknowable to those who walked the land of the well, the land of the living. He was traversing that liminal space between life and death and only time would decide the destination.

Janine pulled the curtain aside and stepped in. "I found a pump for you," she told Victoria, and handed her a hospital-grade model like the one Victoria had at home. "And I brought you something to eat and drink. Please try?"

"Thank you," Victoria whispered. "I will."

"If you need anything else, just press the call button."

Janine gave Victoria an encouraging squeeze on the arm and slipped out through the curtain. Victoria hooked herself up to the pump and tried to nibble at a turkey sandwich but gave up after a few bites. When the curtain opened again, she assumed it was Janine coming back to check on her. But it was Liz's grief-stricken face that poked through instead.

"Victoria," Liz said, her voice heavy with emotion.

Liz rushed in and Victoria stood up, still connected to the breast pump. Wordlessly, they dove into each other's arms, a crush of plastic between them. When Victoria finally pulled away, she saw that Liz's face was slick with tears.

Janine discreetly snuck in with another chair, positioned it next to Victoria's, and left just as quickly. Liz and Victoria sat down next to each other, their chairs screeching against the cold linoleum floor. If Liz had appeared frightened coming into the ICU, now that she had caught a glimpse of Ace, she was a shell of herself. Victoria knew the feeling; it was like looking into a casket, or at a man trapped in amber, on his way to becoming fossilized. It was staring down death.

"Oh God. I'm so sorry, Victoria," Liz said, averting her eyes from the tube taped to Ace's throat and the bits of dried spittle that kept forming in the corners of his mouth.

Victoria reached out and took Liz's hand. It was warm and full of life. She hadn't noticed until now that Liz had the same hands as her father—broad and large but still elegant, with slender fingers.

"How bad is it?" Liz asked. "I mean, is it as bad as it looks? Because it looks . . ." Her voice broke. Liz stole a quick glance over at Ace, then thought better of it and turned away.

"He made it through the surgery," Victoria said. "But the doctors don't know. We have to wait and see if he wakes up."

Liz took this in and briefly shuttered her eyes. She said, her voice breaking again, "This is so fucked. We can't lose him."

Victoria shook her head and felt dizzy. The breast pump made its whirring sound.

"I just got him back in my life again," Liz said.

"Me too," Victoria said. She watched Liz's face pang with recognition and sympathy—a pulse of her features that conveyed how much Liz could relate to Victoria's pain, how they were possibly the only two people alive who could truly understand each other in this situation.

"God, that was insensitive. I'm sorry. Obviously, this is way worse for you."

"It's not a contest," Victoria said with the faintest of sad smiles. "We're in it together."

"I'm sorry, Victoria—about everything," Liz said. "Not just this, but how I reacted in the hospital."

"It's not necessary," Victoria said, shaking her head to disabuse Liz of the notion that she wanted or expected an apology; Ace's heart attack had wiped the slate clean. They were in new territory and any past grievances seemed irrelevant—almost quaint.

"I wasn't ready to admit the truth about me and Preston. I didn't want to hear it and I took it out on you."

"It wasn't my place to force my opinion on you," Victoria said.

"Then whose?" Liz said.

Victoria's gaze traveled from Liz's sincere expression to Ace's frozen state. She reflected upon the friendships she had gained, and the family she had created, and the people she had taken under her wing. She thought about the joy and satisfaction these relationships had brought her and how her life had changed as a result, how her world had grown, how it had become infused with the kind of meaning that a balance sheet could never reflect.

"If not for you, I'd probably still be working for *The Catch* and on the verge of a mental breakdown," Liz said. "I'd probably still be with Preston, ignoring all the reasons we shouldn't be together. I'd be sleepwalking through my life instead of living it."

Victoria looked at Liz; she could detect apprehension in her friend's eyes—fear of the future and of the unknown—but she also saw bravery and determination shining through.

"You broke up with Preston?" Victoria asked.

Liz nodded. "I might need to lean on you, but you can also count on me. Because you're my best friend and my stepmom and that's so insane, but maybe there's also something perfect about it, because you're the family I'd choose, and as it turns out, you're my actual family too."

"You are the family I choose, always," Victoria said.

Victoria reached out for Liz, who buried her head in Victoria's shoulder. The comfort was short-lived. An alarm cut through the air like a siren and shattered any semblance of calm. Victoria's head shot to the monitor at the right of Ace's bedside, which was flaring like a strobe light.

"What's happening?" Liz said, panic clogging her voice.

Victoria knew the answer, but she couldn't summon the words. Code blue.

The curtain was flung aside and doctors and nurses streamed in. Janine came over to Victoria and Liz. "It's best if you wait outside and give the doctors space to work."

Victoria shook her head—she couldn't leave Ace. She couldn't even move. But Liz stood up obediently, wide-eyed with terror, and held out her hand to Victoria. Janine nodded and Victoria knew she had no choice but to comply. Victoria quickly removed the breast pump—the weight of her feelings was so heavy she couldn't bear to be encumbered by anything else. Janine reached for the bottles of milk and indicated that she would take care of them. Victoria put her hand in Liz's.

As Victoria allowed Liz to lead her out, feeling like her limbs belonged to someone else, she heard the doctor counting, "One, two, three—clear," and then the sickening sound of the defibrillator sizzling against Ace's chest, trying to shock him back to life.

"Still in A-fib."

"Resume compressions."

Another nurse appeared and gently led them to the ICU waiting room, a windowless ten-by-ten space that didn't even attempt to muster cheer. Victoria took one look at the clumps of people sitting there quietly—loved ones under siege. She glimpsed their ravaged expressions, their cell phones juicing up with chargers plugged into the walls, their cans of soda and bags of chips from the vending machine, and she couldn't take it. She shook her head, backtracking to the hallway. Liz followed her, a ghastly pallor on her face. The nurse told Victoria and Liz that she would report back with any updates, then briskly walked away. Back into the melee.

Victoria leaned against the wall for support. Liz put her hands up to her eyes as if she could manually shove the tears that threatened back to their point of origin. Victoria shook her head again in disbelief, then found that she couldn't stop. Air-conditioning cycled through industrial vents. Shoes tapped against the floor as people walked by. Elevators arrived in the bank down the hall, their doors opening with a ding. Orderlies pushed carts. Monitors beeped. Victoria had thought that the hovering between life and death might be the end of her, that the not knowing would be her undoing, but now that she was here, on the precipice of a gruesome finality, she would do anything to reverse course and bob in the turbulent waters of limbo. Anything but this.

Victoria's and Liz's gazes connected. Victoria felt her breathing quicken and she choked, trying to get enough air.

"He can't—" Victoria gasped. She couldn't finish the sentence.

"I know," Liz said, squeezing her eyes shut.

Victoria leaned over and tried to put her head between her legs, but panic had overtaken the muscle memory of breath.

Victoria thought she had known how much she loved her husband. She thought she had known when she slipped her hand into his at the hotel bar and said yes, they could move forward. She thought she had known when she swam in the relief of reconciliation and basked in the blissful delirium of life with their newborn son. She thought she had known any of the hundreds of times she had watched Ace putter around their kitchen with precision, performing that special alchemy of turning ingredients into a meal to nourish and please someone because you cared for them, because your heart was inextricably tied to theirs, your fate bound to their well-being. She thought she had known any of the dozens of times when she had gazed into Ace's eyes in the throes of passion and felt a hunger she thought would never abate. She thought she had known when she said yes to a relationship, to marriage, to a life together, even though it was everything she had steeled herself to avoid. She thought she had known any of the hundreds of times she tossed the words out at the end of a phone call or as their heads hit the pillow, sealing in the day with the declaration as a matter of course.

But she hadn't known. Victoria only knew how much she loved her husband as she collapsed into his daughter's arms, her core a molten pit of terror, her entire being paralyzed with the fear of losing him.

26

Liz

THREE MONTHS OLD

Preston stood in the driveway and helped Liz strap Charlie into the car seat and check and then double- and triple-check that it was secure.

"It doesn't look loose to you?" Liz asked, squinting in the morning light outside of Preston's house.

"I installed it the exact same way I did mine," Preston said, gesturing to the garage, where his car was parked inside. "Promise it's good. Are you?"

"Yes," Liz said. "No," she admitted a second later. "I'm nervous."

Charlie had been in the car before, and Liz had been in the car with Charlie before, but Preston had been there with them. Liz had been cleared to drive for weeks, but now that Charlie had gotten his three-month vaccinations, and after everything that had happened with Ace, there were no more excuses to be made. Since Liz couldn't exactly cite fear of being alone with her baby in the wake of her father's heart attack, she was going out into the world with her baby. Alone. Birds were singing and cars were driving by and people were walking up and down the hill as if nothing out of the ordinary was going on, as if another potential catastrophe wasn't about to happen at any second.

"There's nothing to worry about," Preston told her. "You'll be great."

"I don't know . . . It feels crazy that no one's making sure I can do this," Liz said. "You have to take a test to have a driver's license, but there's no one qualifying you to take care of another human being."

"That's why there are shows like *16 and Pregnant*," Preston said. "Anyone can have a baby."

"Is that supposed to make me feel better?" Liz said, her voice reaching a high pitch.

"Yes," Preston said with a laugh. "You're smart and capable and you're completely neurotic, but you're a good mom, Liz. You've got this."

He hugged her goodbye, and then Liz went around to the driver's seat while Preston leaned over and gave Charlie another kiss. Liz took a breath to steady herself. Then she waved to Preston, and he shut the car door, leaving Charlie and her sealed inside by themselves, giving Liz no choice but to face her fear and drive away. *People do this all the time*, Liz told herself. *All you're doing is going out with a helpless human who is entirely dependent on you to protect him from the dangers of the world. His survival is in your hands—no big deal!*

Liz started driving to her favorite coffee shop and darted a quick glance to check on Charlie in the rearview mirror when she was stopped at a red light. He was fine, and adorable, and unbelievably small. Liz tried to imagine being Charlie's age. She tried to picture Angela getting behind the wheel with baby Liz in the back, the two of them headed off into the great unknown.

Liz didn't know if Angela was still living at the Yellow House Foundation or if she had moved on to another artists' colony or meditation retreat or weirdly named love interest. Nevertheless, Liz drove down Sunset, past the bright, sparkly billboards, until the ocean came into view and shimmered on the left, stretching out into the horizon and blending into the sky. Charlie slept peacefully, lulled by the motion of the car, and Liz drove until she reached the turnoff to climb up the canyon into Topanga. Her finger flicked up the right turn signal automatically, as if her body knew where she was headed before she had even realized it herself.

Liz hadn't spoken to her mother since she had cut off communication months ago, before Charlie's birth, and knowing Angela, she could be anywhere. But when she arrived, Liz saw her right away. Angela was painting outside in the dusty, weed-dotted field with another woman. Both were completely naked. *The better to access their art*, Liz thought—you can't let clothes interfere with inspiration. Angela turned when she heard the car door shut and Liz saw her mother's face rearrange itself with surprised delight. Liz had the odd sense that maybe her mother had stuck around town in case of this: Liz arriving without warning, offering the chance of conversation and maybe even more. Angela put down her paintbrush, said something to her fellow nude artist, and started walking over to Liz.

Angela still had twenty strides to cover before she reached the car, so Liz went around and carefully took Charlie out of his car seat. She adjusted his little hat and held him in her arms, and then Angela was standing in front of them. Naked and awestruck.

"Hi," Liz said.

"Liz," Angela said, clasping her hands together in front of her chest.

"This is Charlie."

Angela stared at the baby for several minutes, taking him in, silent and reverent as if she had been granted a private showing of the *Mona Lisa*.

"He's beautiful," Angela said. "A very nice-shaped head."

Liz waited for her mother to bring up her own misshapen cranium, but Angela's focus was elsewhere. She tilted her face down to Charlie. "Welcome earthside, angel boy."

"Do you want to hold him?" Liz asked, wondering if new life could usher in a new beginning.

Angela's head whipped up. "Really?"

"You've done this before, right? I made it to adulthood in one piece."

"I actually did drop you—never mind," Angela said. "But maybe I should put some clothes on first."

"Good idea," Liz said.

"Will you come with me?" Angela asked, and Liz thought maybe her mother seemed worried that the moment would evaporate, that Angela would put on a psychedelic caftan only to discover that Liz and Charlie were apparitions as a result of a different kind of psychedelic.

"Sure," Liz said, and she followed her mother to her yurt, slightly concerned as she stepped inside that there would be an overpowering stench of patchouli or a cloud of peyote smoke that would flood her nostrils like a noxious poison, but her mother's quarters were surprisingly tame and drug-free.

"This is nice," Liz said, looking around at the bare-bones but pleasant space, which was covered with half-finished canvases and sculptures, most of them fashioned out of found objects from nature like feathers and sticks. Liz recognized Angela's artistic oeuvre immediately, which wasn't hard because it hadn't changed in thirty years. The art wasn't good, not by a long shot, but as Liz thought about it, wasn't art completely subjective, after all? A piece of art was worth what someone was willing to pay for it. And besides that, Liz had to respect Angela's commitment to her craft; it took a special kind of stubbornness to fail at something for decades but refuse to give it up. Maybe that was just the madness of the artist.

"Make yourself comfortable!" Angela said. "Oolong tea? Or I might have some fenugreek! Excellent for milk production."

"Just some water would be great."

Liz sat down on a tufted pouf and Angela came over with two mismatched glasses of water that she put on a stack of old *Art World* magazines sitting on the floor.

"Here you go," Liz said, extending the precious bundle in her arms. Angela gingerly took her grandson into her arms.

"Strong aura," Angela said approvingly, looking him over. "September baby?"

Liz knew where her mother was going with this. "He's a Virgo."

"Hmm. Libra is a better September sign—some of my best lovers were Libras—but Virgos are great too! Have you had his natal birth chart done yet?" Angela asked.

"I thought I'd let you do the honors," Liz said.

"Does that mean you're talking to me again?"

"I'd like to figure out a way we can be in each other's lives without me wanting to tear my hair out."

"You're already going to lose a ton of hair because of the hormones," Angela said.

Liz smiled at her mother, who rarely knew the right thing to say but maybe, just maybe, did try her best in her own flighty, chakapa-gifting, gaffe-making, moon-goddess-worshipping sort of way.

"I think you and I have been locked in this dynamic where I'm ten years old, waiting for you to show up for my school play, and you're out trying to chase dreams you'll never catch up to because you have a kid holding you back," Liz said.

Angela's face fell. "That's what you think? That you stopped me from living my life?"

"Didn't I?"

"No, Liz. I didn't stop chasing my dreams. I took you with me."

Liz looked at her mother and realized that this was true, and she had resented Angela for it her entire life. For putting her own needs before Liz's own. For not thinking about what Liz wanted. For dragging her around the country—around the world, really—and making Liz beholden to her whims and decisions. Liz watched Angela coo over Charlie and rock him lovingly in her arms.

"You were so young," Liz said. "Which I knew. I obviously knew how old you were when you had me, but I didn't really realize it, if that makes sense, until I had Charlie. It must have been hard."

"We had great times too, Liz."

"Like when we were living in that cabin in Montana and you woke me up at three in the morning to see the first snowfall of the year."

"We made snow angels in the light of the moon," Angela reminisced.

"I'm sorry I don't always remember the good parts," Liz said. She checked the time, then rummaged through her diaper bag and handed Angela a bottle. Her mother took it and adjusted Charlie's head, tilting the bottle at the correct angle so he would swallow as little air as possible.

"Kids never do," Angela mused as she fed Liz's son. "In twenty years, Charlie will probably come to you with a huge chip on his shoulder and throw your worst mistakes in your face. He won't thank you for all the times you wiped his ass and cut the crusts off his sandwiches and dried his tears when he had bad dreams and fastened his seat belt and did all the million forgettable things in the course of his life to care for him."

"You made me use a seat belt?"

"Sometimes," Angela admitted. "I got some things right, but not all of them. I gave you the kind of life I wanted, but you always preferred to color inside the lines, and I should have held more space for that. I'm sorry for everything I got wrong. I'm sorry I was less than what you deserved."

Liz looked at her mother, shocked that Angela had admitted fault and regret. Liz had been waiting her whole life for her mother to say this, and now that it had happened, she didn't know what to do. Angela looked at Liz and smiled knowingly.

"I know. I'm not great at saying I was wrong," Angela said. "But I've been thinking about it since the last time you were here. I guess you're bound to get reflective when your kid tells you that you're a piece of shit."

"I didn't say that."

"In so many words."

Angela looked off and Charlie kept gulping milk and Liz wondered if that was the end of it, but then Angela returned her gaze to Liz.

"You have every right to be angry. I told myself we were better off so much I think I really believed it. I wanted us to be free to have adventures and I didn't want you to have a father who played the part out of obligation. Both of those things were true. But I was probably punishing your dad too. I resented how he got to pick and choose when he wanted to show up. Men have that privilege. They choose when it's convenient for them to be a father. Women don't have that option. The second you have a baby, you're a mother every second of the day, every day, for the rest of your life."

Liz let her mother's words sink in and thought about telling Angela what had happened to Ace, but it wasn't the right time. "I don't want to be angry anymore," she said. "I can't." Liz looked at Charlie as Angela picked him up, placed him over her shoulder, and firmly tapped his back to produce a burp. She thought about all the ways she might inevitably fail him, and all the ways she would make sure she wouldn't. "I don't want to live in the past," Liz told Angela. "I'm an adult now, and you and I can be different people to each other."

"Out of the two of us, you were always the adult," Angela said. "And it wasn't fair that I was growing up too, right alongside you. And it definitely wasn't fair that you were better at it."

"We both made it out okay. That's what's important."

"Sure," Angela said. "But I'm going to try, Liz, to hear you. To really hear you and show up as the kind of mother you want and need. I don't want to lose you again. Especially now that it's you and Charlie. I get it wrong a lot, but I really do love you."

"I know you do," Liz said, looking into her mother's eyes. Angela would always be Angela and she would probably frustrate and challenge and maybe even madden her in the years to come, but she was also Liz's mother, and you only got one mother in life, and here she was, *trying*. "I love you too." Charlie let out a belch disproportionately loud for his size.

"You're going to be an amazing grandma."

Angela shuddered, jostling Charlie. "We can't call me that."

Liz chuckled. "You can decide what you want to be called."

Angela pursed her lips in thought and then, instead of suggesting Glamma Moonbeam or Nana Aphrodite as Liz feared, she said, "How about we let Charlie decide?"

"Sure," Liz said nonchalantly, although she was aware of the significance that they were mapping out a new and different kind of future. "Just don't break into the house again with that spanking paddle or whatever that thing was. Deal?"

"Liz!" Angela laughed. "Good to know you have some kink in you, but that was a sacred Peruvian chakapa, not a sex toy."

"Actually, definitely don't break in again, because I don't live there anymore. Preston and I broke up."

Angela's eyebrows bounced upwards like they were on a trampoline. Liz braced herself for Angela to ask what Liz had done wrong, or for her mother to say it wasn't surprising but it was a shame because she adored Preston so much. Instead, Angela asked, "How are you doing?" with what appeared to be the genuine article of maternal concern.

"I'm . . . okay," Liz said. "We're going to raise Charlie together and be friends, and even though part of me already feels guilty that Charlie is going to grow up in a broken home, I think that's better than having a broken person as a mother."

"You're strong, Liz. You shape your reality. Only you have that power."

Liz nodded obediently. Even if she didn't feel powerful yet, she could at least envision a world in which she could, one day.

"And you should know, I'm damn proud of you," Angela said. "You're brave and you're smart and you're weird in all the best ways."

Liz was floored. It wasn't only that it felt like she was starting to heal a wound; it was also like Liz had finally begun to locate the source of the bleeding in the first place. "You really don't wish I was more . . . of a Sage?" she asked.

Angela laughed. "Of course not! How could you think that?"

"You told me I wasn't living up to the name."

"You weren't. Because it was a dumb name. But do you remember why we really changed it?"

Liz shook her head.

"You know those personalized license plates on the rotating racks in every rest stop back then, with kids' names on them? Sara and Jennifer and Jessica and Lauren and all those popular, generic names?"

"Yeah."

"They never had Sage," Angela said. "I gave you a unique name because mine was so boring, but all you wanted was one of those license plates. So we talked about it and then we changed it together. You chose Elizabeth."

"I *did?*" Liz said, her mind spinning. "I don't remember that."

"Can you hold him a sec?" Angela asked, handing over Charlie. She went off into the shadows of the yurt.

Liz looked down at her son, caressing the creamy skin of his cheeks with her index finger, deeply relieved to feel affection rather than the need for a psych ward. Angela returned, brandishing two objects. She sat back down and held up the first one: a handmade sheet of metal, warped by time or crafted by a novice, which appeared to be a fledgling attempt at impersonating a license plate. Liz saw that SAGE-143 was etched onto it.

"Metalwork was never my medium," Angela said apologetically. She set aside the homemade license plate, peeled the Bubble Wrap off her other offering, and held up a gleaming, store-bought license plate with ELIZABETH emblazoned across it. Liz leaned forward, her baby tucked under one arm, and flung her other one around her mother.

———————

Liz stepped outside Victoria and Ace's guesthouse with Charlie in tow in his DockATot. Victoria was setting the long wood table with linen napkins and ceramic plates. She looked up at Liz, and even with the marks of fatigue evident on her face, she was still striking.

"Can I help?" Liz asked.

"All under control," Victoria said. "I thought we'd eat outside because it's so nice, but we can always turn on the heat lamps if we need them."

"No, this is great," Liz said, looking around. They were having one of those peculiar winter heat waves in Los Angeles, which was causing an uptick in the news cycle about global warming and sending people to the beaches in droves. The air was warm but not humid, and it had a pleasing, balmy breeze. Tea lights were strung overhead in the backyard, which was technically now Liz's too, at least temporarily, since she had accepted Victoria's offer to move into the guesthouse with Charlie until she found her own place. Liz put Charlie down next to Miles and the two infants looked at each other.

"That's so cute it's gross," Victoria said, and she and Liz instantly pulled out their phones to document the moment. As they snapped pictures, Miles reached out and clenched his fingers around Charlie's hand. Both women shrieked.

"They're holding hands!" Liz said. "I don't know how I'm ever going to move out."

"I hope you never do," Ace said, coming outside with a platter of grilled chicken and vegetables. He was still moving more slowly than usual, but thanks to a strict diet and weekly rehab sessions following his return home, he no longer resembled an invalid. He looked like a man who had cheated death and received a surplus of second chances he would not take for granted.

They waited to sit until Angela showed up, only twenty-five minutes late, which for her was timely. Victoria introduced herself and welcomed Angela graciously, and Liz thought that if Victoria felt at all weird about welcoming her husband's former fling into her home, you couldn't detect any discomfort whatsoever.

"It's nice to meet you, at last," Victoria told Angela.

"Likewise!" Angela said, thrusting a dried (but really just decrepit) flower bouquet into Victoria's hands.

"I'll find a vase for these," Victoria said, excusing herself so Ace and Angela could have a moment. Liz watched with naked fascination, unable to tear her eyes away. Her parents had both said they were up for this, and Liz had verified it repeatedly over the past week, leading up to them all having dinner together: *Are you sure? I know it's weird. Are you positive?* Despite their assurances, Angela and Ace hadn't seen each other in decades, and they shared an undeniably complicated past. Liz didn't know how this would go.

Angela and Ace regarded each other, Ace offering a gregarious but knowing smile; no one thought this moment wasn't loaded, or without nuance.

"Angela," he said. "Thank you for coming."

"Thanks for having me. It's been a minute."

"Since you gave me the boot," Ace said.

Angela threw her head back and laughed, breaking the tension. "It's good to see ya, you old deadbeat," she said, pounding Ace on the back. "Too hard? I heard we almost lost you."

While Ace and Angela discussed the broad strokes of his health, Victoria came back outside and Liz shot her a relieved look. Angela turned around in time to clock it. "What? You were worried? Liz, baby, I've done twenty past-life regressions. I was a waiting woman to Cleopatra in the time of the pharaohs. I think I can handle this."

"There is no person on earth who would deny what a force of nature you are, Angela," Ace said. "I'm just glad I have the chance to tell you what a wonderful daughter you raised."

Angela batted away the praise. "I brought you a pink halite," she said, producing a light pink hunk of crystal from her satchel. "It's a heart opener. Put it next to your bed and sleep next to it, and don't forget to bathe your crystals during the full moon to activate their powers," Angela instructed.

"Thank you, Angela," Ace said. "Very thoughtful of you."

Angela turned to Liz and Victoria. "I use all my crystals in my sound baths. I should do one for that mommy group of yours."

Victoria and Liz suppressed a laugh.

"Sound healing is great for babies and for new mothers," Angela added.

"We're actually taking a break from the class," Liz said.

"Once all the babies arrived, the group chat went from annoying to downright insufferable," Victoria explained.

Angela let out a little huff. "You don't have to explain it to me," she said. "I'm anti anything organized."

Victoria gave Angela a kind smile, then ushered everyone to the table. They sat down with the babies, the light softening into a deep amber through the canopy of trees. Ace sat at the head of the table, Victoria on his left, Liz and Angela on the right. Liz looked around at Victoria, her best friend and stepmom; and Ace, her father and her son's grandfather; and Angela, her mother and Ace's ex; and at the two babies resting next to each other in the idyllic setting of the Los Angeles foothills. Liz realized she was living in a commune of sorts, which was Angela's wet dream of a new tomorrow, and she smiled to herself at how improbable but fitting it was.

All those years railing against her unconventional childhood and bemoaning the untraditional lifestyles Angela had forced on her, only to end up here.

Ace lifted his glass. "If I can say a few words . . ." He smiled at each woman. "I've always been a lucky son of a bitch, but that's never been more true than right now. I have everything I ever could have wanted right here at this table. I am unbelievably blessed and incredibly grateful. Cheers, to the most important women in my life and to the next generation of men who are lucky enough to know their love."

"Cheers," Victoria, Liz, and Angela said, clinking their glasses with Ace and with one another. Liz nearly laughed at the absurdity of the scene, which was something she never could have predicted and hadn't known enough to hope for, but now, looking back, she could see that despite the route it took to get here, Liz was exactly where she was supposed to be. With her stepmom and best friend. With her parents, who seemed willing to move on from their checkered past and coexist in the here and now, for her. With two little boys who were the same age, but who were uncle and nephew. Liz took a sip of the orange wine Victoria had bought because Angela was coming to dinner, and mentally said her thanks for everything that had brought her to this moment.

Victoria looked over and caught her eye, so Liz mouthed the words to her best friend. Victoria's smile stretched across her face, and she mouthed it back to Liz.

Thanks in advance.

Acknowledgments

I wrote the first draft of this novel during the WGA strike in 2023. I told myself I had nothing to lose if it didn't work out, if I was simply not meant to be a novelist and the lesson to be learned was to stay in my lane as a screenwriter. But very quickly that mindset itself became the pipedream; I was undeniably invested. I loved living with these characters in their world and hoped others would want to meet them and spend time there, too.

I am so grateful to all the people who agreed and made that happen. Endless thanks to my editor, Hannah Braaten, for championing this book immediately, finding it the greatest home I could ask for at Gallery, and elevating the manuscript with astute and incisive notes.

I am so appreciative to have a powerhouse of a publisher, Jennifer Bergstrom, who embraced this book with infectious enthusiasm.

Through this process, I learned how many people are involved in the production of a book—a list that could almost rival a call sheet! Thank you to the entire Simon & Schuster/Gallery Books team, each of whom put their effort and expertise into this novel: Jennifer Long, Katy Morreau, Sirui Huang, Laura Levatino, Aimee Bell, Abby Knudsen, Sarah Schlick, Emily Arzeno, Angel Musyimi, Caroline Pallotta, John Paul Jones, Barbara Rivera Nieves, Lauren Wright, Min Choi, Alexis Minieri, Meryll Preposi, Christine Gaba, Paul O'Halloran, Rachel Podmajersky, and Fiona Sharp.

Hats off to Lisa Litwack and Annie Higgie for making a cover so beautiful I want to wallpaper my entire house with it, wear it, or just stare at it. If someone were to buy a book solely based on a cover, I firmly believe this one nails the assignment.

Thank you to Heather Waters, Jessica Roth, and the entire publicity and marketing team for your tireless and spirited work to spread the word.

Thank you to Joe Veltre for your unparalleled representation and for helping me navigate the book world with expertise and aplomb.

Thank you to Eric Garfinkel for believing in me since I was a baby writer, and for your unwavering support as I hopped the fence from screen to books.

Thank you to the entire team at Gersh for advocating for me, nearly twenty years and counting.

I'm also indebted to Dave Ryan and Patti Felker. Law school was never an option for me; I'm glad it was for you and that you're the best at what you do. I appreciate you always having my back with the fine print.

Emily Stone, there is no one I'd rather talk about room tone or share off-the-menu pasta with. I am so glad you're in my life and in my corner.

Loretta Rothschild, you encouraged me to write this book, read first drafts, and then guided me through the process of being a debut author with incredible generosity. It means the world.

Other early readers: Katie O'Donnell, Julia Sonenshein, Ilana Stone, and Liz Hammond. Thank you for your time and invaluable feedback.

I have learned that much like motherhood, bringing a book into the world similarly requires a village. Thank you to my stable of brilliant, beautiful female friends. You know who you are, and I wouldn't be who I am without you. I am so lucky to have these life-affirming friendships and to know women who lift each other up. Thank you for filling my cup with late-night laughs, deep talks, and unbreakable bonds.

My first manager and dear friend, Langley Perer, changed my life professionally and personally, in every way. Any ounce of success feels like hers too, and I miss her every day.

My brother: you were one of the very first readers of a book for which you are quite possibly the least likely audience. Thank you.

My in-laws and extended family. It's a gift to know your love and an honor to carry the Lekkos name.

My parents. I could go on endlessly and yet it would never be enough. You nurtured my early love of reading and writing (even though that may have involved a near-total boycott of TV) and, most importantly, taught me to believe in myself. You showed by example how to live with ambition, compassion, humility, and grace. I will never get over my luck at having parents like you and I can only hope to match the very high bar you set.

My daughter. Motherhood was the most hypothetical, gobsmacking leap into the unknown until you were in my arms and suddenly, it felt like the only place I could ever be. Watching you grow fills my days with awe and joy. Thank you for offering to help me with my work, suggesting alternate titles, and announcing, "And I cleaned my room!" every time someone congratulated me on selling this book. My love for you knows no bounds.

My husband. You told me I could write a novel. Looks like you were right. Thank you for pushing me to believe in myself by supplying absolute conviction and unconditional support. This book would not exist without you. Nor could I. You have shown me what it means to love—and to be loved—in all the little ways. They really do mean everything.